I0653912

SERVANT OF RAGE

Bloodrage

Book 1

ALEX KNIGHT

Edited by BROOK ASPDEN-LI

Copyedited by NAOMI ESPINOSA

Cover art by IVAN VUJOVIC

To

Gray – you *know* what you did.

Brook – you know what you *did*.

Erin – *you know what you did.*

Chapter One

SUBEI

Any great inferno can be traced back to a single moment. A precipitous second where lightning tastes dry grass.

Pitching the plan in the predawn dark, Subei had been holding just such a moment in mind. Could envision that singular heartbeat where brilliant would meet bombastic and all would know it was him who'd made it happen. Would know it was Subei, Son of Kemu Khan, who'd struck flint to steel.

Now that they were several days into said plan, well, it still looked to be a good one. There were just some finer details Subei had failed to consider. Like the special kind of ache that came from hiding in the back of a wagon as it jolted and clattered across the steppe. Or the lack of fresh air beneath two layers of tarp and what that caused in the way of sweat pooling in his every crevice. Also that tent poles made for terrible bedding.

But no one had said catching bandits was comfortable work. Especially not these days.

Time was, a child could walk from one end of the khanate to the other, a pot of gold balanced on their head and not a care in the world. Time was, the Great Baji Khan had united the tribes and all the world had been brought to heel.

Time was gone.

Baji Khan had ascended to the world next and his magic with him. No one had seen anything like it since and, in their absence, the khanate had crumbled. Didn't help that his descendants had fought over it like dogs at table scraps. Fought until what'd once been a feast fit for kings was torn to crumbs not worthy of a field mouse.

And so, the heirs of what'd been the grandest conquest the world had ever seen spent their days feuding. And in Subei's case, hunting bandits from the back of a wagon, clad in armor and soaking in a pool of his own sweat.

He'd just gotten the tent poles arranged below him such that they stopped jabbing into his spine—in favor of digging into his kidneys—when the wagon lurched to a stop. The wooly trovaak pulling it grunted and punched one thick-knuckled fist into the ground in annoyance. Subei had a mind to join it, until a voice carried in on the wind. Clopping hooves came with it. Horses' hooves.

"Hail, travelers of. . . is that the sigil of House Kemu? Ah, so it is. How is ol' Kemu Khan?"

Trying to beat back the excitement bubbling in his chest, Subei peered through the knot hole in his wagon's side. Just ahead, a bearded man sat astride a horse. Beside him were a dozen others, men and women, mounted and with bows in hand. Their clothing bore neither sigil nor colors of the four major houses. Showed no allegiance at all.

"Kemu Khan is strong and fierce, as the ancestors will it," Ghula said from up front. Her bench seat creaked as if she'd shifted her weight. It was all the warning Subei needed.

His prodding toe found Kashi's shoulder down at the opposite end of the wagon.

"Might be time, brother."

"And just when I was getting used to life as a tent pole."

Already Subei could picture the moment this had all been building to. The moment the tarp was pulled back and instead of valuables for the taking, the bandits found an ambush. Armed, armored, and waiting. The perfect moment for a lorecaller to weave a song around, if Subei was being less humble.

"Well, it does my heart good to hear righteous ol' Kemu Khan is well. And well enough to travel to the Kurultai, even?" the rider asked.

"The laws of Great Baji Khan leave no room for misunderstanding. The might of the steppe must descend on Kurul Valley," Ghula answered with a bit too much of a challenge in her tone. The bandit recoiled at that, but wrapped in a lumpy horse blanket, she did look the part of a grumpy wagon driver quite well. Probably helped the grumpiness came natural.

"Nothing quite like a Kurultai. All the houses together once more to feast and trade. And, of course, to win glory in the tournament," the bandit said, his tone back to friendly and sweet. Sickly sweet, by Subei's estimation.

"There a point you're looking to make?" Ghula asked. "Other than making us late?"

"You can afford the delay, old one. Will arrive early, even. Behind me there's nothing but grass for grazing and an easy journey to Kurul Valley. My friends and I ensure it stays that way."

"Such is the duty every Ghangerai owes to the heartland."

"Oh, don't get me wrong. We're more than happy to serve. But you've probably heard, there's bandits everywhere these days. Kick a rock and you'll send at least a few scurrying." A sigh then, and Subei had the distinct impression it wasn't exactly genuine. "My companions and I have worked tirelessly keeping this stretch of steppe open. Had to neglect our herds and hunting, even. Had to start asking for donations to support our efforts."

"Shame you don't hunt half as much as you talk!" Subei shouted through cupped hands.

"Who said that?" the rider called, standing in his saddle. Through the knot hole, Subei could see the other wagon drivers fight back a laugh.

"Sharp tongues for a group of old shits," the rider growled. "Though I'm sure you're willing to donate extra by way of apology."

"Get on with it," Ghula said. "It's bad enough I'm losing my hearing. I don't intend to waste what's left of it listening to you."

Another laugh from the group.

"A whole wagon then," the bearded rider snapped and urged

his horse forward. Most of his companions followed, but three stayed behind, bows at the ready.

"You'll want the middle one. Nothing good in mine," Ghula said. "Just don't tell Kemu Khan I said that."

"Search them all," the bearded man ordered, waving his brigands over. Hooves clopped on the hard-packed earth as horse and rider passed Subei's knot hole, then the whole thing went black when another rider stopped right alongside.

Something ruffled above him, a hand, feeling through the tarp. Subei's heart beat faster. Pounded at the back of his ribcage. Three long, rattling days and finally, the moment was close. That precipitous second the whole plan had been built around.

The hand reached deeper, knocked against tent poles, then his knee. It froze at that, hesitated, then ripped the tarp away.

The shadows burned away in an instant as blue sky seared Subei's eyes—he hadn't accounted for that bit. Made it hard to take in the details of the bandit's face. He squinted enough to make out a broken nose, nostrils flared, and a scar-divided brow furrowed in confusion. Not the dramatic shock he'd hoped for, but probably that was just the sun obscuring his view.

"Greetings! Sorry about your jaw." Subei kicked her across the chin. There was a crunch and she toppled backward off her horse.

"Ouch," Kashi said with a wince, then leapt from the wagon. Sunlight streamed across him and for a moment, Subei was reminded just how boyish he could look at times. Just starting to tip over the cusp of manhood, his brown eyes were bright with life, and his jawline was decidedly beardless. He wore his dark brown hair long—and tied in a hanging braid at the back—but it couldn't fully hide the sharpness of his face. Paired with his reedy frame, he sometimes looked more scholar than warrior. The fighting stance he landed in, however, and the cudgel clasped in his hand, signaled otherwise. Admittedly, it wasn't the best weapon for a fight to the death, but ancestors willing, no one would need killing.

Subei followed his youngest brother out of the wagon. As his feet stomped to the earth, he drew up tall—savoring the moment

4

and sucking in a steadying breath—then pointed his own cudgel at the bandit leader.

"By order of Kemu Khan, lay down your weapons. This shameful behavior is at an end."

The bandit leader stared at him. It would take a moment for him to catch up to what was happening, then the fear would set in across his face. Or, so Subei had expected. Instead, the man laughed.

"What are you lau—"

"Not a step further!" a bandit at the next wagon shouted, blade leveled at the throat of the driver. "We'll kill you a—ah!"

A hand clamped down over his face. A hand that'd shot out from the pile of straw in the wagon. The pile shifted, then fell away as a giant of a man rose from it.

His close-shaven black hair—so short as to be almost bald—was specked with bits of straw, and a few more were caught in his mustache and goatee. His cheeks were full and his face round in a way that was distinctly Ghangerai. Where Kashi's eyes were brown, Bataar's were a fierce black as he put his fearsome strength to use against the bandit.

Subei had long planned his dramatic entrance to the ambush, but as usual, Bataar had done it better. Probably hadn't even planned it. Things always just seemed to work out for him.

Bataar was a big man even without armor, but he wore it today as he clasped his other hand over the bandit's wrist, then squeezed until there was a crunch and the blade fell to the dirt.

"I don't like it when my people are threatened," Bataar said. "You can understand that, right?"

The bandit made a vaguely audible *mmhhhmphh* through Bataar's palm.

"Good. Spread the word." Bataar hefted him overhead, then threw him at the next nearest bandit. They both went down in a pile.

The trovaak harnessed to Ghula's wagon reared up onto its stubby hind legs and beat at the ground with pillar-like forearms, annoyance plain in its smushed-faced features. Ghula worked to calm the beast of burden, and it crashed back down to all fours, pulling the wagon several steps ahead. Around and behind the mounted bandits, as it happened.

"Whoa, whoa!" she called, getting him under control once the wagon was past the bandits.

"Well, isn't this cute?" the bandit leader chuckled as he took in Subei and his brothers standing against them. His lackeys followed suit, grinning and squaring up around him. "Quite the entrance for you lot, but ultimately fruitless. Three brave idiots against all of us?" He spread his arms wide. Even with a few of his number down, eight still stood. Not to mention the three archers on the hill. "I'll take those odds." He drew his sword.

"Shame you didn't run into just three brave idiots, then." Ghula stood, and her lumpy blanket fell away to reveal the armor beneath. Iron lamellar, made of rows upon rows of overlapping, rectangular plates laced together. Accompanying it, she wore a saber on each hip. Didn't draw them, though. Pulled a quarter-staff from her wagon instead, then rolled her shoulders and cracked her neck.

"Ancestors above but that blanket smelled like ass."

"Alright, *four* brave idiots—" the bandit leader began, before noticing the other wagon drivers shedding their disguises as well. All at once, the wagon train was gleaming with armor, weaponry, and even several shields.

"Buncha gray hairs, boss. We can take 'em!" one of the bandits snarled as his horse danced nervously beneath him. The group's leader didn't look so sure.

"Most warriors die young. . . " Subei called out. "So you know what they say about old warriors."

Ghula spat to one side. "You can say their asses are sore, they smell like warmed-over death, and the main thing standing between them and a good bath is this lot."

Some grumbles of agreement from the other warriors at that. The bandits' horses stomped all the more nervously.

"Give up," Subei said, cudgel lowered diplomatically as he walked forward. "I am Subei, son of Kemu. Those are my brothers Bataar and Kashi. Know that we speak with our father's voice when we say the laws of the Great Baji Khan are still

6

upheld in our house. Surrender now and mercy will be managed."

"Ghangerai should not spill Ghangerai blood," Kashi added. "That was the founding tenet of Baji's law. And when we followed it, the world trembled before a united khanate. Those days need not be gone."

"The aftertaste of faded glory isn't going to stop our families going hungry," the bandit leader spat. "And neither is turning ourselves over to Kemu. Yah!" He shouted and spurred his horse forward. Then all the bandits were moving, rounding back to retreat the way they'd come.

Or, they tried to, but Subei hadn't spent three days rattling around in the back of a wagon just to fail to account for such a move.

The bandits made to flee, but they hadn't noticed the rope attached to Ghula's wagon. The rope that, as she'd stirred her trovaak into a panic earlier, had been dragged across the bandit's route of retreat. The far end was attached to another wagon, and now, with a good pull, the rope jumped up to stretch taut.

"You're up, big guy," Ghula said as she raised the rope to her trovaak.

Funny creatures, trovaaks. They bore a passing resemblance to gibbons, or pandas perhaps, but grew as large as elephants, with long, dexterous front arms and stout but strong rear legs. Thick curtains of wooly fur hung from them in most places except the face and hands. Some folks speculated their all-too human hands developed to help rip up the trees and grasses they so loved to eat, but no one could really say. All Subei knew was they were reliable beasts of burden, smarter than yaks or horses, and when offered a thing, *anything*, they had a seemingly irresistible urge to grip it and take a closer look. Ghula held up the end of the rope and her trovaak's massive hand closed around it with a stony, inescapable strength.

The first of the bandits' horses crashed into the pulled-tight rope and went down in a screaming avalanche of muscle, sweat, and panic. The rope broke before the trovaak's casual grip on it did, but the trap had already done its job. The first rank of riders went down, unable to do anything but cry out as the rest of the riders plowed into them and toppled as well. The result was a mass of screaming horses and shouting bandits, and more than a few broken legs. Those still able struggled to their feet and made to flee. Some horses escaped, but no bandits did as Subei, his brothers, and their gray-haired warriors charged in.

The closest bandit pulled himself into a stumbling run as Subei raised his cudgel. It would have been all too easy to strike him in the base of the neck, or higher still and crack his skull. Both potentially lethal blows, but in this moment, unnecessary. No one needed to die this day.

Subei ended the bandit's flight with a blow to the ribs. Nothing lethal, but enough to send him sprawling to the dirt and wheezing to regain his breath.

The next foe wasn't so set on running.

It was the leader, snarling as he charged. There was dirt in his beard, blood in his teeth, and rage in his eyes as he came swinging, sword blade hissing through the air.

Subei side-stepped, leaning back as the attack whiffed past. He ducked under a backhand next, then launched forward into a rising strike. His cudgel caught his opponent in the forearm, breaking it and disarming him. The man staggered back, cursing, but then his offhand flashed out with a knife. Subei deflected the strike with a forearm block then used the man's momentum to guide the knife back to his throat. He pulled up short, though, the blade just pricking the flesh.

There was a moment then, both of them eye to eye, breathing heavy. It would have been the easiest thing in the world for Subei to push the knife just a bit further, and from the leader's expression, he knew it. Instead, Subei swung his cudgel in from the side and knocked the man in the head. A controlled blow, not hard enough to break anything, but enough to double his vision, scatter his thoughts. The bandit leader grunted once, then toppled backward—slowly, slowly—then all at once.

Thud.

A puff of dirt whooshed out from his dazed form. Never a good thing, getting knocked like that. Damn sight better than dead, though.

"The khan might yet be merciful," Subei said, though the

man couldn't hear it. And then a spear came in from the side, nearly caught him through the throat. The hint of movement at the corner of his eye had been just enough warning to dodge, but the attacker wasn't done.

The spear came back, in a barrage of lethal stabs. It was the best Subei could do to backpedal and stay out of reach. Two attacks caught him in the stomach anyway. His lamellar did its job so instead of being skewered, the wind was just knocked from him even as the blows drove him to the ground.

"Today I kill the son of a khan," the spear's wielder said as she stepped over Subei. "Today I meet my ancestors, and they will be smiling."

"What about?" Ghula asked.

Her staff swept the bandit's feet, then followed up with two whistling blows—one to the ribs then another to her right shoulder, which cracked audibly.

Ghula huffed as she spun her staff back into the ready position. Then it was her turn to look down at Subei.

"For a khan's son, you sure do fight like shit."

"You trained me."

"Yeah, well I'm just an old shit wagon driver," she said, as if her face wasn't as beaten as an old shield. As if her hair wasn't shot through with naked lines of scar tissue from fights undertaken, and one way or another, won.

She offered a hand up, and Subei took it.

"Thanks all the same," he said.

Around them, the fight was coming to an end. The bandits that'd tried to flee had been stopped. And those that hadn't were being bound.

"What a waste." Kashi was staring at the corpse of a bandit who'd been caught beneath his horse. "They should have surrendered. We could have avoided all of thi—"

"Arrows!" Bataar swung in from the side and sheltered him as one, two, three heavy *thunks* punched into the wicker face of his upraised shield.

Peering into the distance, Subei spotted the three bandits who'd stayed on the hill. They were fleeing now, but one of them, riding a bay dun with black speckled flanks, lingered a moment to spit in their direction.

"Do we go after them?" Bataar asked as the riders disappeared down the far side of the hill.

"We're not equipped for a pursuit," Subei said, thinking aloud. "But if enough of these horses are healthy, we could make a go of it. Maybe. . . " He'd just started looking around when a hand dragged him back by the collar.

"No." Ghula had that look in her eyes. "You did good work today, but there's little glory in hunting scattered bandits." She turned north, a hand to her brow. "We need to rejoin your father and reach the Kurultai. You three have a tournament to win. For the glory of your father and your house." She smirked then. "And most importantly, the old shit wagon driver who trained you."

Chapter Two

BATAAR

Bataar didn't have words to describe how good it felt to ride again. Subei had the clever tongue, so probably he did. Probably he was lost in his own thoughts, piecing together pretty descriptions. All Bataar knew was riding felt *right*.

And not because hiding in the wagon had filled his body with the kind of aches and pains expected of a person twice his age. It was something else. Something that didn't need to be explained or reasoned. It just *was*.

The rising sun warmed his face as he fell into the rhythm of his horse's gallop. Around, the whole of the steppe stretched away. A vast expanse of grass with gusts of the wild north wind rippling its surface.

The Empty Sea, some called it, with nothing but grass for water and the occasional hill for islands. But this land was only empty to a stranger's eyes. Only empty if one was accustomed to a life filled with useless baubles and overindulgent comforts. The steppe stripped all that away like the north wind scouring a mountaintop.

"Whoa, whoa," Bataar called, leaning back in the saddle and slowing his stolen horse to a trot, then further to a walk. "This'll do." He gave her a pat as they came to a stop beside the packed dirt of an old road. Kashi, Subei, Ghula, and the extra mounts were just behind.

The day prior, they'd taken the bandits' freshest horses and ridden hard. The wagons bearing the prisoners followed at their own pace.

Bataar had chosen a calm-eyed chestnut mare, with brown striping around her legs. She—and the rest of the bandits' horses—looked to have come from the herds of House Tugu, where they bred for speed over stamina or strength. Ghula'd made sure everyone had brought two extra mounts. Speedier horses were prone to tire more often.

At a gallop, they'd chased the sun to the horizon. Then, trusting the sure-footedness of their mounts, trotted through the night. And now, as dawn rose on the steppe, they'd arrived.

"Too late?" Kashi asked, leading the others to the edge of the road. It wasn't more than some old wagon tracks cut along the edge of a hill. "We're too late, aren't we?"

"We are where we should be, when we should be," Bataar said, nodding as he looked at their surroundings with satisfaction.

"We're too early," Subei said from where he was slouched in his saddle. It was a lazy riding position and Bataar made a mental note to correct him in private. After all their years of training, one would think his middle brother would pay more attention to the details required to be an elite warrior. His half-effort was apparent in everything from his posture to his fighting readiness. He was muscular, yes, but in a wiry sort of way that said he didn't eat as much as a warrior should, nor train enough to put it to use. With his height—a finger's length shorter than Bataar—he had the frame to be truly imposing. His brown-black hair was cut short in a warrior's manner, at least, but his beard was sloppy. It was splotchy along the cheeks and jawline, and as such, needed to be kept tidy. Bataar had shown him how last winter, but since then, Subei had let it grow without discipline. Rakish, he liked to call it. Wild, was more accurate. Like a sheep too long strayed from its shepherd.

"We should have stayed with the wagons," Subei continued. "Make a dramatically late entrance, and with our prisoners in tow."

"Should I take a detachment back for the wagons?" Bataar

asked suddenly, concern rising in him. "I don't like the thought of them coming across more bandits without us."

"Those warriors been handling themselves longer than you pups have lived." Ghula's eyes were fixed firmly ahead, not even acknowledging the possibility of doubt in the prowess of those she'd chosen. "Turn your thoughts to the tournament and the honor of your father's house." She nodded toward the far side of the hill where the sky was stained with dust. Moments later, a lone rider appeared, the three-arrow banner in hand. And then, just as thunder followed lightning, the House of Kemu arrived. An avalanche of man and horse, of spear and lance, of bow and whipping hair thundering down the hill.

Concern left Bataar all at once as the spirit of his house filled him. He rose in the saddle to whoop as the front ranks swarmed past. Several called back, and yet more raised clenched fists before them in salute to the sons of Kemu Khan.

The vanguard streamed on like a storm-flooded river. Rider after rider stretched back over the hill and further still, to the distant horizon, as the bulk of House Kemu's number appeared.

Trovaaks pulled wagons, carrying food and drink, gers and fencing, and any other supplies that the seventy-thousand strong pilgrims would need at the Kurultai. Mammoths carried supplies as well, though these were bundled on their massive backs or piled high on sleds behind them. And then, in the distance to either side, the herds drew into view. Fresh horses, foremost. Four or more for every rider. And following further back were the cows and sheep, goats, and even some wide-footed camels from the western border.

A figure broke from the mass, riding toward Bataar and his brothers with a retinue of heavily armored kheshig guards in tow. His horse was plain—a shaggy gray coat adorned only with saddle and cloth—and the rider was dressed just as plainly. He wore a rough-spun deel, one flap of the long-sleeved garment tucked over the other and clasped beneath his right arm. As all true Ghangerai under Baji's law, Kemu Khan wore no fineries. No jewels nor fanciful fabrics, only a blade on one hip and a bow on the other. What more did a person need?

Bataar pressed his fists knuckle to knuckle in front of his

chest, then bowed low in the saddle. Kashi, Subei, and Ghula did the same as Kemu Khan, Blessed of the Great Sky, drew near. His kheshig guards encircled the group, forming a pocket of calm amidst the torrent.

"Torol," Kemu Khan said first, nodding to Ghula and addressing her by the title that marked her as one of his advisors. "Our house is better for your return. Tell me, did foolishness or bravery command my sons on their quest?"

"A potent mix of both, my Khan."

"They are truly their father's sons, then."

"Perhaps more stubborn still."

Kemu Khan laughed at that and clapped her on the shoulder.

"To know wisdom, one must first know foolishness." He was smirking as he turned to Bataar, Kashi, and Subei. "Though I admit, some may be more acquainted with it than others." He nodded then. "Ride with me, my sons. The Kurultai is not far now, and I should like to pass the remaining miles with the tale of your newest foolish bravery."

* * *

Ghangerai cities did not cower behind walls or moats, and their people needed neither kings nor soldiers to protect them. Ghangerai cities were as alive and fierce as their people, because they were one and the same. Anywhere enough Ghangerai stopped for a month, or a season, became a city.

The grass was trodden to streets and the tent-house gers of each family staked out neighborhoods. Herds grazed in the surround, and in a day, any stretch of steppe could become home.

Bataar's breath came quick, though he wasn't winded. His heart beat loud as each stride of the horse carried him closer to the great Kurultai. Already he could feel the mighty tradition of his people giving weight to the air. Weight and meaning and honor.

They climbed the rise and the lowland bowl that was Kurul Valley drew into view. In it, Bataar beheld the largest host of

Ghangerai he'd ever seen. Enough riders and warriors to conquer the world.

"So few?" Kemu Khan asked, frowning. "Would that an ancestor-sent storm swelled the river and washed our pittance away."

Sheltered on two sides by mountains, and on a third by the Chinggon River, the valley was a rare oasis in the Empty Sea. The songs said it was here Baji Khan had convened the first great Kurultai. Now, some one hundred and twenty years—and twelve Kurultais—later, the Ghangerai gathered once again.

A scout waited at the lip of the valley, head already bowed.

"My Khan, we count some twenty thousand from House Arban."

"Hmph. An eighth of their full numbers."

"And the same, if not a thousand less, from House Budai."

"Has a sickness swept their lands? Some plague unknown to us? And what of our proud cousins? What of House Tugu?"

"Thirty-five thousand, my Khan."

"It is easier to move a mountain than to change a person's nature, and yet, my cousins are so changed as this? So strayed from Baji's law that this is all the great houses offer?" He frowned deeper at that, as if the great host sprawled across the valley floor could be in any way a disappointment. "I know my cousins' numbers are not so diminished as this. How little we respect the laws of our ancestors." He shook his head. "Establish our camp beside House Budai. Perhaps the disparity between our numbers will remind them of their duty."

The scout bowed, then peeled off at a gallop to deliver the order. In moments, the word spread and the bulk of House Kemu moved to circle the edge of the valley, chasing the open ground at the far end. The herds moved in the opposite direction, seeking pasture in the steppe. Kemu Khan led his sons and his kheshig guard directly into the camp.

"Forgive me, Father, but even this Kurultai is bigger than I remember," Bataar said. The other houses had established themselves around the wide thoroughfare they now traveled. In each camp, gers and animal pens were arrayed, along with sporting grounds, storage depots, and more than a few feasting tents. It looked as if half the valley was full, what with camps lining the river, stretching across the lowland, and even creeping up the sides of the mountains.

"You were but eight years old at the last Kurultai," Kemu Khan said. "You were small, and the world seemed all the larger for it."

"Subei and I were small," Kashi said with a chuckle. "Bataar was already taller than you, Father."

"I pity his horses daily," Subei added, leaning over to elbow his older and bigger brother. "I still think you should be riding a trovaak."

"You forget the purpose of the Kurultai, my sons. We're not here just to feast and win glory in the tournament."

Bataar shot a glance at Ghula, and from the tilt of her mouth, she'd something to say about that last bit, even as Kemu Khan continued speaking.

"Remind me, Bataar. What is the foremost purpose of the great Kurultai?"

"Baji Khan established the great Kurultai to ensure the readiness of our people," he said, recounting the lessons Mahtma had drilled into them. "To amass the fighting might of each house every ten years for inspection."

"So it has been," Kemu Khan said with a nod. "But no longer. It was bad enough the feuding necessitated we leave ten thousand warriors behind to protect the herds and elderly. Worse now, that the other houses have left far more." Kemu Khan sighed. "In my grandfather's time, Kurul Valley would have been overflowing. This ground. . . " he gestured to the gentle down slope they were crossing, "would have been well within the limits of the great camp. Horizon to horizon filled with warriors and traders, and dignitaries from each foreign king brought to heel by the khanate."

"Now we bring none to heel," Ghula said. Quietly, but no less fierce for it.

"We'll start with the other houses then, when we crush them in the tournament," Bataar said, punching a fist into his palm. His blood was up, and he was eager to add to the honor of their family's great house.

Kashi gave a nod, quick but sure. Subei smirked, but his eyes were distant, no doubt already imagining the adoration that'd follow victory here.

"House Tugu seems to have taken offense to your boasts." Ghula motioned to the side. They were in the valley proper now and the nearest camp was that of their northern cousins, the descendants of Baji's firstborn son, Tugu. A group of shirtless warriors was hacking away at training dummies alongside the thoroughfare and now, looked to be considering how much they'd like to do the same to Bataar.

"The truest lessons are the most painful to learn," he said coldly.

"Attend the tournament and watch us teach your champions *this* particular lesson." Subei added as he gave them a self-satis-fied smile, riling them all the more, but for one in the back. He was brushing his horse. A familiar-looking horse, as it happened. A bay dun with black-speckled flanks. Bataar's gaze snapped to the man, but he was already gone, had slipped away into the forest of gers.

"That bay dun look familiar to you, Subei?" he asked, voice low as he leaned over.

Kashi did the same from the other side. "What are we whispering about?"

"One of the escaped bandits rode such a horse," Bataar said, stroking his chin. Subei nodded, eyes wide now at the memory.

"Bay dun. Black-speckled flanks. Should I. . . " He'd begun to spin to the kheshig when Kashi pulled him back around.

"There's more than one bay dun with black-speckled flanks on the steppe. And between the hundred and fifty thousand Ghangerai here—and five times that many horses—it's a safe bet to say there might even be *two* such bay duns in Kurul Valley."

"Just a unique pattern is all I'm saying," Subei protested.

"You're always looking for the next adventure, brother. Even when one's right in front of you," Kashi said. "The tournament's the day after next. Isn't that enough?"

"Maybe." Subei shrugged. "How's about I let you know after we win it?"

"Ahh, now we're getting somewhere!" Ghula cried from up

front. "Take it in, boys. Fight well, and this field will bear witness to your triumph."

They'd reached the center of Kurul Valley and the tournament grounds. The arena had been carved into the side of the northern mountain such that where previously there had been stone and slope, now there was an oval-shaped field. The hillsides surrounding it had been cut like giant steps to accommodate as many onlookers as possible. Where the stone had been removed from the mountain it'd been reassembled at the fore of the field. Reassembled into the statue of the Great Baji Khan.

Twenty horses tall and still too small a monument to commemorate all the Great Khan had built. The man himself may have ascended to join the ancestors in the world next, but here, in Kurul Valley, at the center of the khanate, the living could once again gaze upon his face.

He sat astride a horse with eyes turned to the steppe where they watched over all his people. His form was captured in strong gray stone, and if there was disdain in how his descendants had let his empire crumble, it didn't show. Instead, the statue of the Great Khan rose tall and proud, one massive fist clenched before his chest and the other hooked to the side. There it waited, palm open and wielding the magic that'd helped build the largest empire the world had ever known.

In Bataar and his brothers' lessons, Mahtma had recounted how some lorecallers argued Baji's intellect and courage had been his greatest strengths. Others, his commitment to rewarding with rank and responsibility any who proved their worth, regardless of birth. All noble facets, Bataar didn't argue. And invaluable to the success of any great conqueror and leader. But it certainly didn't hurt that the Great Khan's already many talents were supplemented by one further.

The lorecallers called it magic, the will of the ancestors manifest upon the mortal world. The khan's enemies called it terror. Bataar's father had only ever called it one thing: power.

Held in the Great Khan's hand was what looked to be an entire boulder. Perfectly smooth but for several jagged lines of carved stone that reached from it and into the Great Khan's upturned palm. Lightning bolts captured in stone. It was said the real thing—Baji's magic alive and furious—had burned as bright as the sun, and caused wounds just as grievous. Even better, that technique had only been one of the Great Khan's many magics. Magics that had united the whole of the steppe and set about bringing to heel all who lived beneath the eternal blue sky. Magics that, to the chagrin of all but his enemies, he'd taken to the grave.

"Great Khan," Kemu said, then pressed his fists knuckle to knuckle and bowed. He held it for a long moment, and when he finally looked up, was smiling. "Father of my grandfather's grandfather. It does me good to see your likeness again. We are but servants before you. Stewards of your legacy." A frown then. "A rather diminished legacy. But just as the winter must be weathered, so too this season. And when the spring comes, the House of Kemu stands ready, by the guidance of your laws, to reclaim the glory of our ancestors."

"So it has been, and so it shall be," Bataar said in time with his brothers.

"So it shall be." Kemu Khan nodded at that, before turning his horse to continue into the valley. "Pay your respects to the Great Khan, my sons. Mayhaps he finds you worthy of victory in the coming days. Ghula, with me. I would hear your thoughts on these bandits." They rode on as, in the distance, the beginnings of House Kemu's camp was assembling. The kheshig followed their khan, and in moments, Bataar was alone with his brothers before the imperious gaze of their ancestor.

"Think he was actually that tall?" Subei asked and Bataar cuffed him in the back of the head. "What? Baji Khan was flesh and blood like the rest of us. I'm sure he appreciated good humor."

"That's the key, *good* humor."

Subei and Kashi swung down from their horses and strode forward, then bowed. Bataar followed, but stopped midstride, when the sun slipped free from a passing cloud and a gleam of light caught his eye. Light not from above, but in front. From the obelisks flanking the Great Khan's statue.

Two of them, their bases made of stone, but further up they changed to a sort of crystal. Reminiscent of the blade of a sword extending beyond its hilt. The crystal was red, like a ruby but angrier, and it had always struck Bataar as odd. The Great Khan, like all Ghangerai, had eschewed fineries. So then why would he decorate his statue with them? Perhaps the crystal had some ceremonial purpose? Bataar had been eight years old at the last Kurultai and hadn't understood how to ask the questions then. This time, he would. But first, there was a tournament to win.

The chestnut mare he'd claimed neighed suddenly from behind. Not an alert, but a greeting. As if welcoming someone it knew. It was a cheerful sound—and enough of a warning to save Bataar's life. He turned in time to duck the slashing blade of a saber. It hissed just overhead as he reached to draw his own. A kick caught him in the chest first and then he was rolling backward.

Subei had his own blade drawn in the time it took Bataar's vision to steady. Kashi's came hissing from the sheath a moment later.

Facing the brothers were two warriors, swords in hand and snarls on their faces. But no, not warriors. Bandits. Those that'd fled the day prior. It didn't escape Bataar's notice that, behind the attackers and at the edge of the field, there waited three horses, freshly saddled and loaded with supplies.

"Kill us and make your escape? Who told you that damn fool idea would work?" Bataar growled.

They didn't waste time on a response.

The first, a woman with a hooked nose, came in swinging at Bataar. Their swords met with resounding rings, each strike flashing in lethal arcs. Bataar wasn't praised for his patience, though, and with his brothers in danger, he opted to lower a shoulder and simply bull into his opponent. To her credit, she met the tackle head-on, even if it did drive her backward, heels digging through the dirt.

Locked in a wrestling match, Bataar could just see out of the corner of his eye to where the other bandit was engaged with Kashi, swinging wildly while he parried repeatedly and gave ground. Subei moved to help his younger brother, but then there was a third bandit. The last of that number was coming around from behind the statue.

Bataar dropped to one knee and shifted his grip to his opponent's legs. With a mighty heave he lifted her into the air then, before she could slash at him, slammed her down to the earth. The blow left her gasping for air—and gave Bataar enough of an opening to warn his brother.

"Behind you, Subei!"

At those words, Subei spun with a wild attack. The sneaking bandit hefted a shield and the blade slashed harmlessly against it, then jolted to the side where it struck one of the obelisks.

For a moment, nothing happened, then a crack shot through the crystal. A brilliant red flash—lightning at ten paces—seared Bataar's eyes as Subei's sword seemed to buck and kick like a horse in a fit of anger.

Subei fought to keep control of it, then reared back to strike again. The shield-bearing bandit was still staring wide-eyed at the obelisk. *Hit him, now!* Bataar shouted internally. *While he's distracted!*

Subei lashed out, but at the last second, the bandit shook himself to the present. His shield came up once more—and Subei's sword cut clean through it. And him.

"Huh?" Bataar gasped, not understanding what he was seeing.

Shock was plastered across Subei's face. Shock, and then revulsion as first the bandit's shield—and then the bandit himself—split in two and fell away.

But then there was light again.

Red, piercing, and emanating from Subei's sword. Bataar squinted to see through the brilliance. The blade of his brother's sword was glowing red midway along its length.

Glowing red right where it'd struck the obelisk.

Chapter Three

SUBEI

"Ancestors above." The words slipped from Subei's lips. He'd never been particularly religious, but then again, he'd also never cut a man in two with a single blow. "What. . . ?"

He looked closer at his blade, but already the searing, angry glow was boiling away. Like hot iron doused in water.

A clang from behind and Subei remembered the bandits. The ambush, right.

Kashi was being overwhelmed by a furious onslaught. Each blow drove him further and further back—and all it would take was one slip up for much worse to happen. Bataar, meanwhile, was getting the better of his opponent. But even as he drove her toward the far side of Baji's statue, more warriors were emerging from the gers at the edge of the tournament ground. Coming to the bandits' aid? Or to his and his brothers' defense? Impossible to say, but so blatant an attack was unprecedented enough. Subei wasn't taking any chances.

"Alright then," he shouted to Kashi's opponent. "You wanted this fight? Let's end it—"

Crack.

Something snapped behind him. Sounded like the statue itself was coming down.

Crack.

He turned in time to see the obelisk breaking apart. Cracks spiderwebbed through it, stretching out in jerks and starts.

And then *something* was wrong. Subei couldn't describe it but to say the air felt. . . anxious. Charged even, as a gust of wind rushed down the mountain and flattened the grass around them.

He wasn't the only one who'd noticed, either. The others had stopped fighting, were staring as well.

"Subei. . . " Kashi called from behind, voice wavering. "What did you do?"

He made to answer, but found he didn't know what to say. And couldn't focus on it anyway as the air was popping and hissing. Quiet at first, then louder, louder—painfully loud—as even more cracks formed in the crystalline obelisk.

An arc of light jumped from his saber's hilt and bit into his wrist with a burning jolt. Then another. And another. Subei choked down a gasp as the jolts built to a frenzy, stinging again and again as the tension in the air continued to build. And yet, he couldn't drop the blade. It was as if he'd lost control of his own hand. Could only clench tighter. The air was so charged now it was as if the world had sucked in a great lungful and was holding it in, waiting, waiting—Subei's hair rose up straight, stretching to stand on end—and then the obelisks exploded.

Both of them at the same moment.

A crystalline shard long as a horse whipped past him and obliterated Kashi's opponent. One moment the bandit was there, the next there was but a puff of blood and a massive hunk of crystal plowing through the earth. Subei'd just had time to belatedly flinch away when the obelisks exploded again. This time there were no crystalline shards, just a boiling red light that blasted him off his feet.

The ground was below, then above, then below once more and rushing to slam into him. The breath was crushed from his lungs in a wheezing gasp. He slid to a stop, coughing, gasping, but the air wouldn't come, was stuck in his throat.

The smell of burning flesh. His flesh.

He raised his right hand to find it was divided by a pale scar. It began at the joint of his thumb and ran down the back of his hand, past his wrist.

And then it moved.

With a sharp jerk, the scar shot forward, cutting a path up his forearm. Another jump and it reached the elbow.

He was already screaming as he grabbed at his arm, squeezing tight as if that would stop whatever was happening. But then the skin was smoking and the scar burned to life in a brilliant shade of red. It spread further, right past his clenched hand and up to the shoulder where it burst into a fiery lattice-work. What felt like streams of molten steel burned all along its length.

Subei's scream ended in a whimper as his voice cracked, then gave out altogether. The strength left him in a rush and it was all he could do to roll to the side, vision wavering.

His world was pain. His mind was fire. And then the edges of his vision collapsed inward, and it all went black.

* * *

It was summer on the steppe, and Subei was a boy again. Out for one of those comfortable nights before the wind's bite grew fierce. Before it swept down from the distant north, leading the mammoths on their yearly migration.

It was summer on the steppe, and the dream was back. It had been gone for some time now. Long enough Subei had convinced himself he'd moved past it.

Not so.

Wind whispered through the grass as he sprawled out in the quiet darkness, eyes turned to the skies. Brother was beside him. Not Bataar, nor Kashi. But his brother from before. The one whose name he couldn't remember, whose face he could no longer see.

Above them, the clouds parted to reveal a vast expanse populated by stars beyond measure. Scattered and swirled, they flickered in constellations too many to learn. But somehow, Brother had. Knew the ancestors they were named after and the stories that made them eternal.

"Altan, He Who Raced the Wind," Brother said, arm outstretched toward a shining point of blue-tinged light. "Fastest rider the steppe ever knew. Even in death he races still. First to rise at sundown, first to reach the far horizon."

"One day, I'll ride as fast as Altan," Subei said, too young to know better.

"'Course you will. And soon, we'll take you hunting. Teach you the ways of Arughai." Brother guided Subei's eyes to a larger sphere of light that Altan had already passed. "The First Hunter, who chases the hart across the sky. Always a step behind, but never hurried. Always patient." He traced the path with a finger, dragging it slowly in an arc from horizon to horizon.

"He must be hungry," Subei said, and Brother laughed. To humor him more than anything, probably.

It was a good dream, almost. Would have been comforting, if it'd ever ended there.

But then came the other light. Not the clean, blue-white of stars, but the lashing, hungry orange of flame. Screams followed, distant, at first. Far across the camp, but drawing closer. And then things got blurry. Sometimes Subei remembered running. Or heard a voice telling him to hide inside. But it always got clear again when the memory of the pain started. Stinging in his eyes, burning in his nose.

He was cowering in the family ger as smoke gathered above, too much for the smoke hole to handle at once. Screams echoed from outside, near drowned beneath the thunder of hooves. The clang of metal on metal.

A figure burst through the entrance of the ger. Brother again. Subei couldn't remember his face, but he couldn't forget the tears.

Ash had caught in the trails they left behind, mixed with them and turned to streaks of liquid black. An open cut on his chin wept blood down his deel.

"Subei!" he called, frantic in his search. "Where are you?"

"Here, Brother! I'm here!" He reached from where he was hiding beneath the sleeping furs.

Brother took a step, hand out.

"Subei—"

Someone grabbed him by the hair, dragged him out of the ger.

"Brother!" Subei ran after him, only to slide to a stop as a warrior ducked through the entrance. Then another, and another still. Big as bears, they were, and cloaked with smoke and sweat.

They were Ghangerai.

They were his people. He should've been safe. Should've rejoiced at the sight. Ghangerai weren't meant to spill Ghangerai blood, but these men's weapons were dripping with it.

The warriors rushed to the family trunk and ripped it open. Upended its contents across the floor as flames chewed through the top of the ger. Subei stumbled backward, and only then did one of the warriors spot him. There was a wild frenzy in the man's eye. A frenzy that, for a moment, subsided.

"Best you run now, boy."

And run Subei did, tears clouding his vision as he plunged through the flames. It was blurry again, then. And sometimes, that was where it ended. But sometimes, not. Sometimes he remembered dawn. Gray and heavy with smoke. Ash puffing up beneath his every step. And in the distance, riders. It was all he could do to limp away from them. All he could do to stay upright with each step.

These riders were also Ghangerai, but different than those who'd come in the night. Their leader swung down from his horse and, as Subei's fleeing feet finally gave out, caught him. Strong arms, lined with scars, but now, gone gentle. Careful, even.

His face Subei could remember. His name, he knew.

Kemu Khan.

* * *

Subei's thoughts came thick and slow as pine sap in winter. As if his mind didn't want to wake. As if it preferred the abyss between dreams and consciousness. But something pulled him back.

Call it a. . . feeling. Or a compulsion? Like there was something he wanted nearby. Something he needed, even if he didn't know what it was.

This feeling, this *pull*, guided him back to consciousness and dragged him from the dream.

"Calm now, calm!" A hand pressed against his shoulder, held him down.

He blinked, but one eye saw only black. The other's vision was fuzzy but grew clearer with each breath that rushed through his lungs. It cleared until he recognized the face above him.

Mahtma. An honored torol in her own right, she was House Kemu's Master of Knowledge, and Subei and his brothers' long-time tutor. She knelt above him, a frown drawn tight with concern and her eyes deeply shadowed. Beside her a healer was preparing salves and bandages.

Subei groaned, his body a mess of pains. Chest throbbing, right arm burning with a deep heat that ached all the way to the bone.

"Don't move too much," Mahtma said.

"What's happening?" he asked, but his voice was hardly more than a whisper. Ancestors above, his throat was dry. Burned something terrible. "Water. . . " he managed to rasp.

The healer's aide pressed a bowl to his mouth and tilted it slowly. Sour water spilled over Subei's lips and down his chin. Still, he drank deeply, chasing the dryness from his throat with the bitter liquid.

"Is that water or horse piss?" he asked between a rush of coughs.

"That'd be all the stomach acid in your throat," Mahtma said, arms crossed as the aide took the bowl away. "Much as you've been vomiting, it's a wonder you've any left."

Subei groaned again as he raised a hand to his head and found a bandage tied tight there. The fabric led down below his ear and then around to the back of his head. A tug and it came loose. He blinked in piercingly bright light as vision returned to his right eye.

"Don't be pulling at things, now. Shape you're in, something might fall off. And I don't mean just bandages." Another voice. Ghula, on the other side of the ger. Beside her, a second pair of healers were tending to someone he couldn't see.

Fear prickled in his stomach and he bolted upright.

"Bataar! Kashi!"

"Calm, boy." Mahtma clasped his shoulder. "They're no worse off than you."

Not saying much, that was. His vision was still coming back, but looking around he could see they were in a larger ger and daylight was pouring through the smoke escape at the peak of the ceiling. Two others lay beside him, covered in furs and bandages.

Bataar was the closest, and by all appearances sleeping peacefully. He seemed normal but for bandages covering what might've been burns on his arms and chest.

Kashi was on the other side, too far for Subei to see in any detail. Ghula was beside him as a healer dabbed his shoulder with a sopping rag.

"They'll be fine," Mahtma assured. "Probably."

"Not much we can do about the scars, though," Ghula added.

Scars? The word hung strangely in Subei's mind. And then he remembered.

The ambush. The obelisks. The explosions.

He raised his right arm to find scars all along its length. Like cracks through a broken pot. As if he'd been shattered and poorly pieced back together. Worse, though, was his vision had finally cleared enough to see Bataar and Kashi in detail. Clear enough to see they too, were shot through with a latticework of unnatural scars.

Chapter Four

BATAAR

Doesn't make any kind of sense.

Bataar turned his arm this way and that to see the scars. In some areas they were exposed, in others, covered by bandages. He pulled at the edges of those, following the streaking lines up his arm, over his shoulder. "Never seen a wound like this. And what sort of scar forms immediately?"

He'd seen the result of arrowheads and saber blades, of horse kicks and brush cat bites. Even a scabbed-over, endless smattering of nicks and cuts from the time Cousin Gerel had tried to ride a rockslide. But none of them came remotely close to whatever the hell had happened to his own arm.

To *their* arms, for they all bore the marks in mostly the same places. The scars all started in their dominant hands—where they'd been holding their sabers—and continued up most of the arm before dissipating around the shoulder joint. Naked, raw lines etched across the skin like someone had taken a needle and ripped it this way and that, carving a jagged course through their flesh.

"*Lot* of things not making sense at the moment," Bataar continued, leaning back into his trovaak pelt sleeping furs. After a few hours of consciousness, they'd been moved from the healers' ger to their own. Smaller, but familiar. And despite the warmth of the day, Kemu Khan had insisted the door stay closed. Too many curious eyes. Asking themselves if the magic of Baji

Khan had truly returned? Bataar looked down at his hands. *A good question.*

It was too warm inside the ger, but at least the smoke escape was open above and a steady breeze was slipping in.

"My saber. . . " Subei said but paused as Bataar waved him quieter. Likely no one would be able to hear them through the mammoth wool felt walls of the ger, but better to be sure.

"My saber," Subei continued, "shouldn't have been able to do that. No blade should. Cleave a man shoulder to hip, all the way through?" Even as his brother spoke, Bataar frowned at the memory. Could still see the body falling apart, each half sliding in opposite directions.

"Whatever it was, there won't be much opportunity to follow up on it," Kashi said. "Seeing as the obelisks. . . " He spread his fingers wide and puffed out a breath of air.

"I've never been the best at Mahtma's lessons, but that's not normal, right?" Bataar asked. "For stone to explode?" For all he knew there had been some lesson that explained all this, which he'd been half asleep for. Luckily, his brothers tended to mostly pay attention to the old monk's words.

"It was some sort of crystal," Subei said. "Which clears up exactly nothing."

"Hold the dog," a familiar voice called from outside, using the traditional greeting.

Dayir and Tayir, the brothers' shaggy old hounds, were piled on top of Bataar. Not much holding needed with those two, but he wrapped an arm around their thick necks anyway. They responded with an assault of wagging tails that beat against the sides of his head.

"Come on in, visit with the invalids," Kashi called and the door swung open. Daylight, for a moment, before a silhouette blocked it out.

Mahtma.

Her ash-gray hair was pulled tight in a small bun high on the back of her head, and her face was as wrinkled as a leaf at autumn's end. Made her seem already half in the grave, but she'd looked that way as long as Bataar could remember. As if she'd aged all at once some years ago, then stopped entirely. Her blue eyes surveyed them with sharp, quick movements as she ducked low through the door frame.

Though she wore a traditional homespun deel there was no hiding her foreign proportions. She was too thin, too tall, as if she had been stretched at birth. Her face was too narrow, her coloring too pale—several shades lighter than most Ghangerai. She was no daughter of the steppe, but the distant Teshkai Mountains. The only foreign region still brought to heel beneath the khanate.

"You three look awfully pleased," she said, arms crossed. "For having so recently destroyed part of Great Baji Khan's statue."

"And here I was thinking we looked closer to warmed-over death," Subei said, raising his scarred arm, then pulling at the bandages wrapped about his face and neck.

"Was anyone else hurt?" Bataar asked. He hadn't seen much before the explosion had knocked him out. If the ancestors were merciful, no one else had been affected.

"A few cuts from flying shards, not much more. Excepting your attackers of course—which is why Kemu Khan sent me. Two of them have decidedly joined their ancestors in the world next. One was seen fleeing, however. A search is underway."

"They were bandits," Subei said. "The few who escaped my trap on the way here."

Mahtma nodded at that. "The survivor will be dealt with accordingly, then."

Bataar stirred. *The bandits don't matter. They're focusing on the wrong things, as always.*

"Mahtma," he said, cutting to the heart of the matter. "What were those obelisks made of? What material could empower a sword like that?" He paused a half second. "And is there more of it?"

Bataar would give his right ball to be able to reliably recreate that supernaturally powerful blow Subei had delivered. It was somehow linked to the obelisk. *That* was what mattered.

Kashi shot him an accusatory look.

"What?" he said in response. "A weapon like that? If we controlled it? It'd put a stop to the feuding immediately."

Imagine it, all the houses unified once more. A power unmatched in the world. The way things are meant to be.

"Weapons tend to cut both ways, brother," Kashi said.

"I'm looking into it," Mahtma interjected before Bataar could reply. "The obelisks have been there as long as anyone can recall. As long as the statue, perhaps. But your father is questioning along similar lines."

Bataar shot Kashi a look.

See?

"It is my role to know such things," Mahtma continued. "And if I do not, to learn them. I am on my way to scour the histories now. Ours I know well, but will check again. It is possible the answer lies among the histories of the other houses, though I doubt they will grant my request to see them. Nonetheless, one must try. Don't break any more priceless artifacts before I return, hm?" She pressed her fists together and bowed, then departed.

"Is there *more*? Really?" Subei shot at Bataar. "One encounter wasn't enough? Nearly killed us."

Bataar prepared to respond, but before he could, another person appeared outside the door.

"Father!" he said, then pushed Dayir and Tayir off of him in his hurry to stand. His limbs were sluggish, though, and his legs unsteady. More than a few joints popped as he straightened, then bowed. Didn't feel great, but all things considered, it could have been much worse.

Kashi and Subei were also standing now and joined him in bowing.

"Come now, don't be ridiculous," another voice said. Turgenei Khatun. Mother. "Dispense with the formalities," she said, tone somehow soft yet stern at the same time. "It's only by the ancestor's mercy that you're all in one piece."

The lines creasing her face were deeper than ever, and her eyes were as fierce as Bataar had seen them. She stepped to the west side of the ger to fuss over Kashi, her youngest, first.

"We're fine, really," Bataar said as she made her way to him.

"I'll be the judge of that," she said, checking his bandages, then grabbing his chin and turning it this way and that. "Guess I

32

should be thankful you didn't manage to disfigure yourself," she huffed, then moved on to Subei. "You haven't looked this poorly since the day Kemu found you." She grabbed his sleeping furs and pulled them over his shoulders.

"You're forgetting about the time he brought a tree down on himself," Kashi laughed.

"It was you who started the cut wrong, as I recall," Subei fired back.

Bataar waved them both to silence with a jerk of his hand and a hiss. This wasn't the time for the usual ribbing.

"My sons." Kemu Khan spoke, voice level. "The ancestors have been kind this past day. Let us show thanks and leave it at that."

"Of course, Father," Bataar said, and Kashi and Subei nodded in agreement.

"Or, we'll leave it *after* your attacker is found." And then Kemu's voice shook with barely restrained anger. "It's against Baji's law to spill Ghangerai blood at any time, but during Kurultai? In this sacred valley?" he growled, and his hand gripped tight to his saber's hilt.

"There is nothing more we can do to them," Turgenei said, voice sharp and low. "The world next must see to their punishment."

"One yet lives," Kemu said. "They will be found."

"It may be a coincidence," Bataar said, not sure if he should. "But. . . the bandits' horses were from the herds of House Tugu. Likely stolen. But yesterday, when we rode into the valley, I thought I recognized one of the horses. It was penned in House Tugu's camp."

"Entirely possible it was a coincidence," Kashi added, voice cautious. "Even if the patterning was similar."

"I don't wish for further conflict with our cousins, Father." Bataar spoke carefully, understanding the weight of the accusation. "But this is what I saw."

"Hm." Kemu grunted it, but somehow the sound itself carried his suspicion. "It has been too long since Tugu Khan and I have spoken face to face. Let us fix that." He turned to the door, then paused. "I will see him now. But tomorrow, you will join me in his camp. Show me where you saw this horse."

"Tomorrow's the tournament," Bataar said at once as his heart missed a beat.

"Of course, you won't be competing," Turgenei said, and Kemu nodded his agreement.

We must compete. To even suggest backing out now is ridiculous. We are no cowards.

Bataar stepped forward, shook his head. "We won the right to represent House Kemu. Bested every team that stepped forward for this opportunity. We can't abandon it now. It'd be an insult to everyone we beat—and bring shame on our entire house!" Bataar said it with rushed words and though he fought it, he was sure his face looked as panicked as his words sounded.

"You're injured. You will surely lose." Kemu didn't soften the words. It was simply a matter of fact. They needed to be in top fighting form, and with all that'd happened, they weren't. "Better to respectfully bow out."

"Better to dare and fail than to never dare at all." Subei stepped up beside his brother. "Your words, Father. And as true now as they've always been."

"Ancestors above." Turgenei rolled her eyes to the smoke escape and the heavens beyond. "How terrible I must have been in past lives to deserve such foolish sons." But then a smile was pulling at Kemu Khan's mouth. Turgenei sighed all the more. "And an even more foolish husband!"

"You'd rather lose with honor—and likely no small measure of pain—than bow out?" Kemu asked. None of them answered. It wasn't necessary.

Kemu laughed, then.

"By blood and by fate, truly, you are my sons."

"And they'll end up as old, achy, and grumpy as you," Turgenei said. "If they don't get themselves killed first."

Chapter Five

SUBEI

"Oof." Subei winced, then tried another swing and was left sucking his teeth as pain lanced through his sword hand. It was still tender from where the bolts of light had bit at it, a deep, throbbing ache like the elders always complained about in their bones.

They'd spent all of the day prior resting, stretching, and willing their bodies to heal, as if it were a matter of effort instead of time.

As usual, time won out.

"Come on, boy. Run the motions. It's going to hurt when you get hit anyway. Consider this extra practice," Ghula said, leading Subei into another flurry of saber slashes, side steps, and lunges.

His body protested with each movement, but she was right. The tournament was fought with blunted weapons, but that didn't mean they didn't hurt. And while no one could make sense of exactly what'd happened when the obelisks had exploded, at the moment, his body just felt incredibly sore. And sluggish, to boot. He'd had worse. And thankfully, while the skin around them was still raw and pink, the scars themselves didn't hurt much.

"Don't shorten your stride," Ghula snapped, spinning around to where Kashi was practicing with a spear. "Step-step, *step!*" she cried, demonstrating as she moved through the quick half-strides of a crow hop and then into a full lunge. "Won't hit a thing if you don't close the distance. Let them think you're outside of striking range until you've already hit them."

"Of course, teacher."

"Bataar, damn it." She hurried to where he was practicing stances, then started fussing over his footing. "Roots, boy. *Roots!*"

"You'd think she's the one fighting today," Subei said, leaning in close to Kashi. "Way she's stressing over every little thing."

As if to drive home his words, a horn blared outside. The droning note reverberated off the mountainside above the tournament ground and rolled across the tent. He could almost see the fabric shaking with the sound. Could certainly feel it through his feet.

"We'll be the ones getting knocked senseless," Kashi said, staring out of the tent and onward to the competitors' entrance. "She'll be the one sitting in the stands having to watch our every mistake. Think she's bad now? Talk to anyone unlucky enough to share her row."

Drums were beating now and the crowd was cheering so loud it sounded like they were in the tent—and still, somehow, Ghula heard them whispering.

"You going to talk your way to a win out there?" she snapped.

"Sorry, teacher." Subei and his younger brother said it at the same time, then tossed in a bow before separating to continue their last-minute preparation.

Slash, slash, duck, step, slash. Spin, repeat. Subei ran through a basic sequence with his training saber. Tried to focus on his grip, the blade's angle, and his weight distribution—and found his mind right back to the obelisks. And the glowing red sword. And the bandit, falling to pieces.

And then the explosion. A rush of red light, of flying crystalline shards, and. . .

Something flashed in his vision. Not in memory, in the present. He looked down, searching for the source. It'd come from below? There was nothing but trampled grass, a few boot

36

prints. He turned, looking around the tent and finding nothing out of the ordinary.

But there'd been a light, he'd seen it. Just for a moment, a flash. And not just a particularly vibrant memory either. This flash had been blue.

Had it come from. . . no. Not possible. He raised his arm, frowned at the scars. They were pink and raw as ever. And certainly not blue.

"Stop admiring your scars, Subei," Ghula snapped. "Odds are, you'll have more before this day's through, anyway."

A horn sounded. Like those before but deeper, older. A horn that'd been blown for one purpose since the great khan himself established the first great Kurultai.

The tournament was beginning.

* * *

It wasn't just khans' sons who fought in the tournament. Anyone could, as long as they brought two teammates and the blessing of their house. Might've been the various minor houses didn't bear the direct lineage of Baji Khan, but their honor was still recognized. Usually, the teams from the major houses won, but not always. And not in this round, as their cousin, Gerel, was learning.

Subei sucked down a wince as Gerel's opponent spun, smacking her spear into the back of his knees and dropping him to the grass.

The crowd erupted into cheers. Spectators were crammed into the stone-cut stands all the way up the hillside. They over-flowed up the mountain as well, and all along the length of the valley's central thoroughfare, everyone stretching tall for a better view. Seemed every person in the valley had turned out to watch and drink and cheer themselves hoarse.

This round hadn't been much of a fight. Gerel's two team-mates fell quick, which was all the worse news for him as now he faced all three champions of Minor House Tergrim at the same time. Not entirely insurmountable. At least, not until a swift kick to the chest sent him tumbling out of bounds.

"The representatives from Minor House Tergrim advance!" the tournament master shouted and the resulting cheers were so loud Subei felt the ground shaking through his boots.

"Hah!" the victorious team cried as one, fists clenched and raised to the sky. Above them, and the rest of the tournament grounds, the statue of Great Baji Khan watched on imperiously. Even from the other end of the field, Subei avoided his gaze. It was just a statue, but even so, those cold, stone eyes seemed focused on him. Just as his own were locked on the empty stone bases where the obelisks once stood.

"Think this is going to be us," Bataar said and clapped his brothers on the shoulders. Subei only winced a bit as the hand came down. The shot of pain passed quickly though, replaced instead with a bubbling excitement as the tournament master waved the crowd to quiet. Or, the closest it could get to quiet at any rate.

"The honorable champions from House Tugu," he shouted. The crowd's roar turned to an echoing chant.

"*Tu-gu! Tu-gu!*"

Drums pounded along to the rhythm, and from the front row, Tugu Khan dipped his fingers into a bowl of airag then flicked the drops of fermented mare's milk into the air. An offering to the ancestors. When that was done, he raised the bowl in one hand and downed its contents.

"And facing them, the honorable champions from House Kemu!"

The crowd's roar was even louder this time, which made sense seeing as their house alone had brought as many warriors as the other three combined.

"*Ke-mu-u! Ke-mu-u!*" the spectators chanted, and the drums followed in a boom, boom-boom rhythm.

"The khan will be proud of you no matter what happens. . . " Ghula hissed, shaking the brothers by their shoulders.

"Of all the times to go soft on us," Subei shot back with a chuckle.

"But *I'll* accept nothing less than total victory. Get out there." She pushed them forward and onto the tournament grounds. Another roar from the crowd at that, and Kemu Khan stood to make his own offering of airag. Turgenei was beside him, and from her expression, she was enjoying herself. That or she was just really good at hiding her concern. Bit of both, maybe.

"Cousins Chimbai, Tahar, and Delbeg," Bataar said, taking the measure of their opponents. "Supposed to be the best fighters here."

Kashi rolled his shoulders and even with the noise of the crowd, Subei could hear them popping. Couldn't have felt good. Probably about as good as his own.

Three weapons were allowed for the tournament. Spear, saber, and shield. Kashi had the spear—though for tournament purposes, the point had been replaced with an unsharpened stone, then wrapped in twine such that blows still hurt, but wouldn't do lasting damage. Bataar carried the shield. With his size and strength, he could make the most out of it. In traditional fashion, the shield consisted of a circular iron base with the face wrapped in coiled wicker. The coils spiraled inward until they met at the center. The shield was held by leather straps across his palm and his knuckles pressed to its inside face. It wasn't strapped along the forearm like the heavy infantry of Mercer, or the knights of those kingdoms in the distant west. No, the Ghangerai style allowed a shield to be used for more precise blocking and even more powerful bashing.

That left Subei with the saber. Blunted, but a fine weapon still. Just the right mix of speed and weight. Subei gave it a casual swing as he strode forward. The excitement bubbling through his gut would have been invigorating if gripping the weapon hadn't already made his palm sore and wrist weak. If every step didn't send a painful jolt up his legs.

"*Ke-mu-u! Ke-mu-u!*" the crowd cheered, but by the time the brothers stepped to the center of the field, House Tugu's supporters were giving it a good fight with their own. "*Tu-gu! Tu-gu!*"

"Cousins," Chimbai said, already smiling in a decidedly unfriendly fashion. "You've looked better."

Subei let out a long, slow breath, steadying his nerves and stifling a retort.

"And yet, still better looking than you." Okay, well, stifling any *more* retorts.

"We'll try not to injure our fragile, southern cousins any more than they've already injured themselves," Delbeg said.

"Great Khan!" the tournament master shouted, and the competitors spun as one and bowed to Baji's statue. "May this fight please the ancestors. May the winner bring honor unto their house."

"I'm surprised you can even face the Great Khan," Chimbai whispered out the side of his mouth. "After you desecrated his statue."

Before Subei could think of a clever response, the tournament master was shouting again.

"Champions at the ready!"

They rose from their bows and faced one another. The chanting and drums boiled to a fever pitch, and then a low, long horn blast cut through it all.

"Fight!"

Bataar rushed forward with the shield and drove it high at Delbeg's head. He raised his own shield to block the blow—and exposed his stomach, which Kashi assaulted with a lunging blow from his wrapped spearhead. Just as planned. The wind went out of Delbeg all at once as he crumpled to the ground. Tahar's spear came stabbing in to do the same to Bataar, but a weighty blow from Subei's saber drove it into the dirt instead—and left him open to Chimbai's slashing strike. It came down across his shoulder, and Subei clenched his teeth against the pain. Or, against the pain he'd expected. Instead, the blow's impact was subdued. As if Subei were wearing a leather jacket instead of the thin fabric of his traditional competitor's tunic. Had Chimbai not put any strength into the blow? *An insult!* He was toying with them.

Subei growled. He'd show his foolish cousin the error of such ego. He brought his saber to bear and found Chimbai frowning, as if confused. The look passed in an instant as he parried Subei's slash. Pain lanced through Subei then. Not from anything Chimbai had done, but from his own movements.

40

Every slash sent shocks through his arm and shoulders, jolting the already sore muscles and bones.

The pain distracted him enough for one of Chimbai's attacks to slip through and catch him in the ribs. Again, a deadened blow.

"You'll regret holding back," Subei snarled, already lunging with a low strike. Chimbai's look of confusion turned to something approaching fear. Misplaced fear, however, as the attack never even reached him. Pain exploded through Subei, and he stumbled to the side. Light flashed at the back of his eyes, bursting to overtake his vision. First it was bright, then utterly, impossibly black. But the moment passed in a heartbeat, and then it was all he could do to groan and stagger away.

Delbeg remained vulnerable—still gasping from where Kashi's stab had taken him in the stomach—but there was no room to capitalize on it. Two on three should have been in the brothers' favor, but it seemed Subei wasn't the only one feeling his injuries.

Bataar blocked each of Tahar's spear strikes with sound technical form, but every movement brought a grunt of pain.

Kashi spun to the side with a sweeping blow—meant to bring Chimbai down—but it should have been faster. Even with momentum in his favor, it was obvious Kashi was laboring. Chimbai parried away the swinging spear, then cracked Kashi across the ribs. It should have been a debilitating blow, but it took three more before Kashi finally went down groaning.

Tahar struck again and Bataar slipped around the attack— pain clouding his eyes—then punched his shield into the side of their cousin's head. That sent him stumbling, and as Chimbai's eyes snapped over to his teammate, Subei had his opening.

He darted in as fast as his legs would carry him, drew back the saber, took aim—and the breath burst from his chest as Delbeg's shield caught him in the stomach. He stumbled back, bracing for a pain that didn't come. An attack like that could have broken his ribs, and he counted himself lucky it hadn't.

The smile slipped from Delbeg's face.

"You wearing armor under there?" he growled, scrutinizing Subei's tunic.

"Maybe you just don't hit as hard as you think you do," Subei spat back before darting in to attack. But as he stomped forward, white hot pain lanced through his leg. It raced up his spine to burst in his skull, and for a moment, everything went black. When the world came back, he was on his face.

In the crowd, the *Ke-mu-u* chants were faltering.

Lying in the dirt, Subei drew in a wheezing breath, sucking hard to fill his lungs. Deep inside, something rattled. No time to wonder what as he coughed, then rolled back to his feet. He had just gotten them under him when Delbeg's leg swept them back out and he was reintroduced to the ground.

Head squashed to one side, Subei had a good view of Chimbai driving back both Bataar and Kashi at the same time. His saber flashed in and out, up and down, hacking at Bataar's shield one moment, then flicking out to smack away Kashi's sluggish lunges the next.

"Come on then," Subei snarled, more to himself than anyone as his feet dug in and just managed to get purchase. His saber didn't come along, slipped from his grip as he rose. It was only then he noticed that his hand had gone numb.

Tahar and Delbeg faced him, their victory all but assured. So why didn't they look pleased? Drawing out the embarrassment, perhaps? Subei wasn't going to let them.

He stutter-stepped forward—planning a feint and reverse into a spinning kick—but his legs crumpled beneath him in a sudden flare of agony.

"*The hell is wrong with me?*" Subei growled into the now all too-familiar ground. His right hand was still dead, but his left clenched a fistful of dirt as he dragged himself up once more. He was already battered and bruised, already weak after the ordeal at the obelisks, but now? Now his injuries cut deeper. Straight to his pride.

Subei didn't need to look to know Bataar and Kashi were being driven further back. He could feel it. As if something inside knew they were moving away. Moment by moment, he was more alone. Must have been what Gerel had felt in the round prior.

All around, the warriors of House Kemu and the assembled

42

might of the Ghangerai cheered. Though, Subei was pretty sure there were laughs mixed in as well now. Above, the Great Baji Khan watched on.

"Stop playing with me. End this with honor," Subei said, and the words came with a growl. A growl he hadn't intended. It was primal, animalistic, like no sound he'd ever made before. It carried him forward and he lunged at Delbeg, fists swinging with renewed fury—even if the right one was still numb.

Delbeg resisted the assault with his shield while Tahar stepped in from behind to swing the shaft of the spear into Subei's now-exposed kidneys. One blow, two. Three. Four. The flurry landed with the sound of a butcher tenderizing meat, each thumping blow reverberating across the tournament ground.

These blows, Subei felt. They hurt and yet, it still felt like Tahar wasn't giving his all.

An angry scream clawed from Subei's throat, and then, as if it knew what it was doing, his body moved. There was no thought in it, just instinct. He swung a backhand blow that sent Tahar dodging backward, then raised his right hand to the sky, palm open wide.

Light, then. Brilliant and blue, it burst from beneath the fabric of his sleeve, growing brighter and brighter with every passing moment. The sleeve slid down his arm, and he stared in surprise as his scars burned with a searing blue light.

The crowd gasped, and a wave of shock rippled through the stands. Warriors who'd known feuds and violence since they were old enough to walk fell backward at the unnatural sight.

Subei himself recoiled. Or would have, were he not frozen in that moment, unable to control his body. A warmth bubbled in his stomach, boiled up inside of his chest. It flowed through his shoulder, then up his arm. His forearm, his wrist, then into his palm where, with a final crackling pop, a burning orb of floating blue light flared into existence.

Screams poured from the crowd, and some spectators fled, sprinting out of sight.

Subei ignored them, fixated on the miracle unfolding. The orb hovered impossibly over his palm, wide as his hand and nearly too big to be held. It bobbed back and forth, as if restless,

43

unable to stay in one place. Tiny bolts of lightning crackled and popped within it, the occasional arc breaking free to snap at his flesh. Where they struck, the skin tingled, but seemed otherwise unharmed.

Subei wanted to stare. Would have spent an eternity in that moment, trying to comprehend what he was seeing. But without intention from him, his arm lashed forward, flinging the orb sidearm as if skipping a stone.

Time seemed to slow as it flew, arcs of lightning in miniature snapping out to rage at the air, the crowd, and then finally—as the orb approached the ground—the dry tip of a blade of grass.

There was an explosion as if the sun itself had fallen from the sky. A wave of heat, then blinding, burning light as the patch of ground beneath the orb disappeared in a plume of flame.

The crowd screamed, scattering, clawing over those that fell in their panic to flee. A shower of debris fell from above, clumps of burning soil slapping back to earth.

Delbeg lowered his shield as steaming soil slipped free from its face. Behind him, Tahar was shaking, eyes wide and mouth slack.

The last of the debris fell amid a pitch-black cloud of smoke. The wind caught it and drove it swirling away to reveal a crater half a horse deep and just as wide. The soil inside was scorched black.

In the wake of the blast, the world was silent. Silent but for a shuddering breath as Subei's hand fell back to his side. He had control of it again. He raised his palm to stare at the brilliant, glowing blue scars stretched across it. As he did, there was another surge of heat from within, and a second orb flared to life.

He froze, staring at it bobbing and crackling just above his palm.

And then, across the field, he caught sight of Kashi. Eyes fixed as he stood, breathing heavy, but rooted in place. Bataar, too. Except, after their eyes met, Bataar's raised to the sky.

No, not the sky. The statue.

Towering above them, the statue of the Great Baji Khan. It stood, one palm outstretched and cradling a stone. A boulder.

An orb.

An orb the songs said had glowed as bright as the sun itself. An orb very much like the one bobbing now in Subei's hand.

Silence, still, blanketing the whole of the tournament ground. A hundred and fifty thousand Ghangerai transfixed.

And then, from far in the back, someone shouted.

"Glory to the Great Khan! Glory to Baji!" A pause. "And glory to his heir!"

Chapter Six

SUBEI

"Subei. Subei!" Kashi was rushing toward him. "What the hell was that?" he whispered, as if the crowd would overhear. As if it would matter. They were chanting again, but neither *Tu-gu* nor *Ke-mu-u*. Instead, it was *Ba-ji Khan! Ba-ji Khan!*

Subei barely heard them though. Barely heard Kashi, for that matter. His eyes were fixed on his hand. On the orb still bobbing there. Kashi looked down to it, then at the still-smoking crater, and took a step back.

Bataar sprinted up a moment later.

"Brother! Are you okay?" He too seemed to remember the orb a step late and froze in place.

"I. . . " Subei paused, frowning at the orb. "Uh. How do I get rid of it?"

"Toss it somewhere safe?" Bataar said with a wince. "Away from the crowd."

Worth a try. But then the orb wavered a moment, spluttering. And likewise, all along Subei's arm, the scars were dimming. They faded like dying embers, dimmer and dimmer. By the moment, the light seemed to slip away, back into his flesh. The orb followed, flowing into him almost like water poured from a bowl until finally, with a little hiss, it disappeared entirely.

It was only then he could finally breathe.

Subei looked up to find the entire crowd chanting and staring and cheering, and immediately his breath was gone again.

"I think. . . uh, I think the obelisks might have done more than just give me weird scars." The looks in his brothers' eyes told him they'd had the same thought. "Done more to *us*," Subei corrected suddenly, and pointed.

Bataar's scars were glowing. And Kashi's. Neither so brightly as Subei's, but enough to see the piercing blue light flickering beneath the skin like a candle's flame caught in the wind.

Kashi immediately tucked his hands into his armpits.

"*Please don't explode, please don't explode,*" he said, a wince drawn tight across his face.

"The obelisks were just the beginning. Think what *this* could do, brothers." Bataar was staring into his own palm now. There was no orb, but he was transfixed nonetheless. "If we could summon it on command?" His eyes crept up to the statue. "Listen. Listen to them." He turned slowly, taking in the crowd.

"*Ba-ji Khan! Ba-ji Khan!*"

"My sons. . . " Kemu Khan was walking toward them, his strides uncertain—shaking, even. "My sons, this. . . this is—"

"Glory to the heir of Baji!" Budai Khan bulled past at a full sprint, dropping to his knees before the brothers. "To the. . . to the *heirs* of Baji!" he shouted, eyes going wide as he spotted Bataar and Kashi's scars. He slammed his fists together then, knuckle to knuckle, and bowed so low his forehead was planted in the grass. "From this day until my last, the House of Budai swears fealty to you, and to the spirit of the Great Baji Khan which so clearly dwells within you."

"Well, uh. . . " The words caught in Subei's mouth. Or maybe he stopped them there. Hard to be sure because what did one say to that? No one had ever sworn fealty to him before and could he even accept? Did he want to? These thoughts and more reeled through his mind and he hadn't even begun to make sense of them—only just managed to look sideways at his brothers—when Arban Khan arrived, breathing hard. He hit his knees as well.

"House Arban rejoices at your return, Great Khan. We stand ready to follow you once more and conquer wheresoever leads your burning fury!" he shouted, eyeing Subei's now empty hand. "Baji's burning fury. . . " The khan said it as if in disbelief. "Let us sweep across the world. Let us restore the legacy of our people." With that, he bowed to the ground. "House Arban swears fealty to you, Great Khan. From this day unto the last."

Two khans, then. Two of the four most powerful leaders of their people, prostrate before him. He'd just wanted glory in the tournament. To bring honor to his house. And now, two khans were—no.

Three khans.

"The House of Tugu agrees with its cousins." Tugu Khan strode forward, head held high. "Tugu was firstborn of Baji, and founded our house. For a century, my fathers and my fathers' fathers have forfeited their birth names and taken up the mantle of Tugu Khan. It was the greatest honor of my life to join them. But now," he spread his arms wide, gesturing out to the crowd which had yet to cease chanting. "As our people look on, and our ancestors watch from the eternal blue sky above, I have found an even greater honor. A higher purpose." He threw a sidelong glance at Kemu Khan. "Long have the houses of the first and second children of Baji sought to outdo each other. Let us put that aside today. Let us both swear fealty to a new house. Or, perhaps, an old one. Restored at long last." Only then did Tugu Khan lower himself, and even then, it was slow. Controlled and deliberate as he eased to his knees. He closed his fists, but stopped short of pressing them together, then stared into Subei's eyes. "House Tugu stands ready to swear itself to the returned khan."

"I'm. . . " Subei couldn't stop his gaze from climbing the great statue. "I'm not Baji Khan."

"Only the Great Khan could wield such magic. Perhaps his spirit has returned to us and you—*you all*—are its vessel," Tugu Khan said.

"I don't know what's happened." Subei raised a hand, studying the scars. "Or what any of this is."

There was one thing he knew, though. One thing Tugu Khan had made very clear. His offer of fealty wasn't to House Kemu. Wasn't to serve Kemu Khan. It was to serve Subei and his brothers. He might not have understood what was happening, but he understood that much. And rejected it.

"Kemu Khan leads our house." Subei grabbed his brothers' shoulders, then raised his eyes to their father. Spoke directly to him. "Without him, I would have died, an orphan in the ashes of my family's ger. He is a wise leader, an honorable father, and above all, he is my khan."

Bataar grunted his approval, and with that, Subei found the strength for his next words. Kashi nodded his agreement, and with that, Subei found the courage to speak for them.

"If this magic inside us is truly the return of the Great Khan, then let it be so. The ancestors smile on our people. But I will not give thanks for this gift by subverting their laws—or our way of life. A son is loyal to his honorable father, and a Ghangerai is subservient to his honorable khan. I am blessed of the ancestors to have that man be one and the same." Subei pulled his eyes from Kemu and down to the kneeling khans. "Your offers honor me, mighty Khans. But I cannot accept your fealty without betraying *my* khan." Subei dropped to his knees, pressed his fists together, and bowed to Kemu. For a moment, he feared he'd said too much. Had acted too quickly, but then Bataar and Kashi joined him and he knew they were in agreement. Always had been. Always would be.

"You do me too much honor. . . my sons." Kemu Khan's words were quiet and, if Subei was being honest, his voice might have broken.

Arban Khan was the first to turn, pivoting to face Kemu.

Budai followed a moment later.

Tugu alone hesitated. A twitch in his cheek and a fire in his eye. But then, even proud Tugu relented and turned.

"Restore our people's legacy, cousin. Use this power and reclaim the might of our khanate. For you are Kemu Khan no longer." He paused, drawing in a breath. "You have become Kemu *Khagan*, khan of khans."

They held each other's gaze for a long moment, until Kemu nodded, and his cousin bowed his head. There might have been a tear in Kemu's eye then. But he clenched a fist and pounded it four times against his chest.

Once for House Tugu, the Soul of the Steppe.

Once for House Kemu, the Order in the South.

Once for House Budai, those Beloved of the Wind.

And once for House Arban, Keepers of the Eternal Road.

Kemu Khagan raised his voice to an echoing shout then, as he spoke to the whole of the assembled warriors.

"The spirit of Great Baji Khan walks among us once more." He paused, and then smiled. "We will not disappoint him."

Chapter Seven

BATAAR

"A gift! Please, I bring a gift for the heirs of Baji!"

A full day it'd been since the events at the tournament ground.

"Great Khan, hear me!"

A full day, but it'd felt like an entire season.

"Spirit of the Great Khan, whatever you need, name it!"

Didn't help neither Bataar nor his brothers had been able to get a moment alone for any of it.

"Allow me to serve you!"

"No, allow me, Great Khan! My lineage is strong, my sword arm stronger still!"

Even in their ger, at the center of House Kemu's camp, they were mobbed with visitors. Come to swear fealty or bring gifts. Some even to volunteer their life in service.

The insanity had everyone frazzled and especially Dayir and Tayir, their normally shaggy coats standing on end and their barking ceaseless as the crowds clamored outside.

"Dayir, calm!" Bataar called at him, as if shouting at a dog had ever solved anything. "And your sister, too. Tayir, come!" He snapped and she whined, but shuffled over, eyeing the door and the chaos beyond with every reluctant step.

"Glory to the heirs of Baji! Glory to the khanate reborn!"

They'd had walls of mammoth wool felt stripped from surplus gers and erected around their section of the camp, and kheshig guards stationed on either side, yet still, the crowds pressed in close. Even here, behind the firmly closed door and with the smoke escape shut and tied, Bataar could feel their eyes searching for him. Could feel how every person looked at them now, as if they had become the ancestors given form and flesh. As if Bataar, Kashi, and Subei were no more. Replaced with. . . whatever the crowds saw. The reborn spirit of Baji Khan, he supposed.

But was that such a terrible thing?

"Will it help, do you think, if I cut my ears off?" Kashi asked after his most recent attempt to plug his ears with wax and cloth had, apparently, failed.

Listen to them. The sound reminded him of the pride he'd felt as the riders of their house thundered past. But now that pride, that honor, was directed at him. Bataar half closed his eyes. His ears were doing the real work now, bringing him sounds more intoxicating than any wine. He drank them in. "Listen to our people, brothers."

"Do we have any other choice?" Subei gave him an angry glance. "Don't get me wrong. It's flattering, but it just feels. . . I don't know, misplaced? Don't give me that look." He turned to Kashi. "You know what I'm trying to say, right?"

Kashi bounced a fist on his knee a moment, then nodded. "It's like, this. . . magic," he raised his palm, studying the scars, "could be something. Could be *everything*, really. But how can we be sure yet? How can *they* be so sure? Certainly doesn't feel like the spirit of Baji Khan has taken up residence inside me."

"Feels a bit more like indigestion, if I'm being honest," Subei said.

"Who says we're supposed to feel different?" Bataar asked as he moved toward the door and considered having another look out at the desperate faces of the assembled masses. "The magic doesn't have to make us feel different to make a difference."

"I don't follow," Kashi said, and Subei nodded in agreement.

"What if the true power of this gift is potential?" Bataar turned to his brothers, stepping away from the door, then paused to gesture back to it. "The potential to inspire belief in

52

our people?" He paused, looked down at the scars lining his own arm. "Inspire fear in our enemies? To inspire—"

"Hold the dog!" A faint cry carried over the din.

"Was that Father?" Bataar turned and cracked the door, nodded, then pulled it all the way open. A wave of noise crashed in, and along with it, their parents.

Bataar shouldered the door shut behind them as Kemu Khagan paused, listening for a moment.

"Wears on you after a while, but, it is an inspiring sound, isn't it?"

"It's inspiring me to go deaf," Turgenei said, then gave them a pained smile. "I can only imagine how our sons feel."

"Kashi was contemplating cutting his ears off," Subei offered. "Only half seriously."

"No one is cutting anything off," Turgenei lectured. "Unless it's those people's tongues." She winced. "Forgive me, that was unkind. But ancestors above, the racket."

"I thought it was funny," Subei said with a shrug.

Bataar punched him in the shoulder. "Those are our people you're talking about."

"Boys, relax," Turgenei chided. "It's been a busy few days for all of us."

"Day," Kemu corrected, and her brow furrowed.

"Ancestors mercy. Has it been only one?"

Kemu laughed. Might be he'd been elevated to the highest status possible—short of the Great Khan himself—but beyond that, he hadn't changed.

"I've been in council with my cousins all day. Most of last night, too. There is much excitement about what comes next."

"What does come next?" Bataar asked, mind already full with possibilities. A united khanate was a powerful thing.

"That's why we came," Kemu said. "To hear your thoughts."

"We came to make sure they're doing okay," Turgenei interjected, giving him a look.

"And hear their thoughts. It's only fair. Great things are underway. An avalanche gathering in the high meadows. It is only fitting now that you, my sons, are the ones to kick the first pebble down the slope." He paced along the edge of the ger, cupped a hand to Kashi's face as he passed, then pulled a stool over and sat. "Cousin Budai remembers all too well the Thijan's betrayal. Believes we should take a united army east into their lands." He shrugged, eyes distant. "And he's not wrong. Traitors must be brought to heel, made an example of. It's what the Great Khan would have done. But Cousin Arban has eyes for the Mercaen trade cities beyond the western border. Not for their shameful baubles and precious metals, but for their roads. Take those, and we control the route to the distant west, to those ripe lands Baji once conquered all the way to the ocean."

"What about the south?" Bataar said, mind turning to their oldest and closest enemy. "The Zhong empire has long sown discord between the houses."

"Instigators and weak-soled scholars," Kemu said, and a hint of venom crawled into his tone. "A fine suggestion."

"Well, I for one say we conquer our own camp first," Turgenei said, rising. "Before we all go deaf." She pulled the door open and waved the nearest guard over. "Assemble a troop of your finest warriors and disperse this crowd. Gifts and offerings can be left, but no more of this shouting."

The guard looked over his shoulder, frowning.

"If it would please my Khatun, this task may require a hundred of my finest men—ten full troops—to complete."

"Whatever is required."

"Khatun," he said, then bowed and strode away barking orders.

"Ten troops?" Kemu laughed. "I fear they'll need more still. A touman, probably. With ten thousand warriors, one might beat back that calamity of noise."

"You are Khagan now," she said, chin high. "And I am Khatun. If a full touman is required, then a full touman we shall have."

The light coming through the door darkened as a guard stepped up outside.

"Returning with news of defeat so soon?" Turgenei asked, but when she opened it, Ghula bowed, then stepped in.

"A message, Khagan. The council requires your presence."

"And so it shall have me."

54

"We've just stepped away," Turgenei said. "Fine, fine. You go. I have a campaign to undertake. Where's my touman?" she asked as she stepped outside.

"She going to war?" Ghula asked, looking to the brothers for answers. Kemu Khagan smirked.

"More swiftly—and likely, more effectively—than even I." The smile turned severe. "Anyway, the council is waiting. Come, my sons. You should be present."

Bataar rose immediately.

"Actually," Ghula said with a slight bow of her head. "I thought the sudden heirs of Baji might enjoy some peace. A ride beyond the camp, perhaps? I've prepared an escort."

"Fresh air, open sky." Kemu Khagan breathed deeply. "Now, more than ever, we must remember our roots." He looked his sons over once more. "Find me when you return. I should like you to take part in the coming decisions."

"Khagan," they said as one, fists together and heads bowed as he took his leave.

Ghula shut the door behind him and for a brief, blissful second, the noise beyond was dampened.

In the relative quiet, she smiled.

"Alright, boys. Subei gave us something of a show in the tournament. Impressive." She nodded. "But a closer look is in order. I've commandeered some training dummies. What say we go find a quiet spot then blow them to pieces? Find out what this magic can really do."

Bataar couldn't stop the grin creeping across his face at her words, the pride of his house still ringing in his ears.

"Yes, let's."

Chapter Eight

SUBEI

"Yah!" Subei shouted, then thrust a hand toward the training dummy. All of nothing happened. Again. A bit of breeze kicked up, and a few pieces of straw slipped free from the sagging dummy. The most damage that'd been done so far.

They'd found a quiet patch of grass out of sight of Kurul Valley. The herds were around, but mostly they grazed idly, only letting out the occasional moo, whinny, or in the case of trovaaks, rumbling grumble. A few Ghangerai moved among them, tending to things here and there, but the kheshig guards Ghula'd brought ensured any onlookers kept their distance.

Not that there'd been anything to see yet.

"Baji's Burning Fury. That was what Arban Khan called it." Subei cursed as he stared down at his palm and its decidedly unlit scars. "I started out slinging explosive balls of light by accident, but now I can't even get the scars to wake up. We're going backward," he said with a cringe. "I'm better rested now, focused, and not aching anywhere near as bad. If anything, it should be easier, right?"

Kashi shrugged. Beside him, Bataar frowned. They'd made exactly the same amount of progress.

"Subei," Ghula said, her voice gentle. "I have an idea."

"Do tell." He looked her way just in time to catch the shield and cudgel she'd thrown.

"Defend yourself!" She charged and swung her saber into his

shield. The impact reverberated up his arm, but for all the force of it, the impact felt almost subdued. Was she pulling her blows?

"I don't understand how this is—"

She cut him short with a slash.

"The magic of Baji Khan lives within you." She landed another battering strike, the force of it throwing the shield to the side and exposing him to a follow-up. "You just have to learn to use it." Her kick caught him square in the chest and lifted him off his feet. Concussive force barreled through him, shaking his vision a moment as he crashed down to the earth. He cursed, steeling himself against a surge of pain, but when it came, it wasn't as bad as he'd expected.

"You just have to learn to use it," he growled, mimicking her words. "That's just the trick, isn't it?"

But then he could feel the energy within, as if it'd suddenly awoken. It was a buzzing deep in his stomach. But any control he had over it stopped there. Stopped with simply feeling that it existed.

"Keep moving!" Ghula roared as her shadow descended from above. Subei rolled to the side as a boot stomped down where his head had just been.

"Is this supposed to help, or have I just become the training dummy?" he asked, rolling into a crouch.

Ghula sheathed her saber. She made as if to speak, then struck forward with a kick instead. It caught Subei in the hip and sent him stumbling backward. Her shield slammed into his shoulder next. The world spun and he found the salty taste of blood heavy on his tongue.

"I concede!" Subei threw his shield down and raised his hands. "I con—"

An open-handed strike caught him on the ear and set his head to ringing. He lurched backward, world tilting.

"Enough!" Subei snarled and clenched a fist. Anger roiled in his gut, buzzing like a hornets' nest given a good kick.

Ghula only smiled. Pleased with herself, apparently.

He spat a glob of blood on the grass.

"The hell are you smiling about?"

"See for yourself." She nodded, then stepped back.

Subei blinked, then looked down.

His scars were alive, blue light shining through the sleeve of his deel. And then, as he focused, he could feel the energy inside tossing and swirling. As if it wanted to be used.

Acting on instinct, he grunted and flexed his core. The energy moved, rushing up his arm—just like it had in the tournament. It built in his wrist, then held steady, waiting just beneath the palm.

"Can I. . . " Subei urged it forward. Willed it, almost, and then light flared in his hand. Nothing but a spark, yet it quickly resolved itself into a glowing blue orb.

"Baji's Burning Fury," Ghula said, still smiling.

In the wake of forming the orb, Subei found a wash of energy had drained from him. Like he'd just hefted a too-heavy barrel overhead. The ache wasn't physical, though. It was almost. . . spiritual? But he wasn't focused on that at the moment. The glowing light bobbing in the palm of his hand had his full attention.

It hovered there, crackling and hissing, the occasional tiny bolt of lightning striking out from it and into his skin.

Elated, Subei nearly jumped to let out a whooping cheer—before remembering dropping the orb would probably not be the best idea. But this was it! He raised his palm, holding the orb out at chest level. He spotted the training dummy next and grinned.

He reared back, threw, then ducked away as a plume of fire burst from the impact site. The dummy that'd been taunting him was there one minute, then nothing more than an echoing boom and hissing, slow falling embers the next.

"Still can't believe I'm actually seeing that," Bataar said, eyes wide.

"Seems you need to get the shit kicked out of you more often, brother," Kashi laughed.

"You might just be right," Subei said, then flexed his core again before the energy buzzing inside could fade. Just as before, if not a bit easier this time, another orb swelled in his palm.

And then, just like that, Subei's aches and pains were gone. He laughed them off, enamored with the swirling ball of light. It was smaller than the two he'd conjured in the tournament. That fact failed to diminish his excitement. He moved his hand to the side and the orb began to slip away. Closed his fingers slightly and it halted, hovering an equal distance between his palm and fingers. He tightened his grip and the orb seemed to shrink, then dim. Opening his hand allowed it to grow back to its original size.

One more good squeeze next. He closed his hand entirely and the orb fizzled around the edges, wobbled frantically, then disappeared with a sizzle.

Subei looked up, breathing heavily, but unable to fight the smile pulling at his cheeks.

"That was. . . amazing."

"How did it feel?" Bataar was in close now, staring at Subei's empty hand. "What is it like?"

"Amazing," Subei said again, too excited to elaborate.

"Now we're getting somewhere." Ghula gave a nod of approval.

"How did you know that would work?" Subei asked.

"Wasn't certain." She shrugged. "But the last time you used the magic, you were fighting, you were losing, and you were—"

"Angry," Kashi said all at once, then nodded as if that'd been some fascinating revelation.

"Desperate!" Bataar said next.

"Okay, well. Yeah, just pile it on, huh? I don't recall you two doing any better."

"Put aside your ego," Ghula said, drawing in close. "We're exploring here. Experimenting. And for the moment, this works. If anger's a trigger for the magic, so be it." She crossed her arms, straightened her back. "You've been given this gift, Subei. Now master it." She snapped her fingers suddenly. "Conjure another orb. Then again, and again. I want to see a hundred repetitions of Baji's Burning Fury until it's second nature." She turned to face Bataar and Kashi. "Who's next?"

Kashi ducked away, hiding behind their bigger brother. He needn't have, though, seeing as Bataar was already advancing on Ghula, shield and saber in hand. "I might give you a bit more fight than Subei."

Ghula chuckled at that.

"Might. But probably not."

The afternoon sun slipped by overhead, passing ever closer to the western horizon. The grunts and groans of Bataar's training were nothing but background noise as Subei focused on the magic within. Urged it to the surface time and time again.

At first, he needed the lingering anger from the fight to conjure the magic. He needed to think back on it, to remember the pain of each blow and provoke the anger to rise. It was like striking flint to steel to create sparks, then hoping they caught.

Only then would the magic come, would rise from its resting place, which felt approximately somewhere between his stomach and kidneys. It was always there now that he knew where to look, but before, he had to really focus to find it. Like digging through a dry riverbed to find a hint of damp beneath.

Once it was found, though, he could draw it forth by activating his core. Could lead it up whichever arm he chose, then on to his palm to manifest as a glowing orb.

The well only ran so deep, though. Every time he drew from it, the next became more difficult. And the deeper he had to search, the more his exhaustion built. It stacked up like a blizzard's snow in a mountain pass. Blanketed his mind, slowed his thoughts. He'd conjured and snuffed ten orbs by the time things started to fall apart. Felt like he was drunk almost, and he couldn't focus long. But there was an idea he wanted to try. Subei sucked down a deep breath and forced his vision steady for one last attempt.

Up to this point, he'd urged the same amount of magic out each time. The orbs that he'd created had been consistently smaller than those from the tournament. Surely that meant he could control their size?

Taking care to move a good distance from the rest of the group, Subei focused on his core once more. It responded to his attention, a dog perking up at its owner's whistle.

Slowly, careful to control how much he called forth, he drew the magic out one more time. It welled up through his body, carrying a warmth with it, then flowed over his shoulder and along his arm. When it reached the wrist, he slowed the flow and focused on letting a continuous, steady amount seep into his palm.

The first hint of light, no brighter than an ember, flared to life. Others followed, a dozen pinpoints growing and multiplying until they merged into one glowing mass. An orb like those he'd been conjuring all afternoon took shape, but when it reached the size of those before it, he didn't halt the flow of energy. It continued to grow, swelling like a storm on the horizon, darker and fiercer by the moment. The tiny bolts of lightning hissing and arcing inside the orb grew larger along with it, tingling his skin with each strike.

Subei let it grow to double the size of the others, almost too big for both hands, even.

But the size proved unstable. The orb began to shake and shudder, its edges wavering as if they would spill out from his hands—and he cut the flow of power.

The ball stopped growing, but still threatened to slip to the grass below. Using his other hand, he snuffed the unsteady orb. Slowly, he pressed his palms together to squeeze the volatile thing from existence. As it dissipated, the magic flowed back into his arm and returned to its place deep in his stomach.

When the danger was past, Subei let out a breath he didn't realize he'd been holding. The orbs in the tournament had been half that size and were still big enough to blow a crater in the ground. He had the sudden urge to discover what the one he'd just created could do, but a healthy sense of self-preservation quelled it.

Subei, He Who United the Khanate—then blew himself to ash and scraps of burnt hair. That song wouldn't ring down through the generations. Probably. Hopefully.

A buffeting wind howled out of the south, and he turned, expecting to see a storm approaching. But then Ghula slammed into the ground and rolled several times before coming to a stop beside him.

She'd left a torn up trail of grass and dirt along the path and, at the head of it, Bataar stood smiling, scars alight. He lowered the open palm he'd been pointing at her.

"Bah. Subei's magic was better, if you ask me," Kashi said,

dismissing his older brother with a wave. "Baji's Burning Fury is way cooler than. . . I don't know, Baji's Breaking Wind?"

Bataar allowed himself a mischievous smile.

"No one's asking you."

He thrust an open palm in their youngest brother's direction and the air around him trembled with an unseen force. Kashi, too, was bowled over and driven backward, sliding on his back across the ground.

When he stopped, he pulled himself up with a groan, followed by a rude gesture at Bataar, who only laughed.

Ghula was up then, smiling as she dusted herself off. "Hell of a hit." She clapped Bataar on the shoulder. "Now do it again." She turned to Kashi. "Ready to find out what you can do?"

Afternoon passed to evening then, as they continued training. Bataar settled on calling the ability he'd discovered *North Wind Scours*, and for once, Kashi was too busy being whooped by Ghula to toss back any clever retorts. The feeling of drunkenness hadn't left Subei though, so while his brothers practiced, he sat in the grass and tried not to focus on how much the world was spinning.

The guards were positioned on horseback around the area, turned outward and watching the passing herds, herders, and occasional birds. Somehow, word that he and his brothers were here hadn't spread to the camp yet, and for the first time since the tournament, there was quiet. Well, quiet enough except for Kashi grunting and cursing as Ghula ran him through the paces.

Bataar approached from behind, his footfalls heavy and tired.

The thought hit Subei as he stared out at the steppe—but, hold on. He looked over his shoulder to find Bataar *was* approaching. But too far off for his steps to have been heard. And Bataar was directly behind him. There was no way Subei could have caught his movement from the corner of an eye.

So how had he known his brother was coming? It'd just been a thought. A feeling, almost.

Instinctual.

"You're feeling it too?" Bataar called.

And then, just like it'd been with the magic within, once Subei knew it was there, it was all the easier to feel. There was a.

. . a *pull*. As if he'd left something behind and felt the urge to return to it. But that something was Bataar. And the closer he came, the more clearly the pull could be felt. Until he stepped within about fifty paces. Then, the feeling evaporated all at once.

"That's uh, strange." Subei looked to the closest guard, astride a horse some hundred or so paces away. She looked, and felt, like a normal person. No connection. No pull.

But there was one more behind. He climbed to his feet, turned to face it.

Kashi.

And he was looking their way, eyes wide beneath a furrowed brow. He jogged closer, then stopped. Backed up. Then forward again. All the while, the pull danced in Subei's head. From Bataar's quizzical expression, he was experiencing the same.

"You're. . . you're both feeling that, right?" Kashi drew within fifty paces and, just as before, the feeling dissipated. He stopped in his tracks, frowning. Then backed up again and the feeling returned.

"This. . . is new," Subei said. There'd been a lot of that lately.

Kashi stepped closer and again, the pull disappeared. Except, no. There was another. So faint Subei had missed it before. So faint it almost wasn't there. But he was reassured it did exist when they all turned to face it.

West, and distant.

"Guess we're headed west," Bataar said.

Chapter Nine

BATAAR

They left immediately, but not without a full escort. Ghula wouldn't have it any other way and, admittedly, Bataar couldn't fault her, even if it did bother him. They'd become stronger and somehow that translated to needing *more* protection.

A good bow, a trusted horse, and my honor's guidance are all I need.

All the same, Ghula and the guards that'd been stationed around the training ground rode with them now as the skies sank into dusk. Twenty warriors in total, armed and armored. A living shield ready to protect them from whatever was ahead.

"We should send scouts first," Ghula said, scowling toward the horizon. They weren't but an hour's ride from Kurul Valley, but she looked as if she were on campaign behind enemy lines.

"They won't know where to go. We don't even know where we're going," Bataar said, then directed his horse with his knees, pointing her a bit more southward. "We're just. . . following the pull."

"I'm sending them anyway. If there's anything out of the ordinary ahead, find it," she ordered, and five riders nodded before pulling away at a gallop.

"It's vaguely southwest," Kashi shouted after them, then closed his eyes, focusing a moment. "Yeah, southwest. Probably," he said more to himself than anyone.

"Anyone or. . . " Ghula paused, frowning. "Anything makes an aggressive move, I want more arrows in it than a hedgehog has quills, understood?"

"Understood, Torol," the guardsmen said, using her formal title. They'd bows in hand and arrows half drawn, even as their horses cantered across the steppe.

"This way," Kashi said, riding ahead. He guided them more south than west and, as Bataar focused inward, he was right. The pull was shifting. Was it moving? Or had they simply passed it and now needed to turn to stay on track?

"There!" Kashi said all at once, and rose in his saddle to point. A rocky outcrop loomed ahead. A hillside really, that'd long been eroding in the wind. And from it, one of the scouts was signaling, lance held high overhead and swinging side to side.

Bataar kicked his horse into a gallop, and they rode hard until they reached the hillside. There, they came to a stop, eyes fixed on the source of the pull.

A person, sagged around a dying fire, and coughing.

"Toss your sword away!" Ghula shouted. The guards arrived beside her, spread along the hilltop with bows at the ready. "I said, remove your sword!"

The figure didn't respond, just stayed hunched beside the embers, tracing a shape in the dirt with one finger. Behind them, a horse grazed idly. A bay dun with black-speckled flanks. Bataar's eyes went wide at that, then fell to the figure. Looking closer, he recognized her. The bandit woman with the hooked nose. The one who'd retreated from the wagon ambush what felt forever ago. Who'd come back to finish the fight at the obelisks. Who'd escaped in the chaos of them exploding.

"And here they are, like hounds on a scent," she said, but her words were cut short by a series of coughs. "I knew you were coming. Could. . . could feel your every step," she finally managed. And it was then Bataar noticed her arm. Burned. Raw. And traced through the flesh, scars. Scars very much like his. Like his brothers'.

"She has the magic, too," Kashi said, and his words rang down in Bataar's mind like a hammer against an anvil. A ringing accompanied them, high pitched and severe.

Bataar swung down from his horse, started toward her.

"Brother, wait." Subei rushed after him, and Kashi after them both.

"Don't approach her!" Ghula shouted, but Bataar didn't stop. Not until he was ten paces from the bandit. He stared her down.

"The ancestors saw fit to imbue *you* with the Great Khan's magic?" he asked the question, but the answer was already obvious. "An honorless bandit?" He tried to contain the bite in his voice, but the last part came out as a snarl.

The woman laughed. It was a broken sound, shot through with coughs.

"The Great Khan's magic? Well, isn't that something? If only father could see me now." She said it flippantly, amusement in her eyes. Through the veneer though, Bataar could see she was in bad shape. Not just burned from the obelisks but stabbed through in several places. Crystalline shards lay discarded on the ground around her, and she'd used cloth from a sleeping roll as makeshift bandages. They were stained with blood, and many of them, freshly.

"This magic is a gift from the ancestors," Bataar said, talking more to his brothers than her. "The magic to unite our people, to reclaim our pride. Our khanate."

"And yet, it was given to one such as this," Subei said, frowning at her.

She laughed again.

"Bet you three thought you were special, huh?" She coughed, then choked down a heavy swallow, pain in her features. "Thought you were chosen? No, boys. You were just in the right place at the right time. Like me." She frowned at that. "Or maybe the wrong place at the wrong time. Call it whichever you want."

"This is an insult to Baji Khan," Bataar hissed. "That she should wield his power? It disgraces us all." She had cast aside her honor, her people. And yet, here she was. Every bit as *chosen* as he. As his brothers.

"This wasn't random," Subei whispered. "Couldn't have been just. . . luck."

"What if it was?" Kashi asked, and then doubt took root in his eyes, souring his expression.

"Does it matter?" Bataar said, the words bursting from him without conscious intent.

"What?" Subei turned to him, confused. There was doubt in his eyes too. Doubt that couldn't be allowed to take root and fester. Doubt that could all too easily spread to others, spread and rot the foundations of everything they were just beginning to build.

Bataar took a deep breath and met his brothers' eyes with his strongest gaze. An iron gaze.

"Does it matter if it was random or not? We have this magic now, and look what we've already achieved." He spread his arms wide. "The steppe is united once more. We achieved what no one since the Great Khan has been able—and without spilling a drop of our people's blood. Generations of feuding swept aside in a day. Already the Houses of Arban and Budai and even Tugu have sent for the rest of their fighting might. Brothers, the whole of our people will descend on Kurul Valley. The way it's meant to be." He sucked in another long breath, then let it out slowly. "That happened because of us. Because our people believed we were chosen." He turned to face the bandit and lowered his voice. "Her very existence refutes that belief."

"If you've the gall to suggest it, at least also have the courage to say it," Kashi said, deadly serious now.

"We kill her," Bataar said, and turned back to the bleeding bandit. "We have to."

A hand clapped down on his shoulder, pulled him back. Subei.

"Ghangerai should not shed Ghangerai blood," he said, and there was no doubt left in his eyes now, replaced with anger. "That is our way."

Bataar winced, not at his brother's words, but at their source. At a night of fire and slaughter that their father had only ever mentioned once, when deep in his drinks.

No, Subei had a point. A fine point. A dangerous point.

Bataar leaned in close to his brothers then. Steadied his

voice. He'd already made his decision, and they needed to understand why. Needed to agree.

"This isn't justice, brother," Subei said before he could speak.

"No," Bataar said as he fought to quash the doubt pricking at the edges of his tone. "But it is necessary."

"Bataar. . . "

"Ancestors above, you going to bicker all day or do something?" The bandit rolled to her side, got her feet under her.

"Stay down!" Ghula shouted, and all around, bow strings creaked as they were pulled taut. The bandit continued to rise.

"Already your philosophizing bores me. Just like the rest of your house, so concerned with right and wrong, *duty* and *honor*, when you finally act, it's already too late." She laughed, took a step toward the brothers. "Let me make it easy for you, children. I'm already dead." She lifted an arm and looked down at her torso, punctured in a dozen places by crystalline shards. "So give me a warrior's death, and let's be done with it."

"She's a problem, I agree," Subei hissed at Bataar. "But killing our own people isn't a solution. At the least, our father must pass judgment."

"We can't have anyone see her at camp," Kashi said, eyes distant as he thought aloud. "So we bring Father here. Keep her isolated until Father decides what's to be done—"

"Ancestors above, get on with it!" The bandit with the hooked nose, and seeping wounds, and scars just like theirs, staggered forward, hands facing each other. Her scars illuminated as an orb glowed to life in her grip.

Baji's Burning Fury! Bataar snarled at the sight. A magic to honor the Great Khan, now raised against them. But. . . no. This wasn't like the technique Subei had shown. This was different, amorphous. And as she pulled her hands apart, it elongated. Clay in the hands of a sculptor. Clay that, if Subei's technique was anything to go off of, could kill all too easily.

The bandit spread her arms shoulder to hip and the light followed, hissing and spitting. Bataar shoved his brothers back and raised his guard as the bandit sucked in a breath and—a rain of arrows whooshed past. They slammed into the woman with deep, thudding impacts, and finished the work the crystalline shards had started.

"There. . . we go. . . " she said, and the light faded, her scars dimmed, and her lips just began to curl into a smile as she toppled over backward.

Silence, for a long moment but for the clattering of arrow against bow as the guards readied another volley in case it was needed.

And then there was light, brilliant blue, pouring from Bataar's scars.

"She's already dead," Subei said, his tone accusatory.

"I'm not doing anything," he retorted, raising his arms to study them.

"Clearly you're doing something!" Subei said, but even as he did, Kashi's scars came alive too. Then Subei's as well.

And the bandit's.

She lay dying, eyes already still, but the scars along her arm were flaring to life. Like sparks catching dry tinder. And then every wound on her was ringed with blue light. Flesh that had been pink and raw now glowing. The light grew fiercer, brighter, then began to spread across her body. Like a pot, dropped and shattering in slow motion. The cracks jumped across her skin. Zigzagged down her arms, up her neck, clawed over her cheeks. And from them, boiling blue light poured out. The air itself sizzled and hissed, and the light manifested into something more. Motes, like floating dust, rose from the cracks. Gathered above her body in a swirling, glowing cloud.

One of the guards panicked, loosed an arrow. It punched through the cloud, opening a hole that lasted all of a heartbeat before closing once more.

"Ancestors above," Ghula said from behind as, like a hound catching a scent, the cloud of light spun and rushed the brothers.

Kashi ducked away, forearms up to block the assault. But it never came. Never crashed into him or drove him back. Instead, the light simply rushed over his palm, found his scars, and joined with them.

With his own as well, Bataar realized, looking down to see a second stream of light rushing into him.

And a third stream, then. It moved for the guards on the hill, then paused, turned, and sought Subei instead.

The light flowed into the brothers, and their scars absorbed it. Drank it deep like a drought-crusted riverbed embracing the spring melt. And just as the snowmelt brought water to the rivers, so too did the light bring life to them. Life. And power.

It grew inside Bataar, down beneath his stomach. The magic there filled and swelled as warmth spread through him. And with it, streaks of adrenaline shooting through his veins. It was. . . euphoric.

The last dregs of light escaped from the bandit's corpse and all at once, her face seemed to darken. The cracks across her body dimmed, faded, and then disappeared entirely, leaving behind an unexceptional corpse.

There was no more light to drink, but Bataar could feel his scars trying anyway. Like a drunk tipping back an empty bottle. And like an angry drunk, when the scars found there was nothing else, rage coursed through him. A surge of it, for just a moment, but enough to drive his thoughts white hot before his legs crumpled beneath him, and he fell to all fours. He gasped for air as the euphoria ended, and the world dimmed. Normal daylight returned, yet somehow, it was darker.

"Is this what Baji felt like?" a voice asked—Bataar's own. He didn't even realize he'd been talking because, inside, the magic was churning. And there was no denying, now there was twice as much as before. What'd once been a thirsty riverbed where he'd had to dig for the magic had become something closer to a stream. And through it, a steady trickle.

"Ancestors above," Subei said, also on the ground. "What was that?"

"The magic. . . came to us," Bataar said, trying to put into words something that his body knew, but his mind didn't yet understand. Something purely instinctual. "Became ours."

"Hey, so, I hate to say this again," Kashi said. He was on his feet and facing south. "But. . . you're feeling that too, right?"

"Yeah." Bataar rose, legs unsteady. "The magic inside, it's grown. Doubled, even. It's incredible. It's—"

"Not that."

"What? *Oh.*" And then he did feel it. A pull. No, not one. Five. Or, wait. Six?

Seven.

Seven more pulls. And if the bandit's had felt faint, these were but a whisper of that. Less still. An echo of a whisper. They felt so far away, it was jarring. As if the whole of the southern horizon was dragging him closer. Was beckoning him to come. Come and claim what was rightfully his.

Chapter Ten

SUBEI

When Kemu Khagan presided over matters of governance, it was often a crowded affair. Beneath the great tent—so large as to fit five hundred people—he would sit on a plain wood throne and conduct the public business of his house. When Kemu presided over matters of conquest, the scene was the same, but only commanders would be allowed into the great tent. Now, not even they were admitted. So sensitive was the discussion at hand the great tent had been avoided entirely. Secrecy was paramount, and the privileged few arrived one by one, slipping quietly into the khagan's personal ger.

As was tradition, the entrance faced south, and the door-frame was carved with ornate depictions of the deeds of House Kemu's ancestors. Within, there was a simple bed, and at the foot of it, a small chest for personal possessions. The middle of the ger was filled with an open fire, smoke rising from it to curl about the central wood pillars before escaping through the smoke hole to the night skies above. Lastly, there was a small family altar against one wall. Small items of significance to Kemu and his direct ancestors rested atop it. Each visitor made sure to pause and bow deeply before it as they arrived.

Arban Khan was the last to do so, and when he straightened, Subei offered him a bowl of airag. The khan accepted it with a grunt, then drank deep from the bowl. When he was done, Subei set it aside, then reached for one himself.

A long drink then, to prepare for what was coming. The slightly sour taste of the fermented mare's milk slipped across his tongue. It cooled him as it went down, dampening some of the past week's anxiety.

"Thank you for being here, honored Khans," Kemu Khagan dipped his head as he said it. "The past few days have been momentous for our people. But the ancestors are not yet done surprising us."

They raised their brows at that, and Subei couldn't blame them. He was still coming to terms with everything himself. It was not the sort of news to spread widely, which explained the evening's small audience.

His brothers, of course, were there, along with the khagan. Ghula, too. And Mahtma, a scroll clutched to her chest. Then it was just the khans of the major houses. Arban, Budai, and Tugu. They'd come with no small number of guards, but at Kemu's request, those had been stationed outside. Close enough to keep any others back, but far enough so their ears would hear nothing. Only the kheshig, the khagan's most trusted guards, stood close to the ger.

"We all beheld the miracle at the tournament grounds," Kemu continued. "Witnessed the return of Baji's spirit—and power—to our people. But, it would seem, that is not the whole of the story. I'll allow my Master of Knowledge to explain further." He gestured to Mahtma. She stepped forward, the glow of the fire lighting her from below.

"Khagan," she said, head bowed, then took in everyone watching her. "I have been working on a theory as to how Great Baji Khan's magic returned. As you all can no doubt surmise, it was linked to the obelisks. Our records have always been. . . " She paused, searching for the word. "Fragmented. But the recent cooperation between the houses has allowed me access to the whole of our collected knowledge. With access to records from *all* of the houses, I believe I can pose the following explanation to you all." She raised up the scroll she'd been holding to show it wasn't just one scroll, but several. A whole bundle of papers, actually. Subei had always found written records were sad things. Dead and stale. Songs were how true knowledge was kept alive and passed on. How it was given new life and fresh belief by every voice that sang it to the winds, every mind that caught the tune and couldn't shake it. But Mahtma was fond of her Teshkai ways, and so, it seemed, were at least a few Ghangerai. Had a lorecaller woven this knowledge into song and shared it with the khanate, perhaps it never would have been lost. No matter, though. It had been found now. The only choice would be what to do with it.

"This account," Mahtma said, holding up a mostly intact scroll. "Was written while the Great Khan was still alive. Though it is heavily damaged and, in many places, illegible, it is obviously a commission to erect a mighty statue here in Kurul Valley." Her eyes flicked toward the door and beyond, to where said statue stood. "It also calls for the creation of obelisks to accompany the statue. '*The bases are to be made of local stone to the dimensions, design, and number previously detailed,*'" she stopped reading to look around the room. "Where this was previously detailed, I cannot say. The document is damaged. But. . . " She cleared her throat, then read on. "'*The length of each obelisk shall be formed of soulstone, mined from Sehymket and inspected personally by Baji Khan.*'"

"Soulstone? Sehymket?" Tugu Khan asked, just as Subei had when Mahtma had first brought the news. "I've never heard of this place, nor this material."

"Neither had I. And I can find mention of neither in the histories available to me here. I have written to the stewards of the Hall of Records in Teshkai, but their reply will surely be some time in coming." Mahtma produced a shard from one of the obelisks, then passed it around the room. "Examination of what remains of the crystals has revealed nothing exceptional. Circumstance necessitates we move forward without a complete understanding, because. . . " she gestured to Subei and his brothers.

"Baji's magic came from the obelisks," Bataar said. "We know that much. *Felt* that much."

Subei nodded in agreement, then stepped forward.

"My sword strike damaged the obelisk, and something came out of it. Some form of the magic. It imbued my blade and, well, we all saw the result of that," he said, thinking back to the body that'd been cleaved in two.

"Not with my own eyes," Arban Khan said, voice gruff. "But many did."

"Too many in agreement for it to be anything other than the truth," Budai Khan added.

"When Subei hit the obelisk. . . it seemed to me like something was trying to get out," Kashi said. "And then the obelisks exploded."

"Both at once," Subei said, emphasizing that key detail.

"And from the explosion, the sons of Kemu were imbued with power." Mahtma was back to rifling through her papers. "It is my belief that somehow, upon his death, Baji Khan's magic was transferred to these obelisks."

"A gift for his descendants?" Arban Khan asked. "A father's sword passed to his sons?"

"Perhaps." Mahtma looked unconvinced. "But then why did he not tell us? Regardless, it doesn't matter. The power, however, it is linked to the obelisks, was released when they broke."

"When they broke *at the same time*," Subei said again, hoping they'd catch on.

Mahtma had found the page she was looking for now. This one had a burned edge and was splattered with wine. Or blood, hard to tell. Either way, she was unperturbed as she flattened it on the table.

"The commission I read from earlier ordered the creation of the statue and its obelisks. This is a snippet from an accompanying document. *'By order of Baji Khan, one obelisk should be affixed in the Teshkai city of Bharmankara, and two further in the ancient southern capital at Ba Seng, thereby to establish for all time the three hearts of the khanate.'*"

"How can two obelisks be sent to Ba Seng and another to Bharmankara?" Arban Khan asked. "There were only two obelisks."

"Ancestors above," Tugu Khan said all at once, eyes wide with realization. "There were only two obelisks *here*."

A murmur went through the room at that, and Mahtma nodded.

"From the records we have with us, I cannot surmise how many total obelisks were commissioned. Only that there were two here, one sent to Bharmankara, and two to Ba Seng."

"There are more obelisks?" Budai Khan frowned, pulling at his beard. "We must protect them then. Immediately! Ba Seng is in the hands of the rebellious Zhong, but Bharmankara—"

"Remains loyal," Mahtma said, her tone severe. A ripple went through the room at her interrupting a khan, but given the circumstances perhaps, no one acted on it. "Already I have written to the regional administrators with instructions. Teshkai remains a vassal state of the khanate."

"It is not enough," Budai Khan said, stroking his wispy beard. "We must send trusted warriors to find and secure the obelisk there!" He dropped to a knee then, head down. "My Khagan, allow my sons this honor. They will leave this very night and not stop until the obelisk in Bharmankara is secure."

"And once it was secured, no doubt it would mysteriously break, hmm, cousin?" Arban Khan raised an eyebrow. "No doubt your sons would accidentally take into them the magic of the Great Khan?"

"You insult not only me but all of House Bud—"

"Enough," Kemu spoke quiet but sharp. "Save your breath. You cannot claim a meal already eaten."

Neither Budai nor Arban seemed to grasp the meaning of that. Tugu did, however. He locked eyes with Subei, then spoke quietly, as if afraid to speak the next words aloud. "Only one of the two obelisks here was damaged, yet both exploded at the same moment. As if they were linked. As if, when one obelisk is destroyed, so too are they all."

"And their magic released into the world." Subei delivered the news that'd brought them all here this night. "We were given the magic of the Great Khan." He raised a palm before him and conjured an orb. The ger lit up with its crackling, blue light. "Baji's Burning Fury." The assembled khans flinched.

Bataar punched forward and a blast of wind burst from his knuckles and set the felt walls to swaying.

"North Wind Scours," he said as the khans gasped.

"And now, Wolf Catches Scent," Kashi added last, eyes distant. All attention shifted to him, expectant, but there was no demonstration forthcoming. "This technique cannot be seen," he explained. "Only felt. Once we began to wield the magic of the Great Khan, we discovered we could feel others who were similarly gifted. The bandit who survived the explosion, foremost. She was empowered like us. Something, maybe the magic itself, led us to her, and when she was dead. . . " He looked down at his palm, at the scars stretching out from it. "The magic she'd stolen was returned."

"Returned to *us*," Bataar said, and Subei knew he was hoping to curb any rising ambitions in the minds of the assembled khans. "Baji's magic did not flow into the guards, nor Ghula Torol, but into us. It recognized the heirs of the Great Khan."

"But there were other obelisks," Tugu Khan said. As expected, their display had not distracted him from the most important news. The most dangerous news. He already knew it, Subei could tell, but was going to wait. Was going to make them say it.

"When the obelisks here exploded," Subei said, voice heavy with the understanding of what came next. "So must have all the others. The magic of Baji has been set free into the world." He clenched a fist. "Even now, it calls to us. Pulls us south."

"South," Kemu Khagan said and there was little joy in it. "Where our ancestor's magic has been stolen. South, where my sons are headed at first light. South, where they will find these false heirs and take back the magic that is rightfully ours." He looked at each of his cousins in turn, taking the measure of the khans before him. "And we will follow. As my sons reclaim the magic that is ours, we will reclaim the land that is ours. Baji Khan anointed the steppe, the mountains of Teshkai, and the fields of the Zhong as the three hearts of the khanate. Two, we control, but for more than a century, the Zhong lands have been in open rebellion. No longer." Kemu strode to the ger's door and peered out into the night. Peered south across the steppe as if even over such a vast expanse, he could see the lands of the rebels. "I have had you all summon the full might of your forces.

House Kemu, as well, has sent for our last touman. When they arrive, I will declare the second great conquest begun. Once again, our united people will ride out from our homeland. And once again, the world will be brought to heel."

Chapter Eleven

BATAAR

"I don't think we'll have time for falconry, Torol," Bataar said, frowning as Mahtma carried yet another bird to her horse. Like those previous, its wings were bound and eyes covered with a strip of cloth. She placed it gently in a gourd-like pouch attached to the saddle. An internal frame gave the pouch structure such that it almost resembled a bird cage, though smaller and with soft leather protecting its winged occupants.

"That the son of the khagan cannot tell a falcon from a messenger pigeon reflects poorly on my aptitude as his teacher."

"My apologies. Never was the best student, was I?"

What use did a warrior have for learning all the different types of birds when there were tactics to memorize, sword strokes to perfect? Still, it was best to be respectful.

Bataar rubbed the sleep from his eyes and gestured to the darkness around them. They'd risen so early, he found himself somewhat unclear on if 'early' was still the word for it or if 'late' was more appropriate.

"Can't tell if I actually slept or just closed my eyes for half a minute."

Mahtma turned to him, not a hint of tiredness in her features.

"We'll be ranging far, and in hostile lands. We'll need a way to communicate with the khagan."

"Perhaps word of our success will precede us," Bataar said as he fought a yawn.

"Better that our success is so swift and subtle, no one hears of it at all—certainly not the Zhong. I should like to ride home with considerably less than the whole of an empire at our heels."

Well, she'd a point there.

"The only people at your heels will be lorecallers weeping for the chance to weave your glory into song," a figure said, emerging from the predawn gloom with a horse in tow.

"And here I thought to outpace you for once." Mahtma gave a slight bow of greeting. "I didn't expect your business among the Yupiak to be concluded so soon, First Rider Tse Su Ren."

"Please, Torol, 'Ren' is fine, at least until we're among the Zhong." She returned Mahtma's slight bow with a far deeper one. "And no business in the north could be more important than this." Then she turned and bowed to Bataar in the Ghang-erai way, fists pressed knuckle to knuckle before her chest. "Let us make history, Bataar Khan."

Bataar's heart skipped a beat at that, but he quickly quashed the feeling.

"Son of Kemu," he corrected her, though there shouldn't have been any need for it. Of course he wasn't a khan yet, even if his father was the khagan. "But. . . yes, let's make history."

"I wished for First Rider Ren to lead our scout contingent," Mahtma said, checking her bags and saddle. "Though I dared not hope she would return in time considering how far afield I sent her previously."

"I believe I've heard a song of your exploits," Bataar said, squinting through the darkness to make out the woman's likeness. "Something about the scout who dropped a landslide on a Mercaen raiding party?"

"Lorecallers and their exaggerations," she said. And was she smirking? It was impossible to tell with still not even a hint of light tingeing the eastern edge of the valley. "Ah, uh, excuse me. Torol, Son of Kemu."

Ren nodded toward each of them in turn, then stepped away as more figures approached. These, Bataar recognized from their stride alone. His father and mother foremost, and behind them, Subei and Kashi.

"Trying to slip off without us, eh, brother?" Subei said. "Steal all the glory for yourself?"

"He just wanted to get up earliest so he could tell us how dishonorable it is to sleep in until dawn," Kashi said.

"Might be I leave you two behind just to find some peace and quiet," Bataar shot back. In the darkness, Mahtma rolled her eyes and returned to her birds.

"Our last morning together, and you all would spend it chiding each other? Is this the memory you'll leave your mother with?" Tugenei huffed. "Your father's sons, truly. Though," she paused. "High spirits travel better than a heavy heart. At least your horses will thank you."

"The whole of the khanate will thank you, upon your return," Kemu Khagan said, words heavy with expectation. It was too dark to be sure, but in that moment Bataar fancied he could see their success reflecting in their father's eyes. Could see the whole of a united khanate cheering their names. "I name this your labor, my sons. All would-be khans must complete one to show their quality. I was your age when I began my own."

"You were sent to hunt a wolf in the northern passes, husband." Turgenei crossed her arms, but Kemu was undeterred.

"And our sons will hunt dogs in the southern fields," he replied, his smile flashing hungry and proud.

"We will not fail you, father," Bataar said, pressing his knuckles together and bowing deep. His brothers joined him.

"You must not." Kemu's words were quiet now as he scanned the vicinity. "We are a khanate united—for the moment. But already I feel the stirrings of treachery in my cousins' hearts. It is in our nature to seek strength, so I cannot fault them. What warrior would not wish to wield Baji's magic? On some level, I might commend my cousins' desire to claim the magic still loose in the world." He raised his eyes to the southern horizon. "Better a Ghangerai wields it than our enemies." He pulled his gaze back down. "But better still, my own sons."

"Then we will not delay a moment longer, Khagan!" Bataar said and looked to the horses.

"I will busy the khans with preparations for war against the Zhong," Kemu continued. "It may buy us additional time. Still, my sons, you must ride swift. Swift as Altan, Who Raced the Wind. Swifter still, if it can be managed."

"We won't fail you, father."

"I know." Kemu Khagan placed a hand on his shoulder. "You are the hope of our people. May the strength of your sword arm be exceeded only by the strength of your convictions."

"I will make it so, Khagan," Bataar said, head bowed.

Kemu turned to Subei next and gave his shoulder a squeeze.

"You are our north star, guiding us ever along the path all true Ghangerai must walk. May your ambition know no limits, and the borders of our khanate follow."

"I aspire to such honor, Father."

Kashi last. Kemu placed a hand on each of his shoulders.

"You are my youngest and yet wisest. Make of this wisdom a spider's web, and all our foes will find themselves caught in it."

Kashi grinned. "I've never been particularly good at weaving."

Bataar slapped him in the back of the head.

"Er, yes, spider web. Wisdom. Will do."

"Smartass," Bataar hissed, but their father only smiled and stepped away. Turgenei came next, fussing at their deels, the way their packs sat on their shoulders.

"Bataar, Subei, I love you as only a mother can. Kashi—"

"But you love me most?" he quipped.

She licked a finger and wiped some unseen smudge from his forehead, then nodded at Bataar.

"Keep that one from overexerting himself," she said, then looked to Subei. "And that one from overreaching himself."

"Keep my older, dumber brothers in line. Got it." Kashi gave a quick nod. Turgenei smiled, then sighed and shook her head. "A touman I would send with you, my sons." She cupped Kashi's cheek with one hand and Subei's with the other. She lingered there a moment, before turning to Bataar, her eyes full of pride. If only they weren't also stained with worry. "Two toumans, even, and still, they would not be enough for this task." She hugged him close then, and he was reminded of just how much he towered over her now, even if he still thought of her as the larger in his mind's eye, just as she'd been when he was a boy.

"Twenty thousand warriors might somewhat defeat the purpose of our stealthy approach, mother," Bataar said with a small laugh as he returned her hug and, for a moment, closed his eyes. She smelled of home, of their ger. Cook smoke mingling with the incense they burned before the family altar. A specific mix, known only to her. One day she would teach it to him, on the day he began his own family and took his own ger. When he brought children of his own into the world and learned the joy of raising them in the ways of their people. Their *united* people. His children would not be brought into the world he'd known; a world of petty feuds and the intangible echoes of long faded glory. No, they would grow strong in a khanate united with borders reaching as far as the eternal blue sky. That world was within his grasp now, waiting just beyond the horizon.

"Look for our return," Bataar said, pulling away and swinging into the saddle. "And the world's changing."

Chapter Twelve

SUBEI

Ghangerai horses were not so large as the war steeds of Mercer. Nor were they so pleasing to look on as the cultivated breeds of the Zhong. But they were hardy even in the depths of winter, needed little pasture for grazing, and above all, their endurance was legendary. Subei and the others put that to the test as they rode, far and fast.

Ghula blew hard on the whistle, and its shrill cry echoed out ahead of the party, screeching across the steppe. In the distance, the relay station was barely visible. It grew clearer by the moment, though, as they approached at a wild gallop. Already it was in motion. Ghula's signal had been heard. Not to mention, First Rider Ren and the forward scouts would have already given them notice.

The attendants crewing the station rushed from their gers and set about saddling fresh horses, and even retrieving extras from the pasture, as well.

Other houses might have let the tyram system fall into decay, but Kemu Khagan had kept the tradition alive. Thriving, even, as had been evidenced today.

It'd been forty miles since the last relay station. Forty miles at full gallop, with brief breaks only to swap onto the extra mounts. Now, for the third time in a day, Subei guided his gasping horse to a stop at a tyram and swung down.

"Highest priority," he said, out of breath himself as he produced the seal of Kemu Khan. There hadn't even been time to update it with his father's new honor as khagan, so quickly had they left. "Remounts and fresh supplies for the whole party."

Saddles were swapped from spent horses onto the well-rested steeds of the station. Waterskins were filled, legs were stretched, and in less than the time it took Subei to catch his breath, the entire party was mounted and underway again.

They'd left Kurul Valley at dawn, twenty in number. It was the largest their party could be and still expect each station to re-equip them with a horse plus four additional mounts each.

The Empty Sea stretched on ahead, seemingly unending. But by the power of Ghangerai steeds and Baji's innovation, its limits would be reached.

Subei turned once to catch a glimpse of the relay station disappearing behind them, then settled back into the rolling gallop that now felt as natural as the beat of his own heart. Bataar was just behind, and Kashi just ahead. Ghula and Mahtma, too. The rest of the party was comprised of First Rider Ren and her scouts—presently out of sight beyond the southern horizon—and Vachir, commander of the nine kheshig guards sent to protect them. They rode on either flank of the group, heavily armed and armored for the days ahead.

There was little time for talk and, as the day went on, too much time alone with his own thoughts. Too much time trying to anticipate what would come next, and if they were ready for it, and how they would reclaim the Great Khan's magic. How their father's expectations weighed heavy on his shoulders, and heavier still because the hope of their people joined it. Eventually, the thoughts faded as Subei entered a sort of waking trance. All of existence blissfully narrowed until there was only the horizon and the rolling rhythm of his horse's strides.

Some two hundred miles passed in this manner. An incredible distance, and entirely unsustainable without the relay stations. Another day of such riding, and they'd be at the borders of the steppe and on their own. Even then, speed would remain of the essence. Every day of delay was another given for the false heirs to discover and master their stolen power, and so Subei and his brothers rode fast and rode far.

Come evening, storm clouds were gathering in the distance. The party could have bedded down at the day's last relay station, but there'd been enough light to press on, and so they had. Another fifteen miles covered before camp was set. In theory, they could have just as well ridden through the night, but as important as it was to be swift, so too was arriving with the strength to fight. The strength to reclaim Baji's magic.

The tents had just gone up when the sun sank behind the hills and the churning storm rolled in. Rain then, carried on a howling wind to lash and bite at anything foolish enough to be caught in the open.

Not that there was much shelter to be had on the steppe. A ger would have weathered a storm such as this, would have even been comfortable inside. Would have lulled you to sleep with the sound of the rain against the roof. A shame then, that they'd left their gers behind in Kurul Valley, Subei thought, as he lay drenched to the bone in his hunter's tent. He'd spent many a poor-weather night in just such a tent, Bataar and Kashi with him. It was made to conserve space, meant to be carried by those with somewhere to go and a mind to get there in a hurry. It was not made for the fury the storm unleashed on it now.

The canvas held the water back for the most part, the wind only half-pulling the stakes from the ground. Not that it made much of a difference. So intense was the deluge the very ground on which they lay turned to mud.

Subei shivered and cursed, wrapped tightly in his drenched trovaak pelt sleeping furs. Kashi lay between him and Bataar, sheltered more from the storm on account of being in the middle. No one spoke, but no one slept. It was a mercy when the storm subsided around dawn. And it was merci*less* when Mahtma pulled their tent flaps open just moments later and chastised them from their sopping furs.

"Starting today, Ghula will train you when the sun is in the west. I will train you when it is in the east. This was the khagan's command." She pulled their tattered, still-dripping tent from its stakes and let it fall to the side. "The sun is in the east."

"Faintest sun I've ever seen," Subei said, squinting toward the near imperceptible rays of pink edging the horizon, but the stern-faced torol had already turned to lead them toward something approaching dry ground.

Subei forced his body to move, grumbling as he pulled himself up, joints refusing to bend, too stiff from the long ride and the seemingly longer cold of the night. A quick look at Bataar revealed more of the same.

"This isn't going to be a regular thing, is it?" Kashi mumbled as he rolled to his feet with a yawn. "I'm fine, obviously. But everyone knows you two need your beauty sleep."

The rest of the camp was still asleep, aside from the guards keeping watch, as Mahtma led the brothers. But for their squelching footsteps, the world was silent, as if in shock in the wake of the storm.

The ground was almost solid atop the hill where Mahtma finally stopped. Subei only sank in to his ankles. Kashi arrived beside him, rubbing at his eyes, then Bataar last, though he was barefoot and cursing. His boots lay abandoned down the slope, half sucked into the earth. Looking down at his own soggy boots, Subei wondered if his brother didn't have the right of it.

Mahtma stood before them, back straight and hands clasped behind her.

"I have long educated you as House Kemu's Master of Knowledge. With this journey, however, the khagan has commanded we begin a new type of tutelage." The faintest rays of dawn reached from the horizon to illuminate her stern features. "I have taught you knowledge of the world so that you may understand it. Today, I begin to teach you knowledge of yourselves so that too, you may understand."

"All I understand right now is I need some actual sleep," Subei muttered.

Bataar nodded in agreement. Kashi seemed too drowsy to chip in.

"The sun is in the east. We train," Mahtma said, as if that was all there was to it. She bowed then, in the Teshkai manner, with one palm placed into the other and both upturned to the sky.

"It is a fine morning, students."

"Dark, cold, and damp, more like," Bataar said under his breath as he and his brothers returned the bow.

"Do you draw breath, Sons of Kemu?" Mahtma asked the question in an even tone, cold, blue eyes locked on them.

"Despite the storm's best efforts to drown us," Subei answered.

"Then count it a fine morning. A little wet and a little mud are far preferable to the cold oblivion of the world next."

"The ride and the storm have not left us in the highest of spirits," Bataar said.

Mahtma turned to him specifically.

"I'm not here for cheerful thoughts. Nor am I here to indulge your complaints. It is understandable you see me simply as your tutor, but thirty years of my service were spent training your father's kheshig warriors in the ways of my homeland." She drew in a breath then, and looked across them all. "I've educated you in matters of the mind. Now I will educate you in matters of the soul. You Ghangerai are headstrong and willful. Both good ways to end up dead. You let your passions control you. Another way to end up dead. That ends today. You have been gifted with the magic of Baji. You are too important to die."

She placed her hands in front of her, preparing for another bow.

"When I say, 'it is a fine morning, students,' you will say, 'it is a fine morning indeed, teacher.'"

She bowed.

"It is a fine morning, students."

Subei bit his tongue and stiffly returned the bow, his brothers following.

"It is a fine morning indeed, teacher," they said in unison.

Mahtma took hold of Subei's arm. She raised it into the dim morning light, sliding back the sleeve of his still damp deel to reveal the scars there.

"You have been imbued with a fearsome magic we do not yet understand. We would do well to remember power of any kind can be a blade that cuts both ways." She dropped Subei's arm and returned to her spot in front of them. "Ghula is here to sharpen this blade. I am here to ensure you don't kill yourselves with it."

Admittedly, Mahtma had always been a tough tutor, but it had been for their betterment. Subei shook off his lethargy and tried to focus. Might be he'd learn something worth knowing.

"If this magic is a blade, self-control will be its sheath. None of us fully understand the forces we're wielding here, but the records say Baji trained long and hard to master his magic, trained as if his life depended on it. So too then, shall we." She turned to Bataar, face expressionless, and spoke two simple words. "Hit me."

Bataar raised an eyebrow.

"I would have to be without honor to strike an elder."

"Honor exists to give guidance for men too weak to govern their desires. You were a khan's son, now you are a khagan's son. You are not allowed to be a weak man. Hit me."

Bataar remained motionless.

"I don't think—"

Mahtma darted forward far faster than Subei would have ever expected from the scholarly woman he knew and cut short Bataar's response with a well-placed foot to the stomach. The air rushed from him in a whoosh as he bent double and stumbled backward. He fell to his knees, coughing.

Mahtma shrugged.

"Hit me, or I hit you."

Bataar cursed as he pulled himself up, wiping the spittle from his chin.

"Just remember, this was your idea." He swung hard with his right fist, hooking it around and toward the old woman's head. It found only empty air as she leaned backward. Bataar was right on her, though, another fist flying in, then another and another. He might as well have been striking at smoke the way she slipped and danced away from each blow. Subei's eyes went wide as he watched. In all the years of droning lectures and forced recitations, he'd never known her to be capable of this. She was fluid as water and twice as difficult to catch, as Bataar was quickly learning.

Another punch missed, and he growled, surging forward for a

full-body tackle. He found only her leg striking him in the shins to send him tumbling to the mud with a sad little squelch.

"Forgive an old woman if her memory is not what it once was. I did say 'hit me,' did I not?" She dug her foot into the sopping ground, then spun into a kick and launched a clump of mud against the back of Bataar's head. "Or am I asking too much of the son of the khagan?"

Bataar jumped to his feet. Something itched in Subei's chest, and he realized his brother's scars were beginning to glow blue, the faintest light stirring in them in sharp contrast to the still dark morning sky.

Another glob of mud slapped into Bataar, this time catching him across the nose.

"Hit me."

Bataar yelled and lunged forward, his scars burning to life. A concussion reverberated through the air as he struck out with North Wind Scours. Mud and earth and water were blasted from the spot where Mahtma was standing. Or, the spot where she'd been standing. Nearly too fast to see, she'd dodged forward and rolled in front of Bataar. He stood scowling and breathing heavily as she rose from the ground and clapped a handful of mud down his shoulder.

"Missed again."

Bataar whipped a hand up to grab her wrist, but she slapped it aside and spun him around. With two quick jabs to his armpits, she left his arms hanging limp. Another jab, this one to his neck, and he collapsed entirely, eyes wide as he lay in the mud. His face passed through several shades of red as he strained to move anything below his neck. Subei couldn't help a smile then. There was a sight: a warrior as big as his brother brought low by the fingertips of an old woman.

"Control over one's body is the most basic form of self-control. We'll start with that. It can be learned in a month, maybe less if a student truly devotes oneself. But to master it takes a lifetime." Mahtma circled them as she spoke. She passed behind Kashi and Subei took the opportunity to poke a bit of fun at his older brother.

"Hear that? About a month and you'll be able to stand

again." He nudged Bataar with the toe of his boot. "Less than that if you really try."

The slightest movement behind him blossomed into a painful jab to his neck.

"Ow—" he managed before his body went numb and he collapsed to the mud beside Bataar.

"This one here," Mahtma said, continuing to pace a circle around them, "Has yet to even learn control over his own mouth."

Subei groaned and fought to lift his face from the mud. Managed to lift it a bit, too, before his neck muscles gave out and he smacked back down wetly.

Only Kashi was left standing and it seemed he'd suddenly nothing to say as Mahtma stopped in front of him.

"Why couldn't your brother hit me?"

"We, uh, hardly slept last night," he offered. "And yesterday was exhausting?"

"An excuse is a lie to yourself even more than those you offer it to. Let's move beyond excuses, Kashi."

"Cause you're more slippery than a fish in a mudslide?" Bataar grunted from where his face was smushed against the ground.

"And why is that, do you think?" She turned to him.

"Spent more of your life dodging than fighting, I suppose?"

If his refusal to cooperate bothered her, she showed no sign of it, eyes as unyielding as ice on a winter's morning.

"You couldn't hit me because I have control over my body. I move only where I mean to, when I mean to. This is the first thing I will teach you. Only once you can control your outward selves will you be ready to control the inward."

Mahtma folded her hands to her chest and bowed.

"It has been a fine session, students."

"It's, uh, it's been a fine session indeed, teacher," Kashi said, and bowed hurriedly. She strode past him, and he only flinched a bit.

"Where are you going?" Subei grunted, using all his strength to turn his head.

She stopped, head turned as she spoke over her shoulder.

"We're done for today. Perhaps you can get a bit of sleep before we break camp."

"We can't move!"

"Oh, it'll come back to you. Eventually." Her words floated back on the wind, barely audible as she disappeared down the hillside.

Chapter Thirteen

SUBEI

The land continued to change with each mile. By midday they were surrounded by short, itchy grass and sharp, sudden hills. Great boulders, too, some so large that wind-blown soil had gathered around them, then plants had taken root and, over time, the boulders were becoming hills of their own. Like great seeds, Subei found himself thinking. The seeds of mountains, maybe. Such was the terrain as he and the others passed from the Empty Sea and into the borderlands.

The storms had all but disappeared behind them to be replaced by a much more familiar sight: the sky. Travelers from afar often called it the widest sky they'd ever seen, but to Subei, it was exactly the right size. It was said the ancestors watched from that sky. Watched from the world next as they judged the deeds and honor of the living. Might be one of Subei's own ancestors looked down from that sky now, he figured, tilting back his waterskin for another long drink as the attendants hurried about the task of re-equipping the party.

"This is the last relay station," Ghula said, breathing heavily as she wiped sweat and caked-on dirt from her forehead. It'd been another day just like the last. Riding, and riding hard. "We're passing beyond the khanate's lands after this."

Subei nodded, and as his eyes came down from the sky, they fell to the southern horizon. The whole of the journey, he'd been pulled toward it. Pulled toward Baji's stolen magic and the false heirs who wielded it.

"Wolf Catches Scent," he said, mostly to himself. Bataar had suggested that as the name for their ability to feel other heirs. It made sense they needed to give the techniques names, if only to keep them straight. Baji's Burning Fury, North Wind Scours, and now, Wolf Catches Scent. A bit dramatic, perhaps, but in this moment, Subei couldn't help but agree. The way he was pulled toward the southern horizon, toward those heirs and their stolen magic, he did feel like a wolf on the hunt. Given, it was rare wolves sought such dangerous prey.

There were at least seven false heirs out there. Seven, but they weren't all together. Two were directly south, and close. The other five were clumped some distance still to the southeast. They didn't feel any nearer now, even after two days and nearly four hundred miles of hard riding. The southern pulls, though, those felt much closer. As if they were just over the horizon.

"Can they feel us too, do you think?" Kashi asked after a long drink from his waterskin.

"The bandit woman said she did," Subei answered. "So, yes. I suspect they know we're coming."

"That'll make things interesting." Bataar groaned as he stretched his back and shoulders, more than a few joints popping loudly. "Assuming we're still able to stand by the time we arrive."

"We'll have to slow beyond here. Thirty, forty miles a day, at most," Ghula said. "These will be the last fresh horses we find. Our five mounts per person will have to suffice, and we'll want some kept fresh just in case."

"In case our quarry flees?" Bataar asked, smirking.

"Or we need to," Ghula said, matter-of-factly. "We'll soon draw into Zhong imperial lands. Expect that they will not take kindly to our return."

"Our rightful return," Subei said. "Those lands belonged to the khanate before the rebels."

"Belonged to the Old Zhong dynasty before that," Ghula said with a shrug. "Right has nothing to do with it. 'Right' has no ground to stand on without *might* to back it up. We were once strong enough that the ancestors saw fit for us to conquer those lands. We are no more." She looked at Subei then, Bataar and Kashi next. "But perhaps, we can be again."

"Hail, Ghula Torol! Hail, Sons of Kemu!" a voice called on the wind. Subei turned to find First Rider Ren approaching on horseback. Since the first time Subei had met her, she'd hardly looked Ghangerai at all. Though, it did seem to defeat the purpose of quietly scouting enemy lands if even your posture betrayed your true nature. Being entirely honest, he wasn't sure which she was more of: scout or spy? She rode in the Zhong style, with a too-straight back and a rigid, unmoving posture. And more, her horse was saddled in fine cloth with tassels hanging from the edges. A shameful finery no Ghangerai would subject themself to under normal circumstances. Worse still, she wore a ring on one hand, its face engraved with some sort of black and white speckled bird. Subei hadn't gotten a close look at it, but it wasn't a hawk or anything. More of a pigeon, maybe? A ridiculous thing.

As Ren drew into the relay station, her posture shifted. She leaned forward and curled around her horse to ride like a true Ghangerai. Other features, though, were less easy to change. Particularly the well-oiled hair that hung to her shoulders, straighter than an arrow in flight. Or the prominent cheekbones and pointed chin that marked her as not purebred Ghangerai. And then, of course, there was the overwhelming smell of perfume and incense. Another shameful finery much loved by the Zhong. Subei recoiled at its sting in his nostrils. Off to the side, Kashi leaned away, eyes watering.

It was said no action performed in service of one's khan could be seen as dishonorable. Ren's indulgent disguise, however, put that to the test.

"First Rider," Mahtma said with a nod as Ren pulled her horse up short, then performed a half-bow from the saddle.

"News from ahead. The wind sighs, the birds sing, and a strange story makes its way to me." Despite her too-oiled hair and excessive fineries, she spoke like a proper Ghangerai, voice confident and strong, if not given to a bit of dramatic indulgence. "There has been an. . . event in the border town of Chobei, though no two people tell it the same. Some saw a flash of burning light, others heard a great clap of thunder from clear skies, and yet others still claim nothing more than a weak earthquake damaged some buildings. All anyone can agree on is there was a disturbance."

"A disturbance, hm?" Mahtma asked, brow raised.

"It was some days past, long enough ago for word to reach the far-ranging herders and my friends among them. Nonetheless, the timeline would match with. . . " Her eyes wandered to Subei's scarred arm and a smile pulled at her lips. "The return of Great Baji Khan's spirit."

* * *

The sun was below the western horizon by the time they stopped. Subei hadn't been off his horse for more than a minute before Ghula was corralling him and his brothers for training. Mahtma sat on the hillside above them, face stoic as she watched.

Thwack! Thwack! Thwack!

Three quick blows from Ghula's quarterstaff, one on each brother, and just like that, training was underway.

"Who's up for seconds?" And then she was swinging again. Subei ducked away, trying to gain distance as she took a moment to strike at Kashi. Didn't work, though. Ghula was too fast, and Subei found himself hit often before he could even process an attack was coming. The blows didn't hurt as much as expected, though.

That thought slowed him a moment.

"You pulling your blows, old woman?" Bataar laughed, backing up under a barrage but smiling anyway.

"You feel it too?" Subei asked him.

"The only thing you should be feeling is the sting of my staff!" Ghula caught Subei in the shoulder with it hard enough to drive him a step to the side. But the blow didn't hurt much. As if it'd been deadened? Subei had to check to make sure he hadn't put on training leathers. But of course, he hadn't. They hadn't even been packed.

"Either the advancing years are getting to you or something's changed," he said, frowning at Ghula.

"You talk tough, boy, but have a look at the welts all over you and let me know. . . " She trailed off, frowning. "Huh."

"What welts?" Bataar asked, and Subei nodded his agreement.

"It's as if I'm armored or, well, not quite. Padded, maybe?"

"Like taking a hit through a winter coat," Kashi said, nodding now. He frowned down at one fist then socked Subei in the ear.

"Hey!"

"I'm experimenting, brother."

Bataar chuckled at that. "I'm not sure you ever hit hard enough for this 'experiment' to mean anything, Kashi."

Ghula spun and chucked her staff at Bataar. It caught him in the forehead with an echoing crack and left his gaze tilted up to the clouds.

"That hard enough?"

"Maybe! Did it do anything?" Bataar's meaty fingers felt excitedly around his head.

"Stop it, no—move! I'm trying to see," Kashi said, slapping Bataar's searching hand away. A moment later, he shook his head in disbelief. "Not a scratch. You and your dense, boulder-like head stand defiant, Bataar."

"Heh. Boulder Stands Defiant. I like the sound of that." He lowered himself into a wrestler's stance then scooped Kashi up. Next, with a great heave, he tossed him flailing through the air. He tumbled to the ground with a *thunk* and rolled several paces away.

"Anything?"

"Dizzying, maybe," Kashi said, sitting up. "But no, not really." He looked quizzically at his hands, up his arms, then shrugged. "It's not like that was comfortable, but it didn't really hurt."

"Boulder Stands Defiant. . . " Ghula said, stroking her chin. "It's like natural armor. Consider me envious."

"Now that I think about it, there was something funny going on during the tournament also," Subei said, a memory pushing to the forefront. "The attacks were deadened then, too, but not so much as this."

"The bandit," Kashi said all at once. "We. . . I don't know, *absorbed* her magic after she died. Maybe we already had this natural armor—"

"Boulder Stands Defiant," Bataar interjected, clearly proud of the name.

"Yeah, Boulder Stands Defiant, whatever. Maybe our bodies were already hardened by this, but with everything going on we didn't notice. Then when we took the bandit's magic, everything got. . . amplified?"

"We were immediately able to feel more distant pulls," Subei added.

"More magic, stronger techniques." Ghula nodded as if it was just that simple.

"More magic. . . more techniques?" Bataar asked, a twinkle of hope in his eye.

"I can think of a way to find out!"

Subei hadn't noticed her pick it up, but Ghula had her staff in hand again and set to whacking Bataar all over.

He put up a guard, forearms in front of him, but it was lazy. More than anything, he just shrugged off her blows, smirking. And then, all at once, his scars were alight.

"First time you've ever been a quick study," Ghula said, then gave him a hack to the ribs. "Wind strikes, five in a row!"

"It's called *North Wind Scours*," he shot back.

Ghula shrugged, uncaring, before turning to chase Subei. A rush of adrenaline coursed through his veins as he brought up his hands, ready to fight. Ghula rained blow after blow on his every muscle, and it was clear that she was really trying now as, despite his newfound natural armor, each strike landed with a dull bloom of pain. He was pushed back beneath the onslaught, and as he lost his balance on a loose stone, she swept his feet. He rolled to stand, and she swept him again. Then, standing over him, blotting out the sun, she raised her staff for a knockout blow.

"Enough!" Subei threw his hands forward and magic surged through his arms. It lit his scars up blue and bowled Ghula backward with a blast of wind. "Whoa," he said, frozen in the wake of the attack. The magic had come easier than before, quicker too, as if it'd been waiting. As if, instead of needing to start a fire from scratch, there'd been smoldering coals all along. Buried in ash, perhaps, but ready to be stoked.

Ghula cackled where she came to rest halfway up a hillside and at the end of a trail of torn up grass and mud.

"Good hit, boy," she said, already rolling to her feet to strike out after Kashi. Subei was left staring at his hands, eyes wide. He hadn't been able to use North Wind Scours before this, but apparently, more magic did mean more techniques, like Bataar had hoped.

"One doesn't mean anything," Ghula shouted over her shoulder. "I want to see ten wind strikes in a row. Better yet, blow that dead tree over!" She pointed with her staff. "Either it's in the dirt when I get back, or you'll be."

Fair enough.

Subei set to assaulting the tree. A gnarled, twisted old thing, it shouldn't have been hard to uproot it, but as he hit it with progressively weakening wind strikes, it only held firmer. Deep roots, probably. Trees with anything but didn't survive in so wind-blasted a place as the borderlands.

"Come on, you old twig!" Subei punched forward with both hands and flexed his core. He dredged the energy up from that riverbed within and stirred it to a frenzy. It rushed through his arms and howled forward. Dirt and leaves leapt into the air on either side, and the grass directly in front of him was blasted down as if a mammoth had charged through. The tree groaned, swayed, and bent away. Its bark popped and snapped, and the ground around it heaved up, roots nearly ripping free. But Subei could only power the technique so long. It wasn't a sustained gale so much as a sudden burst of wind. A gust howling across the steppe. The tree held firm and, as the attack dwindled, bark groaned once more, and the tree straightened.

"Damn it," Subei growled. "Why won't you fall?" Anger came then, rising in his chest. More than he'd expected, but still the damn tree wouldn't fall. Was it really so hard? Knocking down this old, gnarled piece of rotted wood? It was mocking him.

"I'll tear you apart," Subei said, and even he was surprised by his words. But in that moment, indulging the anger felt right. And as he did, the magic surged inside him.

Subei unleashed North Wind Scours over and over, the wind howling as if in the midst of a typhoon. The tree was battered and smashed such that the ground heaved, branches snapped and were whisked away, and the whole thing was nearly pried from the earth. Its roots held strong, but its trunk began to give, splinters popping and flying as it bent ever further down.

"Why won't you die?" His growl was nearly a snarl when, still, somehow, the tree defied him. And then, there was something more inside. Something he hadn't felt before. As if, the magic he'd accessed was but a fraction of what was possible. If he'd been drawing from a stream, this reservoir felt like an entire ocean. Subei probed toward it, feeling his way through more than consciously guiding himself. This. . . ocean was a churning thing, as if itching to be set free. What would happen if he—

A sharp clap from the side. His eyes snapped open to find Mahtma, now standing on the hillside. Her staff was resting heavily against a boulder—the one she'd just struck—but her eyes. . . her eyes were fixed on him, and wide with, was that concern? Finally, she nodded—more to herself than anyone—then strode out of sight.

Subei was left questioning his sudden anger. Where had that come from? But more importantly, what was that vast ocean of magic he'd felt inside? And could he draw from it? He'd only just had the thought when something blue arched down onto the tree—and exploded. Flaming splinters and steaming soil whipped past as Subei threw himself to the ground, covering his face. When the commotion cleared, he looked up to see Bataar smiling.

"Figured out your technique, brother." He laughed and then another orb swelled into his hand as he conjured Baji's Burning Fury once more. He tossed it into the air, and Subei flinched away only to see Bataar catch it easily. "Little more flash, little more fun than North Wind Scours, eh?"

"Please don't drop that on us," Subei said with a wince.

Bataar looked down, as if he'd forgotten. Then he clenched a fist and the searing blue orb was snuffed from existence.

"Oh, oh, watch this," he said then, a smile on his face. "I figured something else out." He scooped a handful of dirt and tossed it high into the air. As it fell, he punched forward with a wind strike. Then, in the same motion, he pivoted to an uppercut—and the wind strike followed. It went forward at first, then hooked upward, catching the soil and blasting it even higher in the air.

"Teach me that," Subei said, rushing to his feet.

And so, as the evening wore on into night, they trained. Ghula spent most of her time with Kashi. He got the wind strikes down quick enough, but was hopeless when it came to making orbs. More than a few whacks and colorful curses came from that direction as the two worked it out.

Subei and Bataar focused on North Wind Scours by using each other as practice dummies. A weaker strike would push them back. A stronger one would leave them dazed on the ground, generally a good distance away. Bataar's curving wind strikes were a pain to predict, and Subei found himself all too often bracing in one direction only to have the attack shift at the last moment and launch him the other way.

North Wind Scours, it seemed, required relatively little effort to produce. Baji's Burning Fury, in contrast, was much more tiring. Drew far more deeply from their internal well.

Something to be noted, Ghula had pointed out. The orbs would be the more effective fighting technique, but not the most efficient, since tiring oneself out in the early moments of a fight was a sure way to end up dead. Balance your attacks, she cautioned them.

There was another technique to be explored, as well, but none of the brothers could quite get a handle on it. Kashi had noticed it first. He couldn't manage Baji's Burning Fury, but he could *feel* when Subei or Bataar were preparing to. Could feel as they called on their magic and drew it forth. Hairs raising on his arms, he said. A tickle in his chest.

Focusing on the concept, Subei found he could feel it too.

Whenever Bataar was preparing to use his magic, he could feel it ahead of time, similar to how he could feel it rising in himself when he was the one conjuring it. They were practicing wind strikes on each other the first time it happened. Bataar had punched forward with his North Wind Scours, and Subei had reacted on instinct. He'd swept both arms down and to the side just as the blast arrived. To their surprise, the strike was deflected, and it slammed into the ground next to him.

North Wind Scours and, apparently, shelters. North Wind Shelters, Subei had wanted to call it, eager to put a name to the ability before Kashi got clever. But what good was a name if he was unable to recreate the sweeping-styled defensive ability? He tried, time and again, and consistently ended up on his ass. Seemed the technique only worked half the time. Or the timing was off, perhaps.

Whatever it was, Bataar remained completely unable to recreate it. The best he could do was to wrap his arms in front of him and push through an oncoming wind strike with a blast of his own. He would still take the brunt of the strike head-on, often driving him back a step or two, but it worked for the most part. And with them exploring completely new territory in the realm of these techniques, all too often that was good enough.

"That's one use of it," Kashi said, watching Subei try to sweep away another wind strike. "But I think there's more here."

"More how?" Ghula asked. When she'd grown tired of whacking them with her staff, she'd pivoted to asking questions. Forcing the brothers to think deeper about what they were feeling with the magic, and how that could be used.

"I don't know," Kashi finally said, shaking his head. "Even when they're not conjuring their magic, I can feel it there."

"It's the pulls," Subei grunted as he threw another wind strike toward Bataar. "Wolf Catches Scent, yeah?"

"No, no. It's deeper than that. I think. I . . . I don't know."

"Think on it," Ghula said and clapped him on the shoulder. "But don't take too long." Her eyes rose to the horizon, where a faint blotch of light was just visible in the night.

Subei turned to stare at it as well.

"Chobei."

Chapter Fourteen

BATAAR

Dawn came with no more ceremony than a boot tapping Bataar on the foot and Mahtma's perpetually stern face staring down at him.

"The sun is in the east."

He grunted and pulled himself from the tent, his body exhausted, mind even more so. Subei was woken next, a groan interrupting his snoring. Last came Kashi, who seemed to have mastered the ability to sleep and walk at the same time.

Typically, Bataar enjoyed the early morning. Dim light, cool wind, and the sounds of the world slowly waking up. It was a great time to set one's mind free and to simply just. . . exist. To be at peace with the steppe, as were all true Ghangerai. But early mornings only worked when preceded by enough sleep, and that'd been in short supply of late.

"Clear air aids in keeping a clear mind," Mahtma said, inhaling deeply as she led them to a hilltop. "One day, I hope you take in the morning air atop the Teshkai Mountains. There, I could teach you properly. But for now, the wind-swept crags of this borderland will make do." She bowed. "It is a fine morning, my students."

They returned the bow.

"It is a fine morning indeed, teacher," they said together, and Bataar's voice was still heavy with sleep.

"Sit with me," Mahtma instructed, folding herself cross-legged in the grass. Bataar sighed in relief as he plopped down. Sitting was close to sleeping, right? Closer than training, at least. But if he was learning anything from the lessons with Mahtma, it seemed the Ghangerai concept of training was entirely different from the Teshkai's.

"Kemu Khagan commanded me here to ensure your magic did not become too much for you to handle. A sword is a magnificent, shining thing to a child—but it will cut them all the same."

"That's why we keep them in sheaths," Kashi said, rubbing one eye.

"Do you fight battles with your sword sheathed?"

"A firm grip, practice, and clear intention are all one needs to control a sword," Bataar shrugged as he spoke. "Why should this magic be any different?" When treated with enough respect, any weapon was safe.

"Saying a thing does not make it so," Mahtma countered.

Bataar gave his core a squeeze and his scars burned blue.

"Words promise, actions prove. One of the foremost sayings of Baji Khan." He raised an open palm and called an orb into existence. He rolled his hand and the orb followed it, dancing around his fingers as he moved them back and forth. With a flick of his wrist, he tossed it into the air.

On his left, Subei rolled away with a wince, but Bataar knew what he was doing. He caught the orb in his other hand, then calmly, casually, snuffed it from existence.

"Sword, meet sheath." He smiled as his scars faded back to a pale pink.

"Do you know how Baji Khan spent his final days?" Mahtma asked. That caught Bataar off guard. Subei and Kashi too, if their expressions were anything to go by. "No? Kashi? Anyone?" Mahtma nodded as if all was as anticipated.

"A sickness," Bataar said. "It took him in his old age."

"That is the narrative, isn't it? It's a half-truth. Your people prefer their oral tradition, and it makes for better stories to focus on his great deeds, his conquests, than it does to recall his internal struggles."

"What do you know of the Great Khan's mind?" Bataar

snapped without meaning to. "Did he confide in you? I know you're old, but not even you are *that* old."

"Bataar!" Subei hissed, and he was right. He hadn't meant for his words to be so cutting, they'd just sort of come out that way. Bataar fought a wince.

"No," Mahtma said calmly. "I did not know Baji Khan, but my forebears did. My people have served the khanate as record keepers and Masters of Knowledge for generations. Would you like to know what they recorded in regards to the Great Khan's death?"

"Yes," Kashi said at once, giving voice to the answer Bataar had wanted to utter, but dared not.

"I fear it is not our place to disparage the memory of the Great Khan," Subei said. "We should tread carefully."

"Or perhaps not at all," Bataar hissed, thinking of how their father would have reacted were he present.

"The world is full of hard truths, Sons of Kemu. Your father knows this well. He also knows what I am about to tell you. But the khagan thought we needn't burden you with the details. It is clear to me now we must do exactly that."

"Our father's wisdom has gotten us this far. Why would you question it now?" Bataar asked.

"Because no one fully understands the magic you wield. But we would be wise to learn from he who wielded it first. Baji Khan's magic was a mighty thing, and not even Teshkai records detail where it came from. He never said, but he did speak at length with his Master of Knowledge and his physicians. They concluded it was a mental issue, that even the Great Khan's mind was not immune to the ravages of time. The lorecallers, on the other hand, called it a Zhong curse, sent to make the Great Khan question himself. To bring him down from within." She paused, looking at each of them in turn. "Baji Khan disagreed with both of these theories. He was sick in his final days, yes, but it was not the sickness that took him. It was something else. A rot, he named it. A fit of madness, always churning deep inside that would rise and turn his mind to terrible acts. Would encourage him to abuse his magic in dark and twisted ways. At the end, he struggled against it constantly. *'The very manifestation of primal desires, unrestrained by logic, or morality, or any of the virtues which separate man from beast,'* he called it, and swore it would die with him."

"This is deceit," Bataar growled, anger turning his hand to a fist before he realized it. All the same, the fire inside was burning hot. "Our father would have prepared us if this was true."

"He did not want your minds burdened with this knowledge, nor poisoned by fear of it. Perhaps the Great Khan's struggles and his magic were not related. He would not have been the first great leader to suffer beneath the weight of responsibility. But your father did not send you unprepared. He sent me, and my orders were to ensure, should this sickness show itself again, that his sons would be prepared to resist it."

"Father should have told us this himself," Bataar said, voice quiet. He felt his face fall into a scowl and tried to fight it. "Would have, were it true."

"*If* this is true," Subei said, his uncertainty clear. "What would you have us do? Not complete our mission?"

Kashi balked at that. "The false heirs have taken magic that does not belong to them. It is the legacy of our people. Our inheritance." Bataar nodded, shooting Subei a glance. *What a preposterous suggestion.*

"And so you must claim it." Mahtma nodded. "I do not contest this, and I will aid you in the journey to do so. But you must be prepared." She smoothed a wrinkle from her deel, then sucked down a deep breath and focused on Subei. "You asked what I would have you do? I would have you trust me. I would have you listen with an open mind to my lessons. And I would have you understand that everything I do, I do in your best interest. My life has been dedicated to serving your father, the khagan, and that has not changed. I swore to him I would prepare you if this rot arose once more. Allow me to keep my word and my honor."

They were silent a long moment then, as they all took that in. It was a reasonable ask, Bataar had to admit.

"You have tutored us for more than a decade, teacher," Subei said, head bowed. "And never led us astray. It seems to me, brothers, we should not stop listening now just because she brings us hard truths."

Kashi bowed as well. "If anything, having the courage to tell us what we don't want to hear is all the more reason we should listen." He was right, but that didn't make the hearing of it any easier.

"Listen is all I'll do for now." Bataar kept his voice as steady as possible. His earlier outburst had been far from appropriate behavior for the son of a khan, and especially when directed at a torol. But she'd spoken against the memory of Baji Khan.

His outburst might not have been appropriate—and he'd never have done that in his father's presence—but at the same time, he would never have had to. Kemu Khan would have shut down any disparaging of the Great Khan's memory. Without his father here, was it not his duty as eldest to uphold those values?

"I don't concede to believe your stories about the Great Khan," Bataar continued. He paused a moment, then forced his next words out, "But if they're true, we should be thankful for your guidance."

"You have your father's wisdom," Mahtma said, taking the three of them in. "Though that's no surprise, seeing as I taught it to him." A flash of a smirk, then. Just a flash, then she was back to her usual, serious self. "Ghula has done fine work teaching you strength. Now it will be my task to teach you control. Do as I do." She straightened her posture, folded her hands into her lap, and closed her eyes.

Bataar mimicked her, making sure there wasn't anything he was missing. But she was just. . . sitting.

"What next?" he asked, and Kashi nodded along.

"Do as I do," Mahtma said again, eyes still closed.

She sat there then, as the sun crept up the horizon behind them. Sat there, unmoving as Bataar stared quizzically, then shot a questioning glance at his brothers. Kashi shrugged. Subei scratched at his chin, then adjusted his posture.

"You have the strength to toss about the magic of Baji Khan like a plaything, but not the strength to sit still, Son of Kemu?" Mahtma said without opening her eyes.

"Sitting still isn't a challenge," Bataar said, and waved her statement away. He paused then, looking down at the hand he'd used to make the gesture.

A slight smile pulled at Mahtma's lips. Or maybe he was imagining it.

"Sit with me, Sons of Kemu. Close your eyes. Control your bodies. Control your thoughts." She inhaled deeply, then let it out slowly.

Bataar straightened his back, let his eyes slip shut, and. . . did nothing. But a muscle was twitching in his back, tired from the prior night's training. And his mind was reeling from their conversation. The grass itched against his ankles. Was that a bug tickling his calf? He moved to swat it on instinct—

"Ah!" Mahtma hissed, but her eyes remained closed. How could she have seen? "Control when one is in motion is easy because there's room to be sloppy. Stumbling forward can still be considered walking, no? But that is not control. Control is utter command of one's body. It is moving only when you mean to. You've shown me your strength, Sons of Kemu. Now prove to me your control."

* * *

By the time camp was broken and the whole party was underway again, the freedom of the saddle was a welcome change for Bataar. Somehow, the simple act of sitting still had been tiring. Or maybe it'd been the weight of what Mahtma had said. He still hadn't made his mind up on that just yet. Either way, the loose, bouncing chaos of a galloping horse was relaxing by comparison.

The landscape stayed mostly the same, but for the appearance of a wood off to the west. It began as scattered thickets of trees, at first, but grew in size and frequency as the sun rose in the sky. In a matter of hours, a full-on forest covered their western flank.

They passed few travelers, thankfully. And those they did, were given a wide berth such that they were no more than distant smudges against the horizon. The Zhong were said to be fond of their roads, but there were none to be found here. Too far from the heart of the rebellious empire, Bataar supposed.

After some hours, a sharp whistle from the front pulled him from his thoughts. First Rider Ren was just ahead, her horse grazing at the base of a low hill. Waving the rest of the group up, she swung from the saddle and walked a few paces toward the forest.

"We'll stop here. Set camp in with the trees," she said as Bataar approached. Kashi, Subei, and the others were just behind.

"In there?" Bataar eased his horse to a stop and turned to stare into the dark of the forest. It was a congested, bulging thing. They had forests on the steppe, sure, but they were positively sparse compared to this entanglement. "Seems a difficult place to keep watch from. Can hardly see a thing in there."

Ren took a long draw from her waterskin.

"Will we be able to see? No. But neither will we be seen. The Longlarch is a labyrinth of shadow and root—and older, fouler things still. But we'll not be going deep enough to disturb anything of note. No, for the time being, that old wood will keep us nice and hidden."

"I must've missed something. Who are we hiding from?"

"Them," Ren said with a grunt, hiking a thumb at the hill over her shoulder before heading into the trees.

Bataar guided his horse the rest of the way up the hill. A few quick steps later, and Ren's reasoning suddenly made sense.

"Ah."

"Ancestors above," Kashi said, arriving next to him. "Ren said it was only a town. . . "

"She did." Bataar's mouth had gone dry.

Chobei was a sprawling mass of houses, courtyards, and towers—and a dozen other structures at whose purpose he could only guess. He couldn't imagine why people would need so many buildings. Some were squat and low, others tall, growing narrower the higher they went. No matter their shape, though, all were packed too tightly together, each seeming to battle its neighbors for another step or two of ground.

Like the scars across Ghula's scalp, streets cut and sliced through the mess of buildings. Specks moved up and down the streets like gnats. Zhong citizens, and no small amount of them either.

"We're supposed to find a false heir amidst all that?" Subei asked.

The entire conglomeration of buildings and streets and people was wrapped in what looked to be a clay wall. No more than a man and a half tall at its highest point, but it'd be enough of an inconvenience to any looking to take the town. It was in disrepair, though. Cracks shot through its red, sunbaked face in many areas, and the gates had long fallen from their hinges, left in the dust at the side of the road.

"Haven't been any wars in these parts for a long time now," Ghula said as she drew up next to them. "The Zhong were among the first to swear fealty to Baji's united khanate. Then the rest of the conquests were west and away, or east to the sea." She spit, and anger crept into her tone. "And when the khanate turned on itself, declaring independence here was merely a matter of saying it. The way my grandfather told it, we were too distracted fighting each other to challenge even a small town such as this."

"Ancestors forgive me for saying so," Kashi said with a wince. "But it's looking to be one hell of a fight if our father's planning to conquer all this." Kashi shook his head. "I've heard the empire stretches all the way to the southern sea. How many other towns like this are there between here and there?"

"How many?" Ghula rubbed her chin. "A lot would be a safe bet. That, and there's a few cities as well. Those are like a half-dozen Chobeis all cobbled together into a single mass of bodies and stink, and with some high walls between them and us."

"With the four main houses under one leader again—and the minor houses falling into line—we can field. . . " Bataar paused, thinking hard. "Four hundred and fifty thousand warriors. A mighty sum, to be sure. But how can we conquer more than a dozen of these? Or a city, even?" It was wrong to doubt their father, Bataar knew. Wrong to doubt his people, too. But nothing had prepared him for the mass of humanity that was, apparently, only a town.

"Yeah, it can look that way," Ghula said, and there wasn't a hint of concern in her voice. "But the thing you don't realize from looking at all that clutter they surround themselves with is these people aren't fighters. Half of them never held a sword before, and even less have an idea how to swing one." She patted her horse, then grabbed the hilt of her saber. "The Ghangerai way of life is an old one, and a simple one. A strong horse, a good blade, and a sure shot with the bow. That's about all a warrior needs. Our people haven't changed the way we've lived for as far back as we can remember. Meanwhile, the Zhong and people like them decided to surround themselves with houses, then surround those with towns, and then those with walls. They shut the world out and live comfortable lives. They field armies only when they must, and even then, they're built on the backs of folk who've spent their whole lives comfortable." She leaned in close. "And that kind of life doesn't make for a strong back."

Well, she'd a point there, Bataar had to admit. And the more he thought on it, the more he agreed. Baji Khan had led their people to conquer the known world. It'd been done once before. Of course it could be done again. That thought steadied his mind, focused his attention, and in that calm, the path ahead became clear.

"Look, there." His voice was steady, his arm strong as he pointed to the southwestern edge of Chobei. Inside the walls, but somewhat removed from the main chaos of the town, there was a sort of courtyard. Hard to say what it was from so far, but one thing wasn't hard to say. One thing was crystal clear.

That was where the pull was leading them.

Chapter Fifteen

BATAAR

If the Longlarch had appeared congested and bulging from without, it was even worse from within. There was hardly room to set up camp between the tangled brush, drooping branches, and ancestors knew what other manner of clutching foliage. But the sun was in the west and that meant training.

It'd taken Vachir and the guards a full hour of enthusiastic gardening to clear enough space for a sparring circle. With the sun sinking now, there was hardly enough light to use it. At least the smothering embrace of the forest would keep any passersby from seeing the brothers' glowing scars, Ghula had pointed out. That and the lamellar armor they'd pulled on. Combined with their bodies' enhanced toughness from Boulder Stands Defiant, well. . . it was a day for testing limits.

Bataar grunted as Subei's wind strike blasted him onto his back. He slid to a stop before Kashi, who looked at him strangely from behind a fistful of twigs.

"Well go ahead, little brother," Bataar said. "Say something clever."

Kashi's eyes snapped into focus. "What?"

"I know you've some insult nocked to that bowstring mouth of yours."

"Oh, uh, not now." Kashi said, and turned his attention back to his twigs.

Bataar sat up, rubbing at the back of his aching head. "You ill?"

No response.

"Kashi. What are you doing?"

His brother had the twigs laid out in one hand and was. . . gesturing at them with the other. Almost wagging his fingers at them? His scars flashed, and the twigs moved, sort of jumping toward each other before falling back into a loose little pile on his palm.

"That's what I thought." Kashi smiled and nodded to himself. "There's something here."

"A puppet show, maybe." Bataar jumped back to his feet. "But that's not going to help us tomorrow, little brother." He raised a fist. "Tomorrow, we fight."

"Milk's not churned in a single stir," Kashi replied, his attention fixed on the twigs again as he strode away.

"The hell's he on about?" Bataar scratched at the back of his head—until another blast of North Wind Scours tossed him into the brush.

"You put on that armor just to look pretty?" Subei taunted as Bataar struggled to disentangle himself. Branches clutched at every gap in his plating and thorny vines clawed at any exposed skin.

"You jealous?" he shot back once free. "Kashi got the brains. I got the looks. What's that leave you?"

Subei laughed. "Leaves me—"

Bataar's orb caught him in the chest. Just a small one, hardly larger than an arrowhead, but still enough to explode in a burst of flame. Subei toppled backward in surprise, cursing and swatting at the flames singeing his collar.

Ancestors above, but that felt good. Not putting Subei on his ass—though that was part of it—but flexing his magic. It was the simplest thing now to call Baji's Burning Fury to hand. It felt right. *Natural*. Bataar shook out his shoulders and smiled.

"I was born for this."

"So was your brother, so please try not to kill him," Ghula said, arms crossed. A moment later, though, she nodded. "Nice shot, all the same."

"So the armor's not just to look pretty!" Subei cheered, back on his feet. "Good." A mischievous smile then, and he conjured an orb in each hand.

"Try not to burn the forest down!" Ghula shouted.

"There's the brother I know." Bataar set his feet and raised his fists. "Come on, then."

* * *

Somehow, they'd managed not to raze the forest. Mostly. And only one or two tents had been blown over. All in all, a success, even if his armor was plastered with soot. There wasn't any real damage, but cleaning it was going to be a pain. A small price to pay. It was one thing to exchange wind strikes with Subei, and a whole other to throw deadly attacks at him. It prepared them for actual battle.

At the moment, though, he had a different sort of battle ahead. A more difficult sort too, as far as he was concerned.

Mahtma's tent sat at the edge of the camp. Tucked into the foliage as it was, it might as well have been a part of the Longlarch itself.

Bataar took a steadying breath and focused his thoughts.

"Hold the dog," he said and gave a half-bow to her closed tent. There was a rush of air and feathers as a bird burst from within, wingtips slapping his ear on the way past. "What in the ancestor's cursed—" He slapped at the thing, but it was out of reach, its black and white speckled form slipping into the night.

"You may enter, Son of Kemu," Mahtma's steady voice came from within. Regaining himself, Bataar raised a flap and stepped inside. Her tent was larger than the one he shared with his brothers. It was just big enough for a sleeping roll at the back, a low folding table set between the support poles, and the soft-sided birdcage hanging from above.

Mahtma was sat on the ground at the table, hands working at a stack of papers. Or, one in particular. A letter?

Ah, that explained the bird.

"The khagan will be eager to hear of our progress," she said, nodding down to the text scrawled across the page.

114

"Play up mine a bit, yeah?" Bataar shot her a conspiratorial smirk. "Oldest brother and all. I have to lead the way."

"The ink is already dry, I'm afraid." And so it was. Bataar frowned at it. He couldn't read the lines and letters, but then again, neither could most Ghangerai, his father included. But that was work for advisors like Mahtma. Learned torols who'd wasted countless years hunched over scrolls and ink. They would relay the message to father, at least, until someone taught pigeons how to speak.

Mahtma folded the paper in half, then in half again. Her hands moved with practiced efficiency, and in moments the page was small enough to fit into a bamboo tube no thicker than a child's pinky. Only then did she reach for the bird cage. With the light inside the tent, Bataar could make out most of a flock in there. Six, seven. . . eight pigeons of pure white and two more with the black and white speckled pattern he'd seen before.

Mahtma carefully withdrew one of the white birds. It cooed softly but stood dutifully still as she tied the bamboo tube to its leg. When that was done, she leaned in close, her voice a whisper.

"Go on, little one. Fly swift."

A flap of wings, and the pigeon burst from the tent. Only stirred air and a feather drifting to the ground marked its passing.

"Now then, how may I be of service, Bataar?" Mahtma turned her eyes to him. They were piercing in a way no armor could protect against.

He bowed his head and spoke his next words carefully.

"I have reflected on your most recent teachings, Torol, and my behavior during them. When you spoke of the Great Khan and the. . . difficulties at the end of his life, it was shocking. I did not wish to believe you. I did not wish to cast doubt on the memory of Baji Khan. But you have my father's trust, and so you have mine. It was wrong of me to react so harshly to the truth, an ugly truth though it was. Going forward, I will conduct myself in a manner that befits my station." He bowed deeper. "Please accept my regret and my sincerest apology as the son of the khagan, as your student, and I hope, as your friend."

Fine words, and he'd only tripped up on the delivery a bit. Subei had helped him get it all polished up and sounding respectable. Turned out his dramatics weren't entirely useless, now and again. Bataar kept his head bowed, awaiting a response.

"Your apology is not necessary," Mahtma finally said.

What? Oh, she's just being polite. Saving face for everyone involved in that way the Teshkai—

"Words promise, actions prove, yes?" Her gaze was still fixed on him, unwavering. "Do not speak your apology. Demonstrate it. Take my lessons to heart and excel in them. Become an example to the others." She folded her hands into her lap. "You are the oldest brother, after all. Lead the way."

A challenge, then. Bataar couldn't fight back the smile pulling at his lips. Apologies were fumbling, awkward things. But a challenge? That, he could do.

He bowed. Properly this time.

"It has been a fine session, my teacher."

Chapter Sixteen

SUBEI

"With all due respect, Son of Kemu, I do not like it." First Kheshig Vachir had led their father's guard for as long as Subei could remember. He was strong of opinion, and everywhere his eyes turned, they found threats. Admittedly, a fine trait most days. Not today.

"I understand your concern, and I share it." Subei tried to keep his tone gentle but confident as the morning sun warmed them. "But slipping a few of us inside that town will be challenge enough."

"Stealth is the order of the day, First Kheshig." Bataar clasped a hand to the man's armored shoulder and met his eyes with a steady gaze. "If the town is alerted to our presence, it won't matter if our number is five or twenty. And I'll not risk anyone more than is necessary. This is our hunt, this is our purpose." He spread his arms to Subei and Kashi. "We know the challenges, and we will rise to meet them."

Vachir sighed. Subei could see the man knew he was beaten, but honor demanded he at least try.

"Our orders are to hunt false heirs. That's dangerous enough in open country, but *inside* Zhong walls?" He said a quick prayer to his ancestors. "It's madness. If something happens while you're in there, my warriors and I will be unable to help."

"Nothing of note is achieved without a little madness." Subei gave him a confident smile. "All the same, keep the horses ready.

If this goes to shit, we'll meet you here and ride hard. But nothing's going to happen. We were chosen of the ancestors, Vachir. We will not fail."

Invoking the ancestors inspired courage, no doubt. But more importantly it allowed Vachir a way to cede his concerns to a higher power. Ghula's arrival next tipped him over the edge.

"They are as headstrong as their father, Vachir. Arguing with this lot is useless," she said. "And anyway, the plan is a good one." She gestured to First Rider Ren who tossed a bundle of cloth to each of them.

Subei unfurled his to find a scratchy wool robe and a wrapped hood meant to be worn over the head and around the face. Teshkai pilgrims often wore them while crossing the steppe.

"Itchy but inconspicuous." Ghula pulled hers on. "It's been a while since they've seen a Ghangerai here, but that won't stop them from remembering what happened the last time our people showed up."

They'd all donned their lamellar armor today and now hid it beneath the lumpy robes.

"Don't think I'm going to make a very convincing monk," Kashi's muffled voice came through the twisted mess of fabric he'd managed to pull on half backward.

"Oh, actually, this is perfect. We can kill two birds with one arrow." Subei smirked as he turned to Mahtma. "Can Kashi take a vow of silence? He'll be extra inconspicuous today, and our ears will thank us every day after."

"I'll give you a vow of silence!" Kashi took a swing at him but missed by a wide margin, only the barest glimmer of an eye poking through his hopelessly twisted hood. He stumbled away, arms flailing before Mahtma caught him and rooted him in place. Her hands worked at straightening his hood as she spoke.

"The only way this is going to work is if you *all* stay quiet. These townsfolk might not be the scholars of Jade Hall, but they'll know a Ghangerai accent when they hear one." She got Kashi's hood on straight then pushed him away. "I will handle the talking. My accent will raise far fewer brows."

"We'll leave our weapons here," Ghula said as she bundled

her shield, sabers, and bow and handed them to a guard. "At least, most of our weapons." She produced a knife that was pretty much a short sword and somehow managed to get all of it under her robe. First Rider Ren followed suit and, in the process of tucking hers away, Subei spotted an assortment of smaller blades strapped tight around her ribs with a harness of fine leather.

"Where can I get a set up like that?" he asked with an impressed nod.

"Duty saw me far along the Eternal road, out west past Mercer. There's a sea there, and the people on the far side of it are renowned for their leatherworking."

"I should like to visit it one day," Subei said, distracted for a moment with thoughts of deserts and seas he'd never seen.

"We'll visit it." Bataar squeezed his shoulder. "And we'll bring the borders of the khanate with us."

"Well, until that day, you might need these." Ren detached three sheathed knives from the harness and tossed one to each of the brothers.

"Appreciated, but this is the only weapon I'll need." Bataar held up his hand and conjured an orb.

"At the end of the day, brother, there's nothing more reliable than a pointy bit of steel," Subei reminded him.

"Have two, then." Bataar tossed his knife over.

Subei rolled his eyes and resigned himself to getting the knife back to Bataar once things got ugly. Dramatic gestures aside, he'd need it.

The last of their number, Mahtma, carried a weapon that was more walking stick than anything. Given, it had an iron cap on the end that looked sturdy enough to crack a skull.

"So then, what are we waiting on?" Ghula clapped everyone to attention. "There's two false heirs down there, traipsing about with Baji's magic. Are we going to do something about that, or hope they choke on their supper?"

So armed and disguised, they followed the slope of the hill down to Chobei. As they drew closer, a path began to take shape, trampled grass giving way to dirt, then hard-packed soil. Ren moved into the lead. She was the only one not wearing a hood.

Her disguise instead consisted of too-oiled hair and too-heavy perfume. To her credit, she played her part well. With each step, her mannerisms changed. Like a lorecaller slipping into a familiar song, she transformed from a Ghangerai scout back to a normal, unexceptional citizen of the Zhong borderlands. She even cleared her throat, tested her voice a bit. All hint of the usual gruffness was gone then, replaced instead by the strange manner in which the Zhong spoke, stressing some syllables faster than others, voice going high at what seemed random intervals. It was a good trick, Subei had to admit.

"I'll consider that as good an invite as we'll have here," Ren said, nodding to the side of the path where the remains of the town's gate lay discarded.

"Not doing much good there, is it?" Kashi nudged it with a foot, testing the rotting wood.

"Everything goes back to the earth eventually," Subei said quietly.

Bataar scoffed.

"Thanks, little brother, for that inspiring thought."

"These walls are halfway back to the earth, too," Ren said, shaking her head. "A good sneeze would bring them down."

She wasn't wrong. From afar the cracks had seemed minor. Up close, they were anything but. Subei was far from an authority on walls—weren't many of those on the steppe—but it didn't take a Mercaen engineer to tell these were in dire need of upkeep.

"Quiet now," Mahtma hissed from the front of their group. "If talking's needed, Ren and I will handle it. After that, you three will lead. Follow the pull. Find the false heirs."

The hood was stuffy in the morning heat, and Subei found he was sweating. Or maybe that was just the nerves. Wasn't every day he abandoned his horse and weapons to walk headlong into an enemy town. Seemed a fool notion when they'd first come up with it. Seemed even more so now that they were here. But again, that was nerves doing the talking. Already he could imagine the song this would make. A far finer deception than his trick with the wagons and the bandits. So, Subei sweated from the heat, and he sweated from the nerves as he followed Mahtma and Ren into the town, the walls looming taller and taller with every step. A tunnel led through them, dark despite the brightness of the morning. The group passed under without stopping, no guards anywhere in sight, and Subei found he didn't much like walking under all that stone and clay. Didn't want to imagine how much weight was looming up there, hanging just above his head. Especially didn't want to think now about all the cracks they'd seen shooting through its sunbaked surface.

The tunnel passed quickly, and Subei's anxiety with it. They stepped into the light at the other end, and the town engulfed them, drowning Subei in an entirely new anxiety. The quiet steppe seemed but a distant memory here, where the noise of the town overtook all. People rushed to and fro, carrying baskets or chests or barrels of ancestors knew what, yelling all the while. Yelling to the person next to them, or at the person in their way. Yelling just to be heard over the yelling. Subei had lain awake, ears ringing from the echoing howls of trovaaks in mating season. He'd felt even his thoughts battered away beneath the rumbling cacophony of a hundred thousand horses galloping across the steppe—and still this sound was greater. Was all encompassing.

The smell hit him next. Ancestors above, the smell. Like nothing he'd ever had the displeasure of inhaling before. Subei considered himself a rather eloquent speaker. Could paint a picture with his words, his brothers always said. But now, even he found himself unable to describe the stench that wafted from every corner of the town. From the people, all sweat and dirt and stress as they hurried about. From the buildings, all that wood and thatch trapped in the confines of the walls. And from the very ground itself, as if the smell had permeated the streets, lying in wait to waft up and suffocate them with every turn of the well-churned mud.

Subei had initially been worried they'd attract attention. That's how it was on the steppe, at least. Easy to spot newcomers amidst all that emptiness. Here, that was far from true. Here, they drowned in a sea of anonymity. Seemed not a single person gave them more than the quickest of glances before continuing on, hurrying to be about their business.

Ren paused briefly to exchange greetings with a man leaning against a wall at a crossroads. They traded only a few words before he pointed to one of the roads. She led the group down it.

Horses pulling wagons laden with all manner of crates and boxes clogged the center of the street, while people on foot rushed past either side. There were even a few mammoths dragging massive, elongated wagons behind them which were all loaded up with people. Every couple of streets, the wagons stopped, and some folks stepped off only to be replaced by as many or more getting on.

Subei kept close to his brothers, and they in turn kept close to Mahtma and Ren, following the gaps in the crowd they made.

"The courtyard Bataar spotted is up this way," Ren said, slowing for a moment. "Seems the best place to start looking. Can you feel them now?"

Subei focused on the magic deep in his stomach and found all seven pulls. Five of those were still very distant. Two stood out, though clearly nearer than the others, and directly ahead.

"Best I can tell, we're heading the right way," he said quietly, careful so that no one overheard. Then he gestured toward the end of the street where the buildings shrunk away to create a wide-open space. "Somewhere up there."

Kashi nodded his agreement. "They're close."

"If there weren't so many people everywhere, I'd be able to spot them already," Bataar said, voice hushed. His fingers fidgeted as he spoke, hands clenching and unclenching with every word. Nerves, Subei figured. He was still feeling them himself.

"This is only the beginning of the songs they'll weave about us," Subei reminded him. "We don't fail here today."

Mahtma shushed them with a look, but kept pace so that they could direct her.

Subei followed his gut now, doing his best to ignore the press of people on all sides. As they drew closer to the town's center the pull continued to grow. Seemed it was leading him straight toward that vast square where, though it seemed impossible, even more people were packed together and, unsurprisingly, yelling to be heard over one another.

Ren stopped for a moment at the edge of the square, eyes scanning the crowd. Subei took a deep breath and prepared to make the plunge. He'd never been packed in with so many people and wasn't relishing the feeling. He took one last look, sucked down a breath—and froze.

The false heir was staring straight at him. Any doubt in Subei's mind was immediately erased. He nudged Bataar and Kashi, but his brothers were already looking.

The false heir stood on the far side of the square. Sixty or seventy paces distant. He looked a bit older than a boy, but not old enough yet to be properly considered a man. Was somewhere in that odd stage in between, the scruff of a beard just starting to sprout around his jawline. Hair as black as tar covered his head, drooping to just above his eyebrows. Despite his youth, there was a ferocity in his eyes, and his mouth was set in a tight-lipped frown. He'd jumped up on the corner of a market stall to get above the crowd, one hand holding tight to its support beam. A thick woolen scarf was wrapped around his neck.

"What are we waiting for?" Bataar growled.

"Don't make a scene," Subei warned him.

The false heir held his ground atop the stall, then gave Subei and the others a calm, slow nod. As if to say he knew why they were there and was accepting their challenge? Or had felt them coming and was ready to talk? Or something else entirely?

The heir jumped down from his spot at the corner of the stall and headed toward the edge of the square.

Bataar lunged to follow, but Mahtma caught him by the shoulder.

"What?" he snarled, turning on her.

"Hold, a moment." She nodded ahead.

An armed patrol was passing through the crowd, people parting to let them by. Zhong soldiers. Subei had never seen one before, and despite the tension of the moment, he could hear his father telling him to wait, to watch. To learn the nature of his enemy.

The united Ghangerai army would be coming south as soon as it was gathered. And once its presence was known, the Zhong would raise their armies to resist. Armies consisting of soldiers like these.

They were heavily clad in armor. Similar to Ghangerai lamellar, but heavier in every way, mail and plate shining cold in the morning sun. It made for an imposing sight. Moving fortresses, each of them, and armed with halberds and spears. Intimidating in a hand-to-hand battle, perhaps, but the strength of the Ghangerai was not in such combat. It was in the lethal combination of bow and horse. A mounted warrior that could rain arrows down on the enemy, then slip away before retaliation was possible. But at the moment, Subei had neither horse nor bow with him. Much less the space of an open battlefield on which to maneuver. And so, the heavily armored Zhong soldiers posed something of a problem. A problem that was best avoided. He kept his eyes down and his demeanor casual as the patrol passed. Several long moments, then they were gone, marching down another street.

Bataar was off in an instant, sprinting through the crowd. Subei broke into a run after him, no longer able to deny the adrenaline pumping in his veins. Long before he'd become an heir of Baji, he'd been a hunter. And now, even with everything that'd changed, the sight of his quarry getting away triggered those primal instincts inside him.

The hunt was on.

Chapter Seventeen

BATAAR

Damned people! Everywhere Bataar turned, there were more in the way. He gave up on weaving around them in favor of simply bowling the bastards over. Cries and curses echoed at his heels, but he paid them no mind as he broke from the town square and darted into the alley after the false heir. He was long gone from sight, but the pull didn't lie. Bataar followed it, vaguely aware of his brothers and the others behind him as he sprinted into a deepening maze of back alleys and side streets. Each turn revealed more of the same—and no heir in sight.

"They breed for speed here in Chobei," Bataar grunted through the exertion. Riding down one's quarry was far preferable to a foot race, but there was no use in wishing for horses they didn't have, so he barreled on, ducking under clotheslines and various piles of detritus perfectly placed to trip him up.

The pull was getting stronger. He was gaining on the false heir. Or the false heir had stopped running. That thought hit Bataar as he turned another corner, and the alley ended against the towering wall of some massive building. There was a hole in the base—just big enough they could duck through. Past it there wasn't much visible but deep shadows inside the cavernous building.

Hiding, are you? It won't help.

Bataar stepped toward the hole, but a hand pulled him back.

Subei.

"Brother, wait. What is this place?"

"Why does it matter?" Bataar pulled free as the others arrived, chests working hard beneath their heavy armor.

"Is this a temple?" Kashi asked, but he wasn't looking at the building. His gaze was off to the side. Bataar followed it to find a gap between the wall of the building and the last house in the alley. Through it he could see some sort of complex. The court-yard he'd seen from outside town?

"That is a temple to the ancestors," Mahtma said. She looked to be the only one not out of breath.

"We don't build temples to our ancestors," Subei said. "We honor them with our actions."

"The Zhong build temples to the ancestors. Or did, when this was khanate land. A mix of the two cultures. But this one has been abandoned for some time."

"Why does it matter?" Bataar growled again. They were wasting precious time. Action was the currency of their people, as well as bravery in the face of uncertainty. As the chosen of Baji Khan, he and his brothers had to exemplify those values. "With me now, brothers. As if Baji himself were watching. Let's go!" He strode forward and his foot sent something clattering along the cobbles.

"Was that. . . ?" Subei asked.

"Soulstone." Ghula scooped up the shard of crystalline mate-rial. And then, as Bataar looked, there were more of them, scat-tered all over the temple complex.

"There must have been an obelisk here," Bataar said, and even as he did, spotted the remains of it. In the center of the courtyard, only its base still stood, but it was exactly like those at the Great Khan's statue.

"The records tell of an obelisk in Bharmankara and two more in Ba Seng. No mention of any here," Mahtma said, brow furrowed.

"Then the records were wrong. But it doesn't matter. There was an obelisk here and now there's a false heir. Let us do what we came to," Bataar said and hurried toward the hole in the wall.

Mahtma wasn't listening, eyes scrutinizing the temple complex.

"There would have been a hall of records here. Ah, there!" She moved toward a building on the far side of the square.

"Mahtma!" Subei hissed after her.

"I am House Kemu's Master of Knowledge, and I have been tasked with discovering the origin and nature of these obelisks," she said without stopping. "If there's information here, it is my duty to find it."

"Very well," Ghula said with a nod, and from how wide his eyes went, Subei must have been shocked. So be it, Bataar figured. They could handle this fight without the monk.

"We're just splitting up now?" Subei hissed.

Ghula nodded. "Information is as much a weapon as steel. Let our Master of Knowledge arm us as best she can. We'll handle the heirs." And with that, she followed Bataar.

"*Thank you,*" he said, exasperated. If Baji was watching, what would he think about such hesitation? Unacceptable.

"I'll watch her back," First Rider Ren said. "Meet you at camp."

"Subei, come on," Bataar heard Kashi say. "Mahtma has her duty, we have ours."

"Get your guards up!" Bataar hissed back at them then advanced on the hole the heir had disappeared through.

The pull was gone now. The thief had to be close. What had they learned with Kashi? Pulls disappeared within fifty paces? An ambush, then. The false heir was no doubt laying in wait.

"You saw the false heir's face," Subei said, breath hot against Bataar's ear. "He knew we were coming. And look at this place."

It was an old building. Some sort of storehouse, but if that was true, it was the largest one Bataar had ever seen. It appeared to have caught fire at some point, too. The sun illuminated only a few steps past the entrance formed by the hole, and all that was visible was charred wood, blackened stone, and deep shadows.

"This looks a trap if ever I've seen one," Subei hissed.

"Let's see their best shot then," Bataar said and ducked inside. *Great Khan, guide us true.*

In the darkness of the building, his magic tingled and churned as if itching to be used. It'd been impatient all day, but now he truly needed it. He kept his clenched fists raised in front of him, ready to rebuff any attacks. If the false heir had learned any techniques, Bataar would feel them coming. Would feel the magic being called like when Subei or Kashi did it. In such darkness, though, if the attack came with, say, an arrow, there'd be no warning.

But no attack came. Instead, silence.

Dim light from outside trickled into the space, illuminating just enough for Bataar to realize the full cavernous expanse around him. The roof was far above, hidden in the unending darkness. The walls were entirely out of sight. Most of all, though, countless rows of shelves filled the space. They were comically large, each level wide enough to hold a horse, and long enough to. . . well, he couldn't truly see their end.

Crates, lumber, and other unidentifiable debris were piled up and down the shelves, most of them burned to some degree. No doubt caught in the flames that had once fed on the building. The air was thick with the residual smell of charred wood and ash. Dust and dirt and other specks of detritus swirled slowly through the space, coating the inside of Bataar's nostrils with each breath. He coughed, and the sound echoed across the vast darkness.

Wordlessly, he led his brothers and Ghula deeper into the darkness. Kashi stumbled then cursed as the plank he'd kicked dragged across the floor with an echoing scrape.

"Having trouble there?" a voice called from the darkness ahead. Or, no, off to the side? Above them? It was impossible to tell, so rapidly did it bounce and echo through the space. Didn't help it the thief spoke quick and high, his voice lilting in that way the Zhong did.

"You may hide from us for a while, but you'll never escape your shame," Bataar said, frustration biting at the back of his throat. "This magic is not yours. You will return it."

"I've felt you coming for two days now," the false heir called out from somewhere. "Wondered at your purpose. Hoped it might be something good, even if the churning in my gut said otherwise."

"Your gut betrays your guilt," Ghula said from behind.

Bataar nodded, before remembering no one could really see each other.

"Everything I have, I've earned." A pause. "Is there even a way to 'give' this back?" A spark of blue light several rows away. Bataar snapped toward it, crouching to look past a broken crate. "It doesn't matter, though, does it? How could I part with it? This magic is life changing."

"Life ending, might be more apt," Subei suggested.

A sigh then, from off in the dark.

"If that's how you want to do things, so be it. I am Yue Jong, and I hope you're ready."

"On with it then!" Bataar called back, still advancing. He squeezed his core, readying his magic as more shelves passed on each side, their heights hidden in the dark.

"Might be you take me down. Probably you will," Yue Jong said. "You have numbers. But I'll give you fair warning: I will take several of you with me."

"Is that right?" Bataar quickened his pace, a good idea where the voice was coming from now.

"It'll be a messy scene for the guards to decipher afterward. Is that what you want?"

"I want my magic back!" And with that, Bataar called an orb to hand. Severe, blue light burned away the darkness as he flung it toward where he guessed the thief should be. Shelves were illuminated as it passed, shadows stabbing out from their darkened sides—and then there he was. The false heir stood at the end of the aisle, far wide of the orb's path.

No matter.

Bataar slashed to the side with his hand, scars shining bright, and the orb hooked toward the thief. His face was lit with its burning light before a second wash of blue blossomed in the room. The reason for the thick scarf around Yue Jong's neck became clear as a web of scars flared beneath it, their light shining through the cloth. The thief extended his hands in front of him, palms facing up, then raised them toward the ceiling as if lifting some great weight. A flurry of movement next, as cracked stones and caved-in shelves and all manner of debris rushed toward him. They slammed together to form a makeshift wall just in time for the orb to explode against it. A burst of angry orange flame lashed out at the shadows. When it faded, half the wall was gone, the sides and top of it reduced to scorched debris. But Yue Jong stood uninjured.

"Glowing, explosive spheres?" Yue Jong pondered aloud. "Hmm, I'd not considered such a use for the magic. I like it."

"The technique's called Baji's Burning Fury," Bataar growled, and conjured another orb. "Have a closer look!"

Another wall intercepted this one's flight, but Yue Jong had angled it such that the orb's explosion and subsequent wash of flame was directed harmlessly off to the side.

"This magic's the best thing to ever happen to me," Yue Jong spoke from behind the remains. "An apology from our parents, perhaps, for succumbing to the plague. Or a gift from the family ancestors to make up for the rotten hand we were dealt. Either way, it will raise us beyond this honorless station. I've worked ceaselessly since this gift was given—and not just so you interloping barbarians can end it all here." He tucked the flap of his scarf in tight, further obscuring the light shining through it, then turned his eyes to the smoldering wall before him. "I don't know what to call this." He clenched a fist, and more debris flew in to fill the gaps the orb had created. He smirked. "But this part? How about. . . Bulwark Breaks Barbarian!" He punched forward in what appeared to be his own version of North Wind Scours—but it wasn't wind that came blasting toward them.

The wall shot down the aisle, individual pieces spreading apart slightly but still hurtling onward like so many leaves in the wind. Except these leaves were made of splintered floorboards, broken pottery, and all manner of other commonplace, but now dangerous, junk.

Bataar crossed his arms in front of him and lunged forward with a growl. The air shook as he unleashed a wind strike. The junk blew further apart, swirling and tossing and bouncing wildly among the tight confines of the aisle between the shelves.

A flash of light from behind as Subei used a sweeping wind

strike to protect himself. The debris nearest him was driven to the ground where it bounced and slid by. The rest whipped past and slammed into the others in a chaos of clanging metal and splintering wood. Kashi cried out in pain, but there wasn't time to check on him.

"With me, Subei," Bataar growled. "I've seen enough."

Chapter Eighteen

SUBEI

"Interesting," Yue Jong said. "You used air to sweep my attack aside. I've not considered that use either. Show me the technique again?"

"This magic doesn't belong to you," Subei said simply. There was no malice to it. No anger. Just a simple truth. He bore no ill will towards this Yue Jong, but the magic had to be reclaimed. It was the rightful inheritance of his people.

Bataar charged with a yell, and Subei followed, his own scars now joining the haptic fanfare of blue light casting the room in its pale, ghostly light.

Yue Jong beckoned as if to raise another wall but cut the motion short. Two long boards were ripped from the floor, nails jutting from them at odd angles. He slung his arm forward, and the boards rushed toward them. Subei tucked his head down and threw himself into a roll, the world spinning as the back of his shoulder made contact with the ground and momentum carried him back to his feet. He stumbled once before regaining his balance and continuing forward.

A sharp crack echoed from behind, followed by a creaking groan. Subei turned to see the boards had crashed into the shelf next to Kashi and Ghula, snapping one of its support beams. The shelf wobbled then groaned beneath the weight of its unseen heights.

"The shelf's coming down!" Subei yelled to Bataar, skidding

to a stop and turning back. But his older brother ignored him, mouth set in a grim scowl as he lunged at the heir.

"Stay back!" Subei shouted as Kashi made to dart forward. Already debris was toppling from the tilting shelf, and Ghula just got ahold of the back of his deel to stop him from being crushed beneath a pallet of charred lumber.

A second support beam shattered, and the entire shelf gave out, a devastating weight of wood hurtling toward the floor. Hurtling toward Kashi and Ghula.

"Gah!" Subei punched forward with a wind strike. He squeezed his core as hard as he could, pumping magic into the attack. A wave force roiled through the darkness and blasted the falling debris back into the shelf, then out the other side. It bought just enough time for Ghula and Kashi to dart away before the whole thing came roaring down. Wood shattered, splinters flew, and when the dust settled, the aisle was divided in two.

"Hold tight," Kashi's voice called from the far side. "We're coming." His head appeared over the top of the pile, but then there was a clatter and the area beneath him gave way. He slid back down and out of view.

"We'll go around, this way!" Ghula's voice echoed from the far side, but even as she said it, another shelf groaned. The debris from the collapse was piled against its base, tilting it to one side.

"Find another way!" Subei shouted at them as he sprinted away from the imminent collapse. He ran then, toward the lights flashing in front of him where Bataar and Yue Jong were exchanging blows.

At the moment, the fight was one versus one. Something approaching a fair fight, maybe. But when it came to matters of life and death, "fair" was just a prettier way to say "foolish." Subei rushed in to join his brother, and the last thing he was looking to do was fight fair.

Bataar was going all in, burning hot on adrenaline and flinging orb after orb at the false heir. The explosions lit up the darkness time and again—but never found their mark.

The very nature of this battleground suited Yue Jong's technique perfectly, Subei realized, suddenly understanding why he'd picked this place. Surrounded by junk and debris, he raised wall after wall. Subei didn't know how draining that ability was, but of those he and his brothers had learned, conjuring orbs required the most magic. Here, one orb was not enough to destroy a single wall, and it didn't take a Master of Knowledge to know that exchange wasn't going to work out. They either had to get a shot around the walls or change tactics.

"Brother!" Subei called as he joined the fight. "This is not a winning strategy!"

If he heard, the continued explosions delivered the message he didn't care. Another orb detonated against another wall, and before the smoke could clear, Yue Jong burst through it and unleashed a wind strike. It caught Bataar clean in the chest and launched him backward to topple over a stack of empty crates. A staggering blow that opened the chance for a lethal one.

The false heir drew a knife and stepped forward—then flung himself to the side just in time to avoid Subei's thrown orb. It slipped past him, and Subei gasped as it nearly hit Bataar. By the will of the ancestors, it missed him and continued along to detonate against the floor some ten paces away.

North Wind Scours, then. Right.

As Yue Jong recovered, Subei lashed out with a wind strike. It winged the false heir, spinning him around. But Subei wasn't done. Once, twice, three times he punched forward, the magic surging through his fists as he struck with his right, his left, then his right once more. The darkness wavered in the wake of the blows, a pond struck by a boulder.

Yue Jong ducked the first strike, but the second caught his legs, and he stumbled. The third bowled him over, cracked his head against the floor, and sent him sliding through the dirt.

Ha!

Yue Jong groaned, reaching into empty air with a shaking hand and unfocused eyes. Subei conjured an orb. It would be a killing blow.

But Yue Jong hadn't asked for this magic.

Subei paused, orb crackling in hand and furrowed his brow. Where had that thought come from? And why now—

Something hit him from below. A wall. It formed beneath his feet then burst upward and launched him end over end. The room was a rushing blur of blue light and deep shadows— then only flashes of pain as he crashed through a shelf, bounced off a crate, and finally rolled to a stop, wood creaking beneath him.

His vision shook a moment, but between his armor and the effects of Boulder Stands Defiant, his empowered body was unharmed.

Good, he thought. Until he realized the world was wobbling. No, not the world, just the ground. But it wasn't the ground he was on, Subei realized. He'd landed on a shelf. Halfway up it amidst the stacks of charred debris.

"Well then." He peered over the edge to find the ground was a good twenty paces below. Yue Jong was there, on his feet now and looking up at him. There was pain in his face still, but his eyes were refocused. Determined. The false heir raised a hand, and then a wall launched him as well. But this wasn't a wild, flailing flight like Subei's. This was a controlled movement. Yue Jong rode the momentum with practiced ease, his knees bent and legs loaded. When the wall reached its full height, he launched off and soared up to Subei. At the top of the arc, he seemed to hang in the air a moment, right hand reared back, knife gripped tight. Then gravity took over and he came stabbing down.

It was all Subei could do to react with a two-handed blast of North Wind Scours. The buffeting wind howled as it drove Yue Jong off course. He came down several steps along the shelf, hair whipped into a frenzy.

He raised his eyes to Subei. Wild, excited eyes.

"Have we ever really lived until this moment?" he asked in a gasp.

How did one respond to that? Subei pondered it for all of a heartbeat before deciding the best answer was an orb. He threw it sidearm, still prone.

Yue Jong dove out of the way—right off the shelf. Then at the last moment, he caught the edge and turned his downward momentum into a swing that carried him through the level below and right back up. He landed with a grin and came slashing in with his knife.

Subei rolled over backwards and to his feet. He ducked one slash then sidestepped another, but his foot found the edge of the shelf and he wobbled, tottering over the long fall below. He only steadied himself when one flailing hand caught a cross brace from the level above.

"Ha!" Yue Jong darted forward and plunged his knife into Subei's gut. It landed with a dull *thunk*. "Huh?" The false heir frowned as the hole through Subei's robe revealed his armor beneath.

Subei caught him in the chin with his knee a moment later and sent him stumbling backward. A leg sweep, and he went down hard. Yue Jong swung his knife then, and Subei met the strike with a kick to his wrist. The sudden impact jolted the blade from his hand, and it tumbled away, disappearing into the darkness beneath them—or would have, if Bataar hadn't snatched it out of the air.

"Drop something?" he asked, snarling as he pulled himself the rest of the way up. "Hell of a climb."

"Hell of a fall, too." Yue Jong clenched a fist. His scars flared, and both Subei and Bataar ducked low as debris whipped in to form a wall.

Bataar threw an orb before it could finish taking shape.

"Gah!"

The explosion blasted Subei back, smacking his head against the edge of a crate. Fire swept over them, searing hot for the two heartbeats it took to burn out. In its wake, smoke. And embers, embedded in the wood of the shelf.

"Did that get him?" Subei asked, squinting to see.

Movement next, as Yue Jong tore through the cloud and leapt off the shelf again. This time he covered the width of the aisle and landed on the shelf opposite them.

"After him!" Bataar shouted, preparing his own leap. He had one foot over the shadowy expanse below before Subei caught him by the collar and yanked him back. At the same moment, a crate whipped past, exactly where Bataar would have been mid-jump.

The false heir cursed. "Almost had you."

Bataar whipped an orb across the gap. Yue Jong stretched his hands in front of him, then pulled them down to the side. His scars flared, and a howling wind swept down from above, catching the orb and driving it wide. It passed through his shelf and detonated against one further back.

"Ha! Now I can do that technique too!" The false heir examined his palms. "Remind me what you call it?"

The only answer was a groan from behind him. From the *shelf* behind him. Two levels down, it was in flames, and a support beam had been blown to bits by Bataar's orb. Even as Subei noticed it, the shelf tipped forward.

"Ah, shit." Yue Jong barely had the words out before the impact drove his shelf off balance. He was carried forward with it —arms swinging for balance—and right toward Subei and Bataar.

"Yes. . . " Bataar growled, bracing to meet him.

"No, you idiot!" Subei tried to shove him out of the way, but the shelves collided. A crate was thrown forward to smash against Bataar's chest. The shelf went out from beneath Subei's feet faster than he could follow, and then everyone was falling. Air roared in his ears and his stomach felt like it was fighting to burst up his throat. He just had time to get his arms around his head as the avalanche of debris, shelves, and heirs crashed to the ground.

Chapter Nineteen

SUBEI

"Subei! Where are you?"

A voice. Ghula.

Distant. Echoing.

"Brothers!" Kashi this time, just as far away.

Subei groaned as he crawled free from the wreckage. The sound was involuntary, some mix of pain and shock and the shuddering reverberations in his chest of whatever the hell had nearly been crushed. Somehow, though, he was still alive.

Armor. . . helped. Subei's thoughts came slow. And Boulder Stands. . . Defiant. One or both had saved him. Still, neither would have stopped a trovaak-sized crate crushing his head. Armor, magic, and sheer dumb luck, then.

He moved to wipe the blood from his eyes and found a splintered length of wood buried in the soft flesh between his thumb and index finger. His stomach went woozy at the sight, and an aching pain lanced down his wrist. Without thinking, he ripped it out.

"Gah!" He curled around the pain, left hand covering its wounded counterpart. A dozen other scrapes and cuts complained all over him, but the warm blood coursing over his hand had his full attention. Not just that it was there, but what it represented. They were losing. To a nobody.

There was a shifting of debris from behind, and Bataar groaned. Panic surged through Subei at the sound of his brother's pain. Panic, then fear, and from that, anger. White hot. He would not let this beggar boy hurt his family any further.

The anger pulsed in his veins, racing through him with each new stab of pain, with each increasingly furious thought of his brothers in danger. Something clawed at his mind, like spectral hands inside his skull. Spectral hands taking hold and clenching into fists. Fists that—

Subei shook his head, forced out a heavy, shuddering breath, and the feeling retreated. Then all that was left was the pain echoing through him—and an injured brother behind.

"Bataar!" He spun to search the wreckage, but his older brother was already standing. He'd one shoulder slumped down and a hand to his ribs, but his breath came steady. And there was fury in his eyes.

"I won't let the bastard escape." He limped as he moved forward, fighting his way over the unsteady rubble.

"Do we even know if he survived?" Subei asked, but even as he did, he spotted the movement. Yue Jong. The false heir kicked and slipped through the rubble as he ran, hardly able to keep upright.

"Come on!" Bataar snarled, and broke into a sprint. By the light of the various fires in the room, Subei was just able to see Yue Jong reach the far wall. A hallway led through it. Tight and narrow compared to the cavern around them. The false heir picked up speed as he limped out of sight.

"Subei!" Another cry from behind. Kashi and Ghula, searching for him.

"This way!" he called back, then joined Bataar in the pursuit. His brother was too far ahead, though, and moving fast compared to Subei's unsteady stumble. Bataar reached the hallway long before him.

"Brother, wait!"

"He went left!" Bataar's shout echoed from out of the hall.

"Damned idiot," Subei growled to himself, then saved his breath for running. He reached the hallway and squinted as he dragged himself down it, the fires' light dimmer here. A dozen paces in, the hallway split.

"Left. . . " Subei said to himself, but something was wrong.

Yue Jong wasn't to the left. He could feel the pull again, and it was clearly leading him right.

"You went the wrong way!" he yelled, but Bataar was gone, disappeared into the darkness. Damn it. The pull was getting weaker, their quarry was definitely to the right. Subei sent one last look after his brother. How could he have not felt it? There wasn't time to ponder. He sprinted in the opposite direction.

The corridor emptied into another large room drowned in shadow. The pull had stopped moving now. Yue Jong was nearby. Preparing another ambush, no doubt. Subei suddenly felt very alone, his breath wheezing in gasps, the only noise in the darkness. He cursed. Why the hell had Bataar taken off down the opposite corridor?

His hand still bleeding a sopping warmth down his side, Subei didn't much fancy the idea of facing their enemy alone. But waiting in the dark to be attacked wasn't going to do him any good.

"We've played this game already," he shouted into the darkness. Then, ensuring his fingers were wrapped securely around it, he conjured an orb and raised it above his head to illuminate the room. It was pretty much the same as the other, but the piles of crates were stacked to the ceiling here, replacing the rickety shelving. The pull directed him toward the back half of the room, but as he drew near, the feeling faded.

Within fifty paces, then.

"I feel you just the same as you feel me. There's no point in hiding. Let's get this over with," Subei called.

Silence, a long moment, then a scuffling of footsteps answered his words. He set his feet apart in a fighting stance and let his injured hand fall to his side.

The false heir appeared from behind a pile of crates—but no. It wasn't Yue Jong. It was a girl. About his own age, maybe a bit younger. She wore a grime-stained shirt and pants several sizes too large, and her dirty hair hung in strands in front of her face, her cheeks smeared with ash. Subei's eyes went wide. But. . . ancestors above. There had been two heirs in Chobei. Two pulls they'd followed here. In the pursuit, though, he'd forgotten that. Had been so focused, so. . . eager for the fight, he'd forgotten the bigger picture. And in life-or-death situations, that was the kind of mistake a person made only once.

"Even from afar, I could feel it in you. The anger, the blood-lust." The girl clenched a fist. "I told my brother there was no hope of a truce, but he held on to hope."

"I. . . uhh. . . " Between the pain, the adrenaline, and the real-ization that he'd entirely forgotten the second heir, Subei's thoughts were left spinning. At the least, he was able to focus a moment and feel Yue Jong. He was distant, but not so much as to be out of the building. And Bataar was there, chasing.

"I can feel my brother still fighting." The girl set her feet back into a fighting stance and slowly raised her fists. "Which means the three of you couldn't handle him. How then, do you think you'll fair one versus one?"

Subei loosened his grip on the orb and pumped more magic into it, light pouring into the room.

"But wait." The girl hesitated, frowning at him now. "You're not Zhong." She blinked, then raised an eyebrow. "That explains why we felt you coming from the north."

It was then Subei realized his hood was gone, must have come off in the fighting.

Her eyes went wide. And then she scowled, lips drawing back to show her teeth.

"You're Ghangerai."

"And you have something that belongs to us."

She swallowed hard.

"Our grandparents told us stories of your kind. More wolves than men, but with none of the mercy."

"Your grandparents were rebels and traitors." Subei advanced slowly, waiting for an opening. "But it is possible to respect one's enemy. To honor them, even if you stand on opposite sides of the battlefield."

"What would you know of honor, Ghangerai fiend?"

Subei shook his head at that. What did they even teach their children here?

"Everything has its place in the world," he said. "The deer is not lessened because it falls to the wolf, just as the wolf is not lessened because it kills the deer. That is their place."

"And your place is scratching a living from the frozen dirt," she snarled.

"My place is wielding the magic of Baji Khan. My *place* is reclaiming the inheritance of my people." Subei growled it with more anger than he'd intended. He leveled his emotions with a steadying breath. "But that doesn't mean we can't face each other as honored enemies."

Why was he hesitating? The khagan had commanded him to find and kill false heirs. And now, one was standing before him. The wolf didn't question its role when faced with a deer. He couldn't question his role now. Subei tensed the muscles in his arm, aimed his throw, and—a tingling rose in his chest. He snuffed the orb and spun to the side, sweeping downward.

His block caught a wind strike and deflected it away.

"Away from my sister, bastard!"

A second wind strike flew toward him, a third close behind it. Subei backpedaled, sweeping quickly to turn both blows aside. Yue Jong was on him, must have snuck up while he was distracted. And Bataar was nowhere in sight, he realized, concern rising inside him. He tried to feel for his brother's presence, but another attack forced his thoughts back to the battle.

"Ru, run!" Yue Jong yelled. "Go to the others!"

"This is my fight as much as it is yours, brother." She raised her hands, and several crates locked together to form a half-wall in front of her. She punched forward, and they shot at Subei.

He saw it coming—couldn't miss that much movement in his periphery—but the onslaught of blows from her brother had yet to cease, forcing him to sweep aside more wind strikes in succession than he ever had before. He was too focused on blocking to consider anything but the next oncoming attack. But he couldn't ignore the wall of crates bearing down on him. Indecision is deadly, Ghula had taught them. Subei saw his chance—Yue Jong miscast one of his wind strikes and created the smallest of gaps in the onslaught. It wasn't much, but it would have to do.

Subei swept aside one more wind strike then spun toward the wall of crates. They were all he could see, were a breath away from smearing him across the floor like a bug beneath a boot. He flung an orb and it detonated so close, flames washed over him

—but the crates blew apart, trailing smoke as they launched in separate directions across the room. At the same time, the orb let out a concussive blast that blew Subei back, his feet digging scuff marks through the hard-packed dirt. His face and neck seared with the heat of the flame, and the smell of his own burning hair clogged his nose.

Still alive. He breathed a sigh of relief. Still—

The barrage of wind strikes bowled into him from the left. The first lifted him into the air, the second slammed him back down, head cracking sharply on the floor, vision flickering to black and spotted with bursts of light. The third rolled him back into a pile of crates. The fourth plowed him further in such that the pile collapsed on top of him. His world was pain and splintering wood and a sharp ringing that screamed in his ears. He groaned, chest and face crushed to the dirt beneath untold weight. His breath came in quick, pained bursts.

This would be his end.

Everything he'd wanted, everything he'd fought for, gone. Ended along with him in some shit town far from home. And worse, thoughts of his brothers sharing the same fate filled his mind. Kashi was already injured, could be picked off with ease. And then it'd just be Bataar.

A true Ghangerai warrior didn't give in to fear, but in that moment, Subei felt himself teetering on the edge.

I will not.

He clenched a fist, sought an escape from the fear, and found his anger. And then, something changed with the magic inside him. Previously, it'd been a riverbed with a trickle of a stream running through it, a steady but infantile flow of magic. Now, he could feel where that magic came from. Could follow it back to its source.

Its. . . blocked source.

It was as if standing on the edge of a spring, but where there should have been a constant rush of water welling to the surface, there was instead a packed-in barrier of debris. That was why the riverbed was so dry. Why his magic flowed in but a trickle.

Can I clear this blockage? Set free the magic?

There wasn't time to wonder. The answer had to be yes.

Could only be yes. And even as he thought it, those spectral hands appeared again. This time they reached not for his mind, but for the blockage. They stretched and shook, fingers bent with effort. But they couldn't get to it. Something was holding them back.

I am.

The realization hit Subei all at once.

I'm holding them back.

He thought about that for all of a heartbeat, then made his decision.

No longer.

The hands tore into the blockage. It was gone in an instant, and Subei found himself staring down into the source of the spring. Down a submerged, wavering chasm and into abyssal depths so dark no light could pierce them. It was from those depths the flood poured forth. It rushed up over his feet, his knees, his waist—then swept him up entirely.

What had once been a riverbed with a trickling channel became a raging torrent, a surging flood in which he was swept along, bashed against the rocks, and drowned. Darkness overtook him then, and in it, he found only those spectral hands. Their clawing grasp wrapped around his mind and clenching tighter, tighter until. . .

A calm settled over Subei. He inhaled one pained breath, and his eyes slipped shut.

He exhaled, and they snapped back open. And then he could only watch as his arms worked beneath him and pushed up with strength he didn't realize he possessed. A growl tore its way from his mouth, body shaking violently as he shrugged the crates off and stood. Any anger he'd felt previously was dwarfed now, a drop of rain breaking through the clouds to find the ocean below and learn it was but the smallest piece of a vast immensity. Such was the rage that overtook him. It grew and swelled and resolved itself into something greater. Something. . . else.

Subei felt himself smile, all teeth and blood and dirt, and found he wasn't in control of his own body. Like his arm, when it'd gone numb in the tournament and acted on its own. Except, now it was the whole of his body. Only his thoughts were his own.

His eyes turned to Yue Jong and his sister. She moved to form another wall, but Subei flicked an orb with the merest twitch of his wrist. It exploded against the wall, tossing her backward to collapse in a heap on the floor. The explosion was so strong it spat a jet of flame to wash against the building's rafters. The room lit up orange as the flames took to the old wood. Their angry, burning light brought to life the fear hollowing Yue Jong's gaze.

"Well then," Subei said, the words not his own but pouring out all the same. "That was a thoroughly invigorating warm-up." He shook out his shoulders, then rolled his head to the ceiling and back down, neck joints cracking one by one.

Chapter Twenty

SUBEI

"Ru, you need to leave. Now." Yue Jong was suddenly unsure, backing away. His eyes were wide, brow furrowed as if considering the problem of the beast before him and liking the answer none too much. "Go to the capital."

Ru—for that seemed to be her name—rose to her feet, blood running from her scalp and into her eyes. Above her, the flames were growing.

"Go, now," Yue Jong commanded.

"I can—"

"Shut up and run, damn it!" he snapped, and Subei had to admit, the false heir had a point. Ru was woozy from the blow to her head, feet unsteady. "Find refuge with the others. Or if they're just as evil, run again. As far as you must. Go!"

His yell seemed to shake her back to reality. She eased backward, guard still up.

"You come with me, Jong," she said. "I'm not abandoning you."

"How far do you think you'll get? Purely out of curiosity." Whatever had control of Subei's body spoke for him. It didn't even pay his opponents the respect of looking at them, staring instead in fascination as he clenched and unclenched his wounded hand. "Do you have good horses, Yue Jong?" He touched the wound to his tongue and tasted the blood, now thick with dirt and ash. He nodded, then raised his eyes to the false heirs. "It won't matter."

What was that supposed to mean? Subei could only wonder as his mouth moved without him, as words that weren't his uttered out. He was but a rider, bound and gagged atop a runaway horse.

"What are you?" Yue Jong said, backing away.

"What am I?" The thing in control of Subei's body laughed. At the same time, Kashi and Ghula emerged from the hall. Subei paid them no mind. "What am I? Pieces, I suppose. Splinters. But you're going to help me with that." A smile pulled across Subei's bloodied face.

"Brother?" Kashi asked. "Are you okay?"

"What is this?" Ghula's voice joined the mix. She and Kashi were off to the side somewhere, but Subei couldn't see them. Couldn't force his head to turn.

"Run, Ru! Run!" Yue Jong shouted, and finally she did, just as her brother lashed forward with a barrage of North Wind Scours. Subei advanced calmly, sweeping each attack away with looping movements of his finger, bobbing back and forth as if it were dancing to some unheard song.

Yue Jong formed a wall of crates next and launched it at him. Subei whistled to himself, a cheery tune, as he extended a closed fist. He snapped it open, and the wall parted, a hole opening so the crates whisking past harmlessly.

The false heir was backed into a corner now. Nowhere to run. He punched forward, a new knife in hand. Subei caught him by the wrist, thumb pushing into the false heir's palm. He pressed forward and Yue Jong's wrist snapped back with a crunch, knife falling away. A punch then, that landed on Subei's lips to stop his whistling. Another and another, each blow connecting with a fleshy thud—but entirely ignored by Subei, who reached out his free hand and wrapped it around his opponent's face.

Yue Jong screamed, voice muffled beneath Subei's palm, and punched all the harder.

"Subei!" Bataar shouted from the side as he arrived, hands on his knees and panting. Barely able to stand, even. Seemed those orbs from earlier had taken their toll. "The hell is this?"

"But a moment, brother."

Yue Jong was mumbling now, something muffled and panicked. One of his eyes slid upward, staring at Subei from between the hand clasped over his face. Their gazes locked, and Subei's heart pounded all the faster, adrenaline pumping through him.

It takes a lifetime to make a man. A mother to birth him, a family to raise him. It takes years and years of watching and learning, growing and living, to make a man.

It took Subei a moment to unmake him.

An orb formed in his hand, one that should have been deadly for him and Yue Jong both. But whatever had control of Subei's body was far more learned in the magic than he. The orb exploded, but directionally. Forward, outward from his palm. It took Yue Jong's head with it.

The headless body collapsed and immediately began to crack and hiss as rivulets of light spread across it. An ethereal, blue glow filled the room, pooling in the air before splitting in three and flowing toward Subei, Bataar, and Kashi. A fourth trail seemed to reach out a moment, as if grasping in the direction Ru had fled. But she was too far gone, and it curled back to join the others.

Subei sighed as the magic touched him, soaking in through his skin. A damned good feeling, that. Any weakness he'd felt was gone, swept away quicker than smoke on the wind. His fists clenched, and the magic inside responded, scars flaring brightly.

Kashi was being charged as well, magic flowing into him. And Bataar, too. Subei's eyes turned to watch as both his brothers were enveloped in the light, their scars burning bright to receive more.

"Water! Send for water!" Several guards burst into the room, armor clanking as they rushed to the far wall, now fully engulfed in flame. Seemed they'd entirely missed Subei and the rest of the party. Somehow didn't see them or the remains of the heir.

"Subei!" Kashi hissed as the magic finished flowing into him. "Let's go!"

Ghula pulled them both behind a stack of crates.

"We got one of the false heirs, that's victory enough. Better now to withdraw and pursue the other than get bogged down here."

Sound logic, all of it, and Subei agreed. But he wasn't steering his own body as it pushed off Ghula's grasp and strode toward the guards.

"Subei!" Bataar this time, hissing in his ear as he dragged him back under cover. "We're far outnumbered. I won't risk our people or our mission just for—Subei!" He growled it this time, words heavy with the anger of being so blatantly disobeyed as Subei pulled free of his grasp. "Listen to me, damn you! I am your eldest br—" Bataar stopped mid-sentence, mouth still open, rage writ across his face. His brow furrowed. "Do. . . do you feel that?" he whispered suddenly, eyes creeping down to look at his hands. "The magic inside, it's. . . there's so much more. Waiting, no, *asking* to be used. It's. . . it's. . . "

"Terrifying," Kashi said, eyes wide as a shudder ran through him.

"Invigorating." Bataar's hands curled into fists.

Two flames flashed to life in Subei's mind, and he was suddenly aware of his brothers. But not aware of them being in the room with him. And not aware of them as in he could feel the pull toward them. This was something more. He could feel his brothers as perfectly as he could feel his own body.

"Embrace it, brothers," Subei spoke words he hadn't thought. "As I have."

"No." Kashi was aghast, revulsion across his face as he eyed Yue Jong's headless corpse. "Subei, this isn't right. This isn't you."

"Embrace this," Subei's mouth said. He looked to Kashi, to Bataar. "Embrace what you are."

"No." Kashi stumbled backward, and then his eyes were shut. He groaned, folded inward. "I won't." And as he said it, one of the flames in Subei's mind extinguished. The other flared all the more brightly.

Bataar stepped into view, and Subei could see he was changed. His scars blazed a brilliant blue, but more than that, his eyes burned with light so fierce and complete, there was nothing but that piercing, stabbing light coming from them.

"What the hell?" Ghula was frozen behind the crates, eyes whipping between Subei and Bataar. Subei paid her no mind, led Bataar toward the guards instead.

"Stop!" Kashi shouted it now, desperation plain in his voice. Though if he was shouting it at them or himself, it was impossible to say.

The guards turned, then drew their weapons. Their expressions changed from shock, to disgust, then finally anger as they saw the remains of Subei's work.

"They're Ghangerai!" one of them shouted, raising his sword but taking a half-step back nonetheless. Subei saw the fear in the man's eyes, saw it and found he liked it. A good thing, to be feared.

The fight didn't last long. Hardly qualified as a fight, really. Several flashes of bright blue light, then silence.

Bataar stepped on the neck of the last guard, crushing it with a sharp crack. The man fell limp, joining the others on the floor. Above them, the flames had spread even further, filling the room.

Subei reached out toward the fire. He could feel it as he never had before. As if it were a thing alive, a hungry, frenzied thing. He channeled his magic into the fire. Wasn't sure how, he just did. The flames roared and swelled, burning all the hotter. In a heartbeat, the whole of the building's roof was engulfed.

"Grow, my friend. Spread. Consume." Once again, Subei spoke with words that were not his own. Then despite his efforts, the muscles in his face tensed, contracted, and finally stretched themselves into a jagged smile. "Show this town, show this world, the bloodrage cannot be denied."

And then that surging river of magic inside him ran dry. The room spun. The energy he'd expended hit him like a wall, and the ground rushed up with a resounding thud.

Chapter Twenty-One

SUBEI

The fire had spread. That was what fires did, after all. That and burn. If the orange horizon and ever-growing black clouds were any indications, the fires Subei had made were doing both exceptionally. Weren't so much fires anymore as a full-on inferno.

When Subei had woken in their forest camp, the first thing he'd heard was the screaming. A hundred hundred distant voices as they called for water, or cried out in pain, or yelled for loved ones trapped in the too-quickly spreading blaze.

The next thing he'd heard had been a softer voice. Gentle as a caress and coming from. . . inside him. From his core? No, deeper still. It crept up out of that submerged chasm, a whisper from deep in the abyssal depths those spectral hands had uncovered. It promised power, conquest, glory. All of it his if only he had the courage to wield the magic he'd been given.

He'd almost answered it then, until Ghula had snapped him from the trance.

"On your horse," she'd shouted, hurriedly packing her saddlebags. "Might be the fire will buy us some time." Apparently, it hadn't been the most discreet retreat from the town, what with them covered in blood and carrying Subei and Bataar's unconscious forms through the streets. Hadn't helped the situation any that Ru had run to the town guards after she'd escaped.

As darkness fell on the day, they rode as far and fast as they could into the Longlarch. The idea didn't sit well with Subei. Didn't much sit well with anyone, based on the looks they'd had on their faces. But the forest would hide their tracks, Ren said. Might even throw off potential pursuers completely.

The Longlarch ran deep, branches interweaving above to form a canopy so thick as to almost block out the sky. No matter how thick it was, though, it couldn't hide the red hell behind them.

"What happened back there?" Kashi asked, pulling his horse near as they hit a stand of trees so dense everyone had to slow to a trot.

Subei made to answer, then frowned instead. One moment he'd been injured and angry, then deep inside he had found a way to access more magic. But as soon as he'd let it flow, he'd changed. Had been taken over by. . . something else.

And so too had Bataar.

"A fit of madness, always churning deep inside," Subei said, voice grim as he recalled what Mahtma had taught them of Baji Khan's final days.

"That would rise and turn his mind to terrible acts," Kashi finished, face ashen.

"That's a frighteningly accurate description." Subei winced at the thought of the words to come. "And this madness, it. . . it named itself."

"The bloodrage," Kashi said simply.

"I found it deep within me," Subei said, frowning all the more. "I thought it was just more magic. A reservoir I needed in that moment to survive. So I. . . released it."

"I did too." Bataar drew up alongside as best he could on the game trail through the denser forest. "Mahtma was right."

"How many families are dead because of us, brother?" Subei could barely stand to ask. "How many will still die?" And not soldiers. Not deaths in defense of one's khan or people. "We unleashed death for death's sake," Subei said. "There's no honor in that."

"Dishonor, more like," Bataar said, quietly.

Subei looked ahead to where Mahtma had drawn up beside

Ghula during the slow down. The two were talking quietly but forcefully.

"Bataar. . . " Subei said, taking in his brother's slumped and bruised form. "We can't let that happen again."

He nodded. "It must be controlled."

"Not controlled, banished." Kashi was staring at the scars along his hand. A hand that clenched into a fist with his next words. "Locked away to never see the light of day again."

"He's right." Subei squeezed the reins tighter as memories of the bloodrage's words filled his mind. "That wasn't magic. That was madness."

"If we could *control* it, though," Bataar began, and his voice had an intensity to it. A desire. Then he was interrupted by pounding hooves ahead. The denser thicket had ended, and Ghula and Mahtma were at full gallop again.

"What do you mean control it?" Subei shouted, but Bataar was already in motion, riding hard. Subei looked to Kashi. "What does he mean?"

Kashi made to shout back, but his words were trampled by the galloping of hooves and the breaking of branches. There wasn't time to delay. Wasn't time to discuss further either, not right now. Not with soldiers likely in pursuit and many miles to cover. Subei tucked into the rhythm of the gallop and found his mind wandering back to Mahtma's lessons. He needed to under-stand—no, to *master*—her preachings about self-control and all that other ethereal Teshkai nonsense. Needed to, if only it would hold back whatever he'd set free.

As the forest whipped past, Subei looked down at his hastily bandaged hand and the bloodstains that still ran along it. He hadn't failed entirely, though, had he? One false heir was dead, and they'd taken his magic. That was something. But for the first time, Subei found he wasn't so sure more magic was a good thing.

He looked from his hand up to his arm. To his scars. In the wake of the fighting, they were pink and inflamed, and ached deeply. Sore from too much use, he figured. Or eager to be used again. Whichever it was, it wouldn't let the fighting leave his thoughts. Wouldn't let the *bloodrage* leave his thoughts.

He could feel it inside him now, lying deep within, at the very center of those abyssal depths. And there, it pulled heavy on him, weighed him down like a stone tied to a swimmer's foot. But it was more than that. Not just a feeling, but a *sentience*. As if a whole other being lay dormant inside him. Had awoken to terrible effect, and now, returned to deep and tumultuous slumber.

Bataar rode just ahead, broad back straight in the saddle. He was a brave warrior, an honorable man, and above all, a protector of his people. Always had been. But then why hadn't he turned to help Kashi and Ghula when they'd been in the path of that avalanche of shelves and debris? Subei couldn't shake the thought, as much as he tried.

They rode on, and the forest was filled with the scent of pine and horse sweat. Did little to mask the stink of death clinging to Subei, though. It was a smell that sent shivers down his spine, left him spiraling back into memory. Back to that nightmare he could never forget. Back to that night where feuding had turned cousins into enemies and family into ash. Even as he shook himself back to the present, he could still smell that night. Or, perhaps, it was just the ash from Chobei, raining down all around them.

Chapter Twenty-Two

BATAAR

"It is a fine morning, my students," Mahtma gave the traditional greeting and bowed.

A pause then, from all three brothers.

"It is a. . . " Kashi started.

"Fine morning indeed, teacher," Bataar finished with him, then waved Subei to join. Ancestors above, but he looked stricken. Probably it was all the ash and road dirt. Though, Bataar didn't see why that would make him so pale.

They'd ridden through the night before stopping sometime near dawn. Bataar had been eager for sleep, but Mahtma had found them first. Now, they were all seated in a small clearing. Ghula, as well. A full meeting, then. Overdue.

First Rider Ren and First Kheshig Vachir were seeing to camp along with the rest of the guards some paces away. Far enough as to be out of earshot.

"I was wrong to doubt you, my teacher," Bataar said all at once to Mahtma. "You spoke the truth." He looked down at his scars, at the blood crusted to his armor. But more, he looked inward, and there he found that flowing spring. He'd thrown himself down it in Chobei and been pulled deeper, deeper into the abyssal depths.

Bataar shook the memory away, refocused on the present to find Mahtma frowning at him. Not surprising, seeing as she was usually frowning, but now it was something softer. Still a frown, but one of empathy, perhaps.

"It was a grim business," Ghula said, her face twisted as if tasting something sour.

"The sort of business," Mahtma added with a wince, "we should ensure never happens again."

Still, there's no denying the progress. Bataar almost felt guilty to think it, but this power would change everything for his people. *Everything.* He squeezed his hand into a fist, and his muscles tingled with the new magic inside him.

"Despite everything," Mahtma continued. "I fear there is worse news still."

"Word from Father?" Bataar asked at once, remembering her messenger pigeon. "Has something happened?"

"This does not reach us from the khanate but the annals of history." Mahtma set a loosely wound scroll in the grass. "There was little left in the Chobei temple's hall of records, but there was this."

It was a beaten, burned thing. As if it'd been damaged in the fire that'd destroyed the rest of the complex.

She tapped the scroll.

"This is a missive from the rebel emperor, sent shortly after Ghangerai rule in these lands collapsed. It congratulates the citizens of Chobei for their bravery in being the first imperial town to cast out the oppressors. As a reward for this bravery, the emperor bestowed upon them a trophy. An obelisk. One of two erected in Ba Seng to *'forever remind the Zhong people of their loyalty to the Great Khan.'*"

Bataar sucked his teeth at that.

"They turned Baji's sacred obelisks into a joke. A war trophy to pass back and forth." *Already that foolishness returns to bite them, even if they don't yet know it.*

"Further," Mahtma said, snapping the scroll open. "This document contains a detailed description of the obelisk, along with the inscription that was sent with it. Originally from the Great Khan himself."

A message accompanying the obelisk? Sent from the Great Khan himself? Bataar sat up straighter.

Mahtma cleared her throat and lifted the scroll.

"*'May they never be joined.'*"

"That's. . . that's it? A message from Great Baji Khan accompanied this obelisk, and that's it?" Bataar furrowed his brow, turning to his brothers.

"No room to misinterpret it, I guess?" Kashi said.

"No room to *interpret* it," Subei said, exasperated. "That's. . . nothing, Mahtma. Doesn't mean anything. Isn't there more text there, around it? I can't read, but I can see the markings."

"Dates of delivery of the obelisk, names and signatures of the officials who received it, and other unimportant specifics," Mahtma explained, waving away the thought with a gesture. "No, Sons of Kemu, you're missing the point here. Baji Khan intentionally separated the obelisks, yes?" she asked. "And the obelisks, we can assume, contained his magic."

"The obelisks were separated so Baji's magic would be as well?" Kashi asked and Bataar frowned.

"What sort of sense does that make? Why would the Great Khan leave us such a weapon if he didn't intend us to wield it?"

". . . gather it all."

"What?" Bataar asked, turning to his mumbling brother.

"He didn't want us to gather it all," Subei said again. "Because of what it might do."

"What it might awaken," Kashi added.

"Even from the world next, Baji Khan watches out for us," Ghula said and looked to the heavens.

"This was Baji's magic, he would have known it better than anyone," Subei said, eyes wide now as he spoke more quickly. "He poured it into the obelisks, then separated them, for a reason."

"We didn't feel the. . . bloodrage," Kashi said, hesitating at the name, "until we gathered more of the magic. First the bandit's, then Yue Jong's."

"There is no doubt in my mind this was the rot Baji Khan described," Mahtma said.

"And we released it." Dread haunted Subei's words.

"But it's gone, right?" Kashi's eyes were frantic now. Snapping from Subei to Bataar and back. "It disappeared when you passed out?"

Bataar felt inward, focusing on his core. At its center, he could see the spring, and if he tried, could peer deeper, down to its source.

"It's dormant." Bataar pulled his thoughts back, unwilling to probe further into those abyssal depths lest they begin their whispering again. "As if the bloodrage is slumbering in the darkness."

"And there we must leave it," Mahtma said. "Baji Khan fought this bloodrage every waking moment at the end of his days. I will not have that be your fate."

"At the same time, we can't allow the false heirs to wield this weapon," Ghula said. "We're walking a knife's edge." She shook her head, then turned to Mahtma. "Can we teach them to use the magic they already have, without waking the rage?"

"You must!" Bataar said without thinking. What other choice was there?

"Look to the horizon, brother," Subei said as he raised one unsteady hand. Even so deep in the Longlarch, there was red reflecting in his eyes. "We did that."

"Yes, we did," the words came out with more bite than Bataar had intended. He took a long breath, steadied his voice. "I regret it. I am *shamed* by it. But I will not be crippled by it." He looked to Ghula and Mahtma next. "The khagan didn't order us to complete this task as long as it was easy. He ordered us to complete this task."

"I. . . can't disagree with you there." Ghula's sour expression grew more sour still, but her words were those of a true Ghangerai. "Shit choices are a warrior's burden, but our duty to the khanate comes before all else."

Subei punched the ground, dramatic as always.

"You saw what happened back there," he shouted. "What's still happening!"

Ghula winced as she shook the statement away. In the motion, her eyes met Bataar's.

"We are Ghangerai," he reminded her.

And then her face was hard, her mouth set.

"There is a balance here, and we must find it. A way to reclaim Baji's magic without turning you all into uncontrollable raging beasts." She turned to Mahtma. "I can teach them to hone the magic for combat, that much we know. Can you teach them to control it?"

"I cannot promise to do what only the Great Khan has. But I will try," Mahtma looked to Bataar, then his brothers. "But in the meantime, we should halt all further indulgence in this magic. We are not prepared for it."

"You don't stoke a fire before you've the means to put it out," Subei said, nodding.

"We can't afford to stop learning. We barely bested Yue Jong —and only did thanks to the. . . " Bataar hesitated, but where was the sense in cowering from a word? From a name? No, if they were going to wield this, they needed to face it head on. "Thanks to the bloodrage." He made sure his voice was steady, confident as he said it. "And still, Kashi and Ghula were nearly killed." And then his voice shook. Just the slightest of trembles, not because they'd a brush with the world next, but because in that moment, he hadn't turned back to help them. Why hadn't he?

Because I trusted my brother. Yes. . . that was it.

Subei had handled it, just as Bataar knew he would. It had been delegation, nothing more. He forced his thoughts to the present situation. "There are six more false heirs left. Our work is far from done. We can't stop learning how to wield this magic."

"Five of the heirs feel like they're in the same place," Kashi said quietly. "That's no small task."

"If we indulge this magic further, what then, brother?" Subei rounded on Bataar. "What happens when we wake the bloodrage a second time? I didn't have control of my body. You didn't either. We weren't controlling the magic." Subei swallowed hard. "It was controlling us."

"An unbroken horse will carry away its rider—the first time. But the second time? The third?" Bataar reached out and clasped Subei's shoulder. "We are Ghangerai, brother. Our people tamed the horse, the *steppe*. At one time, we brought to heel the

159

breadth of the known world. We don't shy away because a thing is hard, we rise to meet it. We rise to best it." He gave him a reassuring squeeze then. "We'll train, we'll learn, and when the rage rises next, we will be the ones in control."

Subei's eyes flicked back to the burning horizon.

"We're supposed to be warriors. Yesterday we were butchers."

"You can't let this guilt consume you, Subei. Fuel you? Yes. Drive you to be better? Yes." Why didn't he understand this? "Brother, we killed a false heir yesterday and reclaimed a part of our people's inheritance."

"And the others we killed? We left barely enough of those guards to fill a saddlebag. We razed an entire town!"

"We did." There was no getting around it. "And I hope we never have to again. But Subei, you must understand. This magic has been set free into the world. There's no going back now. It will be used by our people, or against them."

Chapter Twenty-Three

SUBEI

Another day of riding then. A day for heads to cool, for courses of action to be considered. Another day for the whispers to creep into his mind again too. Subei pushed them aside, drowned them out with the cadence of hooves. That brought him some peace. What he couldn't ignore, though, was the pull toward the escaped heir. Ru.

She was behind them still, somewhere back in the red hell of the northern horizon. In Chobei, probably. Whatever was left of it. All this time they'd spent running toward her, and now they were running away from her. But even with Baji's magic on their side, they could hardly fight through a town's worth of soldiers to get to her. And that was assuming they didn't have half or more of that number already tracking them down.

South it was then, for the time being at least. Get through the Longlarch and break into open ground. From there, they'd be able to put their horses to real use. Would be free to pursue the other heirs. Which. . . Subei still wanted to do. He was sure of that, wasn't he?

The additional five heirs were closely gathered on the horizon and part of that could have been due to distance. Or, it could have been that they were all already together. As best as anyone knew, the Great Khan had seen two obelisks sent to Ba Seng. But by the hands of the rebellious Zhong, one of those had been moved to Chobei. That left the only unaccounted for obelisk in

Bharmankara—and thus far, no one had felt any pulls in that direction. Strange, but it wasn't their mission to investigate what had happened there. Their mission lay south and east. Further into Zhong territory, and directly toward the capital of Ba Seng.

"Bleeding midges!" Subei gasped as another of the little bloodsuckers bit into his cheek. He slapped it, and his hand came away bloody. His own blood, he knew, which the blasted little insect had been in the process of drinking.

A whine in his ear then, as another seemed intent to fly right inside.

"Begone!" he snapped, waving his hand more than necessary. But for every one he chased away, the Longlarch sent another two, swooping and biting at any exposed part of him—until a sudden rush of wind kicked up and swept them away.

"There is no shame in being bested by such mighty foes," Bataar said, smirking at him. It was only then Subei noticed his brother's scars were alight. "But we wield a great and terrible magic now, so perhaps we need no longer be bothered by midges." Another wind strike then, and Subei was once again free of the biting pests. "Alright, that's all you're getting from me. If I solve all your problems for you, you'll never toughen up," Bataar said with a wink. Was the good humor forced? Or had he really gone back to using his magic so easily?

"Uh, right." Subei looked down to his scars. A little release of North Wind Scours here and there would keep the insects off him. Simple enough. Again there was a whining buzz in his ear, so he squeezed his core, called on his magic, and—no.

He released the magic to sink back into that place beneath his stomach. That place where, he now knew, it was not alone. Subei's scars faded back to their usual angry pink, and he was grateful for it.

"Are you alright, brother?" Bataar asked.

"Don't need to waste magic on what a simple slap can solve," he replied, then spurred his horse ahead.

And so passed another day in the forest as First Rider Ren and the scouts did their best to keep everyone heading roughly south. No small feat in the labyrinthine tangle they called the Longlarch.

The group came to a stop just before dusk, to make camp before the canopy above swallowed the last light of day. The guards set about hacking enough of a clearing for them to set up a couple tents while First Rider Ren gave her scouts their orders for the night.

"Same as always, boys," she was saying, waving a third of them toward the brush while the rest collapsed and immediately began dozing. "Three watches, and keep your eyes open. Ears too, out here. And if I catch you sleeping on watch. . . well, I won't, because if you let your guard down in here, I'll be the least of your worries."

"First Rider?" Subei said as he swung down on his horse then gave a bow of his head.

"Subei, Son of Kemu." She smiled, but there was a hesitation in it. "How are you feeling?"

"Bloody."

That brought more hesitation from her, mouth not quite forming words, but definitely moving, as if chewing on what to say in response.

"Yes, well that—"

"Another one, damn!" Subei smacked the back of his neck, then showed her his palm, the squished insect all mixed in with his freshly stolen blood.

"Ah, I see." A flash of a smile then. "Bloody, or bloodless, eh?"

"If I were bloodless, maybe I'd finally have some peace from these damn midges." Subei pulled his hood tight around his head. "Don't they bother you?"

"Oh, they want nothing to do with my blood thanks to the ghuuzeren berries." She frowned. "I didn't tell you? Hold on." She produced a handful of misshapen berries from her pocket that, if Subei hadn't known better, looked more like some sort of tuber. "Take these. Eat a couple every hour, and even your horse will be safe from the midges."

They even felt like tubers as he took them in hand, their little hairs pricking his palm. But relief from the constant biting was a tempting prospect. Subei crunched down on one of the berries and almost immediately vomited so sudden was his gag reflex.

"Ancestors above," he said between coughs, hands on his knees. "That tastes like. . . I don't even have words for it."

Ren chuckled.

"You get used to it."

"I'd rather just leave the midges—and this forest—behind," Subei said, wiping his chin and standing back up. "Which, speaking of, let me ask you about that."

"I am your humble servant, Son of Kemu."

"Before Chobei, you mentioned something about this forest." He paused, eyeing the shadows reaching toward them. Wasn't even night yet, but it might as well have been for as much as he could see through the thicket. "Something about there being 'older and fouler' things in here?"

"Ah, that. Right." She popped a ghuuzeren berry in her mouth and somehow, even the sound of her crunching down on it almost made him gag again. "Let's just say Chobei's walls weren't originally put up to keep out Ghangerai—or other Zhong, for that matter. But these days, the Longlarch has calmed down quite a bit. Doesn't bother anyone anymore, mostly."

"Mostly?"

"Well, long as you stay out of the bits the trees consider sacred." She tapped her temple and smiled. "But that's why I'm here, to keep us on the right path, best as I know how."

"And. . . have we? Kept on the right path?" Subei couldn't help stealing a glance toward the twisting entanglement of foliage around them.

"That's why I'm here." Ren smiled again, then clapped him on the back. "Ooh, I best be off. Ghula's got that look."

What look, Subei wanted to ask, but even as he turned, his question was answered.

"What, just 'cause we've been on the run all day, you thought we weren't going to train?" Ghula laughed as she clapped her hands hurriedly. "Up and at 'em, Sons of Kemu. We've a whole heir's worth of new magic to test and not a lot of time to do it."

"Damn right we do!" Bataar interlaced his fingers, then turned his palms outward in a stretch.

"Subei!" Ghula rounded on him. "You ready to work, or have I been too soft on you of late?" She reached for the quarterstaff strapped to her saddle.

"Hold, Torol." He raised a palm, examined his scars, then gave his core the slightest squeeze. A trickle of light, a tinge of excitement within him. And no bloodrage. No rushing heat spreading through him.

Subei wiggled his fingers, shook a foot back and forth.

Still in control.

"If we train, we have to do so carefully," he said to Ghula, then repeated it to his brothers. "We must not awaken the rage."

"I don't think it works like that," Bataar said, already bouncing on his feet. He threw a few warm up punches next, then followed with a barrage of North Wind Scours. The trees in front of him rained leaves. "Last time, it was a conscious choice, not an accident."

"All the same, we will be careful." Subei gestured forward with a wind strike weak enough it could've been mistaken for a sneeze.

"Best if we keep our scars wrapped up tight, too," Kashi said. Already the sunset was fighting a losing battle against the shadows encroaching from the dense foliage all around. "And no fire tonight, yeah?"

"Right," Ghula answered. "That would somewhat defeat the point of all the running we've done."

"Unless we wanted to draw them to us."

"Huh?" Subei turned to find Bataar still warming up.

"Better to ambush than be ambushed, yeah? Take the fight on ground of our choosing," he said simply.

"Are you so ready for more blood?" Subei snapped. "And you're assuming we're even being pursued through *this.*" He waved his hand at the tangle.

"All I'm assuming is—*ow!*" Bataar was cut off with a crack as Ghula caught him in the elbow with her staff.

Subei snorted.

"Serves you right for making such—"

Crack.

"The hell was that for?" Subei complained, darting away from Ghula with one hand pressed to his ringing head.

"The sun is in the west, boy. We train."

"Ghula. . . " Subei said, risking another ringing crack to the skull as he stepped in close and lowered his voice. "We shouldn't push too hard." He raised his bandaged hand, the flesh beneath still raw and tender from where he'd taken a finger-sized splinter through it. "Anger and pain are what triggered the rage last time."

A nod of understanding then, by way of a response before she clapped her hands again.

"No sparring tonight, boys. Yue Jong did something with his magic we've never seen before."

"Those walls were a pain," Bataar admitted.

"*Fascinating,* more like," Kashi corrected him.

"So what say we figure out how to make them, eh?"

No explosions that evening, then. No gale force winds, either. Instead, they talked and experimented, attempting to recreate the techniques Yue Jong had demonstrated.

"It's similar, I'm sure of it," Kashi said, holding a hand out. "As if the two are related." He'd a bunch of twigs in hand again, like he'd had the first night they'd camped in the forest. Before the events of Chobei. "You have to focus on them, mark them almost, in your mind. Then all at once, you. . . " He gently spread the fingers of his opposite hand then snapped them into a fist. His scars flared and the twigs all jumped up, slamming into one another. But instead of bouncing off, this time they steadied, then lined up. A little fence of sticks all locked together. "You do that," Kashi finished. He lowered his hand, and the tiny fence held its form. Stayed together even after he set it down, too.

"All the World A Shield," he said, admiring his work.

"What's that?" Subei asked, brow furrowed.

"What I'm naming this technique when I master it," Kashi said with a cocky grin.

"A shield against an invasion of ants, maybe," Bataar said with a huff as he bent down to peer at the miniscule creation.

"It's okay, big brother. You can admit I'm better at this technique than you. Your ego needs to be taken down a peg anyway."

Ghula clapped him on the back. "Truly, you are wise beyond your years, Kashi."

"You know what?" Bataar crossed his arms. "You're right."

Kashi positively beamed at that.

"*This time.* Don't get used to the feeling. Anyway, we'll work on learning. . . this," Bataar frowned at the twigs, but even in the dark, Subei could see he was curious, "and you, little brother, can work on Baji's Burning Fury, huh? It's past time you managed it."

"In a bit." Already Kashi had more scraps of foliage in hand and was gesturing at them with scars alight.

"Come on, Bataar," Subei said and flung a handful of sticks at him. "We've ants to fortify against."

Chapter Twenty-Four

SUBEI

Mahtma would wake them for training soon, but already Subei was out of his sleeping furs and stretching. Bataar and Kashi still slumbered in the tent, exhausted from trying to unravel how Yue Jong had formed those walls of his. Hadn't made much progress, though, aside from Kashi, who seemed a natural. Sleep called Subei back to its restful embrace. Another half hour would be a welcome thing, but there would be time for sleep later.

The Longlarch was quiet around him in the predawn hours. That made it all the more difficult to stop from snapping his attention to every sound and bit of movement. Was that a branch stirring in the wind, or an ambush? But Ren's scouts were about the area, and so too Vachir's guards. There was a job Subei didn't envy, sat out alone in that darkness, ordered to watch and listen. No doubt one's mind would run rampant with disquieting thoughts.

No doubt, out there, it'd be even more impossible to ignore the whispers from the abyss. In every quiet moment, they called to him. Enticed him to the very edge of that spring in his mind and urged him another step forward, just *one more*. . .

No.

He shook the image from his mind and focused on the light slipping from Mahtma's tent. The whispers had plagued him all night, had forced him from his sleeping furs earlier than usual. But clearly, not earlier than Mahtma. Did the Master of Knowledge ever sleep? All the same, it was good she was awake. All the sooner they could start training. After Chobei, he needed it more than ever.

"Hold the dog, Torol," Subei said, trying to keep his voice quiet so as not to wake anyone, but also loud enough for Mahtma to hear. Silence a moment, while he waited for a response. A shuffling of papers from within, then Mahtma's voice trickled out.

"You may enter, Son of Kemu."

It was the first time he'd been in her tent, and it was a modest affair. Slightly larger than the one he shared with his brothers, with just enough room for a writing table, bedroll, and hanging birdcage. Six messenger pigeons were nestled in the cage, sleeping on a perch. They were pure white, as were all birds used by House Kemu. Strangely, though, there was a seventh bird, this one with a black and white speckled pattern.

"I did not know you were such an admirer of birds," Mahtma said. "Your dedication is impressive, rising so early just to stare at my flock."

"Ah, uh, apologies, Torol," Subei said, shaking himself back to the moment at hand.

"You're welcome to admire them as much as you want." There was a hint of a smirk in it. "They might enjoy the attention. Certainly better than bouncing against my saddle all day." She set down her quill and folded her hands over the parchment before her at the table. "Or is there another reason for your visit?"

"There was. Er, is." Subei winced. Of all times to stumble over his words. He took a steadying breath, focusing his thoughts. "I wished to hear your thoughts, Torol."

"My bedroll is scratchy, and these old bones no longer take kindly to traveling so roughly." She popped a ghuuzeren berry into her mouth and crunched down on it.

"No, sorry. I meant, about the bloodrage." Subei said the name with a whisper, as if merely uttering it was enough to summon the madness. "I wished to hear your thoughts on it. Your true thoughts. My brothers—well, mainly Bataar—are having trouble with this. He won't admit it, but I know him.

He's honorable and trustworthy, and he'll protect his loved ones and his people above all else. But he's. . . traditional, like our father. What we've learned about Baji, about his magic, well, Bataar's fighting a battle inside. I don't wish to make it any harder for him, so I have been. . . careful with my words around him. I think, perhaps, so have you?"

She considered him a moment, one gray eyebrow raised.

"We do no one any favors by sheltering them from the truth."

"I know, it's just—"

"But neither do we bring down a wall with our fists alone." She shrugged. "Given, that maxim works better for everyone who isn't imbued with Baji's magic."

"So. . . you agree with me?"

"To bring down a wall, one needs strike with the proper tools. To do so without them is but a waste of energy."

Subei nodded along, pretty sure they were thinking along the same lines. Never could quite tell with the Teshkai and their love of complicated analogies.

"I understand what you say about your older brother. There is a wall between his heart and his brain. It protects the ideals he's grown up believing and keeps out the cold reason of logic. I cannot fault him for it."

She sighed, then. Not a resigned sound, but something else. Closer to the breath one might take before settling in for a hard task. "It's easier to trust the things we believe. When swept away in the ocean of uncertainty, they are the anchors to which we cling."

She fixed him with a sharp gaze. "But cling too tightly, and those anchors become weights, dragging us under." She rose then, standing to her full, too-tall height. She shook out her arms, rolled her neck around, the joints popping one by one. "If we are to bring down the wall that separates what is true and what Bataar wants to be true, we must equip ourselves with the proper tools."

Subei nodded at that.

"A warrior is nothing without his sword."

"Indeed." She tidied her writing table. "I am glad you care for your brother so, Subei. Keep that close in your heart. It will serve us well in the trials to come. No one is truly ready when power is thrust upon them, but you, Bataar, and Kashi need not face this new frontier alone. You have Ghula. You have me. Most of all, you have each other."

"Ancestors willing, Torol, it will be enough," Subei said with a bow of his head.

"Now then." Mahtma clapped her hands sharply, the sound cutting through the stillness of the predawn hour. "Unless you'd like to study my birds some more, we will begin today's training. We must equip ourselves with the proper tools, after all."

* * *

Mahtma led them some distance from camp, winding her way through the trees. The guards who'd drawn the last watch nodded as she passed. Subei, Bataar, and Kashi followed, lifting each step high to avoid the entangling branches and vines. Damned things were enough to trip you up by the light of day, and even worse when they could hide in the dark.

When they finally reached a small clearing, the faintest rays of light were climbing into the eastern sky, illuminating the forest just enough to reveal the silhouettes of the trees and bushes around them.

Mahtma turned to the brothers, then bowed.

"It is a fine morning, my students."

They returned the bow. "It is a fine morning indeed, teacher."

She lowered herself to the grass and sat cross-legged. "Join me."

Subei sat, facing her dark form. Kashi and Bataar followed a moment later. They were still bleary from sleep, having more recently awoken.

"Thus far, I've been trying to teach you self-control, starting with control over your body and your movements. It is safe to say our progress has been. . . lacking."

Kashi chuckled at that.

"You're putting it kindly."

And Subei knew he was right. So far, they didn't have much

to show for all the mornings they'd spent with her. That had to change.

"I wonder," Mahtma said. "If we haven't started in the wrong place. The Ghangerai are a people of action. Normally, control over one's body is the best place to start my teachings. But you three, you're different now. More than just Ghangerai. You're also heirs of Baji. That has changed you." She clapped her hands and shook out her shoulders. "To attain true self-control, one must master both control over one's body and control over one's mind. But these are two faces of the same coin. From now on, we'll work on control over one's mind."

Sounded easy enough, Subei wanted to say, but if he'd learned anything from her past teachings, it was that nothing taught in the Teshkai way was easy.

"I imagine that will be much more difficult than it sounds," he said instead. Bataar laughed at that, eyes shining a moment through their sleep-crusted haze.

"You imagine correctly. Now, do as I do." Mahtma lowered her hands to rest on her thighs and straightened her back.

Kashi mimicked her movements, then Subei did too. His back protested at the rigid position, but he ignored it, focusing on what he was supposed to be doing.

"Bataar?" he said when his brother didn't join them.

A long yawn, then a nod.

"Right, right."

"Now, inhale deeply through your nose for a count of three," Mahtma instructed.

She sucked in a deep breath, and they followed.

"No. You're breathing like warriors. Right now, you need to breathe like monks." She let out her breath, then inhaled again, slow and steady. Seemed a ridiculous proposition, but Subei obeyed, forcing himself to breathe more slowly as he sucked in a lungful of air.

"Good. Now hold it for another count of three." She paused. "Then exhale through your mouth, nice and slow."

He let the air slip from him—felt more like a tent collapsing than he did a warrior or monk—but he did as instructed. Kashi's steady breath was audible beside him. Bataar's too, though it was a tad shaky. After a few breaths, though, it settled and was soon smooth enough that Subei was left trying to match it.

"Good. My people call this the soul wind. It is the rhythm of all things. By matching it, we become one with it."

"Huh," Bataar grunted at that, an approving sound.

"Only when you become one with your surroundings, with the rhythm of existence, can you achieve a truly clear mind."

"Okay, what's next?" Kashi asked.

"We're not there yet. Breathe more. Good. Keep breathing."

They fell into a rhythm, inhale, pause, exhale. Inhale, pause, exhale.

"Very good. Now you're breathing like monks."

Inhale, pause, exhale.

"Close your eyes."

Subei let his eyelids droop closed. Wasn't much darker than it had been before.

"Relax your mind, open your ears. Listen to the world around you, and think of nothing."

"Nothing?" The idea sounded preposterous. How was he supposed to think of nothing?

"Don't question. Just think."

"Of nothing?"

"Precisely."

Well, then. Still breathing deep and steady, Subei tried to calm his thoughts. Tried to think of nothing in particular. He'd never tried not to think before. In battle, indecision was deadly, and once he'd slipped into the rhythm of combat, his thoughts would fall away. But that was different. For that, he was operating on instinct and relying on his training. He'd no training for this. No instincts to guide him. Subei tried to clear the thoughts from his mind, but he might as well have been swatting at another swarm of biting midges. Every time he'd chase one away, a dozen others would slip in to fill the gap. The soreness in his back distracted him next, a deep ache building from maintaining his rigid posture.

"My back is killing me. Can we—"

"Ignore it. We're not thinking of our backs. We're thinking of nothing. Just relaxing and listening to the world around us."

Subei grumbled to himself, but pushed the pain from his mind.

"Open your ears. Let your thoughts drift."

From the sound of it, Bataar and Kashi were doing just fine. That thought tipped Subei's mind further off balance.

This was just breathing, damn it. Breathing and. . . not thinking. He could do this!

Inhaling another slow breath, he tried to focus on the sounds of the forest. The incessant chirping of crickets echoed in a chorus all around them. They had crickets on the steppe, and he was no stranger to their songs, but in the Longlarch it was different. They weren't just in the grass, but in the bushes, in the trees. On the steppe, the crickets sang. Here they roared. But there were other sounds as well, filtering through the chorus. The hooting of an owl, deep and distant, its mournful call drifting on the wind. And every once in a while, a howl. Always from far away, it was high-pitched and had a rough, choppy ending. It was answered each time with a series of barks and yips from around the forest. Song dogs, Ren had called them. They'd been singing their howls and yips for many nights now.

The sounds of the forest blended together and wove with one another into a great song. It swelled with the cricket chorus, danced with the owl's call, and every once in a while, a song dog's howl would break out from the rest in a solo all its own. Subei was lulled in. Felt the pain in his back fade as a nothingness overtook him. But it wasn't nothingness, exactly. Rather it was everything, all at once. It a part of him and him a part of it.

"You're not feeling the bloodrage anymore, are you?" Mahtma asked quick, quiet, and soft—and yet it shattered the song. Ripped him free of it.

"What?" The pain in Subei's back burned once more. Thoughts flooded his mind next, as he searched within himself, expecting any moment to find the familiar, lurking abyss below his stomach.

It was gone, as if the spring was blocked once more.

His heart skipped a beat as he searched again.

Those abyssal depths that had weighed him down, that had called him to sink into them, were gone.

And then they weren't. Like a rock crashing through the surface of a still pond, his thoughts scattered. When they settled, the abyss was back. Subei pried his eyes open.

"How did you do that?"

Mahtma opened her own eyes as the slightest of smiles pulled at her cheeks.

"I only guided you. You are the one who temporarily freed yourself from the rage." She turned. "Bataar?"

He didn't respond, though, looked perfectly at peace.

"He is strong with the world around him," Mahtma said, nodding. "Kashi?" She turned to him last.

His eyes too, were still closed, but his face was scrunched up, focused.

"Hold on. There's. . . something." And as he said it, Subei's scars came alight, and not by his doing. He frowned down at them.

"Don't. . . resist," Kashi said. "I'm. . . following something. A stupid idea."

Mahtma's brow furrowed, but she didn't protest. Neither did Subei as Kashi worked at whatever it was.

And then Subei's scars flared brighter, but again, it wasn't him calling the magic. All the same, it rose inside. As if someone had caught it in a net, was heaving it toward the surface. Pulling it out of his body, even. Pulling. . . pulling. . .

"Kashi, are you—gah!"

All at once, the magic snapped back into him. Hit with the force of a horse's kick and threw Subei onto his back. His core scattered, a swarm of flies before a horse's tail. It dispersed for several harrowing moments, but just as Subei realized it was gone, it reformed. Gathered back into a weight deep inside him.

Kashi's eyes were open then, and open wide.

"I could feel your magic," he said, looking to Subei. "Almost as I can feel my own. I don't know what that means." He paused, shook his head. "Don't know what I could do with that. But meditating made it apparent, so I. . . well, followed it, I guess."

175

"Feels like the ancestors themselves just slapped me," Subei said, rubbing his jaw. "Ouch."

"That was interesting." Mahtma was looking between them, first at Kashi, then Subei. "Something to explore further." She nodded to herself. "Hm."

"That was weird," Kashi said, shaking his head.

"Huh? Come again?" Bataar's eyes were open now, though heavy as if waking from a deep and powerful dream. "You said something, Subei?"

"Uh, yeah, but that was. . . a while ago. . . " He trailed off as his mind turned back to the emptiness he'd felt when meditating. "For a moment," he said. "I couldn't feel the bloodrage. Was it gone? Truly?"

Mahtma shook her head, then folded her hands into her lap. "I doubt it. From what I've heard, the bloodrage is not unlike other emotions that cause an imbalance in a person's soul. Learning how to let go of these emotions is the key to mastering self-control. With time and practice, these emotions—greed, lust, even anger—can be released. Can be forgotten. But I fear the bloodrage is more complicated than that. It is a part of you now, as is your magic. But that doesn't mean we can't fight it. While it may not be possible to banish entirely, I know it can be controlled—Baji Khan managed it, did he not? And the first step in that process is learning how to ignore it. Resist it."

Well, it wasn't a pretty answer. And it certainly wasn't the solution he'd been hoping for, but Subei found it hard to fight the excitement growing inside him.

"With practice and discipline, the next time the bloodrage tries to take control you'll be able to fight it. If you can temporarily block it off at those worst, most dangerous times, you'll remain in control." Mahtma stood. "You've all taken your first step today on a long journey. But I think we agree it is a journey worth making."

Damned right, it was. Subei stood as well, and for the first time felt the possibility that he might be able to fight back against the bloodrage. Not entirely, no, but if he could counter it when it was at its worst, that was the next best thing. Was a fine sight from where he was now, living in fear of it rising without warning.

"It has been a fine session, my students."

Subei couldn't help but smile as he, Bataar, and Kashi bowed.

"A fine session indeed, teacher."

Chapter Twenty-Five

BATAAR

"That meditation really worked a number on you, huh, brother?" Bataar asked, nodding toward Subei before continuing to brush the last of his remounts. "Been a while since I've seen you smile that big."

Would be nice to see him smile that big about our progress reclaiming Baji's magic, instead of cowering from it. Must I always lead by example?

"The meditation is one thing, but Ren says we'll be free of this forest today. Should see the sky again soon."

"That'll be a relief," Kashi called, rolling his sleeping furs. A brown-stained bandage was still wrapped around his head from where falling debris had cracked his skull in Chobei. Bataar winced at the sight.

If I'd been stronger, wielded my magic better, he wouldn't have gotten hurt. There is still a lot of progress to be made. We must tame this horse and put it to proper use.

"Getting out of this forest can't come soon enough," Kashi continued. "It feels. . . dishonest."

"Don't think I've ever met a dishonest tree, little brother," Bataar said, forcing good humor. "Nor an honest one at that. The trees are annoying, though, that's for sure. Trying their best to swipe us off our horses." He raised an arm to show the inflamed scratches from where one had nearly dehorsed him the day prior.

"I don't mean the trees are dishonest, smart ass. I mean, if you want to fight someone on the steppe, you ride up and do it.

Not much trickery in that. But here," Kashi looked around, hand not far from the saber at his hip, "here someone could be ten paces from you, and you'd be none the wiser. This place is made of shadows and trickery."

"All the more reason to put the Longlarch behind us," Subei said.

"If any of you want to see the end of this forest, you'll cut the idle chatter and pack your horses," Ghula called. "If we keep south with good pace, we'll find open ground by nightfall, which means we'll ride hard after that. If there's anyone on our tail, we'll put some distance on them—and be able to see them coming from then on."

South? Bataar hesitated at that thought.

"All due respect, Torol, but south isn't our course."

"You a scout now, Bataar?" she said without pausing her work, strapping the last of her bags to her saddle. "Looking to take the First Rider's job?"

"South's the quickest way out of the Longlarch," Ren said, biting at her cuticles. She cursed and pulled her hand away as a drop of blood welled up. She shook it off. "Keeps us away from whoever's after us, too."

Bataar bowed his head in recognition of the scout's skill. It was the best opening move when preparing to contradict an expert. He'd seen his father employ it time and again. In House Kemu, positions were earned, not given. First Rider Ren deserved her title. It was important to show his next words were not born of disrespect, nor inflated ego.

"You know the land, First Rider, and you guide us well. But I know our quarry, and I would guide us to it." Bataar turned his focus to Subei and Kashi next. "Speak up, brothers. I know you feel it too."

The whole of the camp was watching now, and Subei's face went red as their attention turned to him and Kashi.

"Wolf Catches Scent," Bataar said, his eyes looking to the rising sun. He could feel the false heirs, and closest of all, he could feel *her*. Ru. The pull toward her was east a ways, but due east, not northeast back in Chobei. She was traveling. In the open, most like. To let her flee without giving chase? They'd be fools. And worse, they'd be negligent in their duty to their father.

Subei's eyes said he'd caught on. Any smile he'd had was gone now, replaced with a pinched, pained expression.

"This is a dangerous move, Bataar."

"We didn't ride into enemy lands to be safe, Subei."

"What's dangerous, damn it? What are you two talking about?" Ghula snapped, drawing their attention back.

"The escaped heir, she's due east," Kashi answered, eyes still on Bataar. His face said he felt the same about the idea as did Subei.

"Ru," Bataar said, loud enough for the whole camp to hear. Might be some of them remembered their duty. "She ran to the guards after we killed her brother, but now she's left the town. Heading east."

Subei cursed quietly.

"Bataar, this is foolish. I'm all for a good hunt, but not while we've ancestors know how many soldiers less than a day behind us."

"The scouts have seen no sign of them. For all we know, Chobei didn't have the forces to send. Or didn't know where to send them. We can't run from just the thought of the enemy." Bataar stepped forward and forced his face to soften. "Look, brother. I stand by my word to the khagan, to our father. I vowed I would ride south and hunt every false heir I found in the Zhong empire." He took another step. "By the ancestors above, I mean to do exactly that."

Subei looked like he'd a retort ready, but if he did, he choked on it a moment before finally managing a rasping response.

"And when we fight her, what happens if. . . " He winced. "The bloodrage. . . "

"We can't live in fear of what might happen, brother. We can only control what does."

"First Rider," Ghula snapped suddenly. "How many days does the forest stretch east?"

Ren pulled her still-bleeding thumb from her mouth.

"Day and a half." She paused to look at Bataar. "You said the heir's headed due east?"

He nodded.

"If we followed from here, it'd take us longer to break from the forest, but keep us closer to the heir. Going south first, we'd lose ground, then need to make that up with an eastward turn. An extra two nights of riding would do it, probably, though it'd be tough on the horses. All of us, really."

Ghula stroked her chin, eyes distant.

"Bataar has a point. We've a responsibility to the khagan."

"You remember what Jong's last words were to his sister?" Subei asked, arms crossed defiantly. "'Go find the others.' That's probably why she's on the move." He'd a look on his face as he said it, a look that said he thought he'd won the argument. It didn't last long.

"If Ru reaches the other heirs, she'll ruin any surprise we still have," Ghula said.

Bataar nodded. "We can't let her do that."

Subei cursed. "No, wait, that's not—"

"Ru is escaping!" Bataar snapped without meaning to. He took a moment then, to calm his tone. "We can't stay here paralyzed with indecision. The khanate is united, and we must be too. War is coming. Is already here, honestly, after what we did to Chobei. Every day we pretend otherwise, our enemy grows stronger."

"I'm not pretending anything," Subei growled. "Just not chomping at the bit to murder another town."

Bataar stepped in close, lowering his voice so only Subei could hear.

"Nor am I, brother. But if that's what we have to do, can you stomach it? If that's the difference between securing this magic or allowing it to be unleashed on our people, can I rely on you?"

Subei was quiet a long moment, eyes to the ground. When he spoke, he raised them, and there was a snarl accompanying his words.

"You ever had your home razed, brother? Ever had your ger burn down around your ears?"

"I haven't, Subei. And I pray to the ancestors I never will. But they've already answered our prayers." Bataar flexed his core to pump a surge of light through his scars. "This magic makes us strong. Gives us the power to protect our people. To protect each other." Bataar reached out a hand. "Your home will never burn again, brother."

"Protect each other? Like you protected Kashi in Chobei?" Subei pointed to the bloodstains on their younger brother's bandaged head. "He almost died when the shelves collapsed, but you didn't even look back. You were too consumed with fighting the false heir."

Shit.

Bataar winced as Subei's accusation landed with a pulsing stab of pain. He swallowed hard, fighting the guilt rising within him. His brother had a point, and not an insignificant one. But he had his duty. As the eldest, he had to keep them focused on the mission. And on using all the tools at their disposal to complete it.

"We've been given the magic of Baji," Bataar replied, grasping for a response and knowing even as he spoke that it was weak. Hollow. "We. . . we can't hide from this destiny."

"I don't want to hide from this magic," Subei snapped back. "I just don't want to encourage it to take control of me again." Another snarl, and was that a flash in his eyes? His fist was clenched then, and shaking. Light trickled through his scars.

"Do you mean to strike me, brother?" Bataar hadn't meant to ask it aloud, was still processing the thought himself.

Subei recoiled, eyes going wide. He looked down to his fist and recoiled again.

"I—"

Ghula stepped between the two of them.

"Our hunt may not be done yet, but this conversation is." She slapped away Subei's clenched fist. "You want to hit something? Hit a damned tree. Ancestors know there's enough of them here." She wheeled on the rest of the camp then, and her next commands left no room for debate. "On your horses. Ren, take us east."

* * *

East, then. Another long, hard day's ride through the Longlarch. But with each passing hour, they gained on Ru. Even with the overflowing tangle barring their way, they were faster. Good. But even with remounts, rest was needed come sundown. On the steppe, one could ride for days, if needed. But that was easy riding, no trees clawing you out of the saddle, no vines tripping up your horses every other step. Bataar'd had half a mind to burn a path for them. With as much energy as it took to keep weaving through the verdant mess, it'd started to look like lobbing orb after orb would be easier.

By the ancestor's grace, they reached camp before that became necessary. In a natural clearing, pressed up to the banks of a wide and swift flowing river, they set to rest. Ru had stopped an hour previous, and they'd gained on her even more before packing it in for the day. Now, her pull led directly across the river, and there'd be no fording those waters without daylight. Plenty nice to hang one's feet in, though.

Bataar let his head fall back, eyes closed as he relished the sensation of cold, swift water through his toes. The noise of camp being set drifted over from behind him. Footsteps, too.

"That looks like it feels good," Kashi said.

Bataar nodded without opening his eyes.

"Not so cold nor fresh as the waters of the Chinggon, but if we can't be in Kurul Valley, well, this isn't a poor substitute."

Kashi plopped down next to him with a sigh of relief. Bataar peeked one eye open.

"Perhaps a bath, next?" he asked, focus flicking to his younger brother's bloodstained bandage. "It'll be good to wash your wounds."

"You're looking a bit worse for wear yourself." Kashi inclined his head toward Bataar's exposed arms and shoulders.

"Mostly knicks and scrapes from the forest." Given, there were a few deep cuts and aching bruises from the fight in Chobei too. From the hits he'd taken, there should have been far worse, but Boulder Stands Defiant had protected him well. Turned out, having your body become its own suit of armor was awfully handy.

"You know," Bataar said, raising his arm to show one of the

183

nastier scrapes. "I half expected these to heal faster." He forced himself not to look at Kashi's bandage as he spoke. "Thought with our toughened bodies, we might also heal more rapidly?"

"It's a nice thought." Kashi scratched at a scab. "Seems the magic can't do everything, though. Or. . . " He frowned, thinking. "Maybe that's just another technique we've yet to learn."

"Heh," Bataar chuckled. "Well get on with it, then, genius. Those bruises all over your face don't make you look tough, you know." He smirked and elbowed his younger brother. "Not that there's anyone here to look tough for."

There was a flash of blue light in response as Kashi began to work some magic.

"I was joking," Bataar said. "Mostly."

But he wasn't putting actual focus into the magic. It was closer to fidgeting than anything, his gaze staring off into the river. His fingers worked at a couple of vines and with each pulse of magic, they came to life and wrapped around one another. Weaving into a rope, almost. Even when the magic faded, the rope held its shape.

"How are you doing that?" Bataar asked.

"Huh?" Kashi looked down. "Oh. It feels like an extension of walling?"

"I thought you named that technique *All the World a Shield*?" Bataar said, doing his best impression.

"That's what I'll name it when I master it. Besides, this is nothing." Kashi tossed the vines into Bataar's lap. "Watch *this*." He turned his palms toward one another, then scrunched his face up. *Focusing for real now, huh?*

His scars flared, and a spark zapped into existence, hovering in the empty space between his hands.

"Not a very impressive orb," Bataar said.

"Not everything is about blowing something up." Kashi's tongue slipped over his front teeth as it always did when he was concentrating. His muscles tensed—he must have been squeezing his core hard—then he clapped his hands together as if catching a firefly. Were Kashi holding an orb, the motion would have snuffed it out. Instead, a trickle of light made it out through his fingers. Then carefully, carefully, he pulled his palms apart to reveal the spark had morphed into. . . a thread? It was impossibly thin and yet bright as the edge of a blade in the morning sun. Kashi stretched his hands out and the thread followed, lengthening to be as wide as his chest. Then, holding one palm steady, he dipped the other down such that his index finger touched one end of the thread and began to twirl it. Which each spin, the thread twisted in on itself—and grew. As if there were more of them, invisible, but being caught in the motion and all weaving together.

The thread was thick as a finger, then. Another dozen turns, and it was double that.

"What is it?" Bataar said, his brow scrunching up.

"No idea."

"What do you do with it?"

Kashi chuckled, still twirling his finger and thickening the—thread was no longer the right word for it—rope?

"No idea about that, either."

It was becoming unstable now, bucking and kicking each time he tried to grow its size. Finally, Kashi let it be. He smiled then, a glowing, hissing rope of ethereal light stretched between his hands.

"It can kind of survive on its own," he said, and put it down to demonstrate. When his hands broke contact, the rope dimmed but held its form.

"How long can it last?" Bataar asked as he did his best to resist the urge to poke it.

Kashi shrugged. "An hour? Bit less? I don't think the magic can really exist in this world. At least, not without constantly being refreshed. But right now, this. . . thing isn't much more than a glorified torch, so there's no reason to pump more magic into it."

"Keep working on this, little brother." Bataar clapped him on the shoulder. "Father would be proud."

"Of my misshapen glowy rope thing?"

"Yeah. And you."

Silence for a moment then, but for the river sweeping past.

"Bataar?"

"Yeah?"

"Don't let this magic change you."

Bataar laughed and shook his head. "Remember what mother always calls me?"

"Stubborn as a trovaak in mating season?"

"I was. . . just going to say stubborn, but yeah, that works too," Bataar said as he tried to get that visual out of his head. "You have nothing to worry about with me. I'm not creative enough to change."

"Yeah, but you and Subei. . . ever since Chobei. . . " Kashi knocked away the ethereal rope and it slid off the bank, was swallowed up by the river.

"It'll pass," Bataar said, because it was true. Because he knew it was true. Kashi didn't look ready to agree though. "Hey, we're brothers, remember? Sometimes brothers fight. And ancestors know we spend too much time together as it is." He chuckled. "Baji'd already killed his oldest brother by our age." It was meant as a joke, but Kashi wasn't smiling.

"Subei fears he's changing."

"What's that supposed to mean?"

"He told me he can't tell if he's different since the bloodrage, or just worried he is. Like when you're so concerned about something, you start to see problems that aren't actually there."

"Subei's always been too dramatic for his own good. He's fine. I'm fine. *We're* fine." Bataar knew it was true, but in that moment, he realized just how much his brothers needed him. Needed his example. He would be the rock sheltering them from the storm raging around them now. And all storms to come. He had to be.

"Just. . . talk to Subei about it, yeah?"

"Yeah, alright. First thing in the morning," Bataar said as he pulled his feet from the river and stood up. "If I start him talking now, he'll fill our tent so full of words no one'll get any sleep. Come on."

Chapter Twenty-Six

SUBEI

Damned noise. Subei's eyes crept open so stiffly, it almost hurt. He'd just gotten to sleep, hadn't he? He rolled over inside his trovaak pelt sleeping furs and set his mind to searching for a sleep so deep even Mahtma's prodding foot wouldn't wake him come morning.

But there was the noise again.

What was the night watch doing, anyway?

Maybe it was one of Ren's scouts returning. The one that'd been late in getting back?

Subei's body ached with too-stiff muscles as he pulled himself upright in the confined space of the tent he shared with his brothers. He blinked the sleep from his eyes and peered through the entrance flap. Couldn't make out his hand in front of his face, much less the guards working this shift. It was all just darkness.

A horse snorted somewhere off to the side and a light wind whispered through the clearing.

Then, a noise. So faint as to almost go unheard, but it was a sound Subei knew instantly. A sound that raised the hairs on the back of his neck and froze the breath in his throat. A sound as quiet as the blink of an eyelid, yet it hit like a hammer blow. It was a soft squelch, like a footstep in mud, but Subei was no stranger to violence, and this was no footstep.

"No," he said to himself, unwilling to believe what he already knew. He slid out of the tent as quiet as possible, then rushed to his feet. He conjured an orb and raised it high into the air. The clearing lit up with the pale blue light, and Subei's fears were confirmed.

The guard who'd been on watch was slumped against a tree, his neck cut open. Blood ran down his chest as his legs gave out and he collapsed, pale and twitching, next to the body of his watchmate.

The Zhong soldier wielding the bloody knife spotted Subei and froze, eyes squinting in the sudden light. They went wide a moment later, though, as the man took in what must have been his first ever experience with the magic of Great Baji Khan.

It was a short-lived one. Subei caught him in the chest with the orb and the bastard disappeared in a shockwave of flame.

"We're under attack!" Subei shouted, eyes blurry from the explosion. "To arms!"

"Attack? Where?" One of their guards asked, stumbling to his feet on instinct but clearly not yet awake. The others stirred as well, the quicker thinking of them with weapons already in hand.

Another familiar sound, then: the creak of bowstrings being drawn. It came from the trees to the left. A chorus of twangs followed, and it was all Subei could do to unleash North Wind Scours in their general direction. His scars flared bright, and a series of thuds followed as the unseen arrows were driven down into the grass.

The camp was properly stirring now, including his brothers.

"The hell is happening?" Kashi asked, bleary eyed.

"They caught up to us," Subei said, words tumbling out as he searched for his shield.

"Let's make them regret it, then!" Bataar rushed from their tent with a roar. In that moment, he was a bear bursting from its den, all hackles and fury. His scars were already burning, and he was throwing orbs before he'd even properly stood up. The first two detonated at the edge of the clearing, and in the heartbeat of burning light they provided, Subei spotted the Zhong archers half concealed in the brush. Bataar must have seen them too, for his next orbs landed among the attackers. Subei's joined them.

Explosion after explosion burst through the trees, burning soil, flaming foliage, and body parts sent flying in the wake of each blast. After the first few explosions, Subei's vision was thoroughly shot. Nothing visible between the flashes of blinding light, then utter darkness, then back, again and again. Waves of heat swept over the clearing, and the ground shook as if struck by the wrath of the ancestors themselves. Even the very air felt like a weapon, concussion blasts slamming into his chest. By the time it was over there was no doubt everyone was fully awake.

Subei's head ached from the blasts, his ears screaming with a high-pitched whine, and his eyes were seared with the ghosts of the fire. And also with the still-burning fires left in the blasts' wake. An entire section of the tree line was in flames now. By their light, Subei could make out what was left of the archers. Two, maybe three of them were still alive, depending on how liberal one's definition was. One was dragging himself through the steaming soil, a leg blown clean off at the hip joint. Another stumbled past him, face slack and scorched as he reached for. . . more soldiers.

Shit.

Zhong soldiers, and all around. Forty? More? And these weren't archers but armored infantry. The only mercy came in the form of their hesitation, eyes wide at the sudden devastation. If only it hadn't left Subei already choking for breath. That'd been what? Fifteen? Twenty orbs? And all of them heavily charged. But this fight was far from over. He pushed through the exhaustion, forcing his mind to take in every useful detail of the enemy.

Just like the soldiers in Chobei, every inch of these was heavily armored. Shins to heads, all covered in some piece of iron armor or another. They weren't uniformly equipped—some wore the Zhong's version of heavy lamellar, while others had a sort of plate configuration—but even those that were lightly armored boasted thick layers of reinforced leather. Some carried spears and wooden shields, others had swords and shields of steel. Another group had only swords, and it was these, Subei reckoned, that were the furthest from regular fighters. Something closer to militia, perhaps?

Where the hell was his shield? And saber? Both had been with him in the tent. Had they gotten tangled in his sleeping furs? His eyes flicked back to the tent. Could he get to them—

The Zhong cried out as one, and then charged.

"Brother!" Kashi was beside him, and he slammed something heavy into his stomach.

His shield!

Subei pulled it on in one smooth motion, even as Kashi tossed a saber to Bataar.

"You're still injured. Stay out of this as much as you can," Subei shouted to Kashi and put himself between his younger brother and the oncoming soldiers.

"This is my fight as much as yours."

"The hell it is." Bataar shoved past him. "Survive," he growled to Kashi, then lashed out with a sweeping wind strike that buffeted the charging enemies. A couple stumbled, tripping up those behind.

"Loose!" came a cry from the side as Ghula gave the command. A hissing hail of arrows swept past Subei's ears—wind whipping through his hair—and cut into the Zhong front-line. Before Subei could properly process that, there was a voice in his ear. Mahtma.

"You are stronger than the bloodrage!" She held a curved short sword in one hand, and her forearms were protected by iron gauntlets that stretched from her wrist to her elbow. "You're Ghangerai, after all."

"Loose!' Another volley slipped past, and Subei frantically formed a plan. He hadn't gotten a proper count of the enemy's number, but at a guess it was easily forty, maybe closer to fifty—even after the archers' destruction. And their own numbers were already down to eighteen, if not less. But if he and Bataar could hold off the Zhong advance long enough, the rest of the camp could retreat under cover of their own archers. They'd give ground and—the river. *Shit, the river*. It was at their backs. The Zhong had them cornered. And already, the exertion of so many orbs was wearing on him. He'd need to resort to less costly attacks.

"At will!" Ghula shouted, and individual arrows began to zip by. The Zhong ranks had recovered now, though, and were advancing as one, shields raised. Arrows thunked into them or caught shoulder armor or helmets and deflected away.

Subei put an orb in among the feet of the left flank and the resulting explosion blew a hole in their ranks as a good four or five soldiers were knocked down.

"Now!" Ghula rushed past, sabers in hand. She'd either slept in her armor or somehow found enough time to get it on. She led a charge now, along with Vachir and the rest of the kheshig guards, that plunged into the gap.

Not to be outdone, Bataar followed, but straight into the enemy's center.

Subei called an orb to hand and aimed it just in front of his brother to soften the enemies there—but pain stabbed through Subei's ribs and the glowing light fizzled.

"Gah," he hissed, bending at the pain. He'd used too much magic too quickly, was already wringing whatever drops remained in his core. But Bataar was steps from the front rank and the brave idiot was terribly outnumbered.

Subei punched forward with North Wind Scours then curved the attack to rush past Bataar and up into the faces of the Zhong infantry. Dirt and smoke were swept into their eyes, sending a few stumbling back. As the rush of air continued up, though, it stoked the fire in the canopy. Several flaming branches groaned.

"Ah." Subei unleashed another wind strike, this time starting it high then pulling it down. The forced downdraft carried with it swathes of flame that lashed at the Zhong and sewed panic among them. Better still, two large branches came crashing down, their flaming bulk flattening the soldiers directly in front of Bataar.

"Yahaha!" Subei cried, somewhere between a cheer and a taunt.

And then Bataar was in among the enemy, an orb in each hand, and attacking wildly. Ghula's charge had made contact too, and so, with their line of fire obscured, the remaining Ghangerai scouts stowed their bows, drew sabers, and charged. The battle devolved into madness then, both sides mixing among the other in a hacking, chopping, close-pressed affair. The middle and rear of the Zhong were still in something approaching an orderly formation, though, and Subei set his focus on them. He was vaguely aware of Kashi beside him as he threw as many wind strikes as he could and tried to ignore the stabbing pain in his ribs.

Between both brothers' attacks, the flames above the Zhong were stirred into a proper inferno. Like a bellows pumping air into a furnace. Branches began to fall on their own then, tumbling down to crash among the battle. Those that were large enough cut up the battlefield, bisecting it with walls of burning wood and hungry flame.

And still, the Ghangerai were driven back.

Numbers weren't everything in a battle, but they couldn't be overlooked, either. Subei had positioned himself several paces away from the fighting to focus on his techniques, but quicker than he could react, the battle swept over him. What had been a tactical engagement boiled into chaos. Horses screamed and bucked, many pulling free of their ropes to sprint wildly through the battle as, all around, a dozen individual fights raged. Subei saw them in flashes, in parries and cuts, shield strikes and death blows.

A scout brought his saber down between the shoulder and neck of a Zhong soldier. Metal clanged but otherwise the armor was hardly dented. The soldier ran the scout through. A spear caught someone in the hip, and Subei couldn't tell who was stabbing who. He stepped forward to help, but then a big brute came bearing down on him. Subei grimaced through the wracking pain in his chest as he conjured a half-sized orb and threw it. The brute blocked it with his shield, but the resulting explosion was enough to send him stumbling to the side, armor steaming. The face of his shield was red hot, as if fresh from the forge.

Subei didn't have another orb in him, not so soon. He opted for a wind strike, but the brute was on him already. The molten shield was thrust into his face, and Subei jumped backward, skin searing from the heat. Before he could regain his footing, another attack came in low, sword slicing at his hips. Subei whipped his shield in a backhand blow across his body and just caught the sword in time, slamming the blade into the ground. The man leaned in to strike with the still-cooling shield, but Subei's North Wind Scours knocked him backward. The soldier was ready for the second blast of it, though, raising his shield and bracing his stance. Still, it drove him a good pace back, boots tearing gouges in the soil. As soon as the wind subsided, he charged again, sword overhead.

The soldier swung down, blade slicing through the air. Subei punched forward, then turned it into an uppercut. His wind strike swerved upward and slammed into the man's hand, blowing the sword from his grasp. The soldier paused a moment, seemingly confused, staring at his now-empty hand.

The flat of a blade slammed into the side of his face. His metal helmet rang like a bell, and he stumbled to one side, nearly doubling over. A hand ripped his helmet away and another sword swing dispatched him. The body slumped to the ground, lying at the feet of one of the kheshig guards, his beard caked with soot. He gave Subei a nod, then turned back to the fight—and took a spear through the face. A mailed Zhong soldier placed his foot on the fallen man's shoulder and jerked backward, spear ripping out with a sickening pop.

"Bastard!" Subei spat, anger flooding his veins. Adrenaline followed it, and then the bloodrage was stirring down in that pit beneath his stomach. He could almost feel a single claw reaching up from that abyss. In that moment, a fresh surge of magic flowed through him.

"*Piss off,*" he growled.

"Gladly, once you're rotting," the Zhong soldier he hadn't been talking to replied.

Subei extended a hand then, almost as if on instinct. He kept it palm up, as he'd seen Yue Jong do. It hadn't worked in his training so far, so it had no reason to work now, yet his scars flared brightly. And then he could feel the objects around him, could sense them as if they were an extension of his own body. Discarded weapons, broken shields, flaming branches, and more. He clenched his fist, and they all jumped toward him—but came up short, slipping free of his invisible grasp.

The Zhong soldier charged, spear lowered and still dripping blood.

Subei screamed, and then one of the objects snapped to life.

A fallen sword. It jumped off the ground and came screeching in from the side, taking the spearman in the ribs and skewering him all the way through. He was lifted off his feet by the impact and thrown into several of his comrades.

"Ha!" Subei cheered until a dash of movement in his periphery sent him ducking behind his shield. A blow slammed into it, reverberating up into his shoulder and driving him sideways in several off-balance steps. Over the rim of his shield, he saw a flash of light on steel and just managed to adjust his block as the sword crashed into it again. With a grunt, the soldier stepped forward and bashed his shoulder into Subei's chest.

The ground slammed into the back of his head, teeth clicking sharply as his mouth snapped shut. A dull pain bloomed in his mouth and Subei realized he'd clamped down on his tongue. Spitting blood, he rolled backward and scrambled to his feet. The soldier's sword took him in the shoulder. By rights, it should have punched straight through, but Boulder Stands Defiant had toughened Subei's body enough that when the blade bit into his flesh, it was deadened. As if it'd had to cut through a padded jacket first.

Blood and pain blossomed around the wound, but it was the Zhong soldier's turn to cry out then, as Subei wrapped a hand around the blade and pushed it back. The edge of the weapon bit into his palm, but no deeper than the first few layers. Just barely enough to draw blood. The Zhong soldier cursed and released the blade, shock overtaking his features. He made it two steps back before someone's back swing caught him across the face.

Subei spit blood as he rose. Amidst the adrenaline pulsing through his veins and the blood pounding in his head, the abyssal depths were calling to him again, itching to set loose the bloodrage. Subei shook his head and sucked in a deep breath, forcing himself to ignore the madness within. Was a bit harder to ignore the madness without, however.

The forest fire raged above, and beneath it, the world as well. A tumultuous cacophony of metal on metal, of metal on flesh.

For a moment, the chaos parted around him, and he surveyed the battleground, then cursed.

What few Ghangerai there'd been were dwindling. They were easy to spot, often frequently surrounded and cut down by the slashing blows of several opponents at once. This was not their sort of fight. The Ghangerai fought from horseback and on the vast expanse of the steppe where there was room to maneuver, to harass at range with arrows, or bait the enemy into breaking their lines and exposing themselves to a sudden, decisive heavy cavalry charge. This was not the steppe.

"Brother!" Kashi's voice rang out from a dozen paces distant. Subei spun to find him retreating under a rain of blows, bits of wicker flying from his shield with each strike. His foot caught on a corpse, and he stumbled, shield lowered for just a moment. The soldier took the opening and slashed down.

Chapter Twenty-Seven

BATAAR

The blow connected with a resounding thunk.

Kashi blinked once, then mouthed a silent prayer. Bataar nodded down at him, then pushed back with his shield, throwing off the blow meant for his brother and pushing away the soldier who'd delivered it.

The man made to strike again, but Bataar was quicker, his anger a rising tide. He'd be damned if this bastard was going to take his brother. He caught the man's arm with his hand, and then, without letting go, conjured an orb. The explosion should have killed them both, but like muscle memory, it seemed the most natural thing for Bataar to urge the explosion forward— away from his hand and into his opponent's wrist.

The sword fell away, and when the smoke cleared, the man was left with only a blackened stub where once his hand had been.

The bloodrage was churning within Bataar now, teetering on the edge of freedom. He turned his eyes to the soldier.

"He's a brave man that raises his sword against the House of Kemu Khagan. And a dead one."

The man twisted his mouth to respond, but Bataar punched his shield into his face. In the tournament, their shields had been modified to be non-lethal. Where the coiling wicker met in the center, there was nothing but empty space. Now Bataar's shield was a weapon of war, and where the wicker came together, there was a long, iron spike. A spike that he drove into the man's face.

This bastard had tried to kill Kashi.

Bataar punched him again.

And again.

And again.

"*Ancestors above*," Kashi whispered, eyes wide as the man collapsed to the side, his face devastated, punctured, and oozing.

Bataar merely growled and pulled Kashi to his feet, up and away from the heaviest fighting.

"Stay behind me," he barked. He caught Kashi's eyes then, found fear in them. Not of the battle, no, but of *him*. The rage faltered inside him. He took a shuddering breath, forcing himself to calm, and felt the bloodrage slink back into the abyss. Could almost feel its disappointment.

Kashi let out a long, shaking breath. "Your eyes, Bataar. They were different."

A scream burst through the chaos on their left, and a Zhong soldier was tackled to the ground. A flurry of blows rained down on him, denting his helmet and crashing against his face. The soldier clawed back desperately, fingernails pulling at the thick black hair of the woman pinning him down. Ghula, Bataar realized as the old warrior raged. A finger caught her in the eye, and she leaned away, then came back with a dagger in hand. She plunged it down again and again until the soldier stopped moving.

Ghula snarled one last time, chest dripping with blood. Hard to tell, but most of it looked to be someone else's. A spearman yelled and lunged at her.

"Behind you!" Bataar summoned an orb, but a spasm of pain doubled him over, and the technique fizzled before it'd even taken form. "Ghula!" he gasped, one hand clasped over the pain.

She turned toward the spear, and it would have taken her through the stomach, but a blur intercepted the spearman. Didn't hit him so much as sweep past, and he stumbled to one side and collapsed.

Mahtma gave the corpse a dismissive glance then flicked blood from the blade of her short sword. A Zhong soldier came at her from behind, but before Bataar could even cry out, she leaned back into his attack. The movement carried her inside his guard, and she planted her back into his chest. He couldn't pull his slash back in time, and his arm came down on her shoulder, blade well in front of her. Mahtma shifted, aligning his elbow on her shoulder, then snapped his forearm down. The soldier's elbow popped out the wrong way, and he howled, sword falling away.

Mahtma spun and ran her blade up through the soft skin below his chin. He slumped sideways with hardly a sound.

Shaking her head at the sight, Ghula wiped a stream of blood from her face and snatched the sword from the ground. She gave Bataar a nod as she stepped beside him, breathing heavily, her eyes searching for the next foe.

Mahtma darted to one side to slice her blade along the back of a soldier's knees. He collapsed, and the kheshig guard who'd been dueling him dispatched him with a hacking blow. She and the guard joined them, creating a small island amid the sea of writhing bodies.

The last few Ghangerai that had been pushed to the edges of the fighting were cut down now, and the press of Zhong soldiers turned inward to face them.

There was a commotion on the left. First Rider Ren was being driven back. Already she was knee deep in the river. A soldier came swinging at her, and she loosed an arrow into his face at no further than an arm's distance. She'd three more arrows clutched between the fingers of her draw hand, though, so it was maybe half a heartbeat before she'd another nocked and drawn. She caught the next attacker in the neck. He stumbled to one side as she ducked under a slash from a third soldier. She kicked him in the back such that he went face down in the river. That gave her enough time to place a finishing arrow into the other soldier—who was flailing around, hand clutched to his neck—then calmly turn and put one into the back of the other.

Two more drew up behind her, halberds reared back. Ren hadn't seen them, but there was flash of light from Bataar's right, and he turned to see Kashi's scars burning bright. He swept his hands to the side, and a wall of debris—burning

198

branches, dropped weapons, even a bloodied corpse—rose from the battlefield, swept into the river, and broke the two soldiers beneath it.

Ren turned just in time to see her would-be killers crumpled up beneath the onslaught of debris. Her eyes found Kashi, and she nodded her thanks. But another soldier was on her—was there no end to them? She nocked her last arrow, drew, and loosed right as a leaping soldier barreled into her. They went down in a rush of white water and were caught in the current. The last Bataar saw, they were still wrestling, each trying to drown the other while being carried downstream.

"You go to your ancestors with honor," Ghula said, drawing Bataar back to their situation. She was frowning at the corpse of a kheshig guard. She raised her eyes next to the soldier standing over him. "You'll go to yours in pieces."

Fine words, and Bataar knew she'd see them fulfilled. That was the great strength of the Ghangerai—the sheer determination to impose one's will onto the world. Logic was no match for determination, even if, at the present, the odds looked no better than they had before. Worse, maybe, considering all their losses. Ghula, Mahtma, Kashi, and one kheshig were all that stood with him against the too many remaining Zhong soldiers.

"Where's Subei?" Kashi said suddenly.

Bataar's stomach dropped like a rock in water. He swallowed hard but found he'd no spit, mouth dry as the deserts of Mercer. He looked across the forest they'd turned into a slaughter ground. Couldn't find him anywhere. All the Zhong soldiers he could see were facing them, readying for the final push. No other Ghangerai were standing. Which could only mean. . .

No.

Bataar refused to accept the thought. Yet he couldn't stop his eyes searching through the countless corpses sprawled across the red-stained grass. Subei could be any one of those. But no, he'd know if his brother were dead. His and Kashi's scars would have reacted. He felt sick to his stomach thinking it, but he knew he would have absorbed his brother's magic if he'd died. So where was he?

Bataar focused on the magic within and breathed a sigh of

relief as he felt the familiar pull toward Subei, leading his eyes to his brother.

He found him across the battlefield, engaged with five soldiers. Subei'd backed himself into a corner of flame, downed and burning branches at his back and left. He was keeping the soldiers at bay on the remaining two sides with a barrage of North Wind Scours. It was working for the moment, but his heavy breathing and slumped posture made it clear he couldn't keep going much longer. As if sensing Bataar's gaze, their eyes met. In that moment, he could see Subei calculating the distance between them and the number of soldiers occupying it. Too many to break through. And nowhere else to run. There was only one option.

It crept into Subei's eyes first, a burning ring around the edges. Then it moved inward, a wildfire swelling to overtake—

"No!" Bataar screamed and reached out. Not because his brother was wielding the bloodrage, but because he was fighting *against* it. Even as Bataar screamed, Subei shook off the rage. *Idiot!* Was he so proud?

Or was it something else? Was he that. . . afraid of this magic? *No.* Bataar refused the thought immediately. Subei would rather live bloody than die here at the hands of these Zhong dogs.

Except. . . Bataar's heart sank as Subei grimaced with the effort and forced the rage down, back into its abyss. His eyes stopped glowing.

He was a dead man.

"Subei!" Bataar howled, but then there was acceptance in his brother's eyes. They flicked to Kashi, and a short nod followed.

Protect him, Bataar could hear him saying, even if no words were exchanged.

"*No,*" Bataar growled. It was a coarse, guttural sound, borne from deep in his stomach. Lower, even. And then logic was gone, replaced instead with determination.

He closed his eyes, and a burning, impossible heat rose through him.

Chapter Twenty-Eight

SUBEI

"Bataar, no!" Subei just had time to shout before his brother's eyes were consumed by fire. Not actual flame, but the burning, blue light from within. It filled his eye sockets entirely—and the bloodrage wasted no time in setting to work.

An orb burst among the Zhong soldiers immediately in front of Subei, followed by a rain of gore. Subei recoiled, trying not to think about what was splattering down on him.

Bataar smiled as he strode from the safety of the remaining members of their party. But no. That wasn't Bataar, it was the bloodrage.

Soldiers darted in front of him. Four, five, then a sixth too, coming in from the side. That would have been a problem, were it Bataar fighting them.

He clapped his hands together, and there was a resounding boom as a shockwave of blue light burst outward. It hit the soldiers like a wind strike, but with enough force to knock all of them off their feet. And more, they didn't immediately rise again, probably on account of the arcs of light crawling over their bodies. The soldiers panicked and cursed, slapping at the bolts and crying out whenever they bit into their flesh.

Bataar raised an open hand then, wreathed in a similar frenzy of arcing light, and clenched it into a fist. As he did, the sparks covering the men charged to a frenzy too, popping and snapping and hissing all the more. The soldiers' cries rose to a fever pitch as Bataar extended his other hand, then clenched that into a fist as well.

Anyone still fighting paused then, as the screams pierced every ear. Heads turned and stared. Jaws fell open. More than a few prayers were uttered.

And through it all—the screaming, the praying—Bataar smiled. The *bloodrage* smiled and casually extended a hand toward Subei, beckoning. The space between them was filled with crackling energy, though, whatever technique he'd used still hanging charged in the air.

Bataar waved again, and Subei took a tentative half-step into the energy field. His hair stood on end, and gooseflesh shot all through him, but there was no pain. Just a. . . charged sensation, as if all the world had sucked in a great breath and was waiting. . . waiting. . .

Subei ran. He sprinted through the field and passed Bataar to join the safety of the others. A relative safety, perhaps, but still.

It was only then Subei noticed the soldiers writhing on the ground had stopped screaming. Stopped making any noise, for that matter. There was only the occasional zap as the remaining arcs of light snapped across their corpses.

Around them lay the bodies of Ghangerai scouts and kheshig guards the Zhong had slain. Some of the khagan's finest. Hacked and scattered among the trees, yet Bataar was smiling as he looked back at Subei.

"Good, then. We're all in our proper places. Nice and tidy." Bataar spoke the words, but Subei knew it wasn't really him saying them. Could all too easily remember what it felt like to have someone else's voice gather in your throat, to spill from your mouth.

"Bataar. . . " Subei trailed off. What had he wanted to say? What could he say?

Beside him, Ghula tested her grip on her sword. Veteran warrior she might've been, but Subei saw fear in her eyes just then. Fear of Bataar? Maybe. Fear of the battle they still faced? Probably that too. Couldn't say he blamed her. Couldn't say he didn't feel the same fear gripping at his lungs, chasing at his thumping heart.

Mahtma drew in a deep breath, then exhaled slowly. Her normally tight bun had come loose, allowing her shoulder-length hair to fall around her face. A large gash covered her right cheek, all mixed up with dirt and strands of hair. Subei caught her eye, expecting to find fear there too, but she bore no such emotion. No emotions at all, far as he could see. The old monk looked no different now than if she were giving a lesson on meditation. Disregarding all the blood, of course.

"So you're the bastards we've heard about?" a Zhong soldier yelled at them from behind his shield. There was a tremble in his voice. Rightly so. "Them with the glowing scars what razed our town?"

"Only thing worse than a horse-bedding barbarian is a horse-bedding barbarian possessed by an evil spirit," another said, though there was fear in his voice too. They still had greater numbers, but perhaps—with the threat of magic—there was a way to force a truce.

Subei forced himself to breathe. Slow. Calm.

Inhale, pause, exhale—like Mahtma had shown them.

The bloodrage had risen again, was begging to be released. Its warmth spread from his stomach and was working its way up toward his chest.

No.

He focused on his breathing and forced away the feelings.

"You've still got a chance to walk away from this," Subei called to the soldiers as he moved to the front of the group. "No reason you need to die tonight."

"Where's the fun in that?" Bataar stepped up beside him. "Why are we negotiating with worms, brother?"

"We ain't the ones dying tonight," the first soldier shouted, but his sword arm trembled as his eyes darted to the still-sparking corpses. Bataar must have seen it as he gave a little squeeze of his fist then, and the sparks surged stronger for a moment.

"What happened to your town was regrettable," Subei said, trying to ignore the cooking bodies. "It will haunt me for all my years. We didn't intend for any innocents to get hurt. But they did. For that you were owed a debt in blood." He gestured to the dead Ghangerai spread amongst the still-burning trees. "That debt's been paid. Let us end this."

There was a shuffling of feet. None of the Zhong wanted to be the first to accept a truce. Several looked ready to, though.

A soldier near the front cursed. His face looked similar to the one Bataar had bashed all to pieces with his shield spike. A brother, perhaps?

"There'll be no peace between us," he spat.

Bataar smiled at the man. "I like you."

He turned then, and leaned in, right up to Subei's ear. "I could save all of us by myself. Could save our precious, gentle little brother, our stoic monk, our rough-edged but lovable leader." He paused, one long moment. "But I won't. Oh no. You might not want to save yourself, Subei, but if you want to save them, well, you know what to do." A wide smile then, and his tongue licked across the front of his teeth, smearing blood along them. "Release the bloodrage, brother. Wield the weapon inside you."

"Bataar. . . *shit!*" Subei clenched a fist, tendons rising all along his arm. "You're still in there. You can take back control."

"He can? Ehhh," Bataar tilted his hand side to side as if to say '*maybe*.' "He will?" A smile. "He wants to?" Wider, then. "No, Subei. Bataar's already come to realize how useful I am. He wants, more than anything, for all of you to make it out alive. I can give that to him. I *will* give that to him. I *want* to give that to him. But first, I *need* you to release me."

Subei saw a hunger in Bataar's eyes. No, this *creature's* eyes. It wanted him to give in. Wanted it so badly, its breathing ran ragged. Subei knew then with sickening certainty that allowing this thing control of his body might be the last thing he ever did.

"You'll destroy me," Subei said plainly. No anger, no fear. "You're a blade with no hilt. Wielding you cuts me as much as my enemies."

"Oh, but you've already grabbed a sword by its blade tonight, Subei. And look at your hand, it's barely worse for the wear. I'll destroy you? No. I will *remake* you."

"The hell are we sitting around for?" a Zhong soldier shouted. He looked to be gathering the courage to charge in.

"This is insanity! We should. . ." He faltered. "We should end it!"

Bataar flicked an orb without even looking. It caught the man in the stomach and blew him in half.

No! Subei could only watch in horror as the Zhong recoiled at the death. Their expressions of terror turned to disgust, then further bent into anger. And just like that, their minds were lost. He'd had some of them ready for a truce. Now there was no going back.

"For Chobei!"

They shouted as one and charged.

Bataar crossed his arms against his chest and North Wind Shelters burst from him—but it didn't knock over his opponents, it only directed them around him, and stirred the flames above into a frenzy once more.

The Zhong soldiers came in hacking and slashing and once again, battle was joined.

"To the river, go!" Subei cried, using everything he had left to throw a constant torrent of wind strikes against the enemy. His magic was all but spent, though, and even as his group gave ground, several soldiers slipped through to attack. Ghula traded blows with the first. Mahtma engaged the second. The third and fourth took on the last kheshig guard. Their swords clashed once, twice, three times—then a javelin came soaring in to catch him in the shoulder. His armor stopped the brunt of it, but it knocked him backwards, opened his guard.

Subei cried out as the final blow fell, hacking the noble warrior down.

And then another cry, from behind. And flashing blue light.

Kashi.

He'd almost reached the river, but two soldiers had caught up. He knocked the first back with North Wind Scours. The second lunged in, and Kashi sidestepped the blow. His scars burned bright as he raised a hand and—

Baji's Burning Fury! Subei instantly recognized the technique. His little brother had finally managed it!

Kashi's eyes went wide at the sight of an orb in his hand. He reared back, aiming it at the soldier before him—and a blade came slicing down from behind. It might've been aimed to take his hand off, but if that was the case, it missed. Instead, the blade cut right into the orb.

"No!" Subei shouted, but too late. The orb exploded.

Scorching debris whipped past Subei's face—something winged him in the shoulder, spun him around—and he collapsed into the river shallows.

Acrid, stinging smoke, then. He shook it from his eyes, clawed his way through it, searching for Kashi.

There! He was face up in the river, body bloody and smoking and less one arm. The current had him, though.

"Kashi!" Subei waded after him, tripping time and again as the water reached his knees, then his waist. "Kashi!"

There was still time. He could save him! Life without an arm was still life. He just had to reach him, had to stop the bleeding—

Kashi's scars were glowing. But not with any technique. The light from them grew fiercer, brighter, impossibly bright. The water boiled around him. Cracks tore across his skin, raced over his neck, his face, and from them, the magic rose out of his body. It gathered above him in a swirling, churning cloud. A cloud that split in two and rushed toward Subei and Bataar.

Subei hardly felt it, though. Every other magic transfer had been euphoric. Now, there was only pain. Some physical, most emotional. Pain because his brother was gone. Pain because it was his fault. Pain because of everything that'd happened, and fear of what could come next. From that mix, the anger rose. Hot and boiling. Lightning striking dry grass and igniting an inferno.

Subei clenched a fist and took a deep breath. No more. No more talking. No more logic. No more control. Mahtma thought to teach him how to resist the bloodrage, but in this moment, he wanted nothing less. These soldiers had killed Kashi. Had killed his brother. That would not go unpunished. They weren't going to be killed, they were going to be obliterated. Subei let the anger flood into his mind. *Wanted* the anger to flood into his mind. He drowned his thoughts in it.

And then, like some leviathan of the deep catching a whiff of blood in the water, the bloodrage surged forth. A warmth enveloped Subei. It grew until it was a great heat, until the sweat ran from him in streams. He closed his eyes and let himself fall backward into the abyss. When his eyes opened again, he was merely an observer.

* * *

Sticky, covered in blood. Smiling.

The rest of the soldiers had put up an admirable fight, but now they were in too many pieces to be put back together. Nothing admirable about that.

The bloodrage reveled as it sprinted through the Longlarch and Subei was unable to do anything but watch—trapped in the confines of his own mind.

First the soldiers had been fighting, now they were running.

The bastards were running. Had come with arms and armor and numbers and the belief they'd avenge their town. The belief they were due a righteous vengeance.

But that was just the problem. Believing a thing didn't make it so.

The soldiers ran, and Subei and Bataar gave chase.

Mahtma might have called out from behind, but Subei wasn't listening. Didn't care. Two soldiers yet lived—the last two—their weapons cast down in a frenzy and their armor stripped off where possible as they ran. Anything to make them go faster.

Didn't really matter how fast they went, though, did it? Both were injured and trailing blood. Blood that, to the rage, was impossible to miss. Blood that filled Subei's nostrils and led him on. Through the darkness, through the forest, smiling like a madman as he hunted down the last of the bastards that'd killed Kashi.

And then they broke into a clearing. But not a natural one, no. This was the work of people. A place where the forest had been cut back and the soil tilled into a small garden. A pen for animals built beside it. And at the center of it all, a hut. A humble thing, smaller than most gers, and lit softly from inside by the light of a fireplace.

The trail of blood—that intoxicating, beautiful scent—led right into it.

"Hold up there," a voice called out, and Subei slid to a stop to find an older man on the porch. "Don't want no trouble tonight," he said, hand outstretched. "Whatever that commotion was, we've no part of it."

"You're sheltering them," Bataar said, hardly even out of breath from the mad dash, and the old man's eyes went wide at once. Not a good actor, this one.

"Sheltering. . . sheltering who? I don't know what you mean."

Inside the fire and chaos that was the bloodrage, Subei felt a moment of doubt. This was no warrior. Those who killed innocents were—

It wasn't much of a movement, barely a flick of his wrist, but that was all it took for Subei to fling an orb. Not a full-sized orb, but a smaller one. It caught the man in the shoulder. The explosion tossed him back into the house.

"The soldiers are in there," Bataar said, watching the windows for movement. "You can't run from this!" he shouted suddenly, then he lashed forward with a wind strike. The night air wavered and shook as the force of a typhoon slammed into the side of the hut. Shook it to its core such that dirt and sticks and dust tumbled down from the roof. Shook it such that one of the walls cracked.

Bataar struck it again, and someone inside screamed.

And then Subei was attacking, too. And beneath the onslaught, the hut had no chance. The walls buckled, the roof came crashing down, and then there was more screaming. But the bloodrage wasn't done.

Subei charged an orb in his hand—a big one this time. The one before had been meant to wound. This was meant to obliterate.

He threw it. An explosion next, and then the rubble was on fire. And even then, Bataar kept attacking, each blast of North Wind Scours breathing a terribly, hungry life into the flames.

In moments, what had been a home was an inferno. And then there was no more screaming.

The last two soldiers responsible for Kashi's death were off to meet their ancestors. And at least one innocent man with them. The thought punched through Subei's righteous fury, and suddenly it didn't feel so righteous. Suddenly, he found himself wondering if anyone else had been in that house. The screaming hadn't sounded like the old man. The bloodrage faltered a moment. Faltered enough that Subei regained control of his voice again.

"The old man wasn't our enemy. Nor anyone else in that house," he said, quietly. "Anyone besides the two soldiers."

"I don't have enemies," the bloodrage said through Bataar's mouth. "Only victims."

Chapter Twenty-Nine

SUBEI

The fires had all but burned out by morning, and the chill of the night was swept away on a warm southerly wind. Even the birds had arrived to sing, their song flitting and dancing through the forest. It was almost picturesque. Assuming one's eyes were closed. Nostrils, too.

Devastation. Probably that was the best word for it. Subei's memory of the night prior was poor, mostly bloody flashes and piercing screams. The scene before him left little to the imagination, however. Mud, blood, and ancestors knew what else was strewn across the ground, smeared along tree trunks, splattered across his face, caught in his beard, and even stuck in the trees above, somehow.

During the fighting, he'd had a hard time counting the number of Zhong soldiers. Now it was beyond impossible. A few bodies were intact. Most weren't. Some didn't even look to be bodies. Just scraps. An errant finger or part of a leg. Looked like the extras left over from making a man. Except these scraps had once been men. Men who'd had dreams. Men who'd had hopes, desires.

Men who'd killed Kashi.

Subei clenched his fist. Men who'd learned a good hard lesson about the bloodrage.

They weren't the only ones who'd learned a lesson, though. All those that had witnessed his and Bataar's madness had been changed by it. He could see it in their eyes. All those that still drew breath, that was. A day ago, there had been twenty of them on the hunt. Now only five remained. Mahtma, Ghula, Bataar, himself, and Vachir. The last they'd found pinned beneath a burning branch, one arm crushed all to pieces and his helmet mangled. He was a tough old warrior, though, and already up and about. He bore his wounds with a dignity becoming of a kheshig guard.

Ghula was walking with something of a limp as she gathered up what horses could be found, and Mahtma was most certainly nursing a wound or two beneath her robe that she refused to acknowledge, but both still drew breath. Meanwhile, Bataar looked more a training post than a man, covered in all manner of cuts and gashes and bloody openings. Nothing serious, though. Certainly his body was just as magically toughened as Subei's and, as he'd learned last night, even the full force of a stabbing sword couldn't fully pierce it now.

And that was before Kashi had died. Before they'd. . . consumed his magic.

Subei looked down at his hands. They were cracked and blistered, the skin a patchwork of scabs and cuts and bruises. But for the most part, they were fine. As was the rest of him. Bloodied, certainly. But far from broken. Far from injured with any severity. Subei figured he should've felt relieved about that. Figured he should've felt appalled by the scene before him. Instead, he felt nothing. He'd killed ancestors knew how many men and felt nothing. And now his brother was dead, and still he felt nothing. Not despair. Not remorse. Not even pain. Just nothing. A great emptiness. Like looking into the sky on a night when the stars were gone. Void.

"There's not even a body to mourn," Subei said to himself, head hanging as he knelt beside the river. Its swift current rushed ever past, the surface shining in the morning light as if the events of the prior night were already forgotten. Swept away.

Bataar's heavy footsteps approached from behind and a shadow blocked the sun. He took in a breath to speak, but Subei cut him off.

"We need a pyre. For the others."

211

"You know there isn't time."

"Gather some wood."

On the steppe, they would have set the bodies out for a sky burial. Would have left them for the animals, to be devoured and returned to the earth, as were all things in time. But this was not the steppe, and he'd be damned if any Zhong bastards were going to find and desecrate the bodies of their fallen. No, it was best to burn them.

Bataar sighed, and there was pain in the ragged exhale.

"Kashi was my brother as much as yours."

"Don't."

"The scouts, our guards, First Rider Ren. They were our people. *Are* our people, but—"

"Gather some damn wood!" Ah, there was some feeling. Anger. All too familiar these days.

"Subei." Bataar bent over with a wince, a hand on his ribs, then dropped to one knee. "Kashi's death. . . " He fought a rush of sour emotion then, face contorting for several long moments until he got it under control.

Another ragged sigh, then. "There will be time to mourn the fallen. A lifetime to mourn them—and see their sacrifice woven into a mighty and powerful song."

Sounded as much like he was convincing himself as anyone.

He clenched a fist and his eyes went hard. "But we turned east to catch Ru. If we don't keep after her, all of this was for nothing." He gestured to the glade of corpses, then winced again. Not from physical pain this time, Subei suspected.

"I'll not leave their bodies here where their ancestors can barely even see them."

"I. . . still can't even process last night. It happened, I know it did, but it doesn't feel real. I don't have time to feel sorry for myself. Neither do you. Not now. Not yet. Ru cannot escape us."

"That's all you care about, isn't it?" Subei snapped. "In Chobei. Last night. If we'd just kept them talking—" Subei cut himself off. He wanted to hurl the blame at Bataar. To snarl it. Wanted his words to hurt his brother, but he found he couldn't call forth such venom. He was too hollow for more rage. Instead, his words came out slow, quiet. "Find wood. If there's any left unburned."

Bataar's voice boiled with barely restrained anger as he spoke next.

"Our brother is dead, Subei. We can never go back to our old lives." He formed a small orb in hand, then stared at it for a moment. "I saved one brother but lost another in the process. Perhaps. . . " he trailed off, cursed. "Perhaps if I'd embraced my magic sooner, I could have saved you both. I could have *made* the bloodrage help us." He growled then, from deep in his chest. An angry sound, but there was pain in it, too. "This magic is a weapon, and I will make myself strong enough to wield it. If I must be the sword and the shield that separates our people from this?" He gestured to the slaughter with his free hand. "Then I accept. I am prepared to do what I must. Kashi died for this cause. I will not see that count for nothing."

Subei said nothing as he stood and turned away.

Bataar looked up, frowning. "Where are you going?"

"To find wood."

He cursed as Subei left him behind.

The shadows were long, but shrinking as the sun rose higher. Somehow, despite last night's ravages, there was still plenty of unburned wood in the Longlarch. Subei wordlessly gathered an armful, then another, then another and another and still more. The others joined him, one by one. The work was miserably hot and deathly silent.

By midday, the pyre was built and the dead piled atop it.

The five people still drawing breath gathered around it. It was proper that words were to be spoken. For a day, the lorecallers would become woe-speakers and a great eulogy would be crafted. A eulogy that would tell of the dead's deeds and conquests. Their greatest triumphs, and how the world forever changed for their having been a part of it. But there were no woe-speakers here. Even fewer pretty words.

It would have been easy to light the pyre with an orb, but somehow, that felt wrong. Subei lit it with flint and steel. The fire caught fast. It was still burning as the survivors forded the river, then rode east. For the second time in the last week, Subei found himself trying not to think about the smoke staining sky behind as he rode away.

Chapter Thirty

SUBEI

Calm, Subei told himself. Inhale, hold, release. Inhale, hold, release.

Kashi's shocked face as the orb exploded.

The explosion enveloping him. . .

Shit. Subei gritted his teeth hard enough his jaw popped as he tried to push the thoughts away. Meditation had never been easy, but it'd never been this hard, either. In the predawn dark, anger and grief ran rampant through his thoughts and deprived him of even a moment's peace.

After lighting the pyre, they'd broken out of the Longlarch and traveled the rest of the day across wide, open plains. Ridden through half the night, too. By then, everyone had needed rest. And they'd made up any ground Ru had gained, probably. How could they not with so many fresh remounts? Even with just the horses they'd been able to round up, there were too many empty saddles.

All the same, it felt wrong to just continue the hunt. To just leave Kashi and the honorable dead behind. Their loss should have rippled out across the world. Should have changed the course of history. Should have been mourned for a month. More. A season—but the world was wide and uncaring. And while Subei and Bataar might have wept for their fallen, for their lost brother, the world did not.

The Ghangerai army would still be marching.

The false heirs would still be running.

And so what was there to do but be swept along with it? At least it was distracting.

"Quiet your mind, Subei," Mahtma's sharp voice pierced the dark. He'd almost forgotten about her, sitting in front of him, cross-legged in the dim morning. "Follow Bataar's example. He is calm, focused but relaxed. You are tense, your thoughts clouded. I can see that from here."

Subei opened his eyes a smidgen, squinting at the monk.

"Your eyes are closed."

"One who sees only with their eyes blinds themself to the world."

Well, that was helpful.

"Relax, breathe deep. Calm yourself, and let go."

The only thing Subei managed to let go was the sarcastic remark building in his throat as he tried to do as instructed.

"It is more important now than ever before that you master this, Son of Kemu. Do not let pain weaken—"

Subei's eyes shot open at that. His fist clenched.

Mahtma frowned at him, her severe eyes open now too and cutting straight through to his core. "If you're not going to try, we're wasting our time."

"Subei's just anxious, is all," Bataar said, shaking himself alert now. "Take a walk, brother."

Subei pulled at the grass in front of him a moment, teeth gritted.

"Yeah, just a walk." His grip tightened, and he ripped the grass from the ground. "That'll fix *everything*."

"I'll ensure Ghula works you harder tonight, seeing as you've so much energy to burn. Go on, then," Mahtma huffed.

He slipped away into the dark to pace a slow circle around their camp. They'd stopped in a crook between three hills, hidden from sight in pretty much all directions. It was atop the ridge line of these hills he walked now.

The surround was vast and quiet. Chilled still with the lingering mists of night, their translucent forms shifted gently above the knee-high grass. They'd burn off soon, when the sun was up, but for now, their ghostly forms wandered the plains aimlessly. In the distance beyond them, the land sloped upward ever so slightly, the grass-covered earth rising in hills that, unless it was just a trick of the eye, grew taller the further east they went. Might've been Ren could have told them what waited there. Not anymore.

Subei's body ached as he walked, fresh bruises covering him in a dozen different places from the prior night's training. After he'd told Ghula and the others about the sword that'd been unable to pierce his shoulder, experimentation had been required. But the sword that'd barely cut his shoulder, that had happened before Kashi's death. With that additional magic, well, blades weren't enough to cut his skin anymore. Were enough to leave aching bruises—especially when Ghula was the one whacking at him—but not much else. His skin still felt normal to the touch, but any blow that landed on him might as well have had to go through a layer of chainmail before he even felt it. There was a time when Subei would have been ecstatic about that. There was also a time when he'd had a younger brother.

Circuit of the camp nearly complete, Subei spotted Bataar's still form in the darkness ahead. Mahtma must have returned to camp for he was alone.

"Like I said, just needed a walk, right?" he asked as Subei approached.

"It should have been me."

Bataar opened his eyes and scrunched his brow.

"Huh?"

"You let the bloodrage out to save me." Subei stared into the distance as he spoke, eyes seeing nothing but memories of the fighting. "And Kashi paid the price for it."

"I did what I had to, brother." Bataar's tone was guarded now.

"Say what you really want to, *brother.*"

A long pause, then. *Getting up the nerve? Go on, say it.*

"If you'd released the bloodrage too, Kashi—"

"Would still be alive." Subei growled the words because he knew they were true. Knew he deserved the pain they caused. And then there was the further pain. The realization that even if he had given in to the rage when it demanded, it could have chosen to defy them. It could have let Kashi die anyway, if it'd wanted. The bloodrage was sentient and, worse, it was working toward its own ends.

"The damned thing made our peril its leverage," Subei said when he could manage words again. "It used us."

Bataar was silent a long time then, as Subei stood fuming. When he spoke next, though, his words were calm. As if he'd practiced them.

"Fire burns ever toward its own ends, brother, but we use it to give us warmth. To heat metal. To raze our enemy's towns." He set his jaw firm, nodded once. "The difference between fire as a weapon of war and a natural disaster, is control."

"Don't twist this back on me," Subei snapped. "You can't control this. You can't wield it. It has defied *you* already." Subei threw his arms in the air, exasperated at his brother's unconvinced expression. "What might have happened if it had helped as soon as you released it? Kashi's dead because I didn't give in to the rage, but he's just as dead because the rage chose not to help. Have you stopped to consi—"

"Rider approaching," Bataar said suddenly and jumped to his feet. If Subei weren't mistaken, his brother sounded happy for the interruption. To the north, a lone dot was moving toward them.

"Friend, or foe?" Subei asked, feeling the magic rise inside him and not sure if it was in response to his anger or the potential new threat.

But as the rider drew closer, it became clear she was Ghangerai.

"Sons of Kemu," she said, head bowed as her horse came to a stop. A moment later, and she produced the seal of their father—updated now to show he was khagan. "I've been tracking you for several days. The fire in the forest helped." She nodded. "I bring word from the khagan. The United Army is on the march. Has been for some days now."

"Where are they bound for?" Bataar asked immediately.

"I will lead you there," the messenger said.

"Tell the others," Subei said, gesturing sharply toward their small camp. The messenger bowed again, then took off at a gallop. Subei turned on Bataar. "This conversation isn't over. You're a mad man, brother, if you think you can wield this weapon after all its shown us."

"The United Army is on the move," Bataar said, refusing to engage as he squinted ahead.

Subei bit back a curse, but followed his brother's eyes to where a large bank of clouds towered far to the east. A storm waiting for them, perhaps, and they were headed straight for it. Ru was that way and showing no sign of slowing. Hopefully that was the direction of the United Army. It would be good to be among their own people again. Maybe one of them could teach Bataar some sense.

"She's headed straight for the others," Bataar said, breaking the silence. "I can feel them clearly now."

Subei focused inward a moment and pushed a little magic into Wolf Catches Scent. His brother was right. He could feel Ru east of them, and beyond her, he could feel *them*. A group of heirs they'd been calling "the others." Five in total. Ru had been heading straight for them for days now. And they'd been heading straight toward her.

"Her brother told her to go to them," Bataar said. "Probably thinks those are the only people that can protect her."

Subei frowned toward the horizon. "We'll reach her first. But. . . if we don't, it doesn't matter. We'll end this whole hunt in one stroke. Be done with all this."

Chapter Thirty-One

SUBEI

"Ancestors above." Subei stared, mouth hanging open.

At first, he'd thought it a vast storm bank hanging on the horizon. Closer now, he realized how wrong he'd been. But they were so high in the sky, it didn't seem possible they could be anything but clouds. And yet, they were something else entirely: mountains. And not just any mountains, the Ghairkhan range. Might've been Ren had known the land down this way, but it didn't take an experienced scout to mark the Ghairkhan. Mightiest mountain range in the world, people said, and strictly forbidden land. They were the sacred sanctuary of the ancestors. A place few mortals could tread.

But it wasn't the mountains that drew Subei's attention now so much as the sounds coming from them. Or rather, bouncing off them. The clash of steel on steel. The deep thuds of arrows burying themselves in shields. A great battle was underway. Or already lost, depending on which side one was on.

The messenger had led them true, straight to the place where the Ghangerai United Army was punching into the empire proper. An action, it seemed, that had begun by drawing out the Zhong Northern Army.

From where Subei stood atop a rocky hill and looking down into a steep-sided valley, what had happened was all too obvious. To the north, the difficult terrain opened onto plains. Squinting in that direction, he could see panicked groups of Zhong forces in a wild flight back toward the valley. Mounted swarms harried them, darting in with bow and lance time and again. These groups of increasingly small Zhong soldiers stretched all the way to the northern horizon.

"They must have thought they'd won," Bataar scoffed.

"Yes," Ghula said, and such was her enthusiasm the word came out in a prolonged hiss that ended with a smile. "A feigned retreat." Her eyes studied the terrain before them, and Subei could imagine them taking in every detail. She'd been a marshal before a torol, after all. "A regiment would have come first, at least, that's how I would've started it. Not too many warriors, just enough to cause trouble in the outlying villages. Draw attention," she explained. "Then, when the Zhong northern commander sent a force to restore order, I'd have met them with another regiment, maybe two. Not so many as to destroy the force, just enough to raise the alarm, to convince them this incursion would only be put down by the full might of the Northern Army." Her eyes whipped side to side as she spoke, searching for clues in the landscape before them. She nodded then, apparently seeing something to confirm her theorizing.

"And once that army arrived, we'd make a great big show with say, a touman. They'd expect to find us vicious, stupid, and brave, and that's what we'd show them. Because what chance could ten thousand Ghangerai have against the—twenty-five, maybe? Thirty?—thousand strong Northern Zhong Army? Of course, we'd break before their might. And they'd follow, because they'd have to. Honor would demand they drive us back into the wasteland. Remind us of our place." She laughed then. "So we retreat, and they give chase. And maybe they notice when they're led out of the safety of the mountains, but look, the enemy's just ahead! And they're tired, slowing even! So the Zhong chase on, and their army stretches itself out."

Bataar side-eyed Ghula, then smirked. "And that's when we hit them."

"And that's when we hit them. A touman from the east, another from the west. A fourth from the Zhong rear then one right up the middle. At least, that's how I'd have done it with fifty thousand warriors." She turned to Subei then, looking all-too pleased. "The khagan expected how many in the United Army?"

"Four hundred and fifty thousand."

She cackled then and waved a hand at the chaos below.

"And just like that, the Zhong Northern Army would be reduced to rabble."

Had it all happened like that? Subei couldn't say for sure, but it must have been close enough. The only meaningful collection of Zhong soldiers he could make out was in the center of the valley, rallied around a light-blue banner depicting a full moon and a quill. They wore heavy armor and carried large shields, their metal reflecting the midday sun like light off a river. They were packed in tight, backs together and shields up as they fought off encirclement.

Ghangerai riders swarmed them like a disturbed hornet's nest. They swooped in, time and again, to deliver death at the ends of their arrows. Just as they drew within striking range of the Zhong spears, they'd veer aside and melt away. Return arrows chased after them, of course, but it was far more difficult to hit a warrior on horseback than a huddled crowd of infantry.

The mounted archers battered against the Zhong ranks like waves upon a shore, crashing and hammering forward in one moment, then breaking and slipping back the next. The tip of an attack would appear, charging forward, and then—just as the enemy adjusted to repel it—would dissipate, leaving nothing but trampled soil and a few dead Zhong behind.

"This will be a fine victory for our newly united khanate," Vachir said, his injured arm suspended in a sling.

"And perhaps, better yet," Bataar said, eyes turning south. Subei followed his gaze, but even as he did, he felt the pull. The false heirs were approaching.

At the far southern end of the valley, what must have been a Zhong relief force was appearing. Hardly enough soldiers to do anything, but it was almost certain they had no idea what had happened. All they knew, as they drew into view, was their fellows were ahead, huddled up and besieged. The column of infantry doubled their pace, marching to save their comrades. At their rear, Subei spotted riders.

"The false heirs," Subei said, nodding.

"All of them?" Ghula asked, a frown cutting through her mask of glee.

"Yes." Subei focused inward, then nodded again. "I'm counting six. Ru made it to them."

"We didn't have time for the pyre," Bataar said under his breath. Subei chose not to respond to that. Would've liked to, but now was hardly the moment.

"They accepted her into their group, then?" Mahtma stroked her chin. "They're working together, and with the army, no less. It would seem they are aware of their magic, and the Zhong would wield it against us, just as we would them."

"So they haven't killed each other yet," Bataar nodded as he spoke. "What does it matter if we fight six weak heirs or a couple strong ones?"

Subei's hand fidgeted at the hilt of his saber.

"We can end this today."

"As much as it pains me to say, we don't even need to fight," Ghula said, eyes scouring the new Zhong arrivals. "The rest of the United Army won't be far off now. They'll make short work of these reinforcements and the heirs."

"They're mounted," Subei pointed out. "The false heirs will flee as soon as they realize how bad this is. Run back behind their walls and garrisons."

"We'll ride them down," Ghula said as a simple matter of fact, which it probably was.

"Maybe." Subei winced at the thought and fought the scowl pulling at the edges of his mouth. "But every step will bring them closer to reinforcements."

"We set a trap, then." Ghula nodded. "The northern path leads down the mountain. Vachir, you will—"

"Look," Bataar cut her off, but his words were calm, even if there was an undeniable excitement at the edges. He raised an arm and pointed. At the back of the Zhong reinforcements, a woman astride a horse had broken from the ranks. She sat alone, ignoring the battle raging not two hundred paces from her, and stared. Right up at them.

"She knows we're here," Subei said. "Wants us to know it too."

"She's trying to lure us down where she can use what's left of that army to her benefit," Ghula said. "We should not take this bait."

Subei agreed and yet, he was ready to ride right into it if that meant ending this hunt. This was a trap, but they could overwhelm it, strong as they were with the magic now. Before Subei could give voice to these thoughts though, five other riders broke from the Zhong ranks and joined the first. The other false heirs. The foremost of them, the woman who'd rode out alone, raised an arm and pointed. Up the steep slope roughly halfway between them and the heirs, there was a meadow. It ended in an expanse of rock jutting out over the valley.

"She's proposing neutral ground." Bataar cracked his knuckles and smiled. "Ooh, I like this one. She's got guts."

No. It's a safe bet this is still some sort of trap. An ambush will be waiting for us there, surely, Subei knew. But after Kashi, he wasn't ready to be patient. He was ready to be done with all of this. Ready to stop seeing Kashi's death over and over again. Ready to stop fearing he'd see Bataar's next. It could all be over today if they prevailed here, and then maybe he could find a way to wash the bitter taste from his mouth.

"I don't believe this to be an advisable strategy," Mahtma said, but Subei wasn't listening. The Zhong heirs stood down in the valley, posing a challenge, and they would not go unanswered.

Subei stepped from the trees that had obscured them. Staring directly down at the heirs, he raised an arm and pointed to the meadow. And it was done. The heirs broke from their soldiers and led their horses up the hillside.

"It's done," Subei said, trying to keep his voice steady. "Now let's see to it."

Chapter Thirty-Two

SUBEI

Not a soldier in sight. Were the other heirs really so foolish as to come alone?

Subei had expected something, certainly. He and Bataar had arrived well before the Zhong heirs, and with Ghula and Mahtma's help, scouted the surrounding woods.

But here it was. Just them and an empty clearing. As long as their opponents didn't arrive with an armed escort, it seemed the coming fight was going to be an honest one. And if they did arrive with additional soldiers, well, Vachir had ridden to alert the khagan his sons were near. He'd be on his way back immediately with warriors of his own.

"Still don't like this," Ghula said, as Subei and Bataar strode into the clearing. She held back with Mahtma in the tree line, as they'd reluctantly agreed.

"It is a folly of the highest order," Mahtma replied before falling out of earshot. Subei didn't bother with a response. What could she do anyway? Command the sons of her khagan? Forcefully try to stop them? Or worse, join them in the fight? As impressive a fighter as she was, it wouldn't matter. Neither for her nor Ghula. This wasn't a fight they could survive.

Subei reached the center of the meadow, then tried several deep breaths to calm the simmering anger within. It didn't help much. There was a good chance he'd be meeting his ancestors today. He should have been nervous.

Their meeting ground was smaller than it'd looked from afar. He'd envisioned a wide, flat strip of mountain meadow. Instead, he'd found a wispy patch of grass, interrupted all too frequently by fallen trees, rocks, and disconcertingly, the abrupt cliff off to his left. Casting a glance over its edge, he could just see down into the valley. But the remains of the battle weren't his concern now.

A gust of wind swelled through the tree line, setting the leaves off in a chorus of whispers. Crickets chirped all around, and even the birds were singing, their songs floating on the breeze. It was almost peaceful. This place was nothing like the Longlarch. Where those trees had huddled close, creating nothing but shadows and deceptions, here they stood far apart, close enough to shade the ground, but sparse enough to prevent anyone from approaching unseen.

"Today will be a glorious day for the khanate, brother," Bataar said, rolling his neck and shaking out his arms. "Our father will crush the Zhong in the valley, and we'll crush them here."

"'Glory' is far from my mind at the moment." *Revenge feels more appropriate*, he thought, before a hesitation crept over him. *These Zhong heirs have not wronged me.*

He hated the thought even as it surfaced. He turned to his anger instead. Sought solace in its comfortable fury. All the same, he was relieved to see there was no one else around. No huts or farms nearby. No reason at all for regular folk to be about.

Can't hurt innocents if there aren't any to hurt.

"You look worried, brother," Bataar said with a scoff. "But what's Father always say? Easier to move a mountain than change a person's nature?"

Subei readied a biting retort, but Wolf Catches Scent interrupted his thoughts, jumping to the forefront of his mind. "The false heirs are near," he said. And then, a flicker of movement caught his eye. "They're here."

They emerged from the other side of the clearing. Left their mounts with reins wrapped around low-hanging branches and advanced into the clearing as a group. And they didn't have any soldiers with them. Were they suicidal?

"Ooh, I want the big one," Bataar said, shaking life into his hands.

And damned if that description wasn't accurate. Subei looked out to the approaching group but found he couldn't pull his eyes from the giant of a man at their center. Seemed a mistake of the ancestors to allow such a man to exist. The tallest of the other Zhong heirs only rose to the middle of his chest. He towered over them, half shading those that followed. And he wasn't all height, either. A breastplate was stretched across his chest, though it was barely capable of holding in all the muscle beneath. He carried what appeared to be a sledgehammer resting across one shoulder. Looked more like a plaything in his hands than an unwieldy tool. Subei looked to his own shield resting against his leg. Didn't seem much use against a weapon like that. Then again, big, strong men died to Baji's Burning Fury the same as anyone else.

"Hail, Ghangerai invaders," the foremost of the group said as they drew closer. Subei finally managed to pull his eyes from the monster of a man to take the measure of the rest of the group. One was obscured in the big man's shadow, blocked by his bulk. Looked to be a woman, maybe?

In front of the big man stood another woman, the first strands of gray beginning in her long hair. She had a stern face with sharp features and looked them over as she approached. Her mouth was turned down slightly, as if she'd caught a displeasing smell on the wind.

Two men stood beside her. The first looked every bit a soldier, wearing plate mail not dissimilar from those that had ambushed them in the Longlarch. He'd a longsword on one hip, a short sword on the other. A shield rested across his back, and he wore a helmet tucked tight over his head. Only his eyes peered out from within its depths. They weren't the eyes of a scared man, either. That was for sure.

Beside him stood the strangest of the group by far—disregarding the giant, of course, which was a hard thing to do. It'd been a long time since Subei had seen a westerner, their lands far beyond the deserts of Mercer, but this man certainly was one. His skin was pale as mare's milk, and his face was thin and too much longer than it was wide. He'd eyes blue as the eternal sky—a fine blessing, that—and his hair rolled back at all angles in small curls the color of sun-bleached grass. He stood the same height as the soldier next to him and wore a confident smile that said he knew something Subei didn't. From his clothes to his foreign proportions all together, he looked like some strange mix between scholar and adventurer. Though journeying this far from one's homeland was sure to have a strange effect on a man, Subei figured.

The heir that had greeted them stood before the others, a helmet tucked under one arm. He wore plain but fine robes beneath his armor, their silk threads catching in the sunlight. The majority of his chest was covered by steel armor, while the rest of him was protected by thick leather. He carried only a sword at his hip, no other weapons in sight.

He stopped at the center of the clearing, about twenty paces away, and placed his helmet down. Pressing his left hand atop his right, he extended them, palms down, then bowed. His chest lowered near parallel to the ground, but his eyes never left them.

"I am Wu Qian. It's been too long since we've played host to our uncivilized, northern neighbors."

"Hail, Wu, Son of Qian. I am Subei, Son of—"

The man interrupted with a raised hand and a frown.

"Wu is my family name. Qian is my given. You will address me as Wu, or Wu Qian."

"We'll address you as worm food soon," Bataar scoffed.

"Hail, Wu Qian," Subei tried again. "I am Subei, Son of Kemu Khagan, and this is my older brother, Bataar." Subei pressed his knuckles together and returned the bow. "The Zhong rebels have too long forgotten their oath of fealty to our khanate."

"It's been a century since such an oath was sworn and much has changed," Wu Qian said.

"Perhaps time it changed back, hm?" Bataar said.

"Why are we wasting time playing polite with the barbarians?" The person who'd been obscured behind the big man stepped beside Wu Qian. Subei recognized her instantly. The last time he'd seen her, she'd been covered in dirt and clothed in what had pretty much amounted to rags. She'd cleaned up since then, and now wore armor similar to the others—slightly ill-fitting, perhaps, but there was no denying the ferocity in her eyes.

"Ru." Subei nodded to her.

"It's *Yue* Ru to you, barbarian," she snapped back. "Or preferably, nothing at all once I put you in the ground."

Subei side-eyed his brother at yet another correction. Were all Zhong so caught up on names?

"Speaking of in the ground. . ." Her face curled into a cruel scowl then. "Where's the last of you? The younger one. Something happen to him?"

Subei had an orb in hand before he'd even realized it, had already reared back to throw when Bataar caught him.

"Not just yet, brother," he said calmly, but there was a cold fury to his words.

Subei gritted his teeth, then forced himself to breathe out slowly as he snuffed the orb.

Yue Ru spoke to her companions next.

"These men are nothing more than murderers. They'll be satisfied only with violence, and should be treated with such."

Wu Qian placed a hand on her shoulder and eased her back. The anger in her eyes was not stifled in the least. It was obvious she'd felt the touch of the bloodrage. She'd be one to watch out for when it came to blows.

"All of us have been afflicted with this. . . condition," Wu Qian said as he looked down at his own shoulder. No doubt, that was where the bulk of his scars were, Subei thought, seeing as a jagged, white line stretched out from beneath his collar and up his neck. "All of us have felt, to varying degrees, the desire to kill those similarly afflicted. But we've resisted this baser instinct. We are told you have not. Is this true? This is why you've come?"

And there was the plain truth, ugly as it was. One way or another, Subei and his brother had come for blood. But the world wasn't all clear-cut good and evil, right and wrong. It was murky and muddled like a stirred up riverbed.

"You have taken magic that is not yours," Subei said.

"Whether you meant to or not, you have stolen our people's rightful inheritance."

"I would give it back to you, if I could," Wu Qian said, and he looked to mean it.

Truly? He would willingly part wi—

"I don't believe you for a minute," Bataar said, voice quiet but charged. "You may be too noble, or too delusional to admit it, but you'd never give this up." He looked to his own scars, held his arm out before him. "You're addicted."

Wu Qian's mouth bent into a slight frown, but otherwise he did an excellent job of appearing unconvinced.

"Ru says we're here for blood, but so are you. You just don't want to admit it. Want to make us your villains." Bataar took a step forward then. Just a small one, but the false heirs all flinched. "If they could have ridden north and taken our steppe from us, Subei, they'd have done it long ago. But they've never had the strength, so instead they bribe our weaker cousins. They incite us to fight amongst each other, to keep us divided and weak. No more," he snarled and met Wu Qian's gaze. "You're not too noble to resist this magic, you're just worried because we got to it first."

"If that truly is what you believe, I am sorry for you," Wu Qian said. "You may call this magic an inheritance. We call it a curse, and your words now prove we're right."

Damn. Subei found himself starting to nod at that. Stopped as soon as he realized he was doing it, though. These false heirs were no different than their forces down in the valley: fighting a battle they didn't know they'd already lost.

Chapter Thirty-Three

BATAAR

Damned, but this Zhong heir was a dangerous one, with his smooth words and pretty logic. All the better to get him fighting then, Bataar figured. Draw things into an arena where he was advantaged.

"You make everything sound so easy," Bataar said. "So nice and tidy. But not all of you resist this 'curse.' *Ru*," he said, intentionally using the wrong form of address. "I see the bloodrage in your eyes, waiting to take control."

"I'm unfamiliar with this term." Qian looked to Ru, then back to Bataar.

Subei cleared his throat. "It's the compulsion to gather more magic. It's that compulsion given strength and freedom. It takes control of your body and—"

"Perhaps we'll demonstrate it for you today," Bataar said, nodding at his brother's words, then instinctually probing for the now all-too familiar presence in the abyss beneath his core. Didn't feel it at the moment, though. That was strange, but Qian was speaking again, drawing his attention back.

"This compulsion is what brings you here to make war on our lands and people? Just because one can inflict violence doesn't mean they should."

"You want us to be ashamed of our strength? Is the wolf made lesser because he kills the deer?" Bataar asked. "No, that is its nature. And ruling these lands is ours. Everything beneath the eternal blue sky is rightfully ours, so long as we have the strength to take it."

Qian picked his helmet off the ground and pulled it tight over his head. *Now we're getting somewhere.* Bataar withheld his smile.

"I had hoped it would not come to this. But if blood is what you want, blood is what you'll have."

"See?" Bataar said, looking to his younger brother. "They're convinced now that their cause is noble, and we're just savages. Now they can try to kill us without feeling bad about it."

"A proposal, if you please," Qian said, his expression stoic, unconcerned, even. "Our champion against yours? Let us spare what violence we can."

"The big one?" Bataar asked, unable to hold back his smile now.

"Qi Teng?" the seeming leader of the Zhong heirs asked the giant. "Do you accept?"

Teng raised an eyebrow at the sharp-featured woman beside him.

"Teng," she said. "Break the barbarian."

He came roaring in with that sledgehammer of his held high. Bataar snapped his hand open and conjured an orb in one motion. All too easy, now. And it'd put an end to this fight before it'd even properly begun. He took aim at Teng's head—but. . . wait. Bataar snuffed the orb out then dove to the side as Teng's hammer came screaming down. The ground shook where it fell, but Bataar was already back on his feet, behind the giant now.

Killing the false heir immediately would win the fight, but there'd still be the other five. Probably they didn't know how to use their magic—not in any meaningful way—but if he drew this fight out a bit, he might learn what techniques they'd developed. That'd give him and Subei an edge in the—

The hammer came swinging in again, and Bataar blocked it with his shield. It was a glancing blow, but still it ripped the shield from his arm and sent it flying to the edge of the cliff. Bataar's arm ached from even that partial blow.

His body was largely immune to blades and arrows, now, but bashing attacks? Those, it seemed, he could still feel, even if lessened. He shook out his arm as he took the measure of his opponent.

"I'd have drawn my saber if I knew we were sparring," he said. "But I thought we were fighting for real. Show me what you can really do."

The giant's only response was to rush forward again, hammer raised. Bataar called on North Wind Scours as he swept his hands down and to the side. Gale force wind blasted the giant off balance.

"Put down the hammer and fight me like an heir!" An orb next, just a small one. Bataar made sure to land it right in the middle of his opponent's breastplate. The explosion wasn't enough to get through it, and that'd been the point. It was enough, however, to drive the wind from Teng and knock him over. As he landed, his grip on the hammer gave out and the heavy thing fell away with a thud.

Bataar reached toward it, palm upraised, and through his magic, he could feel it laying in the grass. He clenched his fist next, then flicked his hand to the side, and the hammer was tossed away. Jong had used this technique back in Chobei, and then Subei in the Longlarch. It seemed connected to the walling technique. All the World a Shield, Kashi had named that one. This derivative, though, was slightly different. All the World a Weapon, they'd named it.

Teng scrambled after the hammer, and Bataar focused on it again. Would have been better if he could focus on his opponent's body. Would have been better if the magic could wrap him up in its invisible grasp and toss him away, but the technique seemed only able to affect inanimate objects. Good enough. Another flick of Bataar's wrist, and the hammer jumped away again, this time thrown all the way to the cliff's edge. It teetered there a moment, then tipped over and fell from view.

"Now, then. Are there any more toys I need to take from you, or can we fight?"

Teng looked lost a moment, then drew a knife from his belt. Or, it looked a knife in his hand, but was every bit a sword.

He came in slashing then, and Bataar danced away, dodging and ducking each swing. Small bursts of North Wind Scours

233

helped him keep his opponent stumbling and off balance. Surely this was meant as a taunt? Or, no. A stratagem. Teng was refusing to show the extent of the false heirs' magic. The longer it went on, though, the more Bataar doubted. Teng wasn't holding back. Not even the most rudimentary display of magic accompanied his attacks.

"You're really this weak?" Bataar said under his breath. "So ignorant of the might within you? So be it." He raised his voice now, "This magic is more wasted on you than I thought."

Bataar darted in and faked left, then right, then slipped inside Teng's guard. From directly below the giant's chin, he unleashed an uppercut and a double strength blast of North Wind Scours. Teng's head snapped back as he was blasted backward, flipping once then landing on his face. A cloud of dust rose around his fallen form, and he groaned. The fingers on one hand twitched slightly, but he was otherwise still.

Bataar straightened up and turned to face the Zhong heirs. He wiped a single bead of sweat from his brow and smiled. Shock—and more plainly, fear—was plastered across the faces of the five remaining heirs.

Before the bandit's death, Bataar and his brothers had struggled to use much of Baji's magic. Struggled to do things like conjure an orb or unleash a wind strike, forget anything more advanced. If these Zhong heirs hadn't killed yet, then they were still using that barest splinter of magic originally given to them. This would hardly be a fight at all.

"That was your champion? The mightiest of you? Truly?" Bataar asked, then called an orb to hand. He stretched out, holding it above Teng's still form. "I admit, I'm disappointed."

"Our champion has been defeated," Qian said hurriedly. "We concede this ground to you, Sons of Kemu Khagan." He bowed slightly. "Honor dictates we withdraw. We will collect Teng and inform our commander—"

"No one's withdrawing," Subei shouted and there was surprise on his face, as if he hadn't planned to say anything. But Bataar understood all too well. If they won here, now, *today*, then it was over. Kashi's death would have meaning, and Baji's magic would never be used against their people. Better still, once the war was done, there'd be no reason to push themselves hard enough to need the bloodrage. Let it stew in those abyssal depths beneath his stomach, Bataar decided. It could wait there forever, once the magic was reclaimed. Once today was finished.

A few more deaths were all it would take, starting with Teng.

There was the soft but distinct sound of metal hissing across wood as the heir that looked to be a seasoned soldier drew his sword.

"You'll respect the rules of war, or you'll die by them, barbarian," he said to Bataar. "Your magic is impressive, but there's no tool more tried and tested than sharpened steel."

"I once would have agreed with you." Bataar drew his saber from its sheath, gave the weapon a long look, then let it fall to the dirt. "What the ancestors have given us is far more powerful than swords or arrows. Maybe one day, more powerful than even armies. But you wouldn't know about that, would you?" He locked eyes with Qian. "You've resisted this *'curse'*, after all."

The apparent leader of the Zhong heirs, who'd spoken with so much assuredness before, was visibly buffeted by the words. The confidence was gone from his eyes, and he took a half step back before stopping himself.

"How many have you killed?"

Bataar let the orb slip in his grasp, dangling from just his fingertips.

"Not enough."

He let it fall.

Chapter Thirty-Four

SUBEI

The orb exploded in a shower of flame, steaming soil, and decidedly, no viscera. Subei frowned at that. What'd happened? He peered through the lingering smoke to find a shallow crater five or so strides off target, and Teng still in one piece. From among the false heirs, the sharp-faced woman's scars were glowing. She was breathing hard, chest rising and falling, and her hands were swept to one side.

She'd thrown a wind strike, driven the orb off course.

"You *can* use some magic, then," Bataar said. The explosion must have shaken Teng back to his senses, though, for the big man stirred just then.

"Away from him, barbarian!" the sharp-faced woman shouted and sprinted forward, a spear in her grasp. She'd never make it in time, though. Bataar already had another orb in hand. He threw this one, spiking it right down at Teng. It flew through the air, sizzling, popping—screaming almost—then disappeared with a sad hiss.

Wu Qian had his hand out this time, scars alight.

"Now how'd you do that?" Bataar asked with a frown, but there wasn't time for an answer as the sharp-faced woman lunged in with a two-handed thrust. In the same moment, Teng's monstrous hand whipped up to catch Bataar by the throat—or would have, but for Subei's blast of North Wind Scours. It shoved his brother aside such that the woman's blade hissed through only air, and Teng's hand snapped closed on nothing.

An orb, next. Subei sprinted as he threw it, aiming for Wu Qian before he could use his technique to counter it. The fine speaker in his fine robes barely had time to widen his fine eyes. The others were just beginning to lean away, but the soldier among them was faster and threw himself in front of Wu Qian, catching the orb on his shield. The explosion blew him backward, sent him spinning through the air to land several steps away, his shield molten red and hissing steam.

The foul black smoke left in the orb's wake parted as the Zhong heirs charged through it, screaming their battle cries. Corner an animal, and it was like to lash out. One had to admire their bravery in the face of certain death.

Bataar danced away to the right, heading up the slope.

"Brother!" Subei shouted at him but was cut short as the westerner came in swinging.

He was screaming in a foreign tongue, his piercing blue eyes wide as he stab, stab, stabbed with a thin-bladed sword. Its tip might as well have been a pinprick—less, even—as it found the weak spots in Subei's armor.

Confusion clouded Blue Eye's features as Subei gave ground but continued to let the attacks land. The last of them, a two footed lunge with all of the man's weight behind it, might've managed to produce a drop of blood. Could've been mud, though.

Subei retreated another few paces, luring his opponent in, then struck out with an orb in hand. He'd meant to plant it in the middle of the westerner's chest—but that thin blade with its fancy hilt flicked out in a blur to drive the blow off target. He managed to hold onto the orb, though, until the foreigner's scars lit up and a wind strike blasted it free of his grasp.

A wash of heat then, as Baji's Burning Fury detonated off to the side.

Another wind strike came then, but Subei swept it away with hardly a thought. Blue Eyes blinked in surprise, his smug smile wiped away. Subei drew his saber and darted in for a killing blow.

Something flashed in his periphery—Wu Qian coming in with a hacking slash. Subei let it fall across his shoulders so he could finish his strike on Blue Eyes. Both attacks landed, one after the other. Subei hardly felt anything. Blue Eyes, meanwhile, fell away, one hand clasped to his now bleeding shoulder. Not a killing blow, though. In the split second Subei had spent looking at Wu Qian, his aim had slid from Blue Eye's neck to where it met his shoulder. There was still some armor there. Enough to save his life.

Finish the foreigner then handle Wu Qian, Subei thought. He called another orb and even managed to rear his arm back before the crackling ball of explosive magic was snuffed from existence.

"That's getting annoying." He frowned at his empty palm, then raised his eyes to Wu Qian. In one hand the heir held a short and straight blade, very unlike the sabers of the steppe. His other hand was empty, no doubt intentionally so in order to use magic.

"Even the mightiest blow is far inferior to the power of restraint, Subei."

Subei threw his saber at him.

Wu Qian slapped it away with his sword—leaving him open to the wind strike Subei launched with a left hook and the orb that followed it a moment later, thrown underhand from his right.

Wu Qian took the full force of the wind strike so as to focus on the orb. It almost made it to him—little bolts of lightning arcing out to make contact—when the false heir waved a hand, and the attack dissipated like so much water turned to steam.

Subei growled and rushed in, another orb already in hand but was staggered by a series of wind strikes. Blue Eyes. He was back on his feet now and throwing them with everything he had.

Subei snuffed his own orb—couldn't very well use it from the middle of such a gale—and met Blue Eye's wind strikes with his own. The two barrages clashed with howling fury, buffeting winds whipping outward in all directions. To Subei, it almost felt like a good practice session, like the ones he and Bataar shared as they warmed up each night.

The exchange continued only briefly before Blue Eye's strikes began to falter, Subei's lazy, but still more powerful blows beating his back. Subei threw another punch, then spun his momentum into a spinning side kick. He put his full power into this strike. His foot whipped out at chest level and a wind strike rushed from it, blasting through several of the westerner's before bowling him over.

Wu Qian was still staggering back to his feet as Subei turned to face him. He'd have to die first, Subei decided. Couldn't rely on Baji's Burning Fury so long as the bastard was around.

"Wu Qian, you're an honorable opponent. I regret we—"

An orb caught Subei in the shoulder. Blinding light. An explosion. Something ripped into his face, knocked his head backward, and then he was flying. He slammed to the ground and bounced several times, each impact heavy and hard. He was sure of it. Problem was, he didn't feel it. Didn't feel much at all as he rose, feet unsteady beneath him. His ears rang and bitter smoke bit at his nostrils. The world spun. The sky wavered and danced while the ground bucked and kicked like the sea. Amidst it all, a lone figure stood, an orb in her hand.

"Reap what you sow, barbarian."

Yue Ru.

She took a few steps closer, then winced in feigned pain.

"That's going to be a nasty scar."

Subei squinted to see her better, confused as to what she meant. His right eye was blurry, his vision stained red. He raised his fingers to it, and they came away wet. Hot blood ran down his face, stuck to his neck. The pain came then, and he realized the extent of the wound. Couldn't get its exact nature, but it didn't take a physician to know a damned big gash was torn through his face. His tongue felt along the inside of his right cheek, swam through the quickly pooling blood, and found it could feel all the way through. Could feel the tangled, burned mess of hair that had been his beard.

His armor, too, was destroyed. Where the orb had detonated, his shoulder piece was completely gone but for a few swinging plates of lamellae and smoking leather. Subei ripped the remains of the pauldron off and tossed it aside.

"Well, at least you won't have to worry about scars if you're dead," Yue Ru said, then threw the second orb. Subei swept it with North Wind Shelters, and it exploded behind him, steaming dirt raining down in thick clumps. She frowned, then scrunched her brow, visibly straining to conjure another orb. Seemed she was just now learning how much energy it took to make the things.

"Enough," Subei whispered as Yue Ru fought to conjure a third orb.

In the Longlarch, he'd been willing to die instead of releasing the rage. And all that'd done had gotten Kashi killed.

"Enough," he said louder as Blue Eyes got back to his feet and raised his fists.

Kashi was dead, and there wasn't even time to come to terms with it because of this damned hunt. Because these damned heirs were drawing out the inevitable.

"*Enough*," he growled, one final time, as Wu Qian advanced, sword at the ready.

One last time, Subei told himself. *One last time, and all of this can end.*

He focused inward, found himself standing at the edge of that spring and staring down into that submerged chasm.

One last time so I never have to again.

He fell face-first into the spring, let himself be consumed by those lightless depths. And as he sunk down into them, he found. . . nothing.

"Huh?" His eyes went wide at that, then he searched all the more. But he was alone, submerged in the abyss and sinking by the moment. And then he found it, the bloodrage. A great, form-less beast below him. Far below him.

He screamed at it, swam toward it—but it was an impossible distance away. And it gave no indication of being aware of his presence. As if it were sleeping. Hibernating, even.

Every time prior, the bloodrage had come unbidden. Not today. It was down in that abyss, and it didn't even notice him.

Why?

The Longlarch.

The thought hit Subei all at once. Did. . . did the bloodrage work like that? Had it so expended itself that night in the forest that it hadn't yet recovered? Was that possible? He'd thought previously the rage was a bottomless, ever-hungry thing. An unlimited wellspring of magic and fury. In this moment, though, he found even the bloodrage had its limits.

"Lose something?" Yue Ru taunted. "Aside from the piece of your face I blew off?"

Subei threw an orb at her, a senseless, anger-fueled move. Wu Qian snuffed it with a gesture.

In response, Yue Ru clapped her hands together. When she drew them apart, the air split with what sounded like the violent, frenzied buzzing of a thousand hornets, but deeper, and more fierce. Blinding light glowed in each of her palms, and a bridge of lightning arced and spat between them. She turned a hand toward him, and the bridge of lightning followed it, arcing forward faster than Subei could see to strike him in the chest.

It lifted him off his feet, his entire body spasming. An embarrassing mix of scream and shriek burst from him as he shook. The ground slammed into him and forced the air from his lungs. He rolled onto his side, half-coughing, half-gasping for air as smoke rose from his lamellar.

"That was just a taste." Yue Ru advanced further, the lightning crackling between her palms. "This next one's for my brother. I'm going to boil your eyes from their sockets, you murdering bastard."

Blue Eyes advanced on the right as well, and Wu Qian on the left.

"I can't blame you for wanting me dead," Subei said, coughing a puff of smoke. And he couldn't. He'd killed her brother, after all. "But that doesn't mean I'm going to let you see it done."

He'd moved slower than he'd intended—his numb, fumbling fingers barely able to form an orb—but they managed it. Subei rolled to the side and whipped his arm out in a throw. Wu Qian waved to dissipate the orb, but Yue Ru jumped to the side anyway, then struck back with her lightning. But the distraction had bought Subei the time he needed to roll to his feet and sling his shield from his back. He ducked behind it as her lighting struck.

The shield's wicker face popped and spat, then burst into flames. It grew warm, then hot, then hotter still as Yue Ru snarled and pushed forward. The magic surging through her hands intensified, growing brighter, its violent buzzing louder by the moment.

Gritting his teeth at the shield burning against his knuckles, Subei caught sight of his saber in the grass. He reached for it with his free hand, scars flaring blue. It moved in response, and he whipped his hand toward Yue Ru. The blade tumbled end over end through the air. It was a poor shot, but its hilt clipped her shoulder on the way past, enough to break her focus. She cursed, and the lightning blinked out of existence.

She scrunched her brow next, scowling into her hands as she fought to conjure the magic once more. Small sparks spluttered, but didn't catch.

Subei didn't wait for them to. His wind strike threw her onto her back, drove the breath from her with a wheezing grunt.

Wu Qian can't counter those, he realized. Ah. When his life wasn't hanging in the balance, he'd like time to chew on that. Uncover what techniques were susceptible and which weren't. It was exactly the kind of puzzle Kashi would have loved to unravel.

"Three against one, huh?" he said, playing for time as the false heirs advanced, each step cautious. Between the orb blast and whatever the hell Yue Ru had done to zap him off his feet, he'd been driven out of the meadow now. Not ten steps behind, the cliff waited. He could feel it there without even looking. A great emptiness, the thought of which left his gut tingling with nerves.

An explosion burst from behind Wu Qian and Subei was sent stumbling to the side. Qi Teng came sliding toward the cliff's edge, face down and digging a long furrow through the earth. His right arm was scorched and blackened, and as Subei looked closer, he realized the hand was missing. The giant moaned quietly as he fought to get to his knees, shaky and unable to put weight on the stub. The sharp-featured woman was close behind him, spear clutched tight. A single blue scar across her cheek shone brightly as she retreated. She didn't look much better than her ally, however, blood and dirt smeared across her brow, a patch of hair burned from her head to reveal the scalp beneath. Still had both hands, though, so that was something.

The last false heir came next, every step seemingly a decision between regrouping with his allies or charging Bataar—for that was what the sharp-faced heir had been retreating from. He strode forward, all confidence and smiles, and the heirs collapsed before him, drawing into a tight formation with Bataar on one side and Subei on the other.

And the cliff edge just behind him. He tried not to think about that long fall.

"Great, we've had our fun individually, but now we can wrap things up together," Bataar said as he tossed an orb from one hand to the other and back. "Brother, you okay back there?" Hesitation then, for just a moment.

"They've a few good tricks among them," Subei said, wincing as each word stretched and pulled at the wound to his face. "Thankfully, I'm not as fragile as my good looks might suggest."

"All the same, it's past time we wrapped this up. On with it, then."

But even as he said it, the ground began to rumble and shake. Subei looked to his brother, thinking at first that he was conjuring some new magic. But no, he was looking over his shoulder, across the clearing. As Subei turned to follow his gaze, he realized Yue Ru's attack must have been more damaging than he thought because of course he knew that sound, couldn't believe he hadn't recognized it instantly.

It was the thunder of hooves.

Subei smiled. There was a fine sound. He'd heard it many times in his life, and it had always heralded the arrival of Ghangerai reinforcements. Odds were Vachir was returning. But no. He stopped mid-thought, frowning. Mahtma and Ghula were still in the tree line at the edge of the clearing, but they were pointing and shouting now. Pointing and shouting toward the direction the false heirs had arrived from. Toward where riders were weaving through the trees.

Zhong riders.

Chapter Thirty-Five

SUBEI

A dozen or so riders were galloping out of the tree line at the far end of the clearing. The foremost carried a light-blue banner, a gold full moon and quill upon it.

Zhong reinforcements.

"It would appear your force in the valley is winning the field." Wu Qian said, sword down at his side. Blue light poured from the scars hidden beneath his armor as he looked from Subei to Bataar, then the riders storming across the meadow. "We must withdraw."

"Finish this quick, brother!" Bataar yelled, but even as he did, the heirs charged him as one. He was all that stood between them and a swift escape—and he knew it.

Bataar unleashed a cyclone of wind strikes, each one stronger than the next. They were wide, sweeping attacks, aimed at keeping all of the heirs back. But as strong as he was, even he couldn't hold them forever. And worse, the riders had begun to fire arrows now, the first few thunking down around Bataar.

This needed to end *today*. Again, Subei reached out for the bloodrage—flailing in the lightless abyss around him—and again, it did not stir.

He was on his own. And out of time. All he could do, then, was pick off the heirs he could. Most of them were engaged with Bataar, fighting to break through his wall of wind. Subei conjured an orb, readying to hit them in the back but—no. Wu Qian was guarding their rear flank, eyes trained on Subei.

An arrow caught Bataar in the shoulder, bouncing off without doing much damage. Still it staggered him, and his wall of wind faltered a moment. The false heirs pushed several steps ahead, were on the verge of breaking through.

"Damn it!" Subei growled. At a loss for what to do, he flung a barrage of orbs. Poured far too much magic into them, too. Overwhelm Wu Qian, Subei thought desperately. He can't counter them all—but he didn't have to. Even as the orbs approached, they were caught in Bataar's howling wall. Against it, they might as well have been birds in a typhoon. They were dashed and scattered, flung to the ground to detonate randomly all around. The cliffside shook with their impacts and somewhere deep below, the earth groaned.

The spill over from Bataar's wind strikes swept past Subei, and combined with the fire of the exploding orbs, he might as well have been in an inferno. And for a moment, he was, as his mind slipped back to the night Kashi died. That night when flames had roared all around. That night when—oh?

Subei looked down to his hands, tried to remember what he'd seen Bataar do that night. Some sort of clap? And from it there'd come a shockwave and a deadly rush of magic. It'd consumed countless Zhong soldiers because they'd all been bunched up. Bunched up just like—he raised his eyes to the false heirs—like they were now.

"Ancestors guide me," he said, muttering a prayer as he called the magic to each hand. He pulled it up from his core, squeezed out nearly everything he had left. Wu Qian frowned, but kept his feet set, ready.

Light manifested in each palm as Subei spread his arms wide. . . wide. . . then flexed his chest, squeezed his core, and brought his hands together in a resounding clap.

Magic surged through his hands and—spluttered out. Was there one moment, then gone the next. A few fluttering sparks slipped out, then were instantly swept away by the wind. And then it was too late.

The riders were bearing down on Bataar, lances lowered, and

the false heirs were through the storm, even Wu Qian joining their rush as their scars lit up for a desperate attack.

But there was another light, then. Beside Subei. Coming *from* him. From his hand. Subei frowned at it. It was as if he held an orb, except the glow wasn't coming from something in his hand, but the hand itself. As he realized that, he could feel the strength surging through it. Could feel it penned and ready to be set free. But with what? Some sort of super charged melee attack? Not helpful. He was ten paces distant from even the closest of the heirs. How could he possibly reach them with. . .

Ah.

And then it all made sense.

Sometimes, learning new techniques was difficult. It required a fearless curiosity, insightful focus, and then laborious, repetitive practice. Sometimes, learning new techniques came from watching others and trying to recreate what they did. And then, sometimes, it was as natural as breathing. Sometimes—like this moment—everything made sense.

Subei curled his glowing hand into a fist, dropped to one knee, and punched the ground as hard as he could. His magic rushed out in a shimmering shockwave and everywhere it passed, the ground was shattered into bits of loose stone and churned dirt.

The wave swept past the false heirs and the ground went to pieces beneath them. It reached Bataar next, and he too was thrown down. It almost reached all the way to the riders, but they pulled hard on the reins at the last moment, horses panicking.

"Whoa." Subei's eyes were wide as he took in the path of devastation stretching out from his fist.

A groan then, but not from anything living. It came from the earth itself. A shudder next, and something shifted deep beneath Subei. The whole of the cliff face. Bataar just got back to his feet in time to curse as it groaned once more then pried itself free of the mountain.

For a split second, everyone was falling—Subei, Bataar, the Zhong heirs—as the ground itself dropped away beneath them. Then there was a booming, reverberating impact as it slammed into the mountainside and, half a heartbeat later, everyone came crashing down with it.

It was as if they were on an island, then, if islands could be picked up by the ancestors themselves and skipped like stones. Such did their rogue cliff face tumble and skid its way downhill.

Subei was flat on his stomach, grasping for any purchase he could find as momentum and gravity did their best to pry him free, to buck him off and crush him to unrecognizable bits by the impossible weight now on the move.

A crack shot through the already destroyed earth beneath Subei, and then it was all he could do to scramble upward, closer to the Zhong heirs, as the front section of their island gave way all at once.

He'd just pulled himself off as the leading edge crumbled and was ground to pebbles beneath them. Too breathless to even muster a curse, he looked up and caught a glimpse of riders, silhouetted by the sun and already far above as the grating, roaring slide somehow picked up even more speed.

Closer, though, were the false heirs. Most of them were in a similar position to him, prone and clutching to anything they could. But Bataar—ancestors above, Bataar—was rising to his feet. His knees were bent sharply and he'd his weight leaned backward to counter the steep slope. Their island of rock and momentum shook and bucked, but somehow, Bataar managed a step forward. And another.

The sharp-faced woman was closest to him. From her prone position she tried to throw a wind strike. It wasn't much of one, and Bataar crossed his arms to push through it. He responded with an orb, and she just rolled out of the way before it exploded, blasting clean through their island.

"Oh, shit," Bataar cursed as cracks spiderwebbed through their rock. They widened by the moment, and the island began to pull itself to pieces. One opened beneath Yue Ru, and she tumbled in—only to be caught by Blue Eyes. He growled and heaved her out, but then his patch of earth was ripping apart too.

And beneath Subei, as well. All around, the island was

coming undone. But they were still halfway up the mountain, and there was no chance of slowing their descent.

Only one option, then, and it was sure to fail. Better to die trying, though, right?

Subei climbed to his feet, steady as he could. When he straightened, bone-shaking impacts reverberated up his legs every other moment as the island smashed and crashed its way down the mountain. All around, great clouds of dust and debris were flung into the air, the ends of them spun into swirling vortices from the speed and weight of the island punching through them.

Fighting to stay upright, Subei extended his arms, palms up, and let his magic reach out to the world around him. In an instant, he could feel an impossible number of objects within his invisible grasp. Stones, of course, but also a discarded blade, the remains of his pauldron, even an entire tree that'd come down with them. But those were not what he needed. No, instead he stretched his awareness further still, as far as it could go. All the way to the edges of the island. There, he found stones even his magic couldn't lift, couldn't call together to form a wall. But he didn't need a wall, he just needed the island to hold together a bit longer.

Subei squeezed his core for every drop of magic it had. All the World a Shield took hold of the swathes of earth that composed their island, and Subei growled deep in his chest as he strained every muscle to bring his arms inward. The magic resisted him, then. Some sort of feedback in the technique? A natural limit to its potential? He couldn't think straight enough to find out for, a moment later, that resistance became an unbearable force. Subei's arms were pulled out side to side, stretched as if tied between mammoths marching in opposite directions. His shoulders popped and it was all he could do then to scream in pain.

"*Gah!*" The cry boiled into a name. "Ba. . . taar! Help. . . me. . . hold it!"

His brother must have gotten the gist of it, because a moment later he came sliding down, hands clawing into the rock to slow down. He scrambled to his feet, then stretched his arms wide. His scars flashed, and the unbearable force suddenly became that much more bearable. Or maybe it was because, despite their efforts, a large chunk off to the left ripped free to spin off down the mountainside, flattening trees as it went.

"Yahaha!" Bataar let out a whoop, and then he was laughing. The mad bastard was laughing!

Subei would have shaken his head in disbelief if he'd had the energy, but he didn't. So instead, he stood next to his cackling brother, rooted at the leading edge of the island, arms wide and straining not to be ripped from their sockets. The valley floor was just ahead and hurtling closer by the moment. And there were soldiers in the way. The remnants of the Northern Army. They'd been engaged in a fighting retreat, now they were only engaged in running for their lives.

A strand of trees rose up before the island—and was flattened. So loud was the rumbling, Subei didn't even hear their wood pulverized to splinters and dust.

He did hear a scream, though, from behind. Wu Qian's voice.

"Gao Shi, don't!"

Subei managed to get his head around just enough to see a figure hurtling toward him in a stumbling, off balance run. The false heir who'd looked like he was a soldier. There was a distinct lack of fear in his eyes as he flung himself forward, sword raised, and let loose a battle cry.

"You idiot!" Subei just had time to yell before the blow came down on his exposed shoulder. Were his body not toughened by the magic, he probably would have lost his entire arm. As it happened, all he lost was his focus. The island immediately responded, pulling apart.

"No!" Subei fought it back under control, redoubled his hold on All the World a Shield. Bataar strained as well, clearly doing the same. At the same time, the momentum from Gao Shi's leaping attack carried the soldier forward, right to the leading edge of the island where he stumbled, bent low to catch his balance—and lost it all at once. He tumbled out of sight.

A moment later, Subei's scars exploded with light. Bataar's too, and then the false heirs' as a dust-stained cloud of motes seeped up through the island and into them all. The rushing euphoria of a magic transfer doubled Subei over and broke his focus for good. He was thrown down along with Bataar as the island ripped itself in half. The two pieces split in opposite directions—which resulted in only some of the retreating Zhong forces being flattened.

The half Subei and Bataar were desperately clinging to spun to the side, blasted through a small hill, then pulverized the last of itself against the far wall of the valley.

Stones rained down all around, dust hanging heavy in the air, and it was all Subei could do to cover his head as an additional shower of horse-sized boulders came screeching down toward him. They exploded all around, shrapnel hissing through the air.

When the world settled, he peeked out through shaking vision and the complete disbelief he was alive to see the other half of the island. It was jammed up in the sandy remains of a riverbed, its front side dug in deep. But it was still in one piece— and so were the false heirs clinging to the top of it.

At least, Subei could confirm they were for a singular moment before another groan tremored through the valley, this one from so deep down it shook the land in all directions as if it were water.

"On your feet, go!" Bataar dragged him up. "Run," he said next, and they did, a stumbling, limping affair as, behind them, half the mountain came roaring down.

Chapter Thirty-Six

BATAAR

Having seen the valley from above so recently, Bataar expected to recognize its layout. Expected to recall important landmarks by which he could lead them out. Of course, that was before Subei had dropped half a mountain on the place. But the Ghangerai army was vaguely north, he knew, and so he led them that direction, weaving around newly placed boulders the size of buildings and hills of shale and shattered stone that hadn't existed that morning.

"Wait until Cousin Gerel hears about this," Bataar said, laughing despite the limp accompanying each of his steps. "He tried to ride that rockslide once, remember? Turned an old practice shield into a sled?" Bataar elbowed his younger brother. "Remember?"

"I remember."

"Best watch out," Bataar continued as they entered a forest of uprooted trees. "He might want to ride one like that with you." He hiked a thumb over his shoulder to where the valley was completely bisected by rubble. No reply from Subei at that. Bataar looked back at him, stifling a wince as his eyes passed over the jagged wound through his cheek and down his chin. There were burns, too, but nothing gruesome, probably. Was hard to tell through all the blood and dirt, but Boulder Stands Defiant, it seemed, protected against fire as well as blades.

"So when are you teaching me to do that?" Bataar asked.

"Teaching you to do what?"

"Your new technique!" Bataar spun and spread his arms to the ruination behind. "And what are we calling it, anyway? Fist of the Ancestors? No, that's stupid. Fist of the Foe Breaker?" Bataar grumbled. "Come on, Subei, you're better at pretty words than me."

"Can we walk in silence? My head feels how that mountain looks."

"Ooh, Fist that Moves Mountains!" Bataar exclaimed. "Not bad, huh?"

"For the love of the ancestors, brother, can you—"

"Bataar! Subei!" a familiar voice called from ahead. They looked up to find Ghula just cresting a hill. She spurred her horse to a gallop down the near side, and Mahtma drew into view next, accompanied by several warriors.

"Thought you were finally rid of us, eh?" Bataar said, smiling. "No such luck."

"Ancestors above," Ghula exclaimed as she arrived. She swung from the saddle before her horse even stopped and immediately began fussing over them.

"Don't worry about me," Bataar said, pushing away her searching hands. "Subei's the one needs attention. Tried to block an orb with his face."

"And here I thought you were the thick-headed one," she mumbled before turning her attention to Subei.

"I'll live," he said, leaning away from her. "I think."

"That's a nasty wound. I've seen warriors succumb to less," she replied, then paused. "Given, none of them had magically enhanced bodies."

Mahtma and the escort of warriors arrived then.

"Fetch water," she commanded them. "We need to clean those wounds until the physicians can see to them."

"No," Ghula said at once, and Bataar could see she'd an idea. There was that twinkle in her eyes that said she was excited about something. "Leave their wounds." A sly smile then. "Follow me."

She led them at a jog back to the hill she'd just come over.

Bataar followed as best he could, brow scrunched in confusion and one leg stiff from ancestors knew how many small injuries.

They climbed the hill and. . . the breath was stolen right out of Bataar's lungs.

"Ancestors above."

"Yeah," Ghula said, smiling that same sly smile. Then she grabbed Bataar's arm with one hand, Subei's with the other, and raised them both high. "The heirs of Baji Khan return triumphant!" she cried. "The sons of Kemu Khagan return triumphant!" A roar rose up from the masses before them. From the army before them. Looked it was the whole of the United Army, streaming in from the plains. So large was the host, it reached all the way to the horizon and kept on going.

"Ghula. . . this is. . . " *Amazing*, Bataar wanted to say. *Everything*. But his words failed him, tumbled out silently so struck was he. Not that anyone would have heard them, anyway.

"*Ba-ji Khan! Ba-ji Khan!*" Ghula was shouting, pumping a fist to the rhythm as she led Bataar and Subei to the army, who'd taken up the chant. The front ranks, at least. Probably those further back had no idea what was happening. The cry rose higher and louder, though, and they caught the rhythm soon enough.

Bataar and Subei reached the first riders, and they parted, opening a path straight through. Well, not completely straight, considering how many warriors were hanging out of their saddles, arms outstretched to slap the backs and clap the shoulders of their triumphant heroes.

"They'll weave a song about this day, brother!" Bataar said. Subei didn't respond, or maybe he did, but it was drowned out by the cheering. Bataar couldn't tell.

"Honor and glory!" A warrior cheered, jumping from his horse to take Bataar by the shoulders and shake him. They locked hands then, and slammed shoulders in a warrior's greeting. But then Ghula was pulling him onward. More faces, next. More warriors.

"The steppe rides again!"

"Fury from the north!"

A constant barrage of hands slapping his back, squeezing his shoulders. Bataar reached out as much as he could, clasping hands with an uncountable number of warriors and still an even more uncountable number leaned in for their turn. Something caught Bataar's foot, his ankle twisted, and he went down to one knee. There was a trampled corpse beneath him. A Zhong soldier, arrows jutting from his chest and his glassy eyes fixed on the sky.

"The ancestors smile on us this day!" a young voice cheered as a hand took his own and heaved him up.

Kashi, Bataar thought on instinct, before his mind caught up. It was just a younger warrior, didn't even look anything like his brother. And then Ghula was pulling him on again.

A figure was ahead, then. Appeared from the press of bodies like the towering statue of Baji Khan himself back in Kurul Valley. But this man was not made of stone.

"Father!" Bataar punched his fists knuckle to knuckle and dropped into a bow.

"Sorry for the, uh, valley," Subei said, voice barely audible above the cheering.

Kemu Khagan laughed at that. A deep laugh, and in it Bataar heard joy, and absurdity, but most of all, relief. His smile reached all the way to his eyes as he waved them up from their bows.

"A day's labor to clear the way, no more." He spread his arms wide. "United, there's nothing our people cannot accomplish."

"Father. . . " Bataar said, and in an instant all the joy left him. "Father, I'm sorry, I failed you. Kash—"

"I know." He pulled them in close then, wrapped in a frightfully strong hug. "I know, my sons. We will raise our drinks to him this night and share tales of his finest days. The woe-speakers will weave a eulogy to make our grandchildren's grandchildren weep, and so long as I am khagan, a seat will be left open for Kashi at the high table."

Around them, the chant rose to new heights. It bounced off the mountains and echoed through the valley. Buffeted by its thunderous reverberations, and with Kashi's name on his tongue, Bataar couldn't help but imagine that somewhere back the way they'd come, back on the other side of the now blocked valley, the remains of the Zhong army heard the chant.

"Ba-ji Khan! Ba-ji Khan!"

And the false heirs, too.

"Ba-ji Khan! Ba-ji Khan!"

Those that had survived would escape this day, but it was a temporary salvation. The full might of the Ghangerai was coming for them.

* * *

At the Kurultai—what seemed forever ago now—Bataar had beheld the largest host he'd ever seen. One hundred and forty-five thousand. Some of them herders, yes. Some of them crafts-folk, yes. Some of them trappers, or torols, or household attendants. But before any of that, they were warriors.

At the Kurultai, Bataar had witnessed the greatest gathering of his people in a decade. Today, it was easily eclipsed. The sheer scale of it left his head spinning more than crashing down the mountain had.

They rode not in one congested mass of humanity and horse-flesh but divided into groups of toumans. These acted largely independently, the marshal in charge of each overseeing the specifics. And still, there was too much for Bataar to process. Horses and riders passed first, scouting the terrain, marking safe paths, or hunting what animals hadn't already fled. Trovaaks and wagon trains came next, then mammoths and their sleds, all of them hauling support and supply for the forward units. And then there were the herds. These came last and furthest out to either flank. Four extra horses per rider, then the cows and sheep, goats, and the trovaaks and mammoths not fit for or currently needed for hauling supplies.

"How is it possible to have so many. . . " Bataar trailed off. He'd been preparing to say 'people' but that fell short. People, supplies, animals, weapons, food—*things,* even.

"A mighty sight, is it not?" Kemu Khagan said. "The United Army." He rode between Bataar and Subei, all of them mounted now and entering an encampment amidst the rumbling masses. Here, it seemed, their father had established a central position to coordinate the movements further into Zhong territory.

"And still, these two hundred and seventy thousand are but the core of our force," Kemu Khagan said. "Even now, Budai Khan leads six toumans west. They will take Chobei and the surrounding villages, then continue south. Arban Khan and his six toumans, meanwhile, ride far east to where the Ghairkhan range sinks into the sea. A long journey, but the fishing towns and the port of Dangshailan will be reminded how far they are from the central empire." Kemu Khagan gestured directly ahead of them. "And ahead, Tugu Khan prepares to lead the vanguard with six toumans of his own." He chuckled, then. "I fear their journey will begin with clearing a path through the valley you destroyed, Subei."

Bataar tried to keep count in his head as the different armies were listed off.

"Four forces, then," he said. "One to the west, one to the east, one ahead of us, and this core here, with still greater numbers than the other three combined."

"We will be the hammer that shatters the Zhong in the north. But enough of this for now," Kemu said, waving away their thoughts of the grand days yet to come. "You are tired, you are injured, and you must rest. I will see you at the great feast this night. And after, we will speak at length of your journey. Go now."

It was only then Bataar realized they'd arrived at their ger. He hadn't expected to find it here, but why not? Of course it had come with their father. Mother would have no use for it back north, she had her own ger for when the khagan left on campaign. Had all the necessary torols, guards, and resources to ensure the steppe prospered in the army's absence, too.

Bataar made it all of one step inside the ger before he was tackled by a torrent of fur and barks and slobbering tongues.

"Dayir! Tayir!" he laughed, stumbling back into Subei as the dogs licked his face relentlessly. "It's good to see you too, no—gah, ugh. Stop, no! Down!" he laughed, but then it was him on the floor. This pleased the dogs all the more, and the assault of tongue and tail redoubled in ferocity.

"Thank the ancestors they have someone else to smother,"

Kemu laughed. "It's been difficult to look a fearsome conqueror with those two tripping me every other step."

"It's good to be home," Bataar said when the dogs were done licking and settled for trying to sit on him at the same time. "Thank you for bringing the ger, Father. It's exactly like it always was. It does me good to see it."

"Too exact, even," Subei said, speaking up finally. It was only then Bataar noticed there were three sets of sleeping furs arrayed in the room.

"Ah." Kemu frowned as he noticed it too. "I'll have those removed."

"Wouldn't want any painful reminders," Subei said.

Bataar winced. "Subei, it's—"

"I need to find the physicians' tent," he said, cutting Bataar off then striding from the ger.

"He's just tired," Bataar explained as the door closed. But then he'd a sinking in his gut. "Does . . does Mother know?" That thought left him reeling a moment as he tried to work out if a rider could have made it back in time. A bird, maybe? Like one of Mahtma's messenger pigeons? But how was that any way to receive news of a son's death? No, it should be delivered only by another son, or a husband. She was owed that much, at least. But who? Kemu had not been blessed with an abundance of children.

Kemu sighed and sank inward as he spoke next.

"Uncle Jergei rides to your mother with the news," he said, eyes downcast. "I should bear it myself, but. . . " he gestured toward the door, toward the conquest just beginning.

"I understand," Bataar said, because he did.

"Our people," Kemu began to explain.

"Need us here," Bataar finished. "I understand our duty, Father."

Chapter Thirty-Seven

SUBEI

They feasted through the night. A raucous celebration to pay tribute to the honored dead and send their spirits to the ancestors in glory. A night of songs and cheers, dancing and music. Subei heard it all from the physicians' tent. Heard the tutting of the physicians too, and the snip of their scissors as they put his face back together.

By the time they were finished—at least, enough that he could force his way free of their needles and stitches—the sun was rising. A new dawn. A victorious dawn. It was only when the wind blew a certain way that Subei could smell the Zhong dead. They weren't rotting yet, too soon for that, but there were other smells to give away their presence. Earth turned to mud from spilled blood. Bowels that'd been emptied in terror—or after a death blow was struck. Probably, if Subei was drunk, he wouldn't have noticed.

So it was the after battle stench and the pain of his wounds that accompanied Subei through the quiet, smoky camp toward his ger.

". . . not concerned?" A hushed voice somewhere off to his left. A warrior sleeping off the feast probably, and mumbling in their sleep. Subei kept walking.

"It happens in battle, I've seen it before." Wait. Ghula? Why did she sound angry?

Subei held his breath, listening close as he could.

"This isn't regular battle." A terse response. Sounded like. . . Mahtma? Where were they? There was nothing around him but a cluster of gers and the narrow alleys between them. Still, the voices had come from ten or so paces distant, maybe?

". . . a weapon to point at our enemies and step back, but what of the consequences? I fear. . . " The wind picked up, filled his ears a moment. ". . . victory. . . " Another gust, damn it. ". . . their souls."

Victory? Souls? What were they talking about? He needed to get closer. Even as the thought came, he knew it was a wicked one. Few things done in secrecy were honorable. And fewer still that were kept secret from one's friends and mentors. He moved forward nonetheless.

As best he could tell, they were up past the next ger, then to the left. There was a pen of some sort there, and the wide slats of its fence would provide adequate cover. Subei moved fast and careful. He reached the pen in a crouch and tucked up next to it.

". . . give them credit for." That was Ghula again, and yes, clearly angered.

"I would not trust even the Gyakhal Bha herself with this, ancestors forgive me," Mahtma said. "But that doesn't seem to bother you in the slightest."

What didn't? He still couldn't hear well. They were moving away, he realized. Walking through the dawn. He had to keep up. Subei left the shelter of the pen—and kicked a bucket over. He froze, winced, then ducked back behind the fence.

"We'll speak later." Mahtma, that time. Her footsteps squelched through the mud, headed away.

"I'd prefer we didn't," Ghula snapped, then from the sound of it, strode toward Subei's hiding spot.

"Too much to drink there, warrior?" she called, and as she did, the anger was gone from her voice all at once. As if it'd never been there at all. "Best find your furs and sleep it off—oh." Her steps ceased abruptly. "Subei?" She laughed. "No use hiding, boy. I can smell you at ten paces. Haven't had a chance to bathe since we got back, have you?"

She couldn't have seen him, there was still a ger between them. But there was no use hiding. He made a show of walking out fully upright as if he hadn't just been crouched as low as he could get.

"Ghula?" he asked, feigning surprise. "You're up early."

She looked unconvinced, but didn't call his bluff.

"Airag's a fine drink, but damned if it doesn't make for a fitful sleep." She took a swig from a waterskin and swished the liquid in her mouth before spitting it to the dirt. "Quite the feast. Shame you missed it."

He gestured to his face, then winced as he opened his mouth to speak.

"Had to make sure the physicians kept their skills sharp."

Ghula squinted at him for a long moment, eyes following the length of the wound that divided his face. He could feel it even now, the skin stretched tight and sewn closed from his scalp down through his right eyebrow, over his cheekbone and mouth to end at the tip of his chin. His lips were cracked and blistered, constantly bleeding from scabs that broke whenever he spoke. Hurt something fierce, but it was his pride that hurt more. He'd been cocky, and it'd almost cost him his life.

But he still drew breath. His pride would heal, and so would the wound. It'd leave one hell of a scar, though, the physicians had said as much while using ancestors knew how much thread to sew it closed.

"Your first real prize," Ghula grunted. She ran a hand through her hair, fingers slipping across the dozen lines of smooth skin cut through it. "Every one tells a different story, you know. And you never forget them."

"Only story behind this is I underestimated my opponent. Nearly got my head blown off."

She raised her eyes to the shadowy form of the mountains and the valley cutting through them.

"Still, hell of a victory yesterday. For our warriors, and for you and your brother." She paused. "All apologies to your face, of course."

Victory. That's what they'd won, right? That's what you called it when five of the false heirs escaped? When Kashi was dead, and this labor still wasn't finished? Victory. Seemed a funny word for it.

"Something on your mind, Subei?"

"Nothing."

"You're a liar, Son of Kemu," she said as she turned to leave. "Get some sleep. And a bath."

"Could stand for a drink first," he said to her back. Then, after a moment, he continued on his way.

He made it back to the ger without uncovering any more conspiracies in the dark—except perhaps a conspiracy of passed out warriors to trip him every other step. The closer to the center of camp he got, the thicker they covered the ground.

"There's my half-faced brother!" Bataar yelled, wrapping Subei in a hug the moment he entered the ger. His breath reeked of the faintly sour smell of airag—some wine in there too—and his eyes were open just a bit wider than normal. Drunk, then. A good ways beyond drunk, even. He'd a fresh wineskin in hand, too.

"Off to an early start," Subei said, cringing as a scab split on his lower lip.

Bataar paused, blinking several times.

"Not sure I stopped." His eyes went wide as if he'd just remembered something. "We missed you at the feast! Father praised our success before the camp. Many honors were bestowed. Fine words cried!"

"And Kashi?"

Bataar's mouth stopped half open and his eyes went distant, thinking back. No doubt the events were a tad blurry. He held the look a moment longer before the recognition clicked in his eyes.

"Yes, yes, of course! A spot left open for him at the high table, drinks poured to the dirt in his memory. A proper hero's remem. . . " He stumbled over the word, licked his lips and tried again. "Rememerm—"

"Remembrance."

"That!" he said with a contented smile and a sloppy point of his finger. "Oh, and father spoke of the future, as well. Our hunt was successful, but it is not yet done." He clenched a fist excitedly, then slapped Subei on the shoulder. "There's more heirs yet to catch, brother!"

261

"We should have finished it yesterday," Subei said, quiet. It was supposed to be over.

"Worry not, brother," Bataar said, waving away the concern that must've been plain on Subei's face. "It's all already been decided. We'll ride with the core of the army, and if the heirs ever show their faces on the frontlines, we'll be ready for them. But probably they won't. Probably they'll slink back and hide behind their walls. Again, no matter. We'll break their city and hunt them down!" He turned his eyes to the south, a smile pulling across his face. "And if they escape that, well, we'll hunt them still. Ever on, to the ends of the earth if necessary! However long it takes!" Bataar paused his triumphant declaration, noticing Subei's sour expression. "Something wrong?"

"Hunt them to the ends of the earth?" he said quietly. "Are you insane?"

"I don't understand," Bataar said. "Hold on." He took another long swig from the wineskin. "Okay, now let's see if you make more sense." He smirked as he said it, as if this was all a joke.

"Brother," Subei said, words tense, pointed. "Is that truly what you want? More of what happened in the Longlarch? In Chobei? More and more until. . . until what? Until one day, the bloodrage doesn't come when we call, and that gets us killed? Or worse, it comes and never goes back into its abyss?" Subei shuddered at the thought. "What happens the day the bloodrage takes control and never gives it up?" Subei spread his arms wide and laughed. A maniacal, frantic sound. "Yesterday was supposed to end our labor. Was supposed to free us of this damned burden."

Bataar only had a distant look to offer by way of response.

"Burden?"

"Burden, curse—call it what you want," Subei shouted, his fist clenched.

"Hey, hey, quieter, please." Bataar waved him down with an exaggerated gesture, a pained look on his face. "I think I'm hungover and drunk at the same time."

"Then sober up, and maybe your sense will come back too."

A long silence as Bataar stared back at him. His face was still, but his eyes said he was thinking, working on an answer.

"You're afraid of the bloodrage," he finally said, nodding.

"Of course I'm afraid of it."

"You're afraid you're not strong enough to wield it, but it's okay," Bataar said then, and reached a clumsy hand out as if to comfort Subei. "We'll master it together. We're Ghangerai, brother. Everything in this world is ours so long as we have the strength—and the courage—to take it."

"In the Longlarch, it refused to fight until it got what it wanted. The damn thing has *plans*. It's manipulating us! It's. . . it's. . . a blade that cuts both ways," Subei finally said, knowing even as he did that it was a tired argument and weak way to make his point.

"And a sword will kill you if you fall on it," Bataar said simply. "But we're not children, brother. We aren't playing with this magic, we're wielding it."

"I think it's playing with *us*. Can you not see what it's done?"

Bataar took a long, slow look around the ger.

"Our father has been made khagan. Our people have united for the first time since the days of the Great Khan. Yesterday, we won a victory against a Zhong army *and* the false heirs." He looked down at his palms. "This is what the bloodrage has done? Why wouldn't we want this?"

"Because of the cost! Because I'm terrified of what it'll do next. How many innocents it'll use me to kill."

"No one blames you for Chobei, brother."

"*I* blame me, Bataar. I wanted to be a warrior, instead I'm a butcher!" There was a long pause as Subei caught his breath. "I shudder to think what'll happen the next time the bloodrage gets out."

"I shudder to think what'll happen next time you refuse to let it out," Bataar said, voice going cold all at once. "The next time you wielding it is the difference between saving a brother or sending him to his ancestors." Bataar's face softened, then, as if he regretted his words. "It's normal for men to hesitate at the precipice of the unknown, brother. On the verge of true glory. We've been through a lot these past weeks and you're faltering."

He stepped in close then, put a hand on Subei's shoulder. "Don't burden yourself with that concern. Let me carry that worry, that fear, that doubt. I'm the eldest, and I will carry it, so you don't have to." He was quiet a long moment, thinking, then nodded. "Let me lead, and all you have to do is follow. Trust me, Subei. As your oldest brother, trust me."

"As my only brother, you mean."

"That too," he growled.

And then Subei's wound was properly burning. And the anger inside him with it.

"Go back to your drinking." Subei pushed him away. "We'll talk when you're sober." Bataar growled by way of response, but he'd clearly had enough as well. In a moment, he was out the door and gone. But his wineskin wasn't, must've been dropped in the argument.

Subei stared at it. "Said I needed a drink, didn't I?"

* * *

A full day now, or two? Hard to tell from inside the ger. Or, more appropriately, from his brief bouts of consciousness. Bataar had come in at one point? They'd laughed together? Or fought. Argued about Kashi? He wasn't sure anymore.

Far from a respectable existence for the son of the khagan. Ever further from a respectable existence for a man bearing the magic of Baji. But their hunt wasn't complete, Kashi was dead, and the bloodrage. *Shit.* The bloodrage. He'd hoped to drown it in drink, to sink so far into oblivion that he no longer felt it churning below his core. It hadn't worked. It was the last thing he felt as he drifted into a drunken stupor, and the first thing he felt when he couldn't force himself to sleep any longer.

At some point, Tugu Khan and his toumans must have ridden out. The ground had shaken, and Subei's ears had threatened to burst at the sound of thousands of horses ranging south. There was a war on, after all. The rest of the army would follow soon, he knew. But maybe if he drank enough, kept quiet enough, might be they'd forget about him. That was a reasonable plan, right?

A shadow fell across the door as someone stood outside. Subei almost yelled them away, didn't care to see anyone, but he paused. That half-bowed posture, and they appeared to have something in hand? Ah, an attendant, then. He looked to the bottle of wine set atop what remained of the table. He'd plenty to drink. But still, at the rate he was going, there was no telling when he'd need more.

"Enter," he grumbled, squinting and pulling his sleeping furs over his face as the door was opened and sunlight streamed inside.

A hooded figure stepped in with food and drink on a tray.

"Set it down over there." Subei nodded toward the table. It was upside down. When had that happened?

The attendant righted it, then placed the food. An assortment of bread and rice and a few strips of meat. And—wait.

"That isn't airag. Or wine." He rose and scrutinized the bowls. "Water?"

"A fine drink, water. Enough of it will cleanse the body, wash away the toxins within."

Subei frowned. He recognized that voice. Took him a moment to place it, though, in his drunken state.

"Mahtma?"

The attendant lifted her hood, and he saw he'd guessed right. And then immediately regretted it. Her cold, certain eyes cut into him like a blade. He flinched even before the blow was dealt. Her fist slammed into his stomach and bent him double, sent him falling backward.

"What was that f—"

Vomit rose in his throat. He scrambled for the chamber pot, fell, crawled the last few feet, then spewed into it.

"This self-pity ends now." She pointed to the tray she'd brought, a motion he barely saw through blurry eyes.

"Drink the water, slowly. Then eat." She stared at him with eyes that held all the warmth and tenderness of the heart of winter. "Slowly."

"You don't know. . . " he said, rising to his feet and taking a step toward her. "You don't know what I'm—"

"And I don't care." Her words sent him to a spluttering halt.

"Self-loathing. Doubt. Cowardice. I don't care. You've had your time to sulk."

He rose to his full height at that, and remembered he was still a good bit shorter than her too-tall frame.

"I could have saved Kashi if I'd released the bloodrage sooner. But I tried to resist it and now he's dead—and then the rage got out anyway. It's always there now, you know? Clawing its way out of that abyss every waking moment. So tell me, in your infinite wisdom, what was the point?"

"So you're ready to give up then?" she asked. "That's it?" She left the question hanging, leaving him waiting for her next words as she stood and walked to the door. "If you decide you're not yet ready to curl up and die, drink the water. Slowly. Then eat." Their eyes locked, and the intensity of her gaze was almost enough to sober him up on the spot.

"Tomorrow, we train."

The door swung shut behind her. Subei stood alone, the occasional dry heave racking his frame.

He looked to the tray.

"Just a sip of water, maybe."

Chapter Thirty-Eight

SUBEI

Subei cursed as he stepped out of the ger. Sunlight, blazing over the eastern horizon. And there would be more soon. He almost retreated inside at the thought. Considered it for a long moment, then cursed again and shielded his eyes with a hand as he stepped forward.

A cool breeze picked up from the west, set him to shivering. Seemed a particularly cruel contradiction how he could be so hot internally, stomach churning and tossing, and yet still shiver in the morning air. Sweating and shivering. At least in his drunken stupor, he'd only felt one at a time.

He found Mahtma on the training ground. Bataar was there too, though some distance away and already meditating.

Let him stay that way. I'm not ready to deal with him again yet.

"Pay your brother no mind. He has his own training to be about this morning," Mahtma said from where she was surrounded by nearly a dozen training dummies, their canvas sack bodies stuffed with hay. She stood in the middle of them, a quarterstaff in one hand and a variety of weapons lying at her feet.

Wet grass crunched under Subei's feet as he approached, the blades sprinkling dew across his ankles.

"It is a fine morning, my student," Mahtma said with a bow in the Teshkai fashion.

He returned the bow, joints and muscles stiff.

"It is a fine morning, my teacher."

She nodded at his words, then took the quarterstaff in hand and in one sure motion, broke it across a dummy. Half of the staff went to splinters, the other cracked in her hand. She tossed the remains to Subei and he caught it on instinct.

"Today, we hit things."

He raised an eyebrow at that, the scabbed scar on his face stretching painfully and threatening to burst more stitches.

"I expected something more along the lines of meditating and seeking the answers within myself."

"Not today." She scooped a blunted saber from the ground and tossed it to him. He dropped the broken staff to catch it as she nodded to the training dummy.

Subei wrapped a fist around the hilt of the weapon, his lethargic muscles tightening as he did. Felt good to have a weapon in hand once more, he had to admit.

He slashed the nearest dummy diagonally across the chest, the blade cutting through the canvas to nick the wooden pole beneath. A light poof of hay shot into the air and floated to the ground. Subei held back a smile. Felt good to hit something.

"A bit harder and we might actually get somewhere." Mahtma shook her head. "Thought you Ghangerai prided yourselves on strength."

She was baiting him. Might be he was hung over, but he wasn't stupid. Still, if she wanted him to hit harder, that was one thing he was happy to do.

The next strike was a rising blow that caught the dummy in its stomach, tore the canvas belly to neck and sent an armful of hay spilling out. The impact reverberated up his arm, jolting his tired muscles awake.

Mahtma huffed.

Alright, then. Subei breathed deep and raised the saber for an overhead blow. He brought it down with both hands, splitting the dummy's wooden head with a definitive crack and burying the saber in the top of the pole.

Ha! He stepped back with a triumphant smile and a heavy breath to survey his work. Was really sweating now, despite the coolness of the morning. And damn, did it feel good. His churning stomach had settled, felt better than it had in days, and he couldn't help but notice he did too. His muscles complained, but the burn felt good.

He turned to Mahtma with a grin.

"How was that?"

She observed the sword, left in the pole like an axe in a tree stump, and shrugged.

"We're making progress." She used her foot to toss an unstrung bow into his hands. "Let's see your aim."

The muscles in his back protested as he bent the bow with his weight and slipped the string into the top notch. A quiver of arrows lay in the dew-damp grass, and he scooped one up now, nocking it to the string and holding both bow and arrow by his side in one hand. First Rider Ren had somehow tucked four or more arrows into her draw hand such that she could fire them all off in a strumming blur. It was a technique that Subei had barely begun to learn. One day, perhaps, he'd learn to shoot as fast as the best archers did. For now, a single arrow at a time.

Mahtma nodded to his left where a dummy sat waiting two dozen paces away, backed up to a wall of pressed hay.

Subei drew the string and raised the bow, fingertips brushing against his cheek as he took aim. A deep breath, and he closed one eye. He let half the breath out, felt the calm settle over him, and loosed. A sharp thrum of the string, and the arrow buried itself in the target.

A good shot. In the chest, just below the heart. Shot like that would've broken ribs through all but the heaviest armor. Would have likely punctured a lung through anything lighter.

Mahtma grunted her approval.

"Again."

His muscles complained less, waking to their task as he took aim once more. Another whooshing thrum, and this arrow caught the dummy in the neck, just above the collarbone.

"Again."

Nock, draw, release. Chest shot.

"Again."

Nock, draw, release. In the heart this time.

"Again."

He was in a rhythm now, eager for the next shot, had the arrow ready almost before she said the command. Another hit in the chest. Might've been he'd drank himself into oblivion the past day or so, but if his aim had suffered any for it, it didn't show. He loosed again and again until the quiver was empty, sent the last arrow into the dummy's head, punched a hole through its canvas-sack face right under one eye socket. Showing off, more than not. It was an impractical shot to aim for, but he was enjoying himself now.

Mahtma surveyed the results of the onslaught, the dummy looking like a pincushion now and sagged in several places where hay leaked from jagged tears.

"A satisfactory warm-up." She turned to him. "Now use your magic. And don't hold back. Let's make a mess." He could've sworn the slightest hint of a smile crept onto her face then. Probably not, though. Probably just a trick of the growing morning light.

Subei set the bow aside and stretched quickly, several joints in his back and neck clicking as he did so. He interlaced his fingers and turned his palms outward, knuckles cracking to join the chorus of pops.

"You going to stretch all day, or—"

North Wind Scours hit the dummy with gale force, blew the hay from within it and snapped the arrows in its chest like so many twigs. The exertion of magic sent a surge of adrenaline through him, got his pulse going.

The next strike elicited a sharp crack. The pole splintered down the middle, the top half falling away, and the battered remains of the dummy tumbled with it in a shower of hay.

"How's that?" He smiled at Mahtma, but she shrugged it off.

"I count eight still standing."

Ah. She had said to make a mess.

He called on the magic and it surged at his attention, rose like the midsummer floodwaters. Baji's Burning Fury, then an explosion, and the air was filled with embers and splinters. Another orb, another explosion. The ground shook.

Scars flaring bright, Subei turned to the saber he'd left buried in the first dummy. All the World a Weapon, then. It required only a gesture of his hand, and the saber was ripped from the pole, came to hover in the air before him. He shot his hand toward another target and the sword buried itself in it, quivering all the way to the hilt after the impact.

The next three dummies were grouped together and Subei felt the sprouting of an idea, went with it without thinking. He raised his palms and felt the resistance of countless pieces of debris. He forced another surge of magic into his hands and the remains of the already destroyed dummies snapped into place before him, forming a wall of jagged wood and arrowheads, a few rocks and even a stack of firewood were also drawn into the amalgamation.

All the World a Shield. Defensive, useful. Incomplete. Yue Jong had used it another way, too. What had he called it then? Bulwark Breaks Barbarian? A ridiculous name, given in jest. No, this technique reminded Subei of something else. A stampede. But more, still. The way it'd shaken the ground when Yue Jong had blasted the walls forward. . . it'd felt like a cavalry charge. As if standing on a plain as a touman bore down.

"Cavalry in Thousands," Subei whispered to himself then punched forward with a double-fisted wind strike. He put everything he had into it, and the wall shot forward, crashing into the dummies to blow apart in a splintering impact. The dummies were erased from existence in the aftermath, nothing more than a debris field that stretched away at least forty paces.

Subei grinned as he turned to the last two dummies, could almost see them cowering. Sweat poured down his brow now, and his breath came heavy, but damned if he didn't feel good, didn't feel alive. And his work wasn't quite done.

It would've been easy to finish the last two with an orb, or a wind strike. The debris field he'd created probably would've easily reformed into another wall to crush them, but he'd been cursed with a flair for the dramatic, and there was nothing wrong with a bit of experimentation. Where's the fun if you're not trying new things?

He thought back to the fight on the cliffside, to the way he'd imbued his fist with glowing, explosive energy.

"Fist that Moves Mountains," he said, staring at his hand.

Could he do it again? He started by stretching his hands wide, then directing magic down his shoulders, along his arms, and into each palm. From there, he just needed to clap them together, right? It was hard to describe, but each technique had a different feel to it. North Wind Scours was ethereal, but built up in the wrist or ankle, then exploded outward with the momentum of a punch or kick. Baji's Burning Fury was a heavier commitment, pouring magic into one's palm until it solidified into the deadly orb of crackling energy. All the World a Shield felt different still. The magic would build in the air as he raised his palms, then spread out to 'feel' everything around him, and finally, draw it in like a great sucking breath. So what did Fist that Moves Mountains feel like? He tried to recall, but he'd only used it in the heat of battle. Hadn't exactly had time to focus.

"Were the dummies not staked in place, they'd have run off by now." Mahtma watched him with unimpressed eyes. "My instructions were to hit things, not stare at your hands."

"Fair enough." He brought his hands together with a resounding clap and tried to force the magic to gather all in his right fist. It mostly did, though it was sloppy, and he could feel he'd lost a good bit of it, like airag sloshing from an unsteady bowl. It'd have to be enough.

Subei brought his fist down on the earth and a shockwave burst from the point of impact. It rushed forward through the ground, bits of grass and hay kicked up into the air. The dummies themselves were entirely uprooted and toppled. The shockwave caught them in its grasp and carried them a few paces before depositing them all in a pile.

"There we are," Mahtma said, squinting only slightly against the swirling dirt and hay dust.

Subei wiped a wash of sweat from his eyes, then placed his hands atop his head to catch his breath. He'd made quite a mess of the training ground. Given, that had been Mahtma's instructions.

The scar dividing his face complained as he smiled, but he found he couldn't resist. Hadn't known it beforehand, but he'd needed this release. Now he was exhausted, but felt better than he had in a long time.

Mahtma picked up a waterskin at her feet and tossed it to him.

"It's not airag or wine."

"Probably for the best." He took a long drink of the cool water and appreciated how much the world wasn't spinning.

"So, what next?" he asked before taking another long drink.

"Next," Mahtma said, sitting to face the still-rising sun, "we sit."

"Meditate, you mean?" he said, sitting next to her and crossing his legs.

"Straighten your back, no more slouching. And no more words." She took a deep breath and closed her eyes. "Today, we sit."

Chapter Thirty-Nine

BATAAR

Subei's barrage of North Wind Scours came whistling in, but it was weak. So weak, Bataar didn't bother to waste magic on it, just braced his feet and let it wash over him.

"Hmphh," he said, shaking his head, then let a bit of a sting climb into his tone. "You exhausted yourself against those training dummies, brother. Didn't you leave something for me to spar against?" He ended with a cocky smile, knowing the barb would rile Subei up. Antagonize him so they could get to some meaningful practice. And maybe there was a bit of payback in his words, too. He couldn't remember much of their drunken argument, but what he could left his stomach sour.

Subei said nothing, only scowled.

Still not on speaking terms, then?

Another series of wind strikes, then, these fiercer than the last.

Not nearly strong enough, Bataar thought as he dodged and bulled his way through them, respectively. *We can do better. Far better.*

"You might be going through the motions this evening, but I was hoping to make some real progress. Be on your guard, yeah?" Bataar called through the whipping remnants of the last wind strike. An orb came hurtling in by way of response.

"Progress!" Bataar cheered, then hit the orb mid-air with one of his own, resulting in a booming explosion and a wash of smoke. "But hardly original. Come now, brother. Hit me!"

"Don't kill each other, please," Ghula said from several paces off to the side—far enough as to be out of any danger, probably. "Your Father is watching."

Bataar's eyes flicked to the side at that, and he found she was right. The khagan himself had come out to the training ground, a retinue of guards with him, along with Mahtma and some other torols. They all watched now, fascinated by the display.

They haven't seen anything yet.

Bataar focused inward, turned his thoughts to the magic within him. It was fully replenished since the fight on the cliff-side—even despite the nights of drinking and poor rest—and itching to be used.

We'll start with something simple, he thought, then slapped his left hand into his right—the latter balled into a fist—and imbued it with magic. Just as quick, he whipped his left arm out, corralling Subei with wind strikes. They drove him to the side, as planned, and Bataar brought his right fist down to the ground. A shockwave exploded outward, instantly rending the soil. The force of the blast knocked Subei off his feet and he went down on his back hard. A series of *oohs* and *ahhs* drifted over from those watching.

"Fist that Moves Mountains. You never got around to teaching it to me, so I figured it was time I taught myself," Bataar called as Subei fought to pull himself up, his feet finding no purchase in the earth that'd been reduced to loose gravel.

Bataar strode forward, arm extended.

"Need a hand up, brother?"

Subei growled, then rolled to the side and flung an orb. Bataar ducked it, then was forced to throw himself to the side as a second, then a third came hissing in. They exploded behind him, raining soil down all around.

Now we're getting somewhere.

Bataar rolled to his feet, then was forced to duck to the side as Subei lashed out with All the World a Weapon. His magic took hold of the shattered ground and flung it, the shrapnel hissing as Bataar ducked away, one arm up to protect his face. A larger chunk of rock caught him in the hips and spun him around. It wasn't a damaging blow, but that much mass was hard to resist. He was thrown off balance, but regained it as he spun, then planted one foot wide to catch himself.

"That enough for you, *brother*?" Subei said, spitting his first words of the session.

"A moment, please," Bataar called back.

Subei's brow raised at that, and concern crept into his eyes for a moment.

And now for the real show, Bataar thought, then sent a quick prayer to the ancestors. *Great Khan, lend me your strength.*

He focused his breathing, inhaled deep and held it for one. . . two. . . three, then exhaled. Again, then again until he fell into the now familiar rhythm of the soul wind. The sensation of it crept over him, and then it was as if he was meditating—but he stopped short of his mind slipping into blissful nothingness. Instead, he directed his thoughts to his core, to his magic, then onward still. He went further, deeper, until he stood at the very edge of that abyssal spring. In it, the bloodrage stirred. Back from its hibernation, finally.

You are my weapon, Bataar thought as he stared down into that abyss. *I will wield you.*

And then he called the rage forth. He called it to him as a master to his hound—and the rage answered. All at once, initially, but Bataar rebuked it. A squeeze of his core, a blast of the sort of focused, concerted will only possible when in this state, and he pushed it back. Most of it, at least.

The result was a constrained flow of the bloodrage. Unwieldy, yes, and fighting to break, but not so strong that it could slip Bataar's mental grasp. He held it firm, then directed it into his core. It mixed with the magic there, and then, all at once, Bataar felt its heat flow through him. But not an overwhelming surge, no. This wasn't the rising, roiling, all-consuming heat that stole away control and intent. This was something else. A union. A partnership.

An understanding.

The constrained rage surged through him, and everywhere it touched, exhaustion was burned away. Pain, too. In their place, he found only fresh strength and so much magic it practically rushed from him all of its own accord. Took physical effort to keep it fully contained.

But keeping it fully contained wasn't the point of this experiment.

Bataar met his brother's gaze, and Subei took a step backward.

"What've you done?"

"The impossible," Bataar said, and then, even if every moment he had to focus on keeping the rage restrained, he still couldn't keep a smile from crawling across his face.

Bataar unleashed a blast of North Wind Scours then, and it was effortlessly powerful. So strong, it swept up debris as it passed and drove it at Subei. He dove to the side—several chunks smashing against him anyway—and the ground he'd been standing on was scoured. No mere wind had passed there but a driving, howling thing that left the land scarred in its passing.

"Bataar, stop!" Subei shouted. "Resist it!"

"I am, and so much more," Bataar said, reveling in the release of the magic. There was so much his core couldn't contain it. It spilled out, pushed against his palms and feet—his mind even, thoughts swimming with its intoxicating presence—and trickled out of him in little flares of light.

"Fight back! Don't let it control you!" Subei was running toward him now. Bataar hit him in the chest with a wind strike that bowled him backward.

"Ghula!" Subei shouted. "Help me with him! We have to—"

"*I am in control*," Bataar called, interrupting the plea, even if his words were somewhat strained. More than he'd have preferred, but they were true. "I am in control, and we're still sparring, brother. Now hit me."

"Bataar?" Ghula shouted, her voice stiff with authority.

"I am in control," he said again, then lowered his hands and, focusing inward, made to lessen the flow of the bloodrage to demonstrate.

"We can't trust it!" Subei shouted and spread his arms wide. All the World a Shield took hold of the rent earth around them and drew it up into a compacted wall. Subei punched forward and the wall came hurtling in.

Bataar extended a hand toward it, fist closed, then spread his fingers wide. The wall shook, then fell apart as the magic binding it was dispelled. In a blink, what had been a crushing wall of earth collapsed to disparate pebbles.

Subei came soaring past them, a fist reared back and murderous intent in his eyes. Bataar ducked the blow, then gave ground as he parried and dodged the following flurry of strikes.

He thinks he's fighting for his life.

Bataar smirked.

"Let me. . . " Subei grunted, throwing blow after blow. "Stop this. . . " The next strike came aimed at Bataar's temple, but he turned his head so it glanced off. Between his empowered body and the pain-lessening effects of the bloodrage, he didn't even feel the blow. "Help me, Bataar!" Subei cried. "If you—"

Bataar caught the next punch in his palm, squeezed tight. An upper cut, next, and Bataar parried it to the side, then entangled Subei's arm in his own and locked tight.

They were face to face then, and Subei was panting and cursing, his eyes wild with desperation.

Bataar held him locked there a moment, then focused his mind on the controlled bloodrage and, with a long, steady breath, squeezed his core and pushed the rage back into its spring. It didn't go without a fight. It took a second breath and another good burst of concentration, but the rage was beaten back. When the last of it slipped into the abyss, Bataar let out a long sigh, then met Subei's eyes.

"I am in control, brother." A genuine smile then. "I am *stronger* than the bloodrage. And so are you."

Chapter Forty

SUBEI

"It is a fine morning, my students."

Mahtma waited at the edge of the training ground. She greeted them with a bow from amidst the wreckage of the day prior.

Subei returned the gesture and the traditional response as Bataar approached from the opposite side, then did the same. Coming from the direction he was, Subei figured he must've been at the feasting tent. Sneaking in an early breakfast? No. Finishing up a late night.

A storm had blown in after their sparring session the previous evening. It'd howled and ripped at the walls of the ger as Subei sat alone, waiting for Bataar to return. Waiting to discuss what'd happened. He hadn't returned, though. Maybe it'd been the storm that'd kept him out.

That same storm was pinned against the towering Ghairkhan range now, sitting just above them in an unrelenting drizzle. The rain fell in icy drops, tinged with a chill that told of summer's wane.

The exertions of the day prior had been a needed release, but they hadn't solved everything. The guilt, the anger, the fear were still there, knotted and twisted tighter than ever. And buried deep down, its source was still strong. Weakened somewhat now that Mahtma had pulled him from his drinks, but nowhere near beaten. Destroy as many training dummies as he wanted, the bloodrage wasn't going anywhere. But. . . had Bataar found another way? Subei let himself feel the joy of that hope for a singular moment before quashing it. Of course he hadn't. How could it be possible?

"With me, my students," Mahtma said and turned to lead them from camp.

Little puddles splashed beneath their feet as the old monk strode up a hill. She moved quick despite the dark and the rain. Soon she was a shadow, then nothing more than the suggestion of a silhouette in the blowing mist.

"How?" Subei asked under his breath, but he wasn't speaking to Mahtma.

"I can teach you," Bataar said.

"No. It's a trick. It's not possible."

"We're both slow learners, I know." He was grinning now. "But if I can figure it out, so can you. We'll master this, Subei. Together."

"I don't trust it." Subei picked up his pace, slipping on the slope and the mud. When he finally made it up, he found Mahtma sitting atop the hill, facing away from him.

"Sit with me, Son of Kemu. *Sons* of Kemu," she added a moment later as Bataar arrived.

She seemed perfectly content like that, sinking into grass that looked more like a swamp. Subei sighed. Couldn't get much wetter than he already was. He plopped down next to her with a splash, cringing only slightly as the chilly water soaked through his pants and sent gooseflesh rising all across him.

Bataar folded down beside him.

Mahtma spoke without looking at either of them, her eyes focused on the land ahead. The rain was lighter there, mere wisps of water and fog on the wind. Subei could see south for a considerable distance.

"You are heirs. You were given Baji's magic, but there is more to your inheritance." She extended a hand to the land before them.

Subei followed where she gestured.

"South?" he asked.

"The Zhong empire," Bataar said, with a knowing nod.

"Closer than that." Mahtma turned her outstretched hand to a pointing finger and directed their eyes lower. The valley.

Ah. The realization dawned on Subei as he looked closer. Dark shapes were scattered there. The bodies of Zhong soldiers. The remains of the battlefield.

"Anger. Violence. Death," Mahtma spoke again. "You are heirs, and these things are the shadows you cast. No matter where you go, they will follow."

"Anger, violence, and death for our enemies," Bataar grunted. "Peace, glory, and honor for our people."

Normally Subei would have had something clever to say. Some witty retort. He found he'd none now.

Mahtma continued unfazed.

"No one has properly spoken to you of the responsibilities of your magic. I would have sooner, but I did not believe you were ready to listen. I still don't believe you are, but I fear we no longer have time to wait. So today, my students, we talk." She held perfectly still as a drop of rain ran down to hang from the tip of her nose. It shuddered as she exhaled, then with one last shake, plunged down to join the mud and grass.

"Let's start with Kashi."

"What's there to say?" Subei heard the anger in his voice, tried to hide it. "He's dead."

"Truly a peaceful mind you have, if that's how you feel. My people strive for years to achieve such control." She looked sideways at him.

"Ancestors above," he cursed. "I've made what peace I can with my brother's death. Need we dig it all back up now?"

"We haven't talked about it, brother. Not really," Bataar said, his words heavy and his eyes downcast.

"Words won't help the dead," Subei shot back.

"But they may yet help the living." Mahtma poked a finger at her own chest. "The heart is an important organ in a person. Pierce it, and they will most likely die. But for an heir, I believe it is even more important. And even more deadly." She paused a moment, eyes going distant as though thinking. When she continued, her voice had a grave tone he hadn't heard before.

"From what I've witnessed, and from what scant accounts

281

detail, the bloodrage is intertwined with Baji's magic, but I believe it is fueled by the heart. By emotion. In the Longlarch, we started down the path of controlling your thoughts, and thereby your emotions. You must understand how important this lesson is, so that we may complete it."

She looked half drowned as she spoke, what with her soaked-through robes and hair slipping from her bun, but her words were sound. As far as Subei could tell, she was right. The blood-rage had seemed influenced by his emotions.

After Kashi died, it had grown significantly. Normally, killing an heir and absorbing more magic seemed to be the primary way the bloodrage grew in power, in. . . awareness. But even before the Zhong heir's death on the mountainside, he'd felt the rage growing. Almost as if it was feeding off his anger, off his desire for revenge. The whispers from that abyss had been as constant as ever—except for during the fight on the cliffside, when he'd needed the bloodrage most.

"Learn to control your thoughts, your emotions, and you can survive the bloodrage. You can stop it growing stronger, and lessen its effects when it is at its worst."

"You've said as much before," Subei said.

"But she's right," Bataar cut in. "That's how I was able to wield the rage yesterday. Soul wind breathing, paired with intense focus, and sheer will."

"*Wielding* it is not the answer," Mahtma said, and her voice went stern as she did. "You must deny it. Refuse it all together."

"The Khagan seemed impressed enough," Bataar said, and his tone made it clear that was all that mattered.

"The greatest strength of a leader lies in knowing where their own falls short. Your father ordered me to instruct you in these matters because he was wise enough to admit he was ill-equipped to do so."

"I listen to your teachings," Bataar said, tone neutral. "But I listen to Ghula's as well. My father ordered she instruct us too."

"Even your father's wisdom has its limits," Mahtma said, then continued before Bataar could take issue. "I do not condone you *wielding* the bloodrage. But neither can I stop you. If you are intent on continuing down this path, you need to hear this all the more. Knowing how to refuse the rage may be the only thing that can save you from it."

Bataar crossed his arms and did his best to look unconvinced. Subei saw through it, though. You weren't brothers with someone for so long without gaining that ability.

"You have seen the bloodrage released on several occasions now," Mahtma continued. "Have seen, without illusion, what your life could so easily become. When you tracked down bandits for your father, you were fighting criminals. Honorless thieves who had broken the laws of the khanate." She gestured to the battlefield. "The corpses down there are the work of sword and bow, spear and lance. They were soldiers who marched from home knowing they might face their end. The corpses the bloodrage leaves behind, however, are of an entirely different nature."

Subei cursed to himself, but he knew she was right. The rage killed without direction or restraint. Killed, it seemed, for the fun of it.

"Think of Chobei," she said, but he already was. Was seeing Jong's headless corpse lit by flames. Flames that he'd stoked to spread and engulf the town.

"Think of the hut in the forest," she said, but he already was. Was seeing that old man's hand, broken and bruised from beneath the pile of rubble that'd once been his home. Was hearing those screams that didn't sound like they'd come from the soldiers or the old man.

"Think of Kashi," she said. "He—"

"Point taken," Subei said abruptly. Not a train of thought he had any interest in finishing.

She nodded, then spoke again with a voice that seemed, if possible, soft.

"I believe the bloodrage to be a cycle. When it is released, it revels in whatever chaos and bloodshed it can induce. And when it slinks back to its abyss, the memories haunt you. They breed anger, doubt, desperation. All of which fuel the rage and help it to come back stronger the next time."

"So you're saying we should just forget what we've done?" Subei asked, anger hot in his chest.

"*No.*" And her voice was right back to its usual severity. "By no means should you forget what you've done. Just as the blood-rage draws strength from those memories, so should you. Use them to remind yourself what it is capable of. What it can make you do."

Ah.

Subei shifted uncomfortably, ripples rolling out across the growing puddle he sat in. At the same time, Bataar grunted, then nodded as if accepting the logic.

"They can be a steadying hand when wielding the rage. I understand now."

"You must accept what you've done, accept what you've become, and resolve to do *better.*" She locked eyes with Subei. "Resolve to *be* better." Then Bataar next. "Be *smarter.*"

Subei almost laughed. Right, because it was that easy.

"So I just say I'm going to be better, and then I will be? Forgive my saying so, but that sounds like horseshit."

Mahtma almost smiled, and Subei suddenly felt he'd stumbled into some sort of trap.

"The Ghangerai are a people of action, are they not?"

"Always!" Bataar said, almost defensive in tone.

"We are," Subei gave his own answer carefully, thinking back on what had been said and searching for any indication she'd intentionally led them to this conclusion.

"Then no, you shouldn't just say you'll be better. You should prove it through your actions. Words promise, actions prove."

There it was. And well played. She wasn't wrong, not by any means. Everything she'd said had sounded true, had aligned with what he had experienced himself through the bloodrage.

So why then was he so loath to accept it? Why did he want to reject her logic? But Subei knew why. Just didn't want to admit it to himself. He was loath to take her advice because it was the hard thing to do. Because change sounded good and right in conversation but was a damned hard thing to actually achieve. It was the easy thing to sulk in his regrets and fears, to cry and moan about the bloodrage and drink himself into oblivion hoping something would change. But hope without action? What did that count for? Nothing.

"Your magic burdens you with great responsibility, Sons of Kemu. A responsibility not just to yourself, but to the world and all who live in it. I suspect Baji understood this, and that is why he sealed away the magic. Some might call what he did cowardice which deprived his people of mighty strength. I'd argue it was an act of courage. The easy thing would have been to give up, to give in. To let himself fall to the bloodrage, and to hell with the world and all in it when that monster was unleashed.

"Instead, he did the hard thing. He fought it to the last, and somehow, locked it away. His battle is now yours. You will learn to control the bloodrage, or you will kill yourself trying." She paused a moment, eyes drifting across the blowing mists. "Have you ever considered what might happen if the rage were to get free, wreak its havoc, then *not* return to its slumber? What if that horror is unleashed and finds it has the strength to remain?"

A message delivered with all the tenderness and sensitivity the old monk was known for. That being, of course, none. But a message delivered and understood. What would happen if the rage became so strong it could take control and never give it back? It had already razed a town just to send a message. Subei shuddered to think what would happen were it given more than the brief few glimpses of freedom it'd already had.

"No enemies, only victims," Subei said it quietly at first, then louder the second time. "That's what the bloodrage said in the Longlarch."

Bataar looked up at that, eyes hard. "All the more reason it must be controlled."

"All the more reason it must be *refused*, brother." Subei shuddered. "What happens when it runs out of Zhong to kill?"

Will it ever be satisfied?

"Mahtma's right," Subei said, even though he'd never realized it before. "This is much bigger than us. Bigger than the khanate, than the war. Than any aspirations we once had. Like it or not, this responsibility is ours." He shook his head, struggled for his next words. "It might be that leaves us with naught but shit choices, but they're the choices we've been given."

He chuckled then. Didn't know how else to react to the

thoughts rushing through his mind. Didn't know how to process the fact that their desires, their wants and needs, had, in the span of a conversation, been rendered irrelevant.

Shit, for the most part, their own lives had been rendered irrelevant. At least, as far as what either of them wanted to do with them. Mahtma was not wrong. Might be Subei hadn't seen more than this small corner of the world, but now he'd a responsibility to the whole of it. A responsibility to control the blood-rage or die trying.

It was Bataar's turn to chuckle and shake his head next.

"Shit choices, eh?"

"Shit choices, indeed, brother."

It might be they hadn't seen eye to eye about much lately, but that, at least, they could agree on. Even if they went about it in different ways.

Control.

Refusal.

Two paths to the same destination? Or did one lead to a cliff, hidden by brush and so sudden it couldn't be seen until it was too late?

"Well, don't make me say it." Subei leaned back and raised his eyes to the storm clouds. His choice was obvious. Not much of a choice, really. "Only one reasonable way to go about this. Let's beat this damned thing."

Bataar grunted his agreement, one fist clenched.

"Nothing about this is reasonable," Mahtma said. "But that makes the conquest all the greater, does it not?" She trained her eyes south and east, and Subei's followed to where the towering peaks of the Ghairkhan range rose into the clouds, obscured far above the eyes of all on this dreary morning.

"Easier to move a mountain than change a person's nature," he said, eyes lost among the towering giants. "Looks to me like we should've picked the mountain. At least those we know we can break."

Chapter Forty-One

SUBEI

Earlier he'd been wet with rain, now he was wet with sweat. The morning storms had broken and scattered, driven to the far edges of the sky as the sun rose. It brought with it a humid heat that was far worse than any rain.

Subei wiped his brow with his forearm as he rolled the canvas of the ger. Tugu Khan and his toumans had left days earlier to clear the way. Budai and Arban even earlier still. It was time now for the rest to follow. The bulk of the United Army was getting underway, and no man was too good to pack his own ger.

There were attendants, of course, and subordinates, but it was a point of pride for his people, one that stretched all the way back to the distant past. Each person was khan of their own ger, and that meant taking care of it.

Subei's breath came heavy, sweat running down into his eyes and dripping from his nose as he rolled lengthy stretches of canvas into tight bundles. When each was finished, he tied it with a length of rope.

"I should be helping you with that, brother," a voice came from behind.

Bataar.

"Yes, you should." Subei didn't look up from the work, ready for him to join in his usual place and take apart his third of the structure.

Who will handle Kashi's?

It was only after that thought stopped his work that Subei noticed Bataar hadn't joined in.

"Father wishes to speak with us. I've brought an extra horse." He gestured over his shoulder where an attendant stood with two mounts.

"We need to finish packing the ger."

The attendant abandoned the horses and took up the work. Subei balked.

"Each man is khan of his own ger. As a matter of honor, he must—"

"The khagan has summoned us, this is more important. Come on." Bataar turned and swung into the saddle.

They rode in silence and at a trot as they passed among the rapidly disappearing camp. Seemed everyone was in motion, packing gers or readying mounts, sharpening weapons or filling waterskins. Where the night prior a great army had sprawled across the land, grouped around the entrance to the valley, by mid-morning there would be nothing left but trampled grass and smoldering fire pits. Speed was the greatest weapon of a Ghang-erai army, and it seemed the khagan meant to put it to use this day.

"Brother?" Subei asked, side-eyeing him. "Have you ever heard of someone named Gyakhal Bha?"

"Gyakha-what?"

"*Gyah khal bah*," Subei said slowly. "At least, I think that was their name."

"I don't know this person or know of them. Where did you hear the name?"

"Uh, don't worry about it," he said, not wanting to admit he'd been eavesdropping on Mahtma and Ghula several days back.

Bataar made to respond but the reply died in his throat. The khagan was before them now, the host of riders around him opening to let them pass.

"Khagan," Subei said, bowing his head from horseback. Bataar did the same.

"My sons," Kemu said with a laugh, eyes cheery. "An auspicious morning, is it not?" Seemed neither the heat nor the humidity had managed to dampen his spirits. He wore a plain deel, as always, but now accompanied by a light layer of leather padding and a fur cloak about his shoulders. He was a bull of a man as it was, but the furs seemed the last dramatic touch needed to complete the image. Man and beast, wrapped into one.

"Are you rested and recovered from your labor?"

"A bit too recovered," Bataar said with a smirk. "Way I hear it, there's fighting ahead. Better we were a part of it than waiting here."

"I am glad to see your spirits yet burn bright, my sons. But remember, we fight because it is necessary, not because we relish it." The khagan turned his horse and directed them to follow. A host of commanders and kheshig guards trailed a few paces behind as they rode into the valley and the remains of the now days old battle. "All the same, the fighting to come is the reason I asked you here today." Kemu Khagan gestured to the ruination of the valley. "This was a great victory, but in the eyes of the ancestors, it is nothing. We have never had trouble beating the Zhong in the field." He led them further through the valley, their train of horses weaving among the boulders as they followed the semi-clear path Tugu Khan and his toumans had made. "Before the time of Baji, you'll recall our ancestor, Ghatugan, led a united army all the way to the walls of Ba Seng, the Zhong capital."

"The legend is well known, Father," Bataar said.

"Then you also know Ghatugan, for all his strength, and all his pride, could not best the walls of Ba Seng. He won every battle on the way to the capital, but there his conquest ended. The capital stood defiant, and in time, resistance fighters, emboldened by their emperor's courage, drove Ghatugan back to the steppe. All his conquest for naught, because Ba Seng would not fall."

The valley was narrowing now, the ground sloping as they started up a hill. Subei spotted what must've been the looted remains of a Zhong encampment, trampled tents and torn banners half buried in mud.

"But Ghatugan," the khagan continued, leaning forward in

the saddle as the ground rose. "Well, he didn't have the magic of Baji, did he?" He turned at the last words and smiled. Not a happy smile, but a hungry one. The smile of a wolf circling its prey. "That came later, and when it did, Ba Seng was no obstacle. Surrendered without a fight, even."

Subei swallowed hard but forced a grin onto his face. That was what his father wanted to see, after all. Not a son mired in indecision, but a conquest-hungry warrior imbued with the magic of the ancestors. Bataar smiled beside him, and Subei had no doubt it was genuine.

"When we arrive at Ba Seng, they will surrender as they did to Baji, or you will blow their gates to splinters."

They reached the top of the hill, and the khagan reined his horse in and peered out at the lands before them.

The Ghairkhan range paralleled them for some ways to the east before turning back north and dwindling from sight. But that was not their course. South was where they were headed. The land there shallowed and flattened, first into low hills, then something else beyond. Almost looked to be steppe, if Subei squinted.

The khagan took a deep breath and spread his arms wide as he turned his eyes to them.

"What feels all too long ago now, I sent you on a hunt into Zhong lands. You came back mightier than any of us could have hoped. But there is yet another hunt before us." He turned back south, to the distant horizon where, many days away, Ba Seng waited, the Zhong emperor and his armies with it. "By the ancestors above, by the might of Great Baji Khan, let us see it done."

Chapter Forty-Two

SUBEI

The land was changing. Had been for some time. At first, they'd paralleled the Ghairkhan range for several days, but soon the mountains turned east, then back north, and were left behind. The army continued south across a vast plain, dry grass crunching under hoof and kicking a continuous plume of dust into the air. It followed them wherever they went, too thin to provide any shade from the scorching southern sun, but thick enough to catch in every mouth and throat. It covered everything in a perpetual layer of fine, powder-like grit.

The land was passable and survivable, however. Tugu Khan and his toumans had already crossed it, their trail evident. They were several days ahead, the advanced force serving both to hide the true size of the army and to remove any resistance the Zhong offered. Aside from Chobei and the few towns like it in this borderland, the Zhong hadn't much interest in this area, so said the scouts. It couldn't be farmed, nor could it be grazed.

And so they crossed a wasteland of sorts. Nothing so severe as the deserts of Mercer, but a wasteland all its own. Ya Ning's Mire, it was called, after a long-dead emperor who'd lost the whole of his army to the land here. Didn't look it now, but the place was impassable most of the year. When the rains came, it flooded in ankle-deep water and mud as far as the eye could see. Too shallow for a boat to cross, and too treacherous to pass on foot. They crossed it now at the waning end of summer, the land at its driest. Winter would bring storms, and storms would bring rain, then snow. It was only this time of year, for a couple of weeks, that the land was passable.

Some ancient people had planted great stones three times as tall as a horse across the wastes, and it was these that led them now. The Siltway, it was called. A road through the waste. Though "road" was perhaps too generous a word for the path they followed. More a collection of waystones leading on, each just barely in sight of the next.

The crossing also brought a sense of reality to the invasion. Few spoke it aloud, but Subei saw it on their faces as they rode. Heard it in that extra little edge of sharpness in everyone's speech. Might be they'd crushed the Zhong Northern Army, but now they were truly devoting themselves to the fighting ahead. In a few weeks' time, the rains would begin, and the drizzling storms they'd encountered would seem paradise compared to the torrential downpours that would come next.

Ya Ning's Mire would return to its usual state of impassable wetland and the quickest, easiest route back to the khanate would be sealed. The only way home would be far east, around the whole of the mountains to Dangshailan and the coast. What had taken them a week and a half up to this point would then take a month or more. So here they were. Committed.

Morning came early in this place. The steppe was mostly flat with low hills, but this was different. Here there were no hills. Just a flat, unending plain. And so the moment the sun climbed above the eastern horizon, daylight swept across the land. Subei had woken at his usual time, yet the brightness of the morning was astounding.

Made it all too easy to see the pain coming.

Thwack!

Subei could've easily sidestepped the blow or blocked it with his forearms. Even the slightest of wind strikes might've turned it off target. But that was not the point of this exercise.

Thwack!

Mahtma's quarterstaff slammed into his ribs. He felt it too, which was a credit to the torol's strength. It took a lot to get through his toughened body these days. If it'd been strong going

292

into the battle with the Zhong heirs, now it was damn near impervious. The last magic transfer had pushed it to limits Subei hadn't imagined. Blades left behind only scratches, clubs might as well have been pillows, and best of all, infuriating, biting little midges were a thing of the past. Couldn't get through his skin, it seemed.

Crack!

Another blow from Mahtma, and her staff shattered against him, cracked all to splinters. She tossed it aside.

"Third one today," Subei said, eyeing it. "How many do you have?"

"Not enough," she said, breathing heavy. "A change of tactics may be required."

"By all means, do what you—gah!"

She jabbed a fresh staff right into his nose, caught it at his top lip and thrust up against the soft cartilage. The skin didn't break, and the blow didn't feel particularly powerful, but a surge of pain followed it, flashed bright in Subei's eyes.

"Found a spot there," Bataar said, nodding from where he watched to one side.

"It's your turn next," Subei said, voice muffled by the hand pressed to his nose.

Mahtma's next attack came from behind, another heavy jab. This one landed right where his skull met his spine, and again, there was a flash of pain. Subei hissed as he stumbled forward. His teeth clicked sharply as he bit down, but he swallowed the pain. And the anger that rose with it.

Training, Mahtma had been calling this, though Subei was starting to think they'd simply run out of training dummies. For days now, the army had been advancing further into Zhong lands, but for every day spent in the saddle, Subei and Bataar had first spent a morning as Mahtma's stand-in training dummies.

Thwack!

This blow caught him across the knuckles. It hurt, but not like those previous.

"No good there, hm? Oh well." She jabbed him in the nose again and his vision faltered. His feet were swept next, and he slammed down backwards, a jolt running up his spine. Even before he could process it, Mahtma jabbed him at the base of the skull again. His head was properly ringing then, and it only got worse when she planted a foot in his shoulder blades and smashed his face into the earth. Couldn't breathe then, for the dirt choking him as well as the heavy kick that drove the air from his stomach.

"Urgh," Subei groaned as a shudder ran through him. He braced himself, fingers clawing through the earth as they balled into shaking fists. The bloodrage took advantage of his pain. Turned it to anger and used it to climb from the abyss, then rush through him in a flood of adrenaline.

Subei spat and cursed, eyes closed as he forced his thoughts to the rage. He felt he would vomit, lying on his stomach but unstable still as the world spun. A warmth began to spread outward from his stomach, rising over him. He could see it, in his mind's eye, as the bloodrage rose from that spring, crawling up, tentative but hungry.

No.

He redoubled his efforts, doing his best to ignore it while he concentrated on measured, focused breaths.

Inhale, one. . . two. . . three, exhale.

Breathe. Breathe and think of nothing.

But no, not nothing. The memories.

Through gritted teeth, he thought back to Chobei, back to that hut in the Longlarch, back to the innocent people the rage had killed. The innocent people *he'd* killed because he'd let it take control. That wouldn't happen again. Not here, not today. The bloodrage abated some, seemed to hesitate.

Subei spat and focused on the memories. The bodies of the guards who'd come to fight the fire. He and Bataar had left them behind looking more like scraps than once-living beings with hopes and dreams. Their blood ran up and down the walls, covered him head to toe.

Slowly, ever so slowly, the rage receded back into its abyss. His body relaxed, muscle by muscle, and he fell flat to the earth, breath coming heavy, shooting puffs of dust up into the air. Nonetheless, he felt a smile stretch across his face. Might be

Mahtma had replaced him with a training dummy, but damned if it wasn't working. He'd never been able to control the rage. But now, now he could. Well, not control it, but halt it, at least. That was something, wasn't it? It was progress! Subei pulled his head up, smiling. Maybe, if he kept at it, soon he'd—

Thwack!

A heavy blow as Mahtma shattered the staff across his brow and the bloodrage rushed forth again, swept his mind up in the swell of its great flood and drowned his thoughts. The surge of anger and adrenaline blacked out his vision for a moment, and when it returned, he was merely a collection of thoughts trapped in his own mind.

His body rolled to its feet, locked eyes on Mahtma and lunged forward, scars bursting to life with a burning light as he prepared to attack her, kill her, tear her to nothing.

Bataar was moving to defend her, but she didn't need him. Faster than Subei could track, she dodged under his attacks, then sidestepped a wind strike, and slipped behind him. Her arms swept up under his own, her biceps jammed into his armpits. In this position, his arms were trapped in the air, out of reach of her and pretty much anything else. Entirely useless. Except, he could still conjure orbs. The bloodrage did just that then, magic surging toward his palm—but Mahtma was faster.

Her thumb pressed into the base of his skull, just below the ear, and applied a steady, heavy pressure.

The bloodrage snarled and hissed, spit and curses flying from his mouth, but in his thoughts, Subei sent a prayer of thanks to the ancestors as his strength receded, a wave drawing back from the shore. His thoughts slowed, the edges of his vision grew ragged, and unconsciousness swallowed him up.

When he opened his eyes again, he'd no idea how long it'd been. Mahtma was seated facing him, what sweat there'd been on her brow now dried.

"Almost had it that time, Son of Kemu."

She wasn't smiling, but there was a light taunting in her voice. She was baiting him, but damn it, he'd been so close to fighting it back!

His instincts told him to fight the numbness, to struggle, to

295

take back control of his body. His mind knew it wasn't possible. Not yet, at least. It would take a bit to wear off.

"You hit me again, right when I got it under control. That was a cheap trick," he said, forcing his clumsy mouth to work.

"You don't have time in a fight to catch your breath and focus. If you're going to control the rage when it matters most, you have to be able to bury it without lowering your guard."

"And how in the name of the ancestors do you propose I do that?"

"It's the same as moving a mountain, I suppose." She smiled and stood to her full height, impossibly tall above him. "Takes a lot of time and a lot of hard work." She spun to face Bataar, then. "Your turn."

Chapter Forty-Three

BATAAR

Trees, on the western horizon. A wall of them so thick there seemed no way through. Not that anyone in their right mind would enter that place. Bataar had heard stories of it, even as a child. Or, perhaps, particularly as a child.

"The Murkwater," Ghula said, her eyes following his to the shadows on the horizon. "The Zhong say it's haunted." She hiked a thumb back northeast, toward the distant but still-lingering mountains. "If the Ghairkhan Range is the sacred realm of the ancestors in this mortal world, that place's the opposite. A purgatory of damned souls, and worse still."

"Growing up, Grandmother told me it's where nightmares come from. They'd bubble up from that swamp to be carried on the wind, then dropped through the smoke escape of naughty children's gers," Bataar said, lost a moment in memories from long ago. And, staring at the place now, he could see how that myth had begun. An ever-shifting haze seemed to hang over the trees, distorting the air.

"Mahtma told me once it's a maze in there. All swamp and roots and shadows. And there's many-toothed lizard beasts what hide in the water, waiting to take a leg, or more."

"She's been there?" Bataar asked, eyes wide.

"No, read about it."

Ah. That makes sense.

"No reason to have been there before, and no reason to go there," Ghula continued with a stiff nod.

Bataar spurred his horse on at that. "If I'd had even the slightest inclination to poke around in that hell, trust me, the Longlarch cured me of it. I'll stick to open sky, open land, and honest enemies, thank you very much."

"Honest or dishonest enemies," Ghula said. "With you able to control the bloodrage, I don't think it much matters now."

"It's control," Bataar said, nodding and trying not to look *too* proud about his progress. "But it's limited. And fragile. Though, sometimes it feels like. . . " He hesitated then, trying to find the right words. "Never mind. I just have to keep training it."

"You think I was going to accept anything else?" Ghula laughed, then reached from her saddle and slapped him on the back. "I'm going to work you even harder than Mahtma is."

Bataar's eyes flicked to the bruises and cuts from where her strongest blows had managed to cause minor injuries. He grinned, then.

"You're welcome to try, old woman."

"Oh ho," Ghula chuckled. "You'll regret that comment later, boy."

They rode on as the sun and clouds passed overhead. What didn't pass was the Murkwater, as if stalking them on the horizon. In theory, cutting across it would have allowed the army to surprise the Zhong from the far west. They'd be able to sweep down through the unprotected heartland and cut it off from the capital. But the swamp was no place for warriors, or horses, and much less an army of warriors on horses. So they continued south, crossing to the very end of Ya Ning's Mire.

The great cracked plain gave way then, to a low ridge of hills, the first green grass anyone had seen in days. Cheers greeted the sight, starting at the forward ranks and working their way back. A fine sight, living plants. Green meant water, and water was a luxury they'd all come to appreciate. Seemed even the khagan had been sucking the final drops from his waterskin. Around camp, some warriors had resorted to drinking their horses' blood. It was an ancient practice of the tribes that lived in the drier borderlands on the far west of the Empty Sea. Taking too much would weaken the horse, but a bit here and there, taken from different horses over a couple of days kept both rider and mounts healthy.

The cheering at the thought of water was redoubled when the first ranks of the army left the plain, horses' hooves passing into the grass below the hills. It was quickly silenced thereafter, however, when the hills were climbed.

Bataar and Ghula rode just behind the head of the army, a few lengths back from the khagan, when the soldiers were spotted. A force of them was arrayed on the plain below the hills, the blue moon-and-quill banner of the Zhong empire flying over them. And behind their lines, three walled towns waited, one to the east, one to the west, and one right in the center, directly in their path.

"What is this?" Bataar hissed, joining the exclamations traveling down the line. "What of our scouts? The vanguard?" The force before them couldn't have been more than eight thousand soldiers, and only half of those mounted. Still, its mere existence was a problem.

"Tugu Khan has already come this way!" Bataar said, already reaching for his saber as he turned to Ghula. "They were to clear all resistance, or failing that, await reinforcements." And yet, here they had done neither. They were simply. . . gone. No signs of battle, even. Just this armed force arrayed before them. Not to mention the fortified towns waiting on the horizon.

"Patience, Son of Kemu," Ghula said. And was she. . . grinning?

All around, warriors began to call for an attack on the force when the khagan quieted them with a gesture. He turned back to his army, leading his horse to the tallest point of the hill so his voice would carry down across the ranks stretching back across the plain. There was no way they would all hear him, but those that did would spread his words down the line.

"Warriors of the khanate!" Kemu Khagan stood in his stirrups, drew their eyes to him.

"The news of Baji's heirs is a weapon in itself," Ghula said. She was looking up at the khagan with a knowing smile.

What was she talking about? They should be readying for

battle, Bataar wanted to say, but his father was speaking once more.

"Sheath your blades and stay your bows, warriors. The soldiers before us are not our enemies." He pointed down the hill toward the small army. "The ancestors have blessed this invasion. First with Baji's heirs, and now with new allies. Or, perhaps, the return of old ones." He turned as his horse paced, pulling on the reins to face his warriors again.

"Those before us are the Ghanari. Your elders may have told you of them. Long ago, they were brave men and women of the steppe, but greed lured them into the service of the Zhong empire. For years their descendants have served the Zhong as the guardians of the north, kept watch for our armies behind their walls."

The Ghanari? Bataar nodded at that, had heard the tales. When the infighting began, House Ghanari had sided with the Zhong, swayed by greed and gold. They'd been exiled as a result. Stripped of their honor, official titles, and heritage.

"A hundred peoples once bowed before the khanate. Today, we welcome one of them back." The khagan turned to face the Ghanari soldiers. But no, not soldiers, Bataar realized. Warriors.

Kemu Khagan raised one fist high, and the Zhong banners were cast aside. In their place—and with what seemed practiced efficiency—new banners were raised. Khanate banners. Three crossed arrows on a green field.

The front ranks of the force opened, and a bound man was led forward. He wore the battered but still-gleaming armor of a Zhong soldier, and there was an ornate sword at his hip. An officer, then.

"The Zhong commander of the defenses here," Ghula said, nodding toward him. "Defender of the North, they called him."

"The Zhong once thought to pit us against our long-lost cousins," Kemu Khagan cried. "Planned to halt our advance with these defenses. Instead, we welcome another people into the khanate, and tonight, we feast!"

As his words ended, a single sword swing cut the officer's head from his shoulders. His body collapsed, and the army began to cheer again, the rear ranks joining in after the news traveled back. The very earth seemed to shake as even more warriors joined the cheering, sabers clashing against shields, fists pounding against chests. The entirety of the countryside was filled with their roar as the khagan urged his horse forward, and the Ghanari force turned to lead them toward the opening gates of their towns.

Chapter Forty-Four

SUBEI

The Ghanari had abandoned a great many things in service of the Zhong empire. A pure life in favor of greed and gold, their warrior spirit in favor of so-called civilized lives, even their gers in favor of cramped homes stacked atop one another, over and over behind the walls of their three towns.

The Ghanari had abandoned a great many things, but they had not forgotten who they once were. And in time, the khagan had said, they would return to their origins. Would be welcomed back to the steppe. Until that day, they would be treated as an equal people of the khanate. Still, they feasted like Ghangerai. Of that, there was no doubt.

The sun was setting, had only just dipped below the horizon, but the feast was well underway. Cheer, drinks, and drinking songs poured through the streets. Might be the Ghanari had abandoned most of their roots, but those that remained were still strong. They feasted under the open sky, as was proper, so that the ancestors could watch from above and see their descendants' merriment. All through the town, table after table had been pulled into the street and shoved together to host the khagan and the United Army of the khanate. So many were their number, that the celebration spilled out beyond the walls, the light of torches and cooking fires illuminating the grassy meadow all the way to the edge of Ya Ning's Mire. It was the same for the other two towns, Subei saw. The United Army was truly a force beyond comprehension. A force that would have made Baji Khan proud. Didn't seem any way the Zhong could hold them back.

After the long and thirsty trek across the mire, Subei couldn't deny a drink sounded a fine idea. But he couldn't bring himself to the high table, couldn't bear to see Kashi's empty seat and around it, celebration. Instead, he found a quiet side street— quiet being a relative term. Quiet, perhaps, in comparison to the main festivities. But even here, tables were packed together and warriors were singing and laughing.

"A drink, for the heir of Baji Khan!" a warrior cheered as he caught sight of Subei. A bowl was pressed into his hands then, and a good third of it sloshed down his deel.

"To our cousins of old, found again," Subei said as he raised the bowl high.

The street erupted into cheers at that.

"Hear, hear!"

"To the Ghanari!"

"And our victorious dead," Subei said more quietly, then dipped his fingers into the wine to flick away several drops in offering. With that, he raised the bowl to his lips—caught a sniff of wine and his stomach churned all at once. It left him gagging and trying not to show it. Perhaps a drink of water, instead? He tipped the bowl back anyway and made a show of drinking it— even if his lips stayed closed the whole time.

Not the most convincing act, perhaps, but no one was sober that night. The warriors cheered again, then downed their bowls as well. Subei squeezed his core and gave them a flash of light through his scars. More cheering at that as he slipped away and, once out of sight, dumped the wine to the dirt. He rounded a corner. Mahtma was waiting for him.

"Son of Kemu," she said with a nod.

"Torol." He frowned. She carried a wrapped bundle in her arms and three warriors were waiting behind her. Three decidedly unhappy looking warriors, Subei decided. The tallest of them was fighting to keep his eyes from the feasting and merrymaking mere feet away. Behind him, another warrior was bearded, the last one bald.

"It is a fine evening, my student," Mahtma said, and Subei's stomach churned for a different reason. But complaining wasn't going to get him anywhere.

Subei just had time for one longing look at the steaming dishes spilling across the nearest table before Mahtma strode off and he followed. She led them out of the town, then away from the spillover feast. Took them south, a good two hundred paces from the light and noise of the celebrations. She must've deemed that spot acceptable then, for she turned to Subei next.

"It is a fine evening, my student," she said again, this time with a bow. The noise of the feast was still audible, but much quieter here. He did his best to tune it out.

"A fine evening indeed, my teacher." He returned the bow.

One of the warrior's stomachs grumbled loudly.

"You honor us and your khagan with your service here tonight," Mahtma spoke to the three assembled men. "Your dedication will not go unnoticed."

The warriors looked none the happier for her words, but no dissent was voiced. As the khagan's advisor, Mahtma spoke with his authority.

"As soon as we're finished, you may rejoin the feast." The warriors perked up at that. The tallest cracked his knuckles with a nod.

"Let's get to it, then. What'll you have of us?"

Mahtma unwrapped the bundle and tossed him a saber. Not a training one, either. Bearded and Baldy caught similarly sharpened weapons a moment later.

Ah. Subei nodded. He'd been training against Mahtma for a while now, gritting through blow after blow as she tried to encourage his anger, tried to tempt the bloodrage to rise up and take control. She'd been successful more often than not, but he was learning. Was starting to get a handle on how to resist that inner madness.

So now she sought to pit him against a different foe. But he too was a warrior, and had been trained far more than average, at that. And Mahtma was a far better fighter than the four of them combined. Surely, she didn't think a single warrior would be a challenge against him?

"You'll be sparring against my student."

The warriors frowned.

"He will not be allowed the use of any weapons."

The frowns promptly disappeared.

"Right then. Who's first?" Tallest said as he looked from Mahtma to the others.

It was Subei's turn to frown then. He felt it pull across his face, stretch at the stitches holding his still-healing scar closed, as Mahtma spoke her next words.

"You all are."

The men stood shocked for a moment. Subei took advantage of their hesitation.

"Three against one is hardly a fair fight. Even further from a winnable one."

Mahtma turned her gaze to him, eyes holding all the sympathy of a blizzard.

"You win when you learn to control the bloodrage. There is no other victory."

She clapped her hands, spurring the warriors into motion.

"Have at it. There's a feast waiting."

* * *

"Ancestors above," Subei cursed, spitting to one side and reeling back from another blow. Things were going about as expected. His vision wobbled, just beginning to swim as he ducked under a slash, slipping past Tallest. Not that it made much difference. A kick from Baldy caught him in the chest just as he righted himself, sent him sprawling backward into the dirt. A thud as his head slammed down once more and he groaned, vision swimming now.

His body was a mess of fine scratches—the most damage the sabers could manage against him—but the warriors weren't fools. They'd figured it out quick enough and now every blow that fell came with the blade flat. Individually, they didn't hurt much. All at once? It was like going for a run in a hailstorm, if the hail was wide as his hand and aimed mostly at his face.

"In battle, you will not have time to rest properly. You must learn to fight the bloodrage even when you've barely the strength to go on," Mahtma said from the edge of the now-trampled circle of grass.

Subei cursed again as he pulled himself to his feet, willing the world to stop tilting back and forth. Each blow left him more tired. Each blow left the bloodrage clawing to be set free.

"Let me know when you'd like to start trying, Son of Kemu," Mahtma chided. The warriors smirked. Having too good a time of this, they were.

Subei spat to one side and clenched his shaking hand. The scars on his arm were warming now, itching to release the magic imbued within him. That'd give these bastards something to smirk about. A single wind strike would put them on their asses. Another would send them rolling back to the feast, debris caught in a storm. Or an orb. That would do it. Pop them like a blister too long untended—

No. That was the rage speaking. Subei forced the thought away, taking a deep breath to pull his mind free of its influence. He was not the madman it wanted him to be.

One of the warriors caught him across the shoulder with a blunted saber and Subei laughed, made a point of turning to stare the man down.

"Almost tickled, that."

Two blows then, one to the back of each of his knees. Didn't hurt much, but knocked him to the ground all the same. A barrage then, slapping down against his head, his face, smushing his nose one way then the next.

Subei clenched a fist and fought to restrain a growl.

Mahtma had found out every weak spot on him by now. A shot to the nose, dead on, would hurt. Anything to the eyes was uncomfortable, too. The center of his chest, where his ribcage came together was another rough one. These warriors knew none of those spots, but what they lacked in knowledge they made up for in enthusiasm.

"Bastards. . . " Subei growled and fought to regain his feet, but there wasn't much he could do beneath that onslaught. His body might have been toughened, but his strength was still that of a normal warrior. And without use of his magic, well, the beatdown continued.

"Ready to get up and try again?" Tallest laughed from above. Subei's only answer was a slow shuffle of movement as he pulled himself to his knees.

"There you go."

Subei kicked out and caught Tallest in the back of the knees. He was ready for it, though, and fell forward into a roll before rising back to his feet. Subei lunged to one side, but Baldy and Bearded were on him, raining down blows. Not to miss out on the fun, Tallest joined in as well.

Subei gasped as a foot caught him in the stomach, drove the wind from him and rolled him onto his back. A saber came next, swatting away his outstretched arm with the thud of metal on flesh. Another blow, and another, and another until they all melded into one.

Something caught him in the chin and a puff of blood and spit burst into the air as he was rolled back onto his stomach. His open palm slammed into the grass, then clenched closed, raking across the dirt. A warmth rose from deep within him. Subei gritted his teeth and cursed under his breath, the still-constant stream of blows forgotten now that the real battle had begun.

His thoughts flashed red, and he had a vision of how easy it would be to end these men. It wasn't right, someone as strong as him holding back just to get beaten to a pulp. That wasn't how things were meant to be. No, he'd been given this magic for a reason. Been given this magic to put it to use. For the khagan, for his people, and for himself, damn it.

What good was a thing not put to its purpose? A sword wasn't forged to cut wheat. An arrow not fletched to pick teeth. And he hadn't been given this magic just to make flashes of light and impress drunken revelers. What madness was that? What insanity had Mahtma instilled in him to make him believe such nonsense? He was Ghangerai. He was a warrior. He was Subei, Son of Kemu and heir of Baji Khan.

The rage, again. Slipping into his thoughts as it did, trying to trick him into thinking its logic was his own.

No.

Subei took a deep breath, then slipped into soul wind breathing. At the same time, he forced his mind to the wicked things he'd done when he'd released the rage. As he did, the warmth retreated back to its abyssal depths.

He opened eyes he hadn't realized he'd closed and found the blows had stopped. His body was a mess of pain, and his deel was beat to threads, but he'd done it. He'd resisted the blood-rage. Resisted it despite Mahtma's test. He smiled, then slowly pulled himself to his feet and spat a bloody glob of saliva to the dirt.

The three warriors had backed away, were standing with weapons ready, but a look from Mahtma told them they were done. She looked to Subei next.

His heart half-skipped a beat as the impossible happened. Breaking her ever-constant, icy intensity, Mahtma's features warmed for a moment. Lips that had seen nothing happier than a neutral frown were now bent upward in a smile. Even her eyes joined in. For a brief moment, like a beam of sun amid a blizzard, there was a new light there. One of happiness. But more importantly, pride.

Subei blinked, and it was gone. Clouds closed over her expression once more, and she looked like her normal self, unimpressed, unamused, and disinterested. The only remnant of the moment was in her hands, clapping slowly once, twice, three times. She nodded to him.

"You've learned much, Son of Kemu."

Subei couldn't stop the lopsided grin from stretching across his face as she continued.

"In all my years as House Kemu's Master of Knowledge, I've not had so committed a student."

"Would it be too self-aggrandizing if I said, in all those years, you'd never met me?" Subei smiled wider, knowing his response was shit and not caring in the slightest. Everyone needed a victory time and again, and it seemed he hadn't had one in longer than he could remember. He was going to milk this for all it was worth.

Mahtma stared back at him with slightly less of a frown than usual.

"It would."

"Then let's just say. . . yes!" He pumped a fist in the air. "Ancestors above, by the khagan and all who tame the horse, yes!" He celebrated another moment until pain shot through his chest, a new bruise giving him the first taste of the pain to come, no doubt. Stifling a groan as the adrenaline wore off, he turned back to Mahtma and bowed.

"I will not soon forget your lessons, my teacher. You have my eternal gratitude."

She returned the bow.

"You've come far, but there is still much yet to learn, my student."

Subei raised his eyes, then, but found hers were elsewhere. They'd gone hard, staring past him.

Chapter Forty-Five

SUBEI

"Typically, I prefer my nights of feasting to involve more drinking and feasting than, well, beatings," Bataar said, a bemused look in his eyes as he took in Subei's injuries. "But to each their own, I suppose." There was a slur to his words and a sloshing bowl of wine in his hand. Ghula was beside him, though if she was in her drinks too, she hid it far better.

"Ghula, Brother," Subei said and tilted his head to them.

"We raised another song of glory to Kashi tonight," Bataar said, striding forward on not quite steady feet. "A masterwork from the lorecallers, or so I'm told. Never much had an appreciation for songs myself." He clapped a hand onto Subei's shoulder and met his eyes with an iron gaze. "But tonight, again, there were two empty seats at the high table." He leaned in close, then, wine-breath filling Subei's nose. "Father sent me to uncover why only one of his sons bothers to pay the proper respect to the victorious dead."

Subei pushed Bataar's hand off his shoulder, then winced as his body complained at every step of the motion.

"I mourn Kashi in my own way. And I will honor him by fulfilling our task of overcoming the bloodrage." He wanted to say more, but bit it back. "You're drunk, Bataar." He clapped him twice on the cheek. "Get some food and sleep. We'll talk in the morning."

"We'll talk now!" he shouted it suddenly, eyes going wild.

There was a flash burning red in the corner of one of them. Just for a moment. Subei frowned.

A trick of the light?

The pyres from the feast were off to the side, if Bataar had turned just right, their light could have reflected in—

"Look at me, brother!" Wine splashed against Subei's boots as Bataar took him by the shoulders. "What happened to us? What is this?" He looked all around, eyes still wide, then sighed. "When did everything change?"

"The day I destroyed that obelisk. We just didn't know it then."

"No, no, no," he said, shaking his head back and forth. "That was. . . meant to be." He stumbled over the words. "Was. . . the will of the ancestors. No, you changed *after* that. In that damned town, or the forest, maybe. I don't know when exactly, but you're not the brother I knew. Not the brother I loved."

"I'm doing everything I can to stay who I am," Subei said, then gestured to the fresh bruises and cuts, the tatters of his deel. "I refuse to let the bloodrage—"

Bataar cut him off with a groan, a pained sound.

"We are Ghangerai. Everything beneath the eternal blue sky is ours by right, so long as we're strong enough to take it!" Bataar growled the last part. "You're turning your back on who you are. You're running scared from the greatest gift our people have ever been given!"

"A '*gift*' that will devour us. Brother, you—Ghula." Subei looked past Bataar. "Would you take my brother back to the ger? He needs to sleep this off."

"All due respect, Subei, but I think he needs to get this off his chest," she said, then bowed her head and stepped back a pace.

"I'm not arguing with you right now," Subei said, speaking to Bataar again. "Not in this state."

"No more excuses, Subei. I am your oldest brother, and I have shown you the way. The rage can be controlled. Can be wielded. Now that we're sure of this, there's nothing more to debate. This is our duty—to our people, to our father, to *our dead brother*."

"I don't agree—"

311

"I don't care! I am your oldest brother. One day, I will be your khagan. You will do as I say."

"And so I will—when that day comes," Subei said, ice in his tone. "You are *not* khagan, and you are wrong about this. The rage will devour us."

"Devour us?" Bataar laughed, but it wasn't a happy sound. It was something else. Cruel, almost. "But you know what?" he said, lowering his voice to near a whisper. "Words promise, actions prove, right? I will prove you're wrong." He pushed past Subei then, and pointed to the three warriors who'd been standing quietly off to the side, inching their way back toward the feast. "You three," he said, unbuckling his sword belt. "Same thing you practiced with my brother. Let's have it again."

They looked decidedly more concerned about this proposition than they had fighting Subei.

"Subei thinks the bloodrage is controlling me. *Devouring* me. Fight me, and let's prove him wrong."

The warriors were hesitant, but another shout from Bataar, and they obeyed, spreading out in a slow circle.

"This is unwise, Son of Kemu," Mahtma warned, but even as she spoke, Subei knew it was useless. Apparently, she did too. Sometime during the argument, she'd repositioned off to the side. Gave her a good angle to rush him from behind should, Subei assumed, the bloodrage break free.

"Fight me!" Bataar shouted, and the warriors obliged.

Subei grimaced as he watched. It mimicked all too closely the beating he had just received. Skilled or not, three against one were tough odds. But winning in combat hadn't been the point of the training. And Subei had been sober and emotionally balanced. Controlling the rage had been his goal. He'd sought to blunt the blade, in case it were ever drawn. Bataar, on the other hand, had been sharpening it, hoping it would cut his enemies worse than himself.

When Bataar was on his knees, breathing heavy and bleeding from the one cut they'd managed against his toughened skin, the warriors stopped and stepped away. Bataar rose back to his feet, smiling at Subei as he did.

"Ghula, talk sense into him," Subei hissed.

"I didn't say stop," Bataar shouted.

Tallest looked to his companions. They held back, hesitant, fear in their eyes.

"Bataar, this is dangerous," Subei said before another beating began.

"No, brother. I'm tired of hearing how the rage is destroying me. The bloodrage is *my* weapon, not the other way around." He looked back to the warriors. "Continue."

The first few attacks were soundly blocked, but inevitably one slipped through and connected with soft flesh. From there, it was all downhill. Once one got through, more followed, until Bataar was on his knees again. The blows continued to rain down, Subei wincing with each heavy thud of dulled metal on flesh. The warriors finally stopped, Bataar on the ground between them. He lay there for several long moments then, like a corpse back from the brink, his hands clenched, and he rose.

"So, brother," Bataar said, dragging himself back to his feet. He spat a glob of blood off to one side. "How am I doing? Do I pass?"

"I. . . you. . . " *Damn.* He didn't want to admit it, but could it be possible? Could Bataar have really—the red flash again, in the corner of his eye.

Cold realization gripped him. "It's hiding!" Subei said all at once. "It's playing us, even now!"

Bataar frowned and looked down at himself. He raised his palms, showed off his decidedly unlit scars.

"I'm not a good enough actor to trick anyone, brother."

"You don't have to be," Subei said, the realization fully dawning on him. "Think about it, why would the bloodrage rise now? Why would it prove my point? That'd just risk you realizing I'm right, risk you joining me in learning to keep it in its pit."

"I can't believe this." Bataar laughed then, but there was no joy in it. "Ancestors above! I can't win for losing." A growl then. "If I wield the rage to save our lives, then I'm letting it control me. If I prove I can keep it down, then it's not me actually in control, it's just the rage '*hiding*.' That's your argument, right?"

313

And when he put it like that, well, it didn't sound great, did it?

"Maybe, Subei, just maybe," Bataar stepped closer, lowering his voice, "you just can't admit when you're wrong."

"I. . ."

Shit. Subei'd always fancied himself good with words, but in that moment, Bataar had him squarely beaten.

"This is what you want to learn?" Bataar asked, gesturing to the both of them, beaten and bloodied. "This is what you want to believe? *Fine.* I can't change your mind for you. Make your own mistakes, brother. As for me, I will serve my people, my khagan, my father. And you can," he waved a hand at Mahtma, "keep listening to her soft-willed nonsense. There's a reason every nation that once bowed to us rebelled, you know. Our people became weak with infighting and treachery. And yet, even in our darkest moment, the Teshkai were still too cowardly to take back their lands. That's who you want teaching you? That's who you choose to believe over your own flesh and blood?" He shrugged, then gave a sad and exasperated laugh. "Then I can't help you. I can only pray you learn the error of your ways before it gets another brother killed."

And then there was heat in Subei's stomach. Then the blood-rage was rising in him as he imagined losing Bataar as well. Imagined another brother's death weighing him down.

"You—" Subei began, but a hand clapped down on his shoulder. Mahtma.

"I regret it's come to this," she said, looking first at Bataar, then to Ghula. And in that moment, the four of them stood as if on a battlefield, divided down the middle. A monk and her caution. A torol and her courage. A brother and his anger. Another and his disappointment. "I only hope those who are wrong realize it before it's too late."

"I hope you do too," Ghula said coldly.

Chapter Forty-Six

SUBEI

"Why?" Subei asked, taking in the devastation before him. "Is this not wasteful? What purpose does this serve?"

It'd been several days since they'd left House Ghanari's lands, and now they'd entered the Zhong interior. Vast tracts of farmland with small forests scattered throughout. Villages dotted the countryside. All of them were burning.

"Why set Tugu and Budai Khan to such destruction?" Subei asked again, looking to Mahtma beside him. They'd brought their horses to a stop at the crest of a tall hill. Beside them, the United Army streamed onwards.

"Draw blood now to seek peace sooner," Mahtma answered, as if that made any kind of sense. The horizon was nothing but smoke.

Subei looked at her, and he didn't need the dull ache of his scar to know his face was twisted sharply.

"The villagers would not have been slaughtered, if that makes it better," Mahtma said.

"Our enemies are soldiers and mercenaries, the emperor himself, perhaps, but not the people. They're just, well, people."

She shook her head at that.

"I forget, sometimes, how young you are still. You've never left the steppe, and you've never known conquest." She folded her hands into her lap as they sat there, taking in the destruction. "Peace through example, it's named. The lorecallers would have us believe Baji Khan invented the strategy, but Teshkai records report its use, in some form or another, as far back as there have been khans. One might be correct in saying Baji Khan perfected it."

"Perfected *this*?" Subei asked, his tone accusatory.

"The lorecallers don't weave many songs about it, do they?" She let that hang in the air a moment, before continuing. "Still, I have heard it called a more merciful way to conduct conquest. Take the Issiai-ahs of Qaiyur, for example. They were infamous for their brutality in. . . " she trailed off. "Apologies, there is no need for history so old as that. Suffice it to say, the end goal of *'peace through example'* is to minimize casualties. For Ghangerai warriors, yes, but the sooner the fighting stops, so too does the dying—on both sides." She pointed then, to the far horizon. Through the billowing clouds of smoke, Subei could just make out lines of warriors. On foot. So not warriors then, but. . .

"Soldiers?" he asked. "Retreating?"

"Civilians," Mahtma corrected him. "The residents of these villages. They are being driven to Ba Seng. There's no sense in killing them. When all this is over, someone must work the land, after all. And a prosperous empire is a peaceful one. No, these civilians have little value to the khagan as corpses or prisoners, but as a burden on his enemy?" She nodded then, as if she'd just revealed the trick of some grand scheme. "There they may fight for him simply by existing."

"I don't understand," Subei said, trying not to choke on the stink of ash.

"Ba Seng will be besieged. We are only days away now. But a city under siege may hold for many months. Years, even. We will build what war engines we can, but this is an army of rider and horse, not ox-bow and trebuchet. Yet, if Ba Seng has more mouths to feed, and frightened masses crying of the devastation that follows them, well, both the city's supplies and morale will dwindle. A siege may not even be necessary. Through this," Mahtma gestured to the burning countryside, "your father hopes to win the battle of Ba Seng before it need be fought."

There was a logic in it, Subei had to admit. A sour sort of

logic. But then what had he expected? Conquest, triumph, a united khanate. These had been the things he'd dreamed of. Or, perhaps, been told to dream of.

"You look as if you find this all distasteful, my student."

Subei wiped a flake of ash from his saddle and hardened his heart.

"If this means we don't have to fight, means I don't have to risk waking the bloodrage, well. . . "

"It is worth it, then?"

"Something like that."

* * *

The army continued through the hinterlands, ash and dust their constant companions. By the time they stopped for the night, Subei was more than ready to be free of it all. He'd hardly finished brushing down his horse than he was striding from camp. Searching for somewhere free of the hiss of whetstones, the stamp of hooves. Even at a hundred paces distant, the camp was too loud, warriors' songs and boasts of strength carrying on the wind. Warriors being warriors, as it were. There'd been a time when he'd have taken comfort in that. Would've joined them, along with his brothers.

What he needed now was silence, so he turned his back to the camp and slipped away down the hillside toward a rare, unburned field beside the road.

The sun was just beginning to dip below the western horizon as he settled in among the chest-high stalks of wheat, sitting cross-legged a few strides into the field. Before him, the hills rose up and away, swallowed in long, deep shadows from the trees that covered them.

Subei took a deep breath. Meditation, then. A difficult task. Didn't look that way when others did it. He'd seen traveling monks practice the skill. Always looked like a bunch of statues, sitting in their groups, silent and unmoving. Subei figured he didn't look too different. Then figured he was thinking too much. Always was the thinking that made this so hard for him. His thoughts would never shut up.

He took another deep breath and tried to think of nothing like Mahtma had taught. He forced his breath to fall into the rhythm of the soul wind. Slow, intentional, calm.

A breeze swept across the field, a whisper at first, then growing louder as it approached, setting the stalks of wheat to dancing around him. Somewhere nearby, a cricket began to chirp. Somewhere else, a tree frog joined in, adding its own melody to the song.

Through closed eyelids, Subei felt the light of the day slip away as the wind in the wheat, and the song of crickets and frogs, and even the occasional gentle hoot of an owl quieted his thoughts and led him into sweet oblivion.

* * *

"Of course that's them, you fool. Who else would it be all the way out here?"

Voices. Sharp and low, trying to whisper but failing at it entirely. A patrol, most like, their carelessness dragging Subei from the depths of his meditation. His eyes crept open to a world of darkness. The sun had long gone down, the stars now lighting the heavens above in their eternal, flickering dance. Feeling returned to him slowly, his mind seeming to wake from a state not unlike sleep, but somehow sweeter, more comforting. And then the bloodrage was back, its whispers and promises echoing out from the abyss.

"So we go around? Through the field?"

"Seems the only option."

Not a patrol, then. The voices had moved closer now, and through their whispers, Subei could hear the strange, lilting manner in which the Zhong spoke, an almost melodic cadence to the words. He'd just begun to unfurl his legs when the wheat in front of him was swept aside.

A man clothed in tattered and patched robes met Subei's gaze, eyes wide. The newcomer stood frozen, front foot still in the air. Subei rose and the man fell backward, gasping as he scrambled from the field.

"Shit! It's one of them!" A wave of gasps ran through what

sounded to be a small group. Subei stepped from the field and found what was indeed ten or so people huddled in the shadows at the edge of the hillside.

"Gah!" the foremost of them half-yelled as he charged, an old pitchfork in his hands. He stabbed forward several times as Subei watched. The blows landed one after another. Could hardly feel them, though.

A squeeze of his core then, and the whole crowd gasped as his scars lit up. The man with the pitchfork stumbled backward and tripped over his own feet.

They huddled all the closer together, eyes wide and feet seemingly nailed in place. Their robes were tattered, and they carried sacks of what must have been their belongings on their backs.

Subei, still adjusting to the situation, looked down at the man who'd attacked him. The bloodrage stirred at the sight, rumbled from its abyss. It'd be so easy to end him. Hell, he could even do it with the man's own pitchfork. There'd be some irony. Or he could take this chance to practice that lightning technique Yue Ru had used when they'd fought on the cliffside.

Subei picked up the pitchfork. The rage almost purred at that, savoring every moment—until he flipped the tool around and handed it back to the man, handle first.

Subei raised his eyes to the rest of the group. They watched him, frozen still, but ready to bolt at any moment, like a bunch of marmots that'd spotted a hawk.

The group winced as one as he raised a thumb, then gestured over his shoulder.

"You'll want to be heading west. And stay away from any Ghanari you come across, they're with us now."

The farmers simply stared at him. Stood there like a bunch of frightened children.

"*Go*," Subei said, gesturing again. "Get gone before someone sees."

"Ah, quite the catch here," a voice boomed as four warriors emerged from the night. The man with the pitchfork jumped to his feet and rushed to the front of his group, the poor excuse for a weapon held as if it were a spear.

The foremost of the warriors laughed. He looked every bit the part of a fearsome Ghangerai warrior, muscle-bound with a saber in hand and bow at his hip. In the pale light of the moon, Subei could even make out the raised flesh of a scar through one of his eyes.

"Give a man a pitchfork, and he becomes Great Baji Khan himself, eh?" He had another laugh before turning toward Subei. "Good work here, Son of Kemu. Knew there was a reason I liked you. Got a nose for blood, this one," he said, speaking over his shoulder to the rest of his men.

It was meant as a compliment, undoubtedly.

"Out of respect, Son of Kemu, you can have your pick. Was you that found them, after all." Scar-Eye gave a signal to the rest of his patrol, and they raised their bows, arrows already nocked and half-drawn. "We take the rest."

"Peace through example, yeah?" Subei asked, frowning at the warriors. "I thought we were driving them south to Ba Seng."

"They had a choice. South to the city or this." Scar-Eye shrugged. "Shouldn't have been a difficult decision."

The farmers were positively shaking now. The one wielding the pitchfork looked between his group and the warriors, weighing how far he'd get if he charged, no doubt.

Fools. Subei cursed them. He'd given them a chance to flee, to save their own lives, and they hadn't taken it. Now they were a few moments from becoming archery practice. He'd tried to do something merciful.

"Which one you want?" Scar-Eye asked, growing impatient, his men waiting with bows at the ready.

"The khanate united," Subei said, shaking his head all of a sudden. "The whole of the United Army riding south. It should be a triumph. A song to be proud of. Instead, we're in a field killing farmers."

"Hm?" Scar-Eye frowned, didn't seem to follow.

Subei didn't really think the idea through. Probably wouldn't have acted on it if he had, but the rage inside him was clamoring for blood. The man with the pitchfork, it said. Punish that bastard. Maybe it was spite for the bloodrage that overtook him then. Maybe it was guilt, trying to make up for all the others he'd killed. Maybe it was a thousand things. Subei didn't have a clue which. Didn't much care.

"Which one you want, damn it?" Scar-Eye asked again.

Subei locked eyes with the man.

"You."

Chapter Forty-Seven

BATAAR

The wind strike passed through a gap in the farmers and slammed into the Ghangerai warriors, bowled them over all in a line. Several loosed their arrows just before it hit, but the strike turned them aside, swatted them down like fireflies caught in a whirlwind. The merest wisp of the attack reached him in the trees, the air stirring lightly against his chest.

The villagers ran, darting past Subei and disappearing into the crop field.

"The hell was that about?" the big warrior leading the patrol growled as he pulled himself to his feet. He gestured for his men to pursue them. They sprang into action, and Subei lashed out with another wind strike, sitting them all back down.

"So it's true what they say? That monk's made you soft!" His voice carried through the night. "I didn't want to believe the rumors. Told them it was a load of horseshit. But here we are." He spat at Subei's feet. "You're directly disobeying the orders of your khagan, boy. Your own father. Not even the magic of Baji will save you when he hears of this."

"But he won't hear of this, will he?" Bataar said it with a barely disguised threat in his voice as he broke from the shadows of the hillside. The moonlight fell across him, and by its light, he saw the patrol and Subei's shocked expressions.

He clapped a hand down on the leader's shoulder, just heavy enough to make his strength felt, but not enough to be an outright threat. His next words, however, left no room for misunderstanding.

"My brother and I have done difficult things in service of the khagan." He paused a moment, drawing out the man's growing fear. "We carry the weight of these things so our people won't have to. You can understand that, right?"

Scar-Eye nodded, face cast in shadow from Bataar's bulk looming over him.

"So when my brother here has a brief lapse of reasoning, experiences a moment of foolishness, we aren't going to say anything about it, are we?" Bataar tensed his core a moment— just a moment—and his scars flared blue, reflecting in the leader's eyes. The man was shaking.

"Not a word, Son of Kemu," he said.

Bataar nodded slowly.

"Not a word." He squeezed the man's shoulder, then waved him away. "On your way, then. I will handle this."

The patrol left nearly as quick as they'd come, unable to move fast enough as they slipped back into the shadows. After they'd been gone for some time, Bataar turned to Subei.

"What the hell were you thinking?" He stomped forward, throwing his hands up in an exasperated gesture that completely failed to express just how frustrating his brother was. "You want to blather endlessly about the bloodrage and how it's destroying us? Fine. I'm your brother. I'll endure it. But this?" He reached a hand out toward the field. "This is directly against our father's orders. They kill people for this. And attacking one of our own in the process?" He shook his head. "They kill people slow for that."

"They were farmers, brother. What does killing them achieve. . . " He trailed off, hesitating as his eyes took in the myriad of fresh bruises and cuts along his brother's arms. Bataar pulled his sleeves down and tightened the belt of his deel.

"Whoever you've been sparring with is pushing you hard," Subei said, frowning.

"Never mind that," Bataar hissed, angrier than he meant to be. "Do you understand what you just did?"

"I saved innocent lives."

Ancestors above, but he was stubborn. Didn't even look like he felt bad about what he'd done.

"You disobeyed our father."

"By deciding not to kill irrelevant farmers?"

"It's our job to follow orders, not come up with our own!"

"Maybe we should, then? Maybe that's your problem," Subei said, and anger crept into his voice as his fists clenched. But then he took a long, deep breath. "I've known you all my life. All of it that mattered, anyway. I keep bringing this up because I don't want to lose you. Kashi knew the rage was wrong from the start. He resisted it, and now we have to as well."

"You want me to run from it. But I've already mastered it." Bataar said cooly, driving the point home by not letting his anger get the best of him. It'd been easier and easier to keep down of late—evidence of his progress.

"The last time the bloodrage got loose, it was willing to let Kashi die, Mahtma, Ghula—everyone!—just to get me to give in. It's sentient, brother. It's calculating." Subei grimaced then, as if his next words physically pained him. "It's using us."

Bataar sighed then. Ancestors above, but he was tired of this argument again and again. Felt he was all out of words.

"I don't know what else to say, aside from words promise but actions prove." He shrugged. "One of us is right, and I don't think we'll ever agree on who."

Subei took a deep breath, and Bataar noticed they were both sweating despite the coolness of the evening. "We don't have to live like this. Don't have to be victims to that damned madness within. We can beat this thing. So long as we don't fuel it further, we can beat it."

"And what about the false heirs?" Bataar asked simply, knowing there was no good answer. Because of course there wasn't. How could there be?

Subei took a long time to answer, and when he did, well, he might as well have just stayed silent.

"We can't kill them. If we take their magic, the bloodr—"

Bataar scoffed and turned to leave. No more good would come of this. They were talking in circles and getting nowhere. He took a step back toward camp, another, and then Subei's voice called from behind. A surge of heat rose in him. When he spun back around, his mouth was moving before his mind could catch up.

"Our brother is dead because *you* refused to use this gift. How many others are you ready to let die because you don't have the courage to do what you must?" Severe, perhaps, but it was needed.

"Kashi wouldn't be dead if we'd never undertaken this labor," Subei said, coming back just as harsh. "It was *us* that went into Chobei, in case you forgot."

"Stop."

"Us that went looking for blood."

"Stop speaking."

"Our actions razed that town, set those soldiers after us. It was us that killed Kas—"

A clap, magic imbued in his right hand, and then Bataar's punch caught Subei in the jaw. A shockwave burst out, magic rippling through the air, and Subei was launched backward into the crop field. Stalks crashed down one after another as he blasted through them, hit the ground, then dug a trench through it with his limp form.

When Bataar spoke next, it was calm. Icy. And he encouraged it. This needed to be heard. Needed to be understood.

"We do what we have to. For our Father. For our people. We pay this price for them." Bataar shook his head. *This is our purpose.* "Kashi understood this, and he died an honorable death in service of his khagan and his people."

Subei sat up, leaning on one elbow, and spat blood.

"He died in some shit forest, far from home."

Bataar stood there, fist still clenched and shaking. He took several long, heavy breaths, a fire burning in his chest. His scars were glowing now, growing brighter and brighter with his anger.

Silence, then. A long silence. Broken only when Bataar couldn't stand to look at his brother anymore. He grunted and turned. Shook his head and strode back to camp. After a few paces, the darkness swallowed him up. And he was glad for it.

Chapter Forty-Eight

SUBEI

"No staff this morning?" Subei remarked after they'd begun with the traditional greeting. "Not going to beat me senseless today?"

"Though enjoyable, no. I have a question we will consider today."

He groaned. He'd already told her about the night prior, and his jaw still ached something fierce from Bataar's blow.

"I liked when my life had fewer questions and more answers."

Mahtma sat and gestured for him to do the same. Ash from the burned farms and crops kicked up as she settled in, crossing her legs.

"Only when our eyes are truly open do we see how little we know."

"Or when you've a teacher who speaks primarily in riddles," Subei said. "Alright, then. What philosophy shall we discuss today?"

Mahtma drew out the moment. Made him wait. Subei had never much been one for waiting. But the old monk had her ways, and there wasn't much he could do about it. He sat in silence for what seemed half an eternity before she finally spoke again. The question was simple. The answer would be nothing but, he knew. Nothing was simple when it came to the Teshkai.

"Why do you fight, Subei, Son of Kemu?"

It was a strange question. He wasn't sure he understood the answer she wanted.

"For conquest? Because the khagan commands me to?"

"I want an answer, not more questions."

Ironic coming from you.

"We've always fought," Subei said. "Everything we have the strength to take is, by rights, ours. It's the Ghangerai way—and most nations don't just swear fealty because they're asked nicely."

"So you fight because you're Ghangerai?"

"We fight because we're strong."

Silence followed his words. She made him wait again, fingers tapping idly against her knee, before asking another question.

"Why do I fight?"

"You've your reasons," Subei answered. "I don't pretend to know them."

"Why do you think I fight?"

What did it matter what he thought? This was typical Teshkai nonsense, exploring a question for the sake of. . . of what? Creating more questions seemed about the only outcome.

"I'd say you fight because you're good at it. Father knows this, and commanded you to train his kheshig, and his sons. And now that you're," he paused, "older, you train us in other ways. Arm us with knowledge."

"Ah." She tilted her head slightly. "So I fight and I teach because I obey my khagan."

"Yeah, seems so."

"But is he my khagan?"

Subei froze. Dangerous words, those. Especially after the night prior. Subei thought long and hard before speaking next, his words careful.

"The Teshkai people swore fealty to Baji Khan. Their lands are part of the khanate. Kemu is their khagan. Your khagan."

"And should the Teshkai decide we no longer wish to serve a khagan?"

If her previous question had been dangerous, this was down-right lethal.

Subei took a long look around, ensuring they were truly

327

alone. The camp was some distance away, far beyond earshot. To any onlookers, they would appear to be meditating. Nothing unusual there, especially at this hour. And yet still he was wary. The Zhong said words were more deadly than the blade. Subei had found that rarely to be the case. In this moment, though, he was not so certain.

"Should the Teshkai refuse the khagan's grace, they would be destroyed." Subei looked her dead in the eyes. He wasn't speaking a threat, just a fact. A warning, even. She knew better than this, than to speak this way. She was endangering them both. "Should anyone report these words to my father, you'd likely be killed, and your people would suffer as well."

"So you're saying I fight because if I disobey, my people will suffer?"

"Yes."

"You are correct then, Son of Kemu. My people require my subservience to the khagan to ensure their survival. I fight, I teach, I serve, for my people." She gave him a long look. "You have fought because it is expected. It is the way of your people."

He nodded, unsure why she was spouting the obvious, but glad to have that instead of treason.

"But you're an heir now. In many ways, this has already changed you, but it must change you in one more yet."

At that, he grew suspicious, seeing through her many words. The entire conversation had been leading to this point, to whatever she was planning to say next.

"What change is this?"

"Your fighting."

"My fighting?"

She nodded.

"We've spoken of how the bloodrage is fueled by certain emotions. Anger, doubt, desperation. Fighting elicits these emotions, which will only make your battle against the blood-rage more difficult. I fight because my people require me to. You must refrain from fighting because the world requires you to."

"Let us hope the emperor just up and opens the gates of Ba Seng for us then," Subei said, half-joking. But the longer he thought on it, the more the reality of the situation settled over him.

The bloodrage's best chance of getting free is when I'm in a battle. His mind flashed back to that night in the Longlarch. Fire, fear, desperation. These were the tools the bloodrage used as leverage.

"We're in the midst of an invasion, if you hadn't noticed," Subei said, trying to convince himself there was nothing for it.

"All it takes is one mistake—one wrong decision in the heat of battle—and the rage could get free," Mahtma said matter-of-factly. "Will it go back into its abyss when it's done? Perhaps. It always has before. But we both know it'll do anything to avoid that. We cannot risk it being successful."

Subei scratched at his scar as he tried to rationalize her words. A Ghangerai's worth was determined foremost by their skill in battle. He was the son of the khagan, and an accomplished warrior, but now he wasn't supposed to fight? Forget explaining that to anyone else, he was having trouble explaining it to his own mind.

But the more he thought about it, the more he knew she was right. He just didn't want to admit it. He was tired. Deep in his bones, he was tired. Their training had been rigorous and relentless. And he hadn't fought a real battle since meeting the Zhong heirs. He needed all the help he could get.

It was a shameful proposition, but withholding from the fighting to come wasn't a bad idea. The army wouldn't need him, not unless the other heirs showed up. And he'd feel it if they did. Ever since the defeat in the valley, they'd fled south. To the great capital of Ba Seng, most like.

So focus on his training? On controlling the bloodrage? And let the war continue without him?

Subei sucked at his teeth, pondering another moment, then looked up to Mahtma.

"Okay."

Her eyebrows raised in surprise, the most emotion he'd ever seen her show.

"Just like that? I'd prepared a long, moving speech on your responsibility to the world, to beat the bloodrage."

"I've been able to hold down the rage in training, but that's a far cry from a real battle." Subei searched inside himself as he spoke, felt that ever-present abyss lurking below his stomach. The bloodrage lurked within, waiting for its moment.

Subei gritted his teeth against the thought and raised his eyes to Mahtma once more.

"I'm going to need all the help I can get."

Chapter Forty-Nine

BATAAR

"Now *that* is a city," Ghula said. She was a few steps ahead and had crested the hill before Bataar, but he was right behind, was—

"Ancestors above." The two words were all he was able to manage. He'd been overwhelmed at the sight of Chobei all those weeks ago, but this. . . this didn't even compare. If Chobei were a branch, Ba Seng was the entire tree. And he still couldn't even see all of it.

"What was the old saying?" he managed to utter through his shock. "Walls that touch the clouds?" He'd always assumed that an exaggeration. And it still was, admittedly, but not nearly as much as he'd imagined. And all at once, he understood why the city had never been taken by force. How could it be? How could anything short of Baji Khan himself break through such defenses? And yet, around Bataar, the United Army's camp stirred in preparation of doing exactly that.

Ba Seng's walls stood impossibly tall and, composed of layer after layer of stacked brick, they wrapped so far around the city, they dwindled into the eastern and western horizons. A good half of the city hid behind those walls, lying in the shadow of their enormity. But the rest, as Ghula had promised, was built on a steep hill. Further back, the higher sections were visible. Throughout them, smaller, interior walls divided the city into districts. Each one looked a city all its own, the buildings and streets within organized in rigid patterns. From the hilltop, they almost looked a piece of art, meticulously crafted and curated.

"How could man build such things?" Bataar was still in awe of the walls above all else. Chobei's had been cracked and crumbling. These were immaculate. Seemed they could shut out the entirety of the world if they so desired.

"They're impressive, I'll give them that." Ghula nodded as she spoke. "But a wall's only as strong as its gate." She gestured to several spots along the city's edge. "Time was, gates like those would have taken hours to bring down. But now?" She chuckled. "A few good knocks from you and your brother, and in we go."

Seemed a death trap if ever he'd seen one. When one fought a battle on the steppe, there was room to move, to outmaneuver the enemy. Here, looking in at those repetitive, grid-patterned streets, loomed over by multi-story buildings, Bataar was having trouble imagining the fight as anything more than two mobs bashing at one another. Seemed a poor way to fight. More a way to die, really. And that was before he considered the number of archers they could expect to be tucked away, waiting atop every roof, leaning out every window.

The plan would be simple enough, or so Ghula had made it sound. And even from here, Bataar could see their route to the imperial palace. It was mostly a straight shot, though uphill the entire way. The palace sat at the end of the city's widest thoroughfare, and at the very top of the hill. A crowning jewel. It was an entire complex, with its own walls and ground, streets and gardens. From where Bataar stood, it appeared half a thing meant for beauty, and half a thing meant for blood. The patches of green throughout it looked nice enough from afar, but a careful eye would note its tasteful water features conveniently doubled as moats and the gardens were laid out such to allow fine sight lines from the walls and towers overlooking them.

The rest of the city was at the base of the hill off to the west. Here it was all flat ground as a wide river cut through the press of buildings, flowing slow and muddy into a lake larger than any Bataar had ever seen. The walls spanned the river and a sort of water gate beneath them looked able to open to allow passage for the many boats and barges now huddled at the docks behind it.

"It's a fine thing to look at," Ghula said, drawing him from his stunned silence. "But wait until we rule this collection of stone and wood. Only then can one truly appreciate the freedom of the steppe."

Couldn't argue with that. Bataar was sure he wouldn't need to spend long in that city to miss home. Even from here, he could see the press of people pushing and shoving, their chattering, panicked calls echoing out all the way to the hills on which the United Army was encamped.

Seemed the strategy of driving refugees to the capital was working as expected. But that was just the citizens, those who wouldn't be fighting. Another mass of people was evident moving atop the walls and on the rooftops of the lower levels. Soldiers, and a good number of them.

Their number was impossible to tell, but it was safe to say there were many of them. Would have been more if not for Tugu and Budai Khan's armies. Their swift arrival had caught the Zhong by surprise and cut off any chance of Zhong reinforcements arriving overland. Still, the river and lake could pose somewhat of a problem, Bataar imagined, but squadrons armed with oil and fire arrows were already patrolling the banks. Any boat or barge attempting to enter the city that way would have a storm of fire to pass through first.

"How do you like the look of my new city?" Kemu Khagan called from behind as he emerged from his ger and joined them.

"Looks comfortable, my Khagan. And if I've learned anything from my years, it's that a comfortable life does not a good warrior make. These defenses do not scare me, nor do the soldiers manning them. Ba Seng will be a fine addition to the khanate," Ghula said as she bowed.

"Your confidence is inspiring, as always, Torol," Kemu said with a grunt. He stared down at Ba Seng a bit longer before speaking again. "Though, ancestors willing, no blood need be spilled here."

"What do you mean?" Bataar asked at that, not understanding how that would be possible. In its abyss, the bloodrage stirred angrily at the suggestion. Bataar sent a focused burst of will down to it as a warning, and a reminder.

I'm in control here.

"Our goal is not to fight, my son," Kemu Khagan said, and then movement caught his eye. A group entering the camp. "It is to *win*," he finished, then smiled and strode toward them.

Not to fight, but to win. Bataar's thoughts lingered on that a moment, until he too was distracted by the group approaching. They were not Ghangerai, but Zhong. Ten in number, escorted by kheshigs and clad in draping, silk robes of a fine, bright blue. A breeze picked up then, and Bataar winced as the smothering scent of perfume and incense was carried on it. He covered his nose even as Kemu Khagan spread his arms wide.

"Ba Seng is as mighty a city as the songs say. You are wise to covet it," he said, focusing on the foremost member of the group. "I am pleased you accepted my invitation, though. . . " He looked the group over one at a time. "Am I to believe these are the governors and officials of Ba Seng? And your family? I do not see them here. If you are to be my subjects, you must all come before me, without exception, to render service and pay homage. Already you disregard my instructions. This is not an auspicious beginning."

The Zhong officials—for that is what they looked to be, all robes and jewelry with wide, structured black hats atop their heads—bowed. They did so with their hands folded atop one another, palms down and extended in front of them. Their chests paralleled the ground, but their eyes remained fixed at the feet of the khagan.

"My apologies, Great Khan," the foremost spoke, his voice steady, polite.

"The Great Khan has long gone to his ancestors. The world will never know his quality again. You will address me as Kemu Khagan." A stern look then. He waved it away a moment later, however, eyes softening. "Come now." He gestured for them to rise, then nodded to an attendant. "Airag for myself and the emperor." A bowl was handed to the khagan and a second offered to the emperor. He hesitated to take it.

"Drink," Kemu commanded. "I will not hear you pledge fealty with a weak voice."

"My apologies, Khagan," the Zhong emperor said again. "I am but a humble servant of Emperor Taiguang, Chosen of Heaven and Benevolent Father of Civilization. I am entrusted only to deliver his words to you, and yours to him."

Kemu scowled at that, but it passed quickly. When he spoke next, there was a palpable weight to his words.

"Deliver him this, then: Twice I have called you to me and twice you have refused. You will come at dawn tomorrow, your family, your commanders, and the governors of your city with you. You will prostrate yourselves before me and swear fealty. Each season, you will send tribute of food and furs, raw materials and weapons, as is proper from a khan to his khagan. Your soldiers will serve in my armies. Your craftsmen will work in my forges and shops. Do this, and you will continue to rule as emperor, or khan, or whatever title you so choose. Do this, and your people will be welcomed to the khanate as equals under the eternal blue sky. You will practice your religions as you see fit. You will conduct the business of trade, construction, and administration as you see fit. You will live in peace by my blessing. But refuse this, and I will know you as my enemy. Refuse this, and I will unleash unto you such devastation that for a thousand years, all who pass here will cover their eyes and plug their nose so as to be spared the horror of your folly. These are my terms, emperor. I will deliver them to every city and town in your empire. When I do, will Ba Seng be an example of prosperity in our new khanate, or a woe-filled testament to the price of naming yourself my enemy?"

Silence, then. A long silence. Seemed even the wind didn't dare to break it. The only movement came from the Zhong delegate bowing once more.

"The emperor will hear your words, Khagan."

"Leave my camp." He waved them away with a flick of his hand and the kheshig guards closed in, corralling the too-oiled and too-perfumed officials back the way they'd come.

Kemu Khagan strode toward his ger but paused beside Bataar a moment.

"We only fight if we have to, my son. But if we fight, we do so completely. Do you understand?"

Bataar bowed his head.

"I do, Khagan."

"Good." He squeezed his shoulder then. "Ghula, ensure the marshals are ready. We will have Ba Seng tomorrow, through peace or through example."

Chapter Fifty

SUBEI

"Hold the dog," Subei said, pausing outside his father's ger. There was a shuffling from inside, then a line of marshals filed out, bowing their heads as they passed. Subei returned the greeting as he stepped out of their way, and it was then, by the light of his torch, that he noticed a new carving was being added to the doorframe. Unfinished still, but from what Subei could make out, it depicted a warrior in a forest. He fought bravely against a swarm of enemies while a river swept past behind him. Kashi?

"You are welcome inside, my son. Come." Kemu's voice called out. Subei swallowed hard. Had news of his and Bataar's meeting in the field reached their father's ears? There was no point in standing in fear, though. He'd been summoned. He'd answered. But a summons this late was never a good sign.

Subei shook out his hands, then stepped inside.

Kemu Khagan sat beside the fire pit, the flames flickering against his features. It'd been some time since Subei had entered his father's ger, so he paused at the family altar to pay his respects to the ancestors. And to delay a bit longer.

"Every night," Kemu said, breaking the silence. "My dreams take me back to the day we arrived at the Kurultai. To the sight, shortly after, of you and your brothers, unconscious and with those scars all along your arms."

It'd been some time since he'd thought back on it, but

Subei's memories carried him there now. To the obelisks before the Great Khan's statue, to the moment they'd exploded and everything had changed.

"It was a fortuitous day," Kemu continued. "For all of us."

Not Kashi, Subei thought, but dared not give voice to the thought.

"All at once, our world changed. And then, before any of us could process it, really, my sons were gone. Off on their labor." Kemu turned to him now, the fire slipping behind him and casting his face in shadow. "Off to reclaim the magic of the Great Khan."

Subei resisted the urge to wince. This was going about as bad as he'd expected. It was a safe bet the khagan hadn't called him here just to reminisce about the before times.

"I sent with you my most trusted advisors. How did you find their guidance, my son?"

"They are noble and fierce, wise and honest. My brothers and I could not have asked for better teachers."

Kemu nodded at that, and Subei wasn't fool enough to think it meant anything.

"It's good to hear you say that." He rose, then. Frowned. "As I have heard otherwise of late."

Nothing to lose, then, huh? Subei braced himself.

"Admittedly, there have been challenges, Father. But what mighty labor is without them?"

"Challenges, hm?"

Yes, one of them's being carved into your doorframe right now, he wanted to say.

Kemu strode closer, clapped a hand on Subei's shoulder and gave it a squeeze as he circled behind him.

"Ghula is a warrior through and through. She may be coarse at times, and reckless at others, but her heart is Ghangerai, and it has always guided her true. While she may push too hard on occasion, you can rest assured everything she does is in the khanate's best interest."

I'm sure she thinks that, Subei almost said.

A tighter squeeze on his shoulder, then.

"Mahtma is my Master of Knowledge and truly, she deserves

the title. Without her obsessive curiosity, there is much we would not have learned. She is wise and confident. But you must remember, at heart, she is Teshkai." He appeared on Subei's right then, peered sideways at him. "They are a very different people from us. Equals under the eternal blue sky, yes. And in some ways, they are strong beyond measure, but in others, they are deplorably weak." He shook his head. "They do not see the world as we do. So distracted have they become with books and questions and ancient lore, they have lost touch with their roots. They'll spend so long debating *if* a hart should be killed that by the time a conclusion is reached, their family has gone hungry."

He stopped his pacing, then, and turned to face Subei head on. "Clarity of purpose is among our greatest strengths, my son. The Ghangerai people are not feared because we are inherently better warriors than anyone else. We are not feared because we are wiser, or stronger, or more numerous than our enemies. We are feared because we see the world as it is."

"And how is it, Father?" He tried to keep his tone level as he asked it.

"There is no law but that which you are strong enough to enforce, and there is no peace without, first, violence. Mahtma would tell me otherwise. She would—she has—argued some actions are inherently just and others unjust. She may have even convinced me, with clever words and learned texts. But while she lays out her arguments, our enemies would run a blade through my back, because they care not for words or reasons. Violence is the supreme authority of this world, and only by wielding it effectively can we make a place where ideas may take root and safely grow."

It. . . well, his father made sense. Subei couldn't argue otherwise. But his worldview failed to account for one thing.

"What happens, Father, when we wield violence so much it begins to wield us back?" Out with it, then. Enough dancing around it. "What happens when the bloodrage wields *us*?"

"This bloodrage is an enemy like all other enemies," Kemu said, and that caught Subei off guard. He hadn't told their father about the rage, but then how did he. . . Bataar.

"We cannot reason with our foes, my son. And from what I

hear from Ghula, from your brother, we especially cannot reason with this bloodrage."

"Exactly!" Subei nodded now, encouraged by his father's understanding. "That's why we have to resist it!"

"No, my son. That is why we have to command it—and when the time is right, unleash it. That is why, the next time a foe stands against us—be it Ba Seng, be it the city after—you and Bataar will level it."

"W-what?" Subei barely managed to get the word out.

"There will always be other battles. There will always be more enemies, unless they know, irrefutably, that to stand against us will mean utter obliteration. That is why, my son, you must master this rage. You must do as your brother has and make of it a mighty and terrible weapon."

"You mean to make me a monster. . . "

"I mean to make you a savior, Subei!" Kemu spoke louder now, eyes alight with the fires of a future only he could see. "Think of our people. Think of the lives you would save. Who would dare raise their hand against us knowing you and Bataar stood in the way? You two are the answer to everything. We would never need to fight again. The threat of you would end wars before they even began."

Subei found himself too shocked to reply. Could only stand in place, clenching and unclenching his fists as if that would do anything. But then, a thought. It hit him all at once.

"Bataar told you he mastered the bloodrage?"

"Yes. He proved it, too. I watched with my own eyes as ten of our finest kheshig beat him bloody, pushed him to limits a man shouldn't be able to endure, and never once did he lose control."

Ancestors above. Subei's stomach felt ready to fall through his feet.

"It's a trick," he said, panic in his voice now that he couldn't stop. "The bloodrage is using him. It's convinced Ghula, you—*everyone*—that Bataar has it under control! Convinced him, even. But it's just a ruse. The damned thing's sentient, Father. It plots, it *schemes.*"

Kemu frowned at those words, hesitated just long enough Subei felt he'd scored a point.

"Let it."

"What?"

"Let it scheme, then. We will be ready. Ghula Torol will guide Bataar's progress, along with a council of my most trusted warriors. Mahtma Torol will guide his mind, assisted by the finest scholars we can find. An army of physicians will ensure he is healthy and happy. And they all will do the same for you, Subei." A hand then, on each of his shoulders as his Father drew in close. "I know you think me a monster for this plan. But in time, you will come to see its logic. Its mercy. And you won't have to do it alone. I will be here, Bataar will be here, your people will be here to help you, every step of the way."

"And what of the false heirs?" Subei asked all at once. "How do they fit into this plan?"

"They will be offered the same terms their city was. Now that we understand this magic more, they are most welcome to join our cause. If they choose to join us, they'll lighten the burden on your shoulders, Subei. You and Bataar can train them. Together, we'll carve out a paradise here in my khanate."

"And if they refuse to join?"

Kemu sighed, then, but his eyes were hard as stones.

"Peace through example."

* * *

"It is a fine morning, my student," Mahta had said when he'd finally found her. And that was strange because it was still night. Or, it had been night when he'd started looking. Had taken hours after that to find her as he frantically searched the camp. She hadn't been in her tent, nor the mess, nor tending her horses. It was only when he'd taken to sweeping outward in circles around the camp that he finally found her, meditating a hundred paces into the dark woods.

He'd told her everything then, all at once. It all came out in a blurted, panicked affair.

"You must be careful with your words, Subei," Mahtma said from where she sat, eyes still closed.

"I'm speaking the ancestors-honest truth, and no one wants

341

to listen. The bloodrage is using Bataar, using Ghula, my Father even, and I don't know how to stop it!"

"It's a wise person who admits what they do not know."

"What a comfort it'll be to die knowing the bloodrage won but at least I was *wise*."

"You're angry, Subei."

"And I don't understand why you're not! Did you understand what I said? My Father wants to use us to annihilate entire cities. He heard about Chobei, and he didn't think it a cautionary tale, he thought it a great start!" Subei punched the ground, almost put some magic into the blow too.

"You're angry, Subei," she repeated, and that made him all the angrier, because of course he was angry, of course he—*oh*. The realization hit him and even as it did, a wash of heat retreated back down into his core.

Insidious bastard.

"It thrives when I'm angry." He let his clenched fist fall slack, then forced himself to calm with a series of long, controlled breaths.

"Very good, my student." Mahtma nodded at him, and when she raised her head, her eyes were open.

"No, none of this is '*very good*,'" Subei said. "If Ba Seng doesn't surrender, it'll be the first city Bataar and I are ordered to obliterate."

"And will you do it?"

"What?" He recoiled so hard he nearly fell over. "Have you gone mad? Of course not."

"But think how many lives it will save. Not right away, perhaps. First it would pile the bodies higher than the walls. But the next time? The next city? Every time the example of Ba Seng causes another city to surrender, you will have saved thousands of lives. Hundreds of thousands, even. The weight on your soul would lessen. And one day the question would not be how many you killed, but how many you saved."

"I won't do it," Subei growled.

Has she lost her mind?

"You would go against your father, the khagan?"

"When this is his plan? Yes!"

"Good." She smiled then. A long, wide smile. "Then you are ready."

He paused, mouth half open.

"Ready. . . for what?"

"To do whatever we must to stop this madness. In you, in Bataar, in the false heirs, and wherever else it might rear its ugly head." She produced something from her sleeve. A wooden chit? She held it out to him. "You're ready to join me and the Gyakhal Bha in our eternal fight against the bloodrage."

"What?" Subei said, feeling like he'd been saying that all too much of late.

Mahtma placed the chit in his hand, then tapped it. It was a small thing, light and thin as a wafer. On its face, a bird had been painted. A pigeon, with white and black speckles.

"I am Kemu Khagan's Master of Knowledge," Mahtma explained. "I have been in his service for most of my life. That is not by accident."

Subei felt his brow furrow as a dozen questions built behind his lips, but Mahtma was already speaking again.

"When the khanate was at its weakest, the Teshkai people did not rebel. That was not by accident." She folded her hands in her lap. "When you broke the obelisk, the magic of Baji Khan returned. That. . . actually, that one was by accident." She shrugged. "But we were ready. And thanks to you these long weeks, we've learned so much about the bloodrage. Enough, I dare to hope, that we can now send it back where it came from."

"Back into the obelisks?" Subei asked, struggling to keep up.

"No, my student. All the way back." She smiled, then nodded down to the chit in his hand and its speckled pigeon. "We are the Ancient Order of the Gyakhal Bha. The black and white speckled pigeon is our symbol. Long and tirelessly have we worked to overco—look inside yourself, Subei. Only when you look inward can you find true understanding."

What? He felt his face scrunch up, completely lost. Mahtma's eyes flicked up, urging him to look behind. It was only then Subei noticed the pull. Bataar was approaching.

"Brother?" his voice called through the night. But no, not night. Morning. The eastern horizon was edged with pink.

"Subei! There you are," Bataar exclaimed, squinting at them both. "Meditating again? No time. Come on. The sun is in the east." He extended a hand. "Ba Seng is going to surrender."

Subei's heart jumped at—

"Or be destroyed."

Chapter Fifty-One

BATAAR

Ba Seng had not surrendered.

The first rays of dawn had fallen against the city's gates, and they had not opened. The light had crept up the walls, past the towers, and along those perfectly measured and cut streets until, finally, it reached the imperial palace. Lit the whole complex in its golden light. Kemu Khagan had given the signal then, and the trebuchets had loosed. And so, Ba Seng's final day began as fire arced down on it and an army some four hundred thousand strong set to work.

Adrenaline surged in Bataar's veins, left his muscles twitchy with nerves and his hands begging to be put to work. The only work he set them to just yet, however, was wiping the sweat from his forehead as he jogged forward.

Everyone was jammed in around him and huddled low beneath the roof sheltering the battering ram. Arrows rained from the walls, thudding down in wave after wave. Cries of surprise, then often pain, followed each barrage, the warriors that'd been hit crumbling to the ground to be left behind as the front continued forward.

Only so many could fit beneath the roof of the ram and most of those were dedicated to pushing it. Bataar, Subei, Ghula, Mahtma, and their elite escort had been the exception. Were too important to be left in the open with only their luck and shields to protect them, Father had said. There was an irony in that,

Bataar figured, seeing as he and Subei were the only arrow-proof men in the army.

"Almost there!" Bataar called, spurring the warriors on as he joined them in pushing the ram onward, its great wheels creaking with every rotation. Another barrage of arrows came crashing down, the heads of several bursting through the wooden slats a hand's width above his head.

The city was still a hundred paces distant, but the forward ranks of the attack had already reached it. On all sides, impossibly tall ladders were being heaved up to rest against walls just as tall. Warriors waited at the bottom, tying stones around the ladders' bases to weigh them down and stop the defenders from pushing them back. Even before the stones were set, the bravest had begun to climb, adding their weight to the effort.

Bataar's breath came heavy as he jogged along with the ram, armor rattling with every step. Lamellar was, unsurprisingly, the order of the day. Even Mahtma had donned a vest of it.

"What are you whispering about back there?" Bataar called over his shoulder to where Subei and Mahtma had their heads leaned in close. "Help us push!"

Mahtma's attention snapped up to him at that. She nodded, then looked back to Subei briefly.

"I'll explain everything after."

Whatever that meant, he didn't seem happy to hear it. He joined in the effort, though, finding a spot beside Bataar and leaning in to push.

"I'm glad you're in agreement with Father's plan," Bataar grunted to him. He hadn't believed it at first, but then, here was his little brother, on the front lines with all the rest of them.

"How many Ghangerai, how many Zhong, how many civilians will die because the emperor refused peace?" Subei growled, head down as he put his all into the ram. "This all could have been avoided."

There was the brother he knew. Sentimental, perhaps, and prone to overthinking things, but a Ghangerai through and through. It'd been too long since Bataar had seen that man. Felt forever now, really.

"Steel your heart, brother," Bataar said. "This will be avoided next time, and all the other times to come. The example we make today will send shockwaves through all the world."

"Peace. . . " Subei grunted, heaving against the ram. "Through example."

The gates were before them now. A cheer at that, until the roof caught fire as a waterfall of boiling pitch was splashed down on it. Thick black smoke filled the already confined space, choking everyone underneath. But they'd arrived. Bataar staggered forward, one arm across his eyes.

Here were the famous gates of Ba Seng. Monstrous things, all solid wood and iron-capped spikes. Must've weighed more than sixty men each. The songs held they'd stood for three centuries, had repelled countless invasions, the scars of which still adorned their surface. But the only previous time they'd come up against the magic of Baji, the city had surrendered. Not today. Today, the gates would be truly tested.

"Ready?" Bataar asked his brother, shouting just to be heard over the cacophony of battle. A bloodcurdling scream broke from just behind them as boiling pitch hit the ground with enough force to splash up onto a warrior at the rear of the battering ram. She screeched as she ran, flailing and stumbling.

Subei watched her run, transfixed.

Bataar pulled him back around.

"Bring them down!" he shouted, then set to work. He reared back and called on Baji's Burning Fury. Instead of the usual-sized orb, however, he pressed both hands together and focused hard. As the magic took shape, he stretched his palms wider. . . wider. . . wide as his chest. It crackled and spat, sizzling bolts arcing out to rage at the world.

Only then did Bataar throw it. It hit the gate and set its surface instantly alight. Blew splinters and scraps of metal free, as well. And when the smoke cleared, a clear voice rang out through the chaos.

"Ram at the ready!" Ghula yelled, and the warriors who'd pushed it this far released it from its bindings so the great iron-tipped mass of wood could hang free, suspended by ropes from the ceiling of its covering.

Subei had his own massive orb conjured by then. He

347

launched it into the gate and another resounding explosion blasted out.

Another hit from Bataar, next. With every massive orb he conjured, he could feel exhaustion rising in him. But without the magic of Baji Khan, this task would have taken hours. Days, maybe. Now, it took only heartbeats.

Another blast from Subei, and splinters plinked off Bataar's helmet, smoking as they whipped away. The gates were fully engulfed in flame now. Another volley of orbs and they were noticeably groaning and sagging inward.

Bataar continued with the orbs as Subei switched to wind strikes. Punching forward, he sent a blast against the gates. They groaned louder as they shook, buffeted by the blow. Another blast and one of them popped a hinge, collapsed half to the dirt with a savage crack.

Around, warriors were continuing to climb the ladders, but more had gathered about the ram now, were huddled in close, shields above their heads as arrows, pitch, and even sizable rocks rained down.

"As one!" Ghula shouted, and the warriors heaved back all together, a collective groan escaping as the ram was pulled into position.

Bataar clapped his hands together then and trapped a rush of magic in his right fist. Subei did the same, as planned.

"Release!" Ghula's cry echoed out and the ram swung forward. At the same time, Bataar and Subei charged, fists raised. All three hit as one.

Might be the gates of Ba Seng had stood for three centuries. Might be they'd repelled countless invasions. Might be they could have repelled countless more. Not this one.

Three withering impacts echoed out across the battlefield, and the gates of Ba Seng did not fall—they were blown from their frame.

A formation of Zhong soldiers stood waiting on the other side, and that seemed a poor idea all of a sudden as the gates came crashing through and crushed half of them.

Just like that then, the way into Ba Seng was open.

Whistles sounded across the Ghangerai ranks. Bells clanged

back at camp, and as one, the feints at the other gates turned and flooded toward the breach.

For a moment, the warriors around the ram stared in awe at the city. Staring back was the somewhat diminished formation of Zhong soldiers. They were amassed in a courtyard, the first buildings of the city several steps behind them, and beyond that, the main thoroughfare that led up the hill to the imperial palace. The soldiers looked at the warriors. The warriors looked at the soldiers.

Bataar laughed, and charged.

The soldiers readied their shields and tucked in tight to their ranks. It was a good formation, shields all interlocked, separated only by spearheads protruding like quills from a hedgehog. It was a good formation, but it was not prepared for Bataar.

Screaming like the men before him had each been responsible for killing Kashi, he unleashed another volley of orbs. The first exploded just short of the assembled soldiers. The foremost of them cowered back, visibly shaken by the explosion. The second and third orbs landed among their ranks in deafening booms. And then it was hell. Men and blood and pieces of men went flying. Bataar leapt into the middle of it, pushing right into the gap he'd blown in their formation.

A dozen spearheads stabbed toward him. They were not fast enough.

Bataar brought his hands together in an echoing clap and, instead of trapping the magic in one hand, he forced it out. Baji's Thunderous Might, he'd named it ever since the technique had come to him that night in the Longlarch. It exploded forward now in a wave of crackling, blue light. The force of it alone knocked half of the Zhong soldiers over. The other half were left stumbling away, slapping at their armor as arcs of light snapped and hissed, biting into flesh wherever it was found.

"For Kashi," Bataar said, then clenched his fist. Magic poured into afflicted men and their screams quieted quickly.

"Yaahh!" A scream from behind.

Bataar turned to find a Zhong soldier bearing down on him, sword high. Subei's Fist that Moves Mountains caught him in the side and the man exploded through the side of a building.

"You're in rare form today, brother," Bataar said, eyes wide at the aftermath. A soldier by their feet groaned, still alive despite the lightning crackling across him. Bataar pressed a small orb into his chest and the explosion silenced him.

For a moment then, the small square was clear. Bataar looked back to find their warriors standing as if confused. They'd charged in for a fight to the death, but their work was already done.

Or, the first part of it. Whistles sounded from streets further into the city, then stomping boots followed as ranks and ranks of Zhong soldiers appeared, jogging in formation, armor clanking.

"The spirit of the Great Khan is with us this day, my brothers," Bataar said, raising a fist. "Let us make him proud." And then he turned and charged.

Chapter Fifty-Two

SUBEI

Subei's orb exploded in a wash of heat, and a splatter of blood slapped against his face. Smoke stung his eyes, but he blinked through it, shield in hand now as the fighting descended into chaos.

The initial soldiers must have just been a delaying force, meant to hold out long enough for the main body of the defenders to respond to whichever gate was breached. They came in great numbers now, regiment after regiment. Their father's warriors were streaming in through the gate now too, and the fighting grew so thick Subei could barely keep sight of his brother.

The soldier just ahead had his sword raised high for a killing stroke. Subei brought the edge of his shield down on the man's hands. Bones cracked and the sword fell to the cobblestones. A wind strike next and the soldier was bowled away to slam into a wall with an echoing crack.

"We need to stay together," Subei yelled to his brother.

A wicked smile in return.

"Try to keep up, then."

Bataar spun back into the crowd, redirecting a spearhead on his shield as he put his saber through its wielder's throat.

"Damn it, brother!" Subei spat. He spared a quick glance behind, but Mahtma was nowhere to be seen. Ancestors above, where was she? If their plan was to work, he'd need her.

A sword near caught Subei in the face, sent him stumbling backward as it whooshed down. It slammed to the cobbles in a spray of sparks, then came stabbing inward as the soldier on the end of it struck again.

Subei punched the stab away with his shield, then drew his saber from the loop on his belt. Magic was an effective way to fight, but far more tiring than using a weapon. The battle had just begun, and the Zhong heirs were somewhere nearby, surely waiting for their turn.

He and the soldier exchanged several blows, Subei's blade leaving clean slash marks on his opponent's shield while pieces of wicker were hacked off the face of his own. They were almost evenly matched in swordplay. Unfortunately for his opponent, Subei was armed with far more than swordplay.

The soldier slashed quickly and wildly, each blow less precise than the last, but effective through their sheer number. Subei blocked them on instinct, before remembering he didn't really need to. He stepped into the next slash then, the blade cutting along the thinly armored spot between his neck and shoulder. The soldier's eyes went wide, thinking he'd scored a lethal blow, no doubt. He'd just begun to smile when Subei put his saber through his throat.

Before the dead man could even hit the ground, a spear was darting into Subei's chest, caught him on the left breast and pushed him stumbling backward as it scraped off his armor. The spearhead withdrew, then just as quickly came back in a flurry of stabs. Stab, stab, stab, all in quick succession. The blows hammered Subei's chest like frantic drumming. Annoying, more than anything.

Another jab and Subei leaned into it. The spear snapped with a sharp crack. The soldier threw it down and made to draw the knife at his hip. He pulled it from its sheath, elbow raised high, and Subei's saber came down on his shoulder. Didn't do much through the armor, but the man panicked all the same, falling back.

Subei stepped in for the killing blow, and then he was sideways, saber spinning from his hand, helmet slamming against the cobblestones, dirt in his mouth, his eyes, his nose. The man who'd tackled him scrambled to untangle himself, kicking at Subei as he got free and scrambled away.

Someone screamed to the left, and a Ghangerai warrior spun around, blood gushing from a wound in his stomach. A sword blow caught him between the shoulder and neck, and he collapsed on top of Subei, the weight slamming into him and driving the wind from his lungs again.

He struggled to lift the dead man, but his hands were slick with blood, couldn't get a grasp on the limp body. The man who'd tackled Subei was upright now, had scooped a two-handed hammer from the ground. He reared back, raising it high overhead like an axe man preparing to split wood. From deep within, the bloodrage moved, growling to be set free, to end the man above.

No.

Subei pushed that madness back into its pit, then flung an orb into the soldier above him. It blew him backward in a burst of fire that forced Subei to turn his head, eyes shut tight against the wash of heat.

Subei grunted as he heaved the Ghangerai corpse off of him. As tough as the magic had made his body, and as strong as it had made his attacks, it hadn't increased his general strength at all. A weak spot, that.

He pushed the corpse up enough for it to slip off to one side, and then he was back to his feet. He recovered his shield then searched for his saber and spotted it several feet away. Too far to reach. Someone would certainly be on him before he could take more than two steps.

But no, he realized, looking around the courtyard. The fighting was slowing, the Zhong soldiers retreating in some semblance of a line back toward the buildings and the main thoroughfare. Ghangerai warriors harried them every step of the way, slamming into them with shields and swords.

Their attack stuttered, however, when they neared the buildings. All across the road, shuttered windows were thrown open as archers leaned out and let loose a volley of arrows into the Ghangerai ranks. Countless warriors collapsed, and those still standing ducked behind their shields, then advanced more cautiously.

Subei grabbed his saber and turned back to the walls. Mahtma was striding toward him, a splash of blood on her armor, but otherwise seemingly untouched. She nodded as she arrived.

"You've kept the rage at bay."

"I have a good teacher," he said, allowing himself a moment to realize how easily he'd done it. He'd swatted it away like a fly. He would've celebrated in that moment, but a man splattered onto the street behind them, blood spraying up the stone of the walls.

Subei turned as another fell, screaming the whole way down. And then Mahtma was pulling him out of the courtyard and beneath the overhang of a nearby house, its front closed up with boards and spare wood.

Looking up, Subei realized the battle on the walls had been lost, in this section at least. The fighting had slowed, and the Zhong archers were turning inward now.

"Find cover!" Subei yelled to the Ghangerai moving through the courtyard as the first arrows clattered down around them. The gates were flooded with warriors now, the main body of the United Army pushing into the city. Cries went out among them, and they raised their shields, arrows thudding into them in ever-increasing volleys.

One particularly clever group had secured the ram and were using it as moving cover. Along with them were several officers, shouting orders above the chaos, directing warriors here and there. Ghula broke from her position on the front lines to sprint to the quickly forming circle of officers. Her armor was filled with dents and blood, though none of it seemed to be her own. She'd lost her helmet somewhere in the fight, the scars through her hair plainly visible.

She shouted at the officers, who shouted at the warriors, and then the stream of Ghangerai split in two, the larger number moving toward the main thoroughfare while the other line made for the stairs beneath the wall. There, they worked their way up to the archers above.

Subei waved to Ghula, to show her they were up and ready to move with her, when an explosion from the side nearly knocked him over. Two Zhong soldiers who'd been backed up against a wall were launched into the air by Bataar. They fell back down with a crunch, then were quickly set upon by several warriors. Bataar strode past and surveyed the square, shield held casually over his head. Seemed he was using it for shade more than protection.

"Bataar!" Subei shouted to him. "Form up! We make for the palace next," he added, as if his brother needed a reminder. They all knew the plan. The khagan's plan, that was. Subei and Mahtma had another, hastily crafted though it'd been.

"Bataar!" Subei cried again when his brother didn't respond. And then Bataar turned sharply, head shooting to one side like a hound catching a scent. He jogged toward the edge of the square and stopped beside a three-story house, the height of it hiding him from the archers on the walls. The road there led uphill through a narrow street, away from the main thoroughfare.

Where was he going?

"That's not the plan," Subei said, looking to Mahtma. "The khagan's, or ours."

"Is he still himself?" she asked, squinting for a view of his face. Subei did the same and. . . yes, Bataar's eyes were still his own, right? Yes. And focusing inward, he could feel his brother had not released the rage.

"It's still him," he confirmed.

"Then what's he doing?"

"I'll find out." Subei darted after his brother. Another volley of arrows clattered down, a couple of them staggering him, but doing no damage. He grabbed Bataar by the shoulder as he caught up, stopped him from heading off up the street.

"What are you doing? We're supposed to be with Ghula." Subei pointed as he spoke, gesturing to the main thoroughfare where the warriors were still advancing under a barrage of arrow fire. Those were the orders. "We're supposed to be headed for the palace," Subei said again when Bataar didn't respond. He was still staring up the road, eyes fierce, angry.

"They're not at the palace."

"What?" But even as he asked, Subei found his answer. The Zhong heirs. Sure enough, five distinct pulls led up the road ahead of them. He could feel Yue Ru among them, her pull familiar at this point. The others were more cloudy, wasn't sure who was who, but they were the same ones he'd felt at the battle in the valley.

"They're up there, waiting for us." Bataar's gaze was distant. He was considering going after them.

"Brother, this is a trap. We were ordered to stay with Ghula and take the palace. Then we unleash the rage on this place. We have to stick to the plan!" *Or my plan won't work*, he added internally.

Mahtma caught Subei's eye then from across the courtyard. Arrows clattered down between them, stopping her from running over. She nodded at Bataar, though. Quick, easy to miss. But Subei knew what she meant.

No, not here. He shook his head. For their plan to work, they needed to be closer to the palace. Away from the main body of warriors.

"Come on, brother. With me," Subei grabbed his arm, but Bataar didn't move but to lean a bit in the other direction. Almost as if he were being pulled up the hill. "Don't make me drag you back!"

A shrill whistle then, and Subei turned to find Ghula with her pinkies in her mouth. She waved them over impatiently. Yelled a curse, too. He didn't hear it, but reading her lips was easy enough. She pointed to the main thoroughfare. Several paces away, Mahtma raised her shield and rushed across the open square, arrows striking all around.

"Destroying this city will be fun," Bataar said all at once. "But there'll be plenty of time for that after the Zhong heirs are consumed." Even as he spoke, his eyes turned to flame, to light so bright Subei stumbled back, hand in front of his face.

Chapter Fifty-Three

SUBEI

A burst of wind slammed into Subei's chest and sent him tumbling down. North Wind Scours, he realized, then immediately raised his shield, ready for a follow up attack. But the bloodrage in control of Bataar had no interest in him. As with every time before, he was seemingly not its target. Not for killing, at least.

Would doing so give Bataar the strength he needs to break free of its hold?

Bataar was running. Away. Up the street.

"He has turned." A voice in Subei's ear, then Mahtma was there, helping him up. "This is not how it was supposed to go."

"The rage was waiting," Subei began as he took off after his brother. "Like we thought. It took him over so easily just then. We weren't even in a fight!" And then, something was wrong. Something was very wrong. As if responding to what it saw in Bataar, the bloodrage inside Subei was churning now, boiling and rising, fighting its way to the surface. Subei took a deep breath, forced himself to calm, and fought back, pushing the rage into its abyss. It went, but not without a fight. Put up more resistance than it had for a while.

Mahtma opened her mouth to respond but was cut off by a shout from behind.

"The Torol demands you return to the courtyard!" A warrior,

her drawn bow aimed at Bataar's back. "Another step and you'll be considered a deserter."

Bataar didn't even break stride, just whipped a hand out behind him. Subei dove to one side and Mahtma to the other as a section of cobblestone ripped itself from the street and hurtled between them. It caught the warrior in the face, broke over her in a spray of dirt and stones. She collapsed heavily to the ground.

"Your brother is gone," Mahtma said again, laying on her side as she watched Bataar sprint away.

"I won't accept that." Subei scrambled to his feet. "Our plan can still work. We'll just change the location. Make do." And with that, Subei took off after him again.

The street wound through the city, ever steeper with each turn. The courtyard was long behind now, forgotten as Subei's breath came heavily. Bataar was still ahead, but he was moving like a man possessed. Hadn't slowed a bit the entire run up.

The houses loomed over them now, three or four stories tall on either side and leaning over the street such that they almost blocked out the sky. Every so often an alleyway opened up on either side, winding away into darkness and concealing ancestors knew how many hidden enemies. An ambush could come at any moment.

The false heirs were close, too. Subei could feel them waiting somewhere just ahead. His slapping, irregular footsteps were overtaken by the steady pace of Mahtma's as she drew alongside him.

"This is a trap."

"Almost certainly," he managed, wheezing.

She sighed, then.

"Tairhrin of Summoner's Summit."

"Huh?" Subei asked.

Mahtma's gaze focused ahead as she spoke next, her eyes set on Bataar's back.

"A man. A place. I will lead you to both, if I am able. If not, you must find them yourself."

"What?" he asked, but she'd increased her pace and had already pulled enough ahead as to be out of earshot. Or, perhaps, simply chose not to respond. Either way, Subei fought to keep up as they both followed Bataar. He passed out of sight down a side street, and they just turned the corner in time to see him pause before a doorway, then pass through.

"Brother, wait!" Subei called, but he was already gone. "Damn it!" he cursed, pausing at the edge of the doorway and peering in, Mahtma just behind.

Beyond the door, the building opened up into a two-story courtyard. The floor was open to the sky and empty but for a fountain, some benches, and an ill-tended garden. Along the walls, several doors led to darkened rooms that could've held a hundred soldiers. And above, the upper level of the courtyard was lined with wooden balconies.

Bataar stood in the center of the courtyard, eyes locked on the door directly across from him. Subei concentrated for a moment, but he could no longer feel the false heirs. Within fifty paces, then. In this building, certainly.

Here was their trap. Had to be. It was the perfect ambush location. Archers on the balconies, most like, and soldiers waiting just behind the doors. How could Bataar have just marched right into this? And now he was in too deep. The trap was already sprung, or would be in a moment.

"Where's your brother, Bataar?" a voice spoke from the centermost door.

Bataar didn't respond but to throw aside his shield and crack his knuckles. After a long moment, a figure emerged from the doorway, hands tucked behind his back. Wu Qian, Subei recognized the well-spoken Zhong nobleman from the valley. He'd seemed the leader of the Zhong heirs then, and nothing seemed to have changed now. Except they were probably a bit more pissed off, considering they'd seen one of their own crushed to death on the mountainside.

"I know you're near, Subei," Wu Qian said, looking past Bataar and toward the doorway.

No sense in hiding now. No sense in taking an orb to the face again either, though. He leaned just far enough into the door to yell through it.

"I'd say it's good to see you again, Wu Qian, but I'd hoped to meet under different circumstances."

"Ah, and there's your younger brother." Wu Qian raised his palm in a gesture of welcome. "You are welcome to come in."

"I'll be staying here, if it's all the same to you."

Wu Qian sighed.

"Very well." He clapped his hands and a dozen bowstrings groaned as they drew taut, archers appearing on the upper balconies. Footsteps followed as what had to be fifty soldiers filed out from the side door, followed by the rest of the false heirs. The sharp-featured woman, Blue Eyes, and even Yue Ru, looking as angry as she had at their last meeting.

The big man, Qi Teng, came last, so large he had to duck to fit through the doorway. Subei noticed his missing hand—the one Bataar had blasted off at their last meeting—had been capped at the wrist with an iron plate. It made him appear even more unnatural.

Bataar seemed entirely unconcerned in the face of their new adversaries. Subei could only see his back, but he'd hardly moved as they appeared.

"Subei," Wu Qian said again with no pleasure in his voice. "Come join us, or we're going to kill your brother. I really don't want—"

Several archers cried out as the balcony beneath them groaned. They stumbled, then loosed their arrows all at once. Bataar had a hand pointed at their balcony, and as his fist clenched, the supports holding the structure up collapsed. The arrows were in flight though, and on target—not that it mattered. Bataar let them slam into him, punch through his armor, bounce off his skin where they found it. The last one caught him on the cheek and the arrowhead broke off, spinning one way while the shaft went the other.

A collective gasp from the Zhong heirs at that, then the balcony came down. Archers and wood and all manner of debris crashed to the floor to send a whooshing plume of dust and dirt into the air.

Bataar lowered his hand, scars burning bright, and turned to look at the other soldiers.

"You're in the way," and as he said it, his scars changed. Their brilliant blue boiled away and was replaced with a deep, angry red. His scars extended then too. They clawed their way up his neck, got all the way to the base of his skull and whereso-ever they spread, the skin around them grew inflamed.

The soldiers surrounding Bataar rushed forward at the sight, but not fast enough.

Drawing his hands up before him in the style Yue Ru's brother had used, Bataar formed a wall, the remnants of the balcony flying into place before him. Another gesture and the debris shot across the courtyard, swept the soldiers away and plastered them against the buildings.

All the while, Subei couldn't stop staring at his brother's scars.

What new hell is this?

"Subei?" Mahtma was at his elbow.

He took one last breath, gave her a nod, then rolled off the wall and into the courtyard, scars bursting to life.

"So be it." Wu Qian's scars flared as well. Subei had barely blinked before an orb left Bataar's hand. It burned red as it flew hissing through the air. Wu Qian thrust a hand before him like he had when countering Subei's attacks previously. It wasn't enough to dissipate this red orb, however. It weakened it, but then the attack exploded all the same and Wu Qian was launched backward in a trail of acrid smoke. He hit the ground several paces away, groaning. Soot stained his face as Bataar threw another orb.

"No!" Subei punched forward with North Wind Scours. It swept past Bataar, then, as it reached the orb, Subei hooked it hard to the right. It was just enough to drive the explosive ball off course. It detonated against a wall with an echoing boom.

The other heirs sprang into action, but Bataar, fueled by the bloodrage, was quicker.

Blue Eyes threw an orb of his own, and that was new. He hadn't shown the ability to use that technique in the last fight. All the same, Bataar made as if to sweep it away, hands ready in front of him. But as the orb arrived, he sidestepped and swung both arms in an arcing loop.

The orb changed direction, seemed caught in the movement, then followed his hands as Bataar swung them back to Blue

Eyes. It exploded at his feet and lifted him into the air. He'd barely slammed into the ground when Bataar let the momentum of his spin carry him to face the sharp-featured woman.

He swept his arm in an underhanded arc and lunged at her. She had just brought her hands up to guard herself when a sizable chunk of the tiled floor ripped free and caught her in the leg.

"Gah!" she screamed, bending over as the leg broke with a jerk. Bataar flicked his hand, and a wind strike swept her up and slammed her into the wall behind. Her head snapped back with a crack, and she lay still, unconscious.

Ancestors above, Subei thought, watching the display. His brother was using the magic in ways neither of them had seen before. Where was this coming from? But he already knew the answer, just didn't like it.

The big one, Qi Teng, charged in with a roar as Yue Ru attacked from the side, conjuring balls of lightning in each hand as she had against Subei.

She pointed her foremost hand at Bataar, and the lightning shot forward, arcing toward him with a snarling hiss. The arc struck Bataar, steaming as it ripped across his armor, jumping to and fro, back and forth, as if searching for a weak spot. Bataar's body shook where it touched him, spasming almost. He raised his left arm and flicked his wrist in her direction. His scars flared briefly, and then the fountain ripped from the garden and flew across the courtyard. Yue Ru dodged at the last moment, the lightning between her hands fizzling as she fell to one side. The fountain exploded when it hit the wall, stonework flying in all directions.

His attention still on Yue Ru, Bataar was distracted when Qi Teng reached him. The big man swung one meaty fist and caught Bataar in the stomach. A flash of light then, like some lesser version of Fist that Moves Mountains. Another new technique from the Zhong heirs. The blow lifted Bataar off his feet, sent him flying through the air to crash down on one of the benches, crushing it.

Qi Teng made to follow up, striding forward and reaching his one massive hand toward Bataar's head, but Subei was on him. Or, at least, he started forward to attack, but then hesitated.

What side was he on? Both were fighting to kill, and neither could be allowed to. He needed to get Bataar under control, but he couldn't do that with the heirs attacking him. At the same time, he couldn't deal with Bataar and watch his own back.

Indecision wracked Subei as he struck a stinging blow, the flat of his blade catching Qi Teng across the knuckles of his last good hand. The giant howled as he reared back, several fingers seemingly broken.

The scars across his torso flared to life then, and Subei backed away, shield up. His chest tingled in that way it did whenever magic was being summoned. A wind strike, perhaps? Or an orb? Maybe even a wall. Either way, he'd be ready.

Qi Teng raised one foot, his scars still burning bright, and slammed it into the floor of the courtyard. As he did, a flash of blue light ran through the ground. The tile shattered in its wake, cracks bursting across it. When the wave passed under Subei, he was swept off his feet, falling forward on his face. He rolled to one side on instinct and a massive foot crashed down into the spot he'd previously occupied. Subei rolled forward and to his feet, passing beneath the giant and rising behind him.

Qi Teng roared again as he turned, then was cut short. Something hit him from behind, sent him stumbling forward. Another blow, and the giant was on his face. Bataar stood behind him, then stepped onto the giant's back and unleashed a flurry of wind strikes into his head, each blow smashing the giant's face into the cracked tile with a crunch. To finish, he called an orb to hand.

"Brother, don't!" Subei blasted it from his grasp with a two-fisted wind strike.

"What are you doing, little Subei?" Bataar asked, eyes burning with that angry, red light.

"This is for Jong, you bastard!" Yue Ru was up now, the lightning back in her hands. She moved to strike but was stopped as Bataar hit her with his own bolt of lightning, mimicking her attack. She cried out as her body was sent into a convulsive dance. Subei cringed, all too familiar with the feeling from their last encounter.

"I like this technique," Bataar said, and as he did, Subei noticed his voice had changed. His, but not entirely. Just a tinge off. Bataar held the arc on Yue Ru for several long moments, until her eyes rolled up in her head. Only then did he withdraw the attack and let her slump to the ground. She lay still, smoke rising from her as silence filled the courtyard.

"Well, shit," Subei said, turning to look at the devastation. The balcony was gone, reduced to a pile of debris and groaning soldiers pressed into one corner. The fountain had been ripped from the earth, leaving behind a gaping hole. And everywhere else lay the broken and unconscious bodies of the Zhong heirs.

Bataar didn't look to have even broken a sweat.

Chapter Fifty-Four

SUBEI

"Bataar," Subei said, turning to his brother and looking into his eyes. They weren't his eyes anymore, though. They were red-rimmed and burning.

Subei licked his lips, nervous.

"You in there, brother?"

A voice answered, but it was not Bataar's. Wasn't just a bit off anymore, either. It was entirely different. Deeper and coarser, as if it came from deep down inside his chest. And it was something else too, almost. . . older? As if it hadn't spoken in a long time. It croaked the first few words, then spoke more clearly.

"You have so much potential, Subei. But you squander it, cowering from what you can become. What you're meant to become. It pains me to see you this way." As the voice spoke, something struggled in Subei's own throat. His mouth moved of its own accord, trying to speak in unison with the voice.

Subei choked the feeling back down.

"I tire of your games, Subei. Release me. Make this easy on yourself."

Subei swallowed hard, then took a step back and raised his shield in front of him. The bloodrage spiked within. Damned near took over as it surged forth, the familiar warmth rising with it. Subei shook his head, fought the feeling back down. He barely managed it this time, barely pushed it back to its pit.

"Who are you?" he said, voice shaking.

"I'm you. I'm Bataar. I was Kashi too, though only for a short time." A smile stretched across Bataar's face, slow, taking its time. "Or more appropriately, perhaps, you are all me. You just don't know it yet." He looked down at the unconscious bodies of the Zhong heirs. "I'm them too. Until I kill them. We'll both absorb their magic, and then it'll all make sense." Bataar's smile only widened as he stepped closer. "So I give you one last chance, stubborn child. Release me willingly. Let us begin our new partnership smoothly, hm?"

"A tempting offer, but I'll have to pass all the same," Subei said.

"Stubborn to the last. I can respect that," Bataar said with a dismissive wave of his hand, then turned back toward the fallen Qi Teng.

Subei's eyes flicked across the courtyard to where Mahtma was crouching low, had just passed through the doorway.

"Wait!" Subei shouted the word, and his brother—or the thing that was wearing his brother—turned back to him.

"Reconsidering?"

Subei fumbled for words. *Shit.* Hadn't thought that far ahead. This wasn't how they had planned to do things. They'd meant to lure Bataar from the others, incapacitate him until the battle was over, then handle the consequences as they came. Not a good plan by any means, but compared to obliterating the city? It was something.

"I. . . uh. . . "

"A simple yes will suffice. Or better yet, don't say anything at all. Simply take your mind to the edge of my domain. . . and throw yourself in."

Subei searched for something to say, fighting to keep his eyes from betraying Mahtma's approach. Whatever had happened to Bataar, she was pivotal in undoing it. If she could get close enough, if she could paralyze him, then maybe, *maybe* they could find some way to fix him. She seemed confident that was possible with the help of her order. She was almost within arm's reach then, moving low and steady, not the slightest sound betraying her presence.

"Oh, you were going to warn me, weren't you?"

Subei had always thought himself clever, always had a response ready for any situation. Except for this one, it seemed.

"Warn you?"

"About Mahtma, of course." Bataar spun and threw an orb at the approaching monk. She darted to the side as it exploded, but Bataar was faster. He swept his other arm up in an underhanded blow and a volley of broken tile shot into the air to slam against her stomach and chest.

It shattered against her lamellar, some pieces embedding in the armor, but not deep enough to do any significant damage. Still, she stumbled forward, then slumped against the wall, exhaling one wheezing breath. A single drop of blood dripped from her neck and Subei's stomach fell out from beneath him. A shard of tile was embedded deep in her throat.

She coughed, wincing as she did so, and a spurt of blood ran down her chin. She'd never looked so old as she did in that moment, all the years she seemed to shrug off each morning suddenly settling back onto her and bringing with them the weight of a lifetime.

She raised her eyes to Subei, and he found they were as fierce as ever. As determined as the last freeze of winter resisting the onset of spring, knowing it was doomed but fighting on nonetheless.

She coughed again, then opened her mouth to speak, the words rasping in her throat.

She frowned, then opened her mouth to try again and—

An orb caught her in the side, exploded with such force as to shake the entire wall. And then it collapsed, horse-sized chunks of stone breaking and tumbling as the entire structure gave way, slamming down to shake the earth.

"No!" Subei yelled, lunging forward, but she was gone, buried beneath a mountain of crumbled stone and scorched wood.

"No dramatic last words today, I'm afraid, huh." Bataar chuckled. "Kashi didn't get any either, come to think of it."

Subei stood frozen, staring at the settling dust, unwilling to accept what had just happened. She was gone. Just like that. She'd always seemed unstoppable. A force of nature, almost. Not even time had slowed her down. And yet, she was mortal. Just like everyone else. And now she was dead. Dead like Kashi. Like Ren. Like all the honorable Ghangerai warriors he'd seen put in the ground. Like the poor bastards he'd put there himself.

Subei exhaled a long, slow breath. As he did, he felt the warmth rise inside him. Felt the bloodrage churning and boiling as it fought its way to the surface.

"Ooh, now you're getting it," Bataar said.

Subei closed his eyes and stopped fighting the rage, let it rise within him. All his training he'd been ignoring it, resisting it. Trying to control it, lest it control him. But he was done with that now. Mahtma was dead and Bataar was gone, had succumbed to the rage. What did he have left to fight for? What did he have left to care about?

The rage surged up from his stomach, over his chest, rose through his throat, burning as it did, and finally slammed into his mind. It hit his thoughts like a burst of flame, blinding, painful, and searing hot. He stumbled backward, the world outside spinning and shaking.

What did he have left to fight for? The question repeated over and over in his mind as the rage seared through his thoughts. Why resist anymore? What had that earned him but the scorn of his people and the deaths of those he cared about? He'd struggled all this time, and it hadn't saved Kashi. Hadn't saved Mahtma. Shit, hadn't even saved him. Not really.

And then he was angry. Terribly angry. He clenched his fists, felt his teeth grind together, harder and harder until something popped in his jaw.

All of this, everything he'd been through, and it was for nothing. What had been the point of it all? Why even fight if this was going to be the outcome?

And then a thought cut through his mind. His entire consciousness was fire and anger, burning with the intensity of the bloodrage, but this one thought resisted. It was a snow-capped mountain peak, high above the world, still icy and frozen despite summer's heat below.

Why resist? Why fight? Because if he didn't, nothing else mattered. Because Kashi's death would be for naught. Because

Mahtma's death would be for naught. Because this monster that had consumed Bataar would be right, would be vindicated. And damned if that was going to happen.

No, Subei thought, as long as he drew breath, he would not let the rage win. If for no reason other than spite, he would not give in. If it killed him, right here and now, so be it. But he would not become a servant of rage. Would not let the deaths of those he loved be for naught.

Ancestors damn the bloodrage. It had ruined his life. Destroyed those he loved. Might be it was winning right now, might be it would win in the end too, but damn it all, he wasn't going to go down without a fight. Let it be spite alone that drove him. He would not give in.

Subei opened his eyes to find he was no longer afraid.

Cower from a blow and it hurts all the more. Subei was done cowering. He wasn't afraid of the bloodrage anymore. And he was ready to strike back. He didn't understand it in that moment, but that realization caused a shift. A shift from fear to determination. To defiance at all costs.

Everything became very simple then.

The fear inside him evaporated and as it did, the bloodrage lost its strength. A fire running out of fuel because—he suddenly realized—the bloodrage didn't run on anger. It used it, yes. But it was fueled by fear. And Subei was no longer afraid.

If he died here, then he would die fighting. And he could take comfort in a warrior's death, fighting for something he believed in. Fighting not for his own glory, fighting not to conquer, but to protect.

Something burst from beneath his armor, and Subei looked down to find his own scars were sizzling with a new light. Not red like Bataar's, no. White. Brilliant as the sun and every bit as bright. And as they lit up, a rush of magic followed. Magic untainted with the touch of the rage. Magic pure as water from a mountain stream. The magic of Baji free from the bloodrage.

"It's fear," Subei said, then laughed. "Fear, not anger."

"*What?*" Bataar's face scrunched up in confusion.

"In Chobei, when I first released the bloodrage, it was out of fear, not anger. Fear that I would die there. But worse, fear that my brothers would too, far from home and forgotten." Subei shook his head, unable to believe he'd been so thickheaded. "In the Longlarch, the night Kashi died, I gave in not because of rage and the desire for revenge, but because of the pain of that loss—and the fear of losing more still."

He let his saber clatter to the ground. Next he tossed his shield aside, then raised a hand before him and flicked his wrist. Bataar was thrown off his feet, a wind strike more powerful than any Subei had ever conjured carrying him across the courtyard. He landed heavy, then rolled, slamming into the wall separating the courtyard from the street. It shook from the impact, puffs of dust shooting into the air.

Bataar rose to his feet, red-rimmed eyes staring in confusion for a moment.

"Well, this is new," he said, seeming unsure. "You're. . . confident all of a sudden."

"You wield anger as a weapon, but you feed off fear," Subei said, setting his feet for what was to come. "I see that now." He nodded to himself. "You cloud my thoughts with the fear of you, and it weakens the magic. Tricks me into thinking I can't beat you. But I can." He laughed then, and for the first time in what felt forever, he meant it. Felt truly free. "And now I will."

If he was wrong, the bloodrage didn't bother to correct him. Instead, it snarled through Bataar's throat, then unleashed a barrage of orbs, a wind strike, and—before any of them had connected—a wall as well, raising his hands before him and ripping the very earth apart to throw it at Subei.

Subei reacted on instinct, feeling fresh, unpolluted magic flowing through him. It was as if he'd never truly used the magic of Baji before. Had always been wielding it with thick, clumsy gloves on.

No longer.

He moved to sweep the orbs away, but instead of throwing them off course, when his wind strike hit them, the orbs simply. . . fizzled. They glowed white around their edges, then were whisked away like a candle's flame before a gust of wind.

Subei's eyes just had time to go wide at that before Bataar's own wind strike arrived. Subei crossed his arms in front of him and pushed through it with North Wind Shelters. His feet dug into the earth, then he strode forward and unleashed North Wind Scours. It washed against the oncoming wall of earth which lost speed, sagged inward, then collapsed.

"This magic," Subei said, smirking as the wall reached him as no more than a topple of soil, like a kicked-over ant pile, "is the antithesis of yours."

"Weaker, you mean!" And then Bataar was on him, lunging through with a ball of lightning in each hand. A bolt arced out and caught Subei in the chest, drove him backward, body shaking, armor rattling at its touch. But he gritted his teeth and pushed through.

It hurt, yes. But now, instead of being dragged down by fear of that pain leading to defeat, he saw through the illusion. It hurt, yes, but that didn't really matter. Pain was temporary, and he need not fear it.

Locking his eyes on his discarded shield, he flicked his wrist at Bataar. His scars flared white, and the shield took flight, hurtling in from behind. It caught Bataar in the back of the head, broke his concentration, and the balls of lightning fizzled from his hands. Orbs reappeared near instantly, though, and Bataar grinned as he punched forward with both of them.

Subei extended his own hands to meet the blows. He forced magic into his palms as if to make his own orbs, but instead, his palms came alive with white light. Bataar's orbs met that light and once again fizzled. Except, no. It was better than that. The magic wasn't just dissipated, it was absorbed. Subei felt it rush into him, then down into his core, waiting to be used.

Suddenly orb-less, Bataar's hands punched into Subei's palms, and he caught them, holding tight. For a moment, they stood like that, face to face. Bataar snarled. Subei smirked—then planted a kick in the middle of his brother's chest and blasted a wind strike out of his foot.

Bataar was launched back, skipping like a stone across a pond.

He hardly seemed to notice, however, tucking in tight, then rolling to his feet as he dug in to bleed off the last of the momentum.

"This is ridiculous," he snarled. "You would reject the magic inside you? Corrupt it into this. . . mockery?"

"I think *you're* the corruption," Subei said, feeling inside himself. "Actually, I'm sure of it." He smiled then, and it was genuine. "You're a rot, and I've found the cure."

Chapter Fifty-Five

SUBEI

Bataar advanced step by step, hands working furiously as he did. The tangled remains of the balcony—half-buried soldiers and all —came first, rising into a wall and rushing at Subei from behind. He reacted on instincts he hadn't known he'd had. Instincts that had been obscured and polluted by the bloodrage.

Free of that now, he turned, set his feet, and leaned a shoulder into the attack—while pouring magic into the same shoulder. Nothing happened until the wall struck. As it did, an invisible shield around Subei flared to life. The wall broke around it then fell back to loose dirt and debris—as if Subei's block had stripped all malice, all aggression from the attack.

"Huh," Subei said, smiling at the translucent shield as it dissipated and faded away. He remembered something Wu Qian had said to him, then. "I guess even the mightiest blow is inferior to the power of restraint."

Before the debris was even still though, another barrage was on the way, the rubble that had buried Mahtma hurtling toward him. Subei didn't have time to recreate the shield, so he threw himself to the side as a series of stones as large as his chest flew across the courtyard and slammed into the far wall.

One of the stones caught him in the shoulder though, and tendrils of pain spiked out from the impact. He half cried out, then clenched his teeth, silencing the sound. And as he did, he felt magic flow through him, rushing to the site of the injury. As it arrived there, the pain lessened, numbed. Didn't heal it but took away the pain.

When he climbed to his feet, his right arm hung limp, the shoulder joint protruding from the socket at an unnatural angle.

"First blood to me, then?" Bataar asked. But he wasn't done yet, continued forward with wind strike after wind strike, each changing direction, swirling and spinning and curving as they hit him, each fiercer than the last.

Subei set his feet firm and swept away as many of the strikes as he could, but there were too many and they were too frequent. His one remaining good arm had no hope of keeping up. They finally broke through and bowled him over, the barrage far from ending as they swept him across the courtyard.

He caught a glance at Yue Ru as he rolled past. She was stirring, groaning as she started to move again. For a moment their eyes met, and then he was gone, bowled away to slam into the wall with such force he nearly brought the whole thing down. In the wake of it, his vision shook, tossing back and forth. His thoughts were muddled, coming slower after that blow, and jumbled.

He tried to roll to his feet and found the world was all wrong, wouldn't sit still. He stumbled to the side and collapsed, then pushed himself back up, dead right arm flopping around uselessly. Something warm was running down his face now, stinging in his eye. Blood, he realized as the smell hit his nose. Must've split his head against the wall. Would explain why everything was spinning, at least.

If there was mercy to be found in the world, it wasn't here. Bataar attacked all the more now, nostrils flaring, smelling victory close at hand. He came in close, striking with open palms, orbs crackling on the end of them. Subei threw a wind strike that fizzled the orbs, which gave him just enough time to dance back, blocking punches with all the grace one could expect from a one-armed warrior that had just had his head cracked like an egg. But it was enough, at least, the slipping, stumbling, just-staying-alive dance he did, backing away in the face of Bataar's onslaught.

Amid their fight, one of the archers groaned and pulled

himself to his feet, eyes going wide at the sight of the two of them exchanging blows, one's scars burning red and the other's white. He made to grab his bow from the rubble and Bataar casually flicked an orb in his direction. The man yelped and squeezed his eyes shut—and a gentle rush of air blew past his face as Subei's wind strike arrived and extinguished the orb.

Bataar pressed the advantage, palms striking in again and again. Subei dodged those he could, blocked those he couldn't. His right arm was still limp, useless. Forced him to get creative. Bataar leaned in too far for a strike and Subei ducked under it and rose up inside his guard. He raised a foot as he did, managed to plant it on Bataar's hip.

For a moment they were face to face, snarling and spitting, and then Subei kicked back, shoving Bataar away initially with just his foot, but following with a wind strike. It forced Bataar back for a moment, giving Subei the breathing room he needed.

Raising his left arm before him he conjured a wall, one more powerful than he ever had before. Previously he'd only been able to create walls out of debris scattered around him. Now, free of the rage's corrupted magic, when he raised the wall, it was a manifestation of the magic itself. Not detritus and battlefield scraps, but almost crystalline. It was gaseous at first, then solidified into a diamond-like material.

Subei called the wall and raised it beneath Bataar. It burst through the soil and carried him up to two times, three times the height of a person, the thing that had once been his older brother struggling to maintain his balance. And then Subei dropped the wall and as quickly as it'd solidified, it turned to mist.

Bataar tumbled forward, arms flailing, then landed hard, the breath rushing from him in a resounding *oomph*. He pushed himself up, but Subei had the momentum now, and couldn't afford to lose it again. The magic inside him was pure now, but just as draining as before—and this fight was taking too long, was wearing him out. And his wounds were no doubt taking their toll. He couldn't feel them much as his newfound magic did its work, but damn, they were going to hurt when this was over.

Bataar had just about gotten to his feet when Subei's wind strike knocked him over backward. From the ground, Bataar launched an orb, but Subei swiped it from the air and turned it to no more than a fleeting sigh.

Another orb and Subei used the same move again, spinning to the side. But Bataar was ready this time, got him with the same trick he had Mahtma. As Subei finished his spin, the ground in front of him exploded upward, shattered and jagged tiles launching into his face. Ducking away, he raised his good arm in front of him. The flat of a tile caught him across the forehead, planted him backward on his ass, lights flashing in his vision.

Arm still raised, Subei gasped for air as he saw double, his vision going in and out of focus. Something was stinging in his palm. When his vision finally focused, he could make out why. A shard of tile had embedded itself in his hand. A single sharp corner was staring out at him, the previously beige tile now smeared a bloody orange.

Well, shit. There went his other arm, he thought as he shook his hand, ignoring the stabs of pain and trying to loosen the tile. Already, his magic began to numb the pain, but the hand remained mostly useless.

"I'd say you're going to feel that in the morning, but you won't live until morning."

"That so?" Subei asked, all out of clever comebacks.

"Ancestors-honest truth," Bataar said with confidence, but then something rose in his eyes. Doubt? Strain? No, *struggle*, Subei recognized. Was his brother fighting back from inside? Challenging the bloodrage for control? If that was the case, it passed in a moment, and then Bataar was advancing, arms held out at his sides, hands clenching and unclenching.

Subei fought to get back to his feet, but between his dead arm, impaled hand, and unsteady vision, he didn't make much progress.

Damn it, he needed another trick. Had thrown everything he'd had at Bataar, and even several things he hadn't known he'd had. All to the same end. His older, bigger brother—or rather, the bloodrage that had consumed his older, bigger brother—was still going to win.

Subei cursed, feeling the rage draining from him by the moment. The adrenaline was wearing off now and his magic reserves were low, too. His scars were fading, the white leaving them as they faded back to pink flesh.

He searched for anything else he could do, reaching out to feel around him with his magic as he had when he'd conjured the wall. But there was nothing. He wracked his mind next. For any technique he'd seen the false heirs use, or he'd tried to practice and not mastered. Or. . . no. That wasn't anything, was it?

His mind flicked back to one of his earliest training sessions with Ghula. Back to when he and Bataar had been exchanging wind strikes, but Kashi had been focused on something different. Had mentioned something about being able to feel his brothers' magic. And then, he'd mentioned it again, that time in the Longlarch when he'd learned to meditate with Mahtma and Subei. And that time, Kashi had pulled on Subei's magic. Pulled on it like a thread and called it to the surface.

The memory hit Subei as he realized he now felt what Kashi had meant those times. He felt Bataar's magic nearby just as he felt his own. Hadn't noticed it before, but now that his own felt so different, there was no missing how angry, how boiling, Bataar's was.

His big brother was drawing closer now, that mad smile back on his face. He'd won, and he knew it. Had proved he was stronger, and now he was here to claim the kill.

The furious roil of Bataar's magic grew stronger as he drew nearer, and with no other real options left, Subei focused inward, then followed the feeling toward Bataar's magic. It was like following a pull, but somehow, stronger. Deeper. As if his mind could reach out and *touch* Bataar's magic. Could reach out and grab hold of it.

"Stay with me, Subei," Bataar said, only a few steps away now. "I'd like you to be conscious when I kill you. I'd like you to—" He stopped. Frowned. "What are you doing?" But even as he asked it, his scars burned brighter. Burned brighter as Subei focused and *pulled*. Not physically, but spiritually. Didn't really understand what he was doing, but it felt right. He had Bataar's magic held tight in an invisible grip—as if he'd reached right down into the core of his brother's being and clenched a fist around it.

And then there was a shift in the air. Subei fought back a smile; he had it now. Had a firm grasp and was pulling it out, out, out. . .

Bataar's scars flared all the more brightly, and then an aura began to swell from him. A great, swirling, hissing cloud of red light. It welled up through his skin, like sweat but gaseous, and as Subei pulled harder, it began to separate itself from Bataar.

Bataar looked suddenly unsure.

"What're you doing?" He swatted at the aura, at the light rising from him.

Subei's only answer was to pull harder, put everything he had into this last-ditch attempt.

"Stop!" Bataar shouted, but it was the bloodrage speaking more than anything. "What is this? *Stop!*" There was panic in his voice now as he swatted and grabbed at the light, as if he could snatch it up and force it back inside. His arms passed clear through it.

"It's not physical, brother," Subei said through his intense focus. "It's. . . spiritual, I think." And then he yanked harder. Yanked with everything he had. Took that invisible, grasping grip of his and pulled it so hard as to rip the magic, and the blood-rage, clear from Bataar's body.

Subei could see it happening in his mind's eye, and then reality followed as the light began to separate from Bataar's body. His scars dimmed as a full cloud of burning red light— vaguely shaped like his silhouette—was dragged forth. And then the top formed into a head. Manifested a face. But it wasn't Bataar's face. It was someone else's. Something else's.

"*Stop!*" Bataar shouted and the ghostly face did as well, its jaw distending as it howled defiance. Bataar clenched his core, half bent over with the effort and a portion of the aura split from the rest, gathered around his hand to form an orb. "*Stop!*" he shouted again, then threw it.

"No." Subei gritted his teeth, all his focus centered on pulling the rot from his brother's body. But the orb was flying toward him, miniature bolts of lightning hissing out of it to rage at the world around.

Subei had to divert focus to swell one palm with white light, then groaned as he got the arm to move, got the hand to rise, and just managed to catch the orb. It hit his palm, crackled once, then fizzled away.

But the distraction was enough to break his concentration and all at once, the aura stretching from Bataar snapped back into him. Hit with the force of a tsunami and he was carried off his feet.

He flew backward across the courtyard, slammed into one of the benches, only to bounce off and keep going. He landed hard on his back, rolled end over end, then tried to turn the momentum so he could rise to his feet but stumbled and slammed right into the far wall. His head cracked back against it, and he staggered once, twice, then went down in a heap on the ground.

Subei pulled himself to his feet, completely spent after his. . . attack? Technique? He didn't know what to call it. Didn't even rightly know what it was but for the fact that, for a singular moment, it'd felt like he could have pried the magic from Bataar. Could have ripped the bloodrage free of him completely. Was. . . was that possible?

He had to try again. He sucked in a breath, stumbled forward, leaking more blood than he cared to think about as he closed the distance to his brother.

Somewhere deep inside, the faintest voice hoped that when he arrived, he'd find Bataar back to normal, the bloodrage gone.

But then he was standing there over his brother and reality set in. Bataar blinked slowly as he opened his eyes. His burning, red-rimmed eyes. Subei's brother was gone, and he knew it. But with this new magic, this new technique, he could fix that, right? If only his thoughts weren't so fuzzy. If only the world would stop spinning.

Bataar was still in shock, every hair on his body standing on end. His head lolled to one side, eyes blinking slowly.

Subei extended his hand, the tile still stabbed through it, and scraped the dregs of his remaining magic to reach out and grasp Bataar's magic once more. To reach into his spiritual core.

It took everything he had, and as he called on all of the magic inside of him, the reserves that had been numbing his various injuries were all drained at once. The pain came rushing back, and Subei cried out, teeth grinding together as he fought to keep his concentration.

This was it. He could end this. Could save his brother, if only he could focus. Could only find the strength to—

"Subei?" Bataar asked, words slow, confused. But his voice was his own. Not the croaking, scratching abomination that had spoken through him.

"Where are we? What happened to you?" Bataar winced, then looked down at himself. "What happened to me?"

And Subei faltered. His concentration broke, and his grasp on Bataar's spiritual core slipped entirely. In its place, exhaustion rushed in, and it was all he could do to stay upright.

"You lack the resolve to do what you must. One day, this will kill you." The voice was back. Bataar's face scrunched with effort then as he punched out with a limp wind strike. Weak, compared to the blows they'd been exchanging earlier, but enough to knock Subei back several steps.

Bataar scrambled to his feet then, stumbling as he did so, struggling for purchase. He finally pulled himself up and managed to fall and stagger his way toward the exit.

Bataar fell against the doorframe, then pulled himself out with one last glance back. For a moment, Subei saw his brother's eyes looking back at him. As if the fires there had gone out. But they were back in an instant as Bataar slipped into the street. And then he was gone, around the corner and out of sight.

Subei swayed in the wind, less standing than just not immediately falling. He could barely breathe from exhaustion as what little strength remained drained from him. His scars faded altogether until they were nothing more than faint, pink lines raised ever so slightly above his skin.

In the shock of everything that'd happened, he found himself thinking about his people. About the army he'd abandoned when they needed him most. Granted, that hadn't been a choice he'd wanted to make, but the end result was the same. Probably the army was still fighting down there. Probably the battle hadn't been decided yet. But without him and Bataar, the Ghangerai weren't much better off than their ancestors who'd tried, and failed, to capture Ba Seng.

His feet went out from under him and he collapsed as pain pulsed through his body from his numerous injuries. The gash somewhere on his forehead was still bleeding down into his eyes and mouth. A series of deep cuts were torn through his cheeks and neck. His right arm still hung limp, and his left wasn't much better. And his armor was still hot to the touch, scorched where Bataar's lightning had bitten and clawed at it.

These and a hundred other pains washed over Subei as he stared up at the sky, thoughts a muddled, jumbled mess somewhere between too overwhelmed to think straight and too tired to think at all.

Some rubble toppled over from behind, and a figure rose up over him.

Yue Ru.

Her brows were furrowed. One hand clenched open and closed, almost reaching for the dagger at her hip. But then she made up her mind, raised one foot and brought it down between Subei's eyes.

Chapter Fifty-Six

SUBEI

So the Ghangerai had lost. Subei couldn't think of any other reason for so much cheering outside. The small gap at the top of his cell, no bigger than the width of his hand, was his only contact with the outside world. And today it brought him the sounds of celebration.

Couldn't say he was surprised. Hard to win when your initial plan is betrayed by a secret plan, then both are tossed out in favor of the bloodrage's plan.

How many had died? Subei couldn't stop the thought. How many had given their lives for a cause that was lost the moment he and Bataar had abandoned it? And what of the United Army? Cast back out to their camp licking their wounds, no doubt. But Kemu Khagan would not give up so easily. He still had one son, after all.

But fall was full here now, and winter would come soon after. Even in the depths of his cell he could feel it in the air, in the chill of morning and of late night. The preferred fighting season was drawing to a close. So what then? What next? He wished he'd the answer, then found he didn't much care. Found he'd had his fill of this war business. Was tired of losing people he loved.

Kashi.

Mahtma.

Bataar, he thought of last. Still alive, perhaps, but in what condition? What had the bloodrage done to him when it'd burned red like that?

And what of his own magic? It too had changed. For the better, Subei dared to hope as he looked down at his palm. Could he replicate that technique? The way he'd reached out and taken hold of Bataar's magic, or the bloodrage, or both? If he could do it again, could he succeed in pulling the bloodrage right out of his brother? More questions and fewer answers.

His captors had stripped him of his weapons, his armor. Left him his pants at least, and the chains and guards, of course. Those were ever-present, never less than twenty fully armed and armored soldiers watching his every move through the bars. All the while, the chains held him tight, up against the dank wall, arms pulled taut.

They'd set his shoulder first though, he'd found when he awoke there. Tended his other injuries as well, for the most part. Probably that was a good sign, right? No point in healing a man you meant to kill? Unless they only meant for him to heal so they could break him again.

Torture. Now there was a prospect he wasn't too fond of. Hoped it wouldn't come to that. He'd saved the lives of every Zhong heir, after all. Maybe that hadn't been his only motivation at the time, but they were alive because of him. Yue Ru at least knew that, saw him fight his own brother over their bruised and broken bodies.

Maybe that would count for something. Maybe it wouldn't. Wasn't much he could do about it either way but hope. And what was the old saying about hope? Spit in one hand and hope in the other, see which filled up first? Seeing as both his hands were chained to the wall, he couldn't very well spit in either. Guess that left only hope, then. Whatever that counted for, anyway.

Hope, and that little chit Mahtma had given him. He'd secreted it away in a hidden pocket before the battle and, best he could tell, it was still there. Couldn't really get a hand free to check, but when he moved his leg just right, he imagined he could feel its edge press into his thigh. But what good was the thing now? Mahtma was dead, and all the explanations she'd promised had gone with her. All she'd left him with was a place and a name.

Tairhrin of Summoner's Summit.

What am I supposed to do with that?

A door creaked open somewhere out of sight, and the flickering light of a torch pierced the gloom. Footsteps followed, several sets of them.

The jailer came first, a man Subei recognized all too well. He'd seen him twice a day, every day since he'd woken. The man had unlocked the cell to tilt a bowl of some sort of broth down Subei's throat. Pathetic, to be fed like that. But when the choice was to sip down your soup like a good prisoner or starve, well, that was an easy enough decision to make.

Subei recognized those that came next as well, though they were covered in enough wounds and stitches they must've had a dozen physicians working on them each day.

Wu Qian was first, crutches aiding his movement and tap-tapping as he swung his way to the front of Subei's cell. He wore the same well-made but plain robes as he always did, but beneath them, Subei could see all manner of bandages wrapped and tied across his chest and shoulders. Apparently, he'd survived the orb to his chest. Must've been his magic and armor had saved him, if only just.

Blue Eyes followed next, looking the least battered of the lot. His face was littered with long, thin scrapes, all scabbed over now—the remnants of the orb that had exploded in front of him. His arm was bandaged along the wrist, and he'd a head wound leaking through its bandages, but otherwise he seemed fine. Still had enough fire in him to glare at Subei through the bars.

Last was Yue Ru, arms crossed as she entered. She'd a heavy robe on, hiding any potential bandages, but her movements were stiff, labored. Nursing a number of injuries, no doubt. The side of her head had been shaved, Subei noted, a short length of stitches running along the bare scalp there.

All in all, they looked a sad lot. Had been through hell and just managed to be pieced back together. Subei figured he probably didn't look much better himself.

They each stared at him through the bars, expressions

ranging from disgust to curiosity and, for Yue Ru, anger tempered with confusion. She was having the hardest time of all this, he figured. After all, it'd been him that had killed her brother back in Chobei. She wouldn't soon forgive him that, and he didn't expect her to.

"So," Wu Qian said, breaking the silence. "Yue Ru says we're alive because of you."

"Well," Subei said, voice cracking at first, too dry from lack of water. "Humility has never been my greatest strength, so yeah, safe to say I'm the sole reason you're alive."

Blue Eyes scowled at that, looked like he wanted to get through the bars and get a few good hits in. Yue Ru simply frowned all the more.

Wu Qian rested his crutches against the wall and grabbed the bars for support.

"Considering you intervened on our behalf, it'd probably be in poor taste to execute you."

"As a horse-bedding barbarian, I'm not sure I get a say in what's tasteful. But I do prefer my head attached."

"I say we kill him anyway," Blue Eyes said with his gruff, westerner's voice.

"No," Yue Ru quieted him. "We have use of him yet, dangerous though he might be." She leaned in, face pressing against the bars. "And when the time does come, when he is no longer useful, it'll be me that puts an end to him."

"Fair's fair," Subei said. "Though I must warn you, I am incredibly useful."

"Heh," Blue Eyes laughed. "We'll see."

"That we will," Wu Qian said, regaining his crutches as he turned to leave, the others following. Yue Ru was the last to go, her eyes lingering. Lot of emotions in those eyes. Mostly anger. Colored with a bit of hate too, perhaps. But something else, something she was trying to hide.

Doubt.

Subei noted that as she finally turned to leave. Now there was something he could work with. Hope was fine and all, but doubt? Doubt was a bit more promising.

The door to the dungeon creaked closed once more, and Subei leaned his head back against the wall and closed his eyes.

Well, at least they probably weren't going to kill him, he thought. And maybe tomorrow the broth poured down his throat would come with some seasoning. That'd be exciting, now wouldn't it? Subei forced himself to imagine what that'd taste like. Forced his mind away from what he really wanted to think about as the distant sounds of celebration poured in from the streets of Ba Seng above.

Bataar was lost.

Mahtma was dead.

Kashi was dead.

He was a prisoner.

Chapter Fifty-Seven

KASHI

If this was the world next, why did it hurt so much? And why did the towering spirits of his ancestors, come to welcome him to the hereafter, look so much like monks?

They weren't even glowing. Bit of a disappointment, that. He'd always figured the ancestors would be a marvel beyond marvels. One of them had dirt smudged on his cheek.

"Well, it's about time," that one said. "We really should be underway."

"Give him a moment. He can't be feeling very well," the other, on his left, said. He pressed his palms together in front of his heart, then raised them to his bowed forehead. "Hail, friend Kashi. I am Li of Asp Den Monastery. My companion and I have been caring for you for some time. It is heartening to see you finally conscious."

"Con-scious?" Kashi managed, though his voice didn't want to come. "But. . . I died." He remembered it vividly, despite the haze slowing his thoughts, clouding his mind.

His arm had been blown clean off. Water next, flooding his lungs, and the magic had rushed from him, pulsing out with every faltering, unsteady beat of his heart. The magic of Baji Khan had gone, left him shivering and his vision fading as the river had carried him away.

"Well, if we're being exact, I suspect you did actually die," the monk on the right said. There was a canopy over his head.

Trees and leaves, and sunlight shining down through it. "Oh, apologies." He repeated the pressed-palms bow of his companion. "Mai-Qual of Ascendant Song Monastery." He bowed and a necklace swung out from his robes. A wooden medallion hung from it, some sort of bird with black and white speckles painted on it.

"K-kashi, Son of. . . Kemu," he croaked, returning the greeting as best he could.

"Right, as I was saying, you probably did die, just not for very long. Just long enough for the bloodrage to panic and flee from you, cowardly opportunist that it is."

"You know about the bloodrage?"

"More than you do, I'm sure," Mai-Qual said with a chuckle.

Li smiled, then, apologetic with a touch of sadness in it. No, not sadness, Kashi realized, empathy.

"We'll explain it all on the way."

"Way to where?" Kashi asked and tried to sit up, pushing out from a pile of scratchy sleeping furs. He pressed his right hand to the ground and missed it entirely. No, didn't miss, there just wasn't a hand to push with.

Ah, right.

He tried to roll to his other side and use that arm, but his body couldn't manage it. Was all shaky and weak. His breathing too, for some reason. He wasn't winded but all the same his breathing was ragged, shallow. As if he'd just sprinted long and hard.

"On the way to where?" Kashi asked again through his shaking breath.

Another empathetic smile then, as Li eased him back down and rearranged the scratchy bedding. When he spoke again, there was a new light in his eyes.

"Teshkai."

Afterword

Ancestors smile on you for reading *Servant of Rage*! It would bring great honor to my house to know you enjoyed this story. If you did, please send your swiftest rider to the land of Amazon where rules the fearsome House Bezos. Reviews need not be long—but even a couple of lines can make all the difference in getting this book recommended to more readers.

https://www.amazon.com/dp/B0DK4ZFRSX

Should you find yourself longing to spend more time in the world of *Servant of Rage*, you can get a FREE prequel novella by signing up for my mailing list at:

https://authoralexknight.com/more.

Keep your courage close, should you tread this path.

If community is what you seek, you may find myself and all the honorable members of House Knight online at:

https://www.facebook.com/groups/alexknightreadersgroup.

Finally, if you've enjoyed the style of magic and progression in this book, you may wish to explore further. You can find fans, news, and discussion of cultivation/progression fantasy novels at:

https://www.facebook.com/groups/cultivationnovels/
https://www.facebook.com/groups/WesternWuxia/about

My sincerest thanks to you for reading *Servant of Rage*. This book was a journey that started almost a decade ago now. I think, finally, I'm ready to continue that journey in the next two books. Care to join?

- Alex Knight

Also by Alex Knight

Fantasy

Wriggly Little Hands

A cozy, comedy fantasy. Oli and his goblin family are sent on a world-ending quest for the Dark Lord—and accidentally do good at every turn.

Launching May 27th, 2025

The Far Wild

A tense, fantasy thriller. A swashbuckling hero, a timid scholar, and their crewmates are trapped in a primordial jungle. Big predators, a big mystery, and one ego bigger than them all.

LitRPG

Rise to Glory

A fantasy-themed VR LitRPG. Bash the Berserker's dreams of going pro are shattered—unless he can cobble together a rag-tag team, win the biggest tournament of his life, and do it all as a three-foot-tall support class.

The Nova Online Trilogy

A sci-fi-themed VR LitRPG trilogy. Wrongly imprisoned, Kaiden can earn early release by serving as a Warden in the massively popular Nova Online. Or, he can use this newfound digital freedom to prove his innocence, and maybe bring down the government.

Also available in a digital ebook and audiobook boxset.

Acknowledgments

This has been one of the most difficult books I've ever written. Also the first. It might seem strange to think my ninth published book was the first I ever wrote, but well, that's what re-writing it five times and editing it for just about a decade will do for you. A lot of that work was necessary because of bad luck, indecision, and crippling perfectionism. The rest of it was necessary because, in many ways, this is the truest book I've ever written. I set out to write a cool-looking action story with big fight scenes and dangerous magic, but somewhere in the process, this fiction became one of self-exploration. I learned a lot about myself writing *Servant of Rage* (and not *all* of it was that I really, really like glowing, explosive orbs). If not for the following folks, it's very possible—likely, even—that this book would never have been finished.

In no particular order, thanks of the highest order are owed to: my wife, Erin Anthony, for her extraordinary efforts in brainstorming and plotting with me, and for not leaving me somewhere between rewrite three and four; Brook Aspden-Li (author of *Gamified*), for his extraordinary editing, cherished friendship, and for also not leaving me between rewrite three and four; G.D. Penman (author of... just so much, but we'll go with *Witch of Empire*), for their eternal wisdom, innuendo, and general mentor character energy (which *will* see them killed off in act two of my life); my parents, Diane and Greg Anthony, for fostering my love of reading at so young an age and encouraging me to pursue my dream of authorship; Michael R. Miller (author of *Songs of Chaos*), for writing me as a badass knight in *Ascendant* (and maybe for helping so much with this book and being an awesome dude); Taran Matharu (author of the *Summoner* series), for his advice, guidance, and constant friendship; and Jonathan

Smidt (author of again, so many books, but *Flamespitter* is my favorite), for the constant writing chats, industry nitty-gritty, and meme exchange.

In addition, I owe a debt of gratitude to those folks who welcomed the first incarnation of this book—and myself—onto the writing stage all those years ago. Many of you have since become close friends and all of you have supported my writing efforts in ways that have been more meaningful than you can imagine. Among this treasured group, I am grateful to count Bethan Hindmarch, Laura M. Hughes, Michael Everest Evans, Kitvaria Sarene, Debbie Grimm, and Professor Mark Zeigler.

Lastly, any finished book is the product of the hard work of just so many people. It's honestly insane. I'm the keyboard jockey who typed this thing up, but so many talented people helped bring it to life in ways I never could. A huge thank you to Naomi Espinosa, for finding the too numerous typos I hid throughout as well as fixing so much of my weird sentence structure; Ivan Vujovic, for applying his artistic genius to create the cover (and Taran Matharu a second time, for guiding the art direction); Matthew Prince, for formatting this bad boy; Tim Gerard Reynolds, for speaking this story to life with his golden tongue; all the folks at Portal Books who I failed to mention; and everyone at Podium, for taking a chance on producing the audio-book edition. You have my enduring gratitude.

And so, after thanking approximately half the population of the northern hemisphere, I think I've gotten everyone. Except of course, I haven't, because I haven't yet thanked *you*. Your enthusiasm and support, dear reader, means more than I can voice. More than I can type. The best I can put it into words is to say: your support allows me to keep doing the job of my dreams. It's my favorite thing in the world and I couldn't do it without you.

Thank you.

About the Author

Alex Knight is filling good books with bad jokes one sentence at a time. As an author, his work includes *Wriggly Little Hands*, *The Far Wild*, and the *Nova Online* trilogy.

As an aspiring twin, he's not making much progress (but remains determined).

Alex grew up a sunbaked, outdoorsy Floridian and has lived in several places around the world including many of the on's— London, Boston, and currently, Houston.

When he isn't writing, he's likely lost in a wetland, falling down in his novice hockey league, or playing competitive pinball. Oh, and gaming. Lots of gaming.

Catch him online at: www.authoralexknight.com

Portal Books - Newsletter and Group

Portal Books is a digital publishing house that specializes in LitRPG, Dungeon Core, Cultivation and Progression Fantasy. Our mission is to bring you the best possible novels, with professional editing, copywriting and cover design.

We only work with authors who have a real passion for the genres and we think this shows in the novels we publish. We know that the heart of LitRPG is solid games mechanics and ensure every story is based on the kind of game system we ourselves would love to play.

If you'd like to try out stories from the other fantastic Portal Books authors, you can sign up to our mailing list for 80,000 words of FREE LitRPG stories. Whenever we add more, you'll get the update, absolutely free.

https://portal-books.com/sign-up

You can also find us on Facebook. Join our group to stay up to date on all our upcoming books, cover reveals, author interviews, giveaways, promotions and more!

https://www.facebook.com/groups/LitRPGPortal/

We also have a Discord server where you'll have a chance to chat with some our authors, members of the Portal Books team, or our community of readers as a whole!

https://discord.com/channels/815688886197551104/
816053544817131532

For more general discussions about the genre, these groups may be useful to you:

www.facebook.com/groups/LitRPGsociety
www.facebook.com/groups/LitRPG.books
www.facebook.com/groups/LitRPGGroup

Best wishes,

The Portal Books Team

www.portal-books.com